"HAVING FUN, SAM?" HE ASKED WITH FEIGNED INNOCENCE.

"It's a blast, Steele," she returned, ignoring the made-to-order opportunity to explain just what she thought of him. Here she was, sitting calmly in a wrecked vehicle eating a three-dollar meal with an ill-mannered trucker while dressed in two-hundred and fifty dollars worth of fancy clothes. She couldn't believe it.

"Careful, Sam," he warned. "Your outfit's elegant enough for a millionaire. Be a shame to ruin it before you have one."

"I already have!" she shot back. "Three of them! Sorry to disappoint you, but I'm only interested in wealthy men."

"You're an impudent brat, Sam. You need a firm hand on your delectable backside more than you need a meek, well-heeled male."

"You arrogant beast! Don't—"

"Don't what?"

"Don't, er . . . don't kiss me . . . you . . ." Sam stuttered in a helpless plea. What was the matter with her? She barely had time to question before her hands came up of their own accord and held on to his broad shoulders. She felt like she was drowning, and he hadn't even touched her mouth. She was sinking . . . sinking slowly into an abyss of desire.

A CANDLELIGHT ECSTASY SUPREME

1. TEMPESTUOUS EDEN, *Heather Graham*
2. EMERALD FIRE, *Barbara Andrews*
3. WARMED BY THE FIRE, *Donna Kimel Vitek*
4. LOVERS AND PRETENDERS, *Prudence Martin*
5. TENDERNESS AT TWILIGHT, *Megan Lane*
6. TIME OF A WINTER LOVE, *Jo Calloway*
7. WHISPER ON THE WIND, *Nell Kincaid*
8. HANDLE WITH CARE, *Betty Jackson*
9. NEVER LOOK BACK, *Donna Kimel Vitek*
10. NIGHT, SEA, AND STARS, *Heather Graham*
11. POLITICS OF PASSION, *Samantha Hughes*
12. NO STRINGS ATTACHED, *Prudence Martin*
13. BODY AND SOUL, *Anna Hudson*
14. CROSSFIRE, *Eileen Bryan*
15. WHERE THERE'S SMOKE . . . , *Nell Kincaid*
16. PAYMENT IN FULL, *Jackie Black*
17. RED MIDNIGHT, *Heather Graham*
18. A HEART DIVIDED, *Ginger Chambers*
19. SHADOW GAMES, *Elise Randolph*
20. JUST HIS TOUCH, *Emily Elliott*
21. BREAKING THE RULES, *Donna Kimel Vitek*
22. ALL IN GOOD TIME, *Samantha Scott*
23. SHADY BUSINESS, *Barbara Andrews*
24. SOMEWHERE IN THE STARS, *Jo Calloway*
25. AGAINST ALL ODDS, *Eileen Bryan*
26. SUSPICION AND SEDUCTION, *Shirley Hart*
27. PRIVATE SCREENINGS, *Lori Herter*
28. FASCINATION, *Jackie Black*
29. DIAMONDS IN THE SKY, *Samantha Hughes*
30. EVENTIDE, *Margaret Dobson*
31. CAUTION: MAN AT WORK, *Linda Randall Wisdom*
32. WHILE THE FIRE RAGES, *Amii Lorin*

MAN IN CONTROL

Alice Morgan

A CANDLELIGHT ECSTASY SUPREME

Published by
Dell Publishing Co., Inc.
1 Dag Hammarskjold Plaza
New York, New York 10017

Copyright © 1984 by Alice Morgan

All rights reserved. No part of this book may be
reproduced or transmitted in any form or by any
means, electronic or mechanical, including photocopying,
recording, or by any information storage
and retrieval system, without the written permission
of the Publisher, except where permitted by law.

Dell ® TM 681510, Dell Publishing Co., Inc.
Candlelight Ecstasy Supreme is a trademark of
Dell Publishing Co., Inc.
Candlelight Ecstasy Romance®, 1,203,540, is a registered
trademark of Dell Publishing Co., Inc.

ISBN: 0-440-15179-1

Printed in the United States of America
First printing—July 1984

*To Kay Garteiser and Monique Baux—
two wonderful fans who
became very special friends*

To Our Readers:

Candlelight Ecstasy is delighted to announce the start of a brand-new series—Ecstasy Supremes! Now you can enjoy a romance series unlike all the others—longer and more exciting, filled with more passion, adventure, and intrigue—the stories you've been waiting for.

In months to come we look forward to presenting books by many of your favorite authors and the very finest work from new authors of romantic fiction as well. As always, we are striving to present the unique, absorbing love stories that you enjoy most—the very best love has to offer.

Breathtaking and unforgettable, Ecstasy Supremes will follow in the great romantic tradition you've come to expect *only* from Candlelight Ecstasy.

Your suggestions and comments are always welcome. Please let us hear from you.

        Sincerely,

        The Editors
        Candlelight Romances
        1 Dag Hammarskjold Plaza
        New York, New York 10017

CHAPTER ONE

"Fifteen minutes I've sat here," Sammi complained impatiently. For one quarter of an hour she had been forced to wait while traffic zipped by on the busy freeway and not a single—not one—man stopped to change her obviously flat tire.

"Rude chauvinist!" she called out when the driver of an elegant silver-gray Mercedes tooted and threw up a hand on his journey north.

She should have known better than ever to loan her jack to a neighbor's irresponsible teen-age son. Now she was stuck. What really galled her more than anything, though, was being dependent on some male for a job she was fully capable of completing herself.

Interrupted in another glance at her watch, she stared wide-eyed as a semi-truck and trailer pulled to a stop fifty feet in front of her leaning Datsun sedan.

Not above using any advantage possible, if it assured a speedy tire change, Sammi carefully undid the top button of her sapphire silk blouse. With deft fingers she tied the shirt tails beneath her breasts before looking up to see just who her benefactor would be. As the door of the tractor was opened, she only had enough time to hope it was an older, happily married man with the boundless desire to help out females with car trouble.

Her eyes widened when a giant of a man barely hit the metal steps on his way to the pavement and started toward her.

"My God, a redheaded beast!" Sammi exclaimed in dismay. "A damned good-looking redheaded beast to boot!"

The hairs on her nape rose, an instinctive reaction to men with that color hair. She hated them all—had done so since childhood—and this one seemed particularly disconcerting.

Before she could decide whether to roll up her window and pretend she neither spoke English nor had anything that prevented her from driving like the rest of the maniacs whizzing by, the longest legs she'd seen in weeks had carried the broad-shouldered figure to her car door.

Both tanned hands gripped the window frame with a sinewy strength taken for granted as he leaned down to see inside.

Another thing Sammi detested was tall men. It always gave her a feeling of superiority to meet her dates at eye level, or if she was in a particularly mischievous mood, she'd wear her highest heels and tower over them. Standing three inches less than six feet while barefooted gave her that privilege with most men she met.

She was rarely intimidated by anything or anyone, and eyes that perfectly matched the color of her blouse clashed head-on with a penetrating gaze of the deepest hazel she'd ever seen.

"Having trouble or do you always drive around on three good tires and one flat one?"

Annoyed that his voice matched the rugged masculinity of his features, she gave him her sweetest smile and lied in a honey-coated voice, "Actually, I'm waiting for my *very jealous fiancé* to come by in his patrol car. It's a shame the highway patrol are so busy today."

Sammi lowered her lashes demurely, figuring she might as well act her most innocent while giving the trucker the brush-off. He was so damned close she could see a mischievous twinkle light up his eyes and the sun glint off his beastly bright hair.

"My fiancé will be here in a few minutes and fix my flat."

No way was she going to let this big brute change her tire. The way his eyes were boldly wandering over her body, she had no doubt he'd expect payment in the sleeper of his cab the moment he finished. As the brazen assessment continued, she wished desperately she'd worn a loose-fitting shroud instead of revealing summer wear.

"No need for the man to get his uniform dirty," he persisted. "I'll have it taken care of in no time."

His eyes went to Sammi's well-manicured hands clasping the steering wheel with unnecessary force and lingered deliberately on the unadorned third finger of the left hand.

"What's your fiancé's name?" the stranger asked with pointed inference.

"Er . . . Whit," Sammi stuttered, taking the name Whit from Whitfield Interstate Trucking Company painted in gleaming bronze letters on the back of the truck before her. "Whit Smith." Considering her rare lack of composure, it was the only last name she could think of with him staring so intently.

"Don't know him," he replied smoothly.

"Why should you?" Sammi shot back, trying hard to avoid the intriguing way his muscles rippled as he flexed his arms. "I doubt very much that you know each of the fifty-five hundred uniformed personnel in California."

She faced him smugly. That fact certainly made her sound more knowledgeable than she was. He didn't need to know she'd read it in a magazine article last night because everything on TV was too boring to hold her interest.

His laughter was filled with devilry as he replied with sudden amusement. "I don't know them all, but the ones I do aren't too strapped to give an engagement ring to the woman of their choice."

"We, er, just got engaged yesterday," Sammi stammered, heaping lie on top of lie.

Another thing she hated was impertinence. She withdrew her hands from the wheel to clasp them in her lap. It was no stranger's business to question her lack of a ring. Maybe it'd be better for her with her easily aroused temper to ignore his remarks, to let him change her tire and then be on his way. She was running late as it was.

With forced good humor, Sammi bit back the impudent retort on the tip of her tongue and lowered her lashes in a pretense of feminine confusion. Letting them rise and fall slowly had never failed her before.

"My fiancé must be delayed investigating a traffic accident. Would you be so kind, sir? I am in a hurry," she asked with an angelic smile that barely showed a glimpse of her gleaming white teeth.

"That's why I stopped my rig." His voice was as roguish as his glance. "Another thing, honey, fluttering those lashes won't get your tire fixed a second faster. I've been immune for years."

He'd seen through her insincerity from the first moment of eye contact. The impudent minx looked like a handful for any man.

Sammi raised her shapely chin, met his entertained glance squarely, and prepared to sass back. Who cared what the beast thought of her anyway? She'd never see him again, that was certain. She eyed him keenly. He was the epitome of everything she disliked in the male sex, and she was damned glad they'd never meet again.

He had the wrong color hair, was too tall, too forward, too poor, and too too arrogantly masculine. She favored slender men of medium height with blond hair, lots of class, and even more . . . those with a bank full of money waiting to indulge her slightest whim.

"Get out, woman," he commanded, interrupting her thoughts with abrupt speed. "No need for you to sit on that delectable little backside while I do all the work." He stepped back, opened the driver's door, and waited for her to stand up.

"I'm surprised a sassy-looking female like you even needs a man's help in such a simple thing as fixing a flat tire."

"I don't!" Sammi spoke with emphasis, staring up as he stood with both arms across his chest in a dominant male stance. "But even a *man* can't change a tire without a jack and I loaned mine to a friend."

"Hmm, independent and generous too. You're looking better all the time," he teased, while his eyes continued to assess lazily the most obvious attributes of her shapely figure.

"You seem to forget I'm engaged to, er, Whit!" Sammi reminded him.

"Engaged or not you'd better move it," he suggested. "Women's lib being strong in this state, you'd probably be insulted if I didn't insist you help."

Taking a deep breath, Sammi forced herself to count to ten as she stepped onto the pavement.

A deep whistle, blown through lips that were much too nicely shaped for a man she disliked so intensely, escaped in obvious appreciation while she straightened up before him.

"A little far from Dallas, aren't you?" he asked thoughtfully. His voice broke off while sweeping over her bare limbs with the thoroughness of a connoisseur.

Confused by his comment, Sammi looked away, wishing she had dressed in something far less revealing. His bold glance was scanning her figure from her flat-heeled sandals, up the naked expanse of golden legs, across the brief hip-hugger shorts, the alluring midriff exposing a dainty indented navel, and over a narrow waist and rib cage bared below exquisitely formed breasts outlined with tantalizing sensuality in the thin material of her blouse. His scrutiny stopped, lingering appreciatively on the stormy features of her anger-flushed oval face.

Sammi's eyes flashed frosty sparks, a look that normally cowed any man and gave her complete control of the most traumatic situation. This confrontation was obviously one-sided—*his side*—and she didn't like it one bit.

"What do you mean far from Dallas? I'm from California!" she snapped with a toss of curls framing her face, which shone as much as his hair did.

"You look like a Dallas Cowboy cheerleader," he explained

with calm indifference. "Except for a vest and boots you're wearing their uniform."

"If you haven't noticed up there in your monster truck, the weather at this level is exceedingly hot for May."

"Not hot enough to be driving on the freeway half naked," he shot back, his voice deep with censure.

As if in answer to his comment, a man in a pickup truck tooted his approval of her shapely body while his young passenger banged on the door and yelled a suggestive remark as they sped on by.

"See what I mean," he grumbled. "Get around the off side of your car and try to look inconspicuous. You'd be in one hell of a dangerous position if you'd had a flat at night while wearing that skimpy outfit."

"Since it happens still to be morning and I'm only an hour or so from my destination, that will never occur." She spoke in a miffed voice to his long back as he rooted through her trunk to free the spare. With one tug he pulled the tire loose and set it near the rear fender.

Sammi could see the disgust on his face as he glanced from her expensive set of luggage to the bald, retreaded tire. Unlike most of her male friends, she figured spending money on a car a waste, especially when chic new fashions came out each season.

"You're lucky I have a jack that will work on a car." With long strides he loped to his tractor, leaving Sammi to stare after him with narrowed eyes while his chastisements lingered in her mind.

"Brute!" she fumed. "Giant redheaded brute." She hated to admit he was also a most magnificent, sensual-looking male animal too. Her many girl friends would think him quite a virile hunk in fact.

He must have towered over her by at least seven inches, every bit perfectly proportioned, she was forced to concede. Fortunately she hated his type. Strong-looking, overly masculine men had always turned her off. She preferred well-heeled, clean-shaven, attentive professional men. No hairy truck driver eking out a living on the road for weeks at a time would ever cause her heart to skip a beat. Perish the thought, she reminded herself, making certain deliberately to avert her censuring eyes from his lithe torso when he returned.

Giving Sammi a thoughtful look, he squatted on his heels and with one wrench each had loosened the nuts of her hubcapless wheel.

"Don't worry about it, woman," he teased, obviously aware of her disapproval of him. "Ill-tempered, lying innocents are off limits for me, especially *engaged* ones. Just as you imagine you are immune to the charms of a brawny eighteen-wheeler."

"Well, I never!" Sammi spluttered furiously beneath her breath before turning to storm back to the inside of her car.

"Too bad, honey. That's probably why you're so touchy," he laughed, with the innuendo blatantly clear. "Hold it!" he demanded as she took another step away. "I said I'd need your help and I meant it."

Sammi's footsteps halted the moment the trucker's stern command was given. Something in his deep-voiced injunction warned her it was best to stop. As she spinned around to give him a tongue lashing, their eyes met; she thought better of it and returned to his side in silence.

"I'm almost finished," he told her. "You can get me a rag to wipe my hands on."

Trying to ignore the rippling muscles visible beneath his clinging, sweat-stained shirt as he removed the flat tire then placed the spare on the hub, Sammi glared at the back of his well-shaped head. Pleased he couldn't see her childish, impertinent expression, she opened the passenger door and reached into her canvas shoulder bag. She rooted through its cluttered interior and removed a dollar bill from her wallet and cupped it in the palm of one hand.

With natural grace she straightened up in time to catch his lingering glance assessing her rounded bottom with devilish appreciation. Without saying a word he stood up, threw the flat in the trunk, slammed it shut, then turned to gather up his tools.

Standing straight, Sammi faced him boldly, at the same time furtively trying to pull the back of her shorts below the swell of her bottom.

"I don't have a rag. Wipe your hands on your jeans. They look like they need washing anyway."

With fluid ease of motion he placed his jack and handle on her car roof and turned to loom over her with alarming power. Undaunted by her saucy reply, he covered the short distance separating them. His eyes narrowed, pinning her widening gaze with a sense of purpose that left her limbs suddenly useless.

"Thanks and er, er, here," Sammi stuttered, thrusting the dollar into his outstretched, grimy palm. Instinctively knowing she would be better off leaving as soon as possible, she spun around, intent on getting in the driver's seat. She didn't like the sudden darkening of his hazel eyes at all.

Before she could take a single step, she felt a sharp tug on the long single braid hanging down between her shoulder blades.

"Quit!" she yelped in surprise, reaching a hand up to loosen the grip of his fingers. She found herself easily spun around and brought within an inch of his heaving chest. It had clearly been the wrong thing to offer him money and remark on his dirty jeans.

She arched her back to avoid touching any portion of his large frame. He was the first man who had ever awed her with such apparent ease of control. With her glossy braid still held in his firm grip, she stared upward.

"Let go of me this instant!" She couldn't remember ever being so mad.

"And if I don't?" he answered with calm acknowledgment of his own superior strength. He gave her hair another brief jerk.

"If you don't I'll darn well cave in your ankle bone," Sammi retorted, undaunted. "Now take your damn dollar and get the hell out of here," she continued, undaunted by the amusement in his expressive eyes changing to anger. "I detest chauvinistic yokels like you!"

"You've made two mistakes, honey," he warned. "I don't accept money for helping anyone in trouble and I don't like women who swear."

"Tough—" Sammi snapped, breaking off when she felt one large palm cup her bottom and the other pull her braid down with a sharp tug. Ready to finish her crude retort, she felt her lips crushed beneath his mouth in an unexpected kiss. This brute's audacity left her momentarily helpless.

She was taken totally by surprise, and one leg went back to kick his sensitive shin while both hands were raised to pummel his chest.

Without releasing her lips he shifted her closer, his long fingers splaying out over the swell of her buttocks, constraining her. Before she knew what was happening, his fingers left her braid, took both feminine hands into his, and held her motionless while his mouth parted her lips to deepen the forced caress.

Twisting her head proved useless, causing him to exert additional pressure on her lips as well as her rounded bottom. It was the most disturbing embrace she'd ever endured, yet she raised on tiptoe to meet it.

With shocking expertise his mouth played with hers, breaking off word after word. Each expletive was muffled, incoherently swallowed as he drew in her breath, savored its sweetness, and exchanged it with his. He toyed leisurely, with no apparent effort and in total control from the first moment of intimate contact.

Suddenly it didn't matter that he was a total stranger. Forgotten were the sounds of the cars on the freeway, the raucous tooting and the fact they were exposed to every passerby. Even more extraordinary, completely erased from her mind was the fact that she loathed all red-haired men.

She didn't know what was the most confusing—the stirring touch of his hard body pressed the length of hers with an imprint explicitly male, or the endless pursuit of ardent lips that were ceaseless in their desire to arouse a response. Without thought her body grew soft, molding pliantly to his. A deep sigh escaped her throat as her lips formed to his—exquisitely cushiony, satin smooth, and passionately shaped lips that complemented his wider, finely chiseled mouth.

When he felt her receptivity, he raised his face. Smiling at the dazed shimmer in her jewel-toned eyes, he kissed the tip of her straight little nose and reluctantly withdrew his fingers from her curved bottom.

"That was pretty fair for the first time," he told her huskily. One hand rose to cup her shoulder, the other released her fingers to slide intimately across her heaving breasts. Deftly he inserted the dollar bill in the deep cleavage displayed so provocatively in the opened neckline of her blouse, then picked up his tools.

"See you around, kid." He started toward his truck, stopped three paces away, turned around, and added with arrogant nonchalance, "Tell, Whit, er, whatshisname, he's a fool to let his fiancée kiss other men. It's no telling who she'll respond to."

Before Sammi could scream in outrage at his actions, she was standing alone on the freeway shoulder, while he was inside the tractor's cab with the motor started, exhaust smoke belching out the twin stacks, waiting for her to get back on the freeway.

"I hate you!" Sammi screamed, rushing to her car. She awkwardly scrambled inside, slammed the door, and nervously fumbled with the key, trying to start the ignition. Her stomach was churning with such agitation it was difficult to breathe.

Forcing herself to meet his nonchalance with equal composure, she raised her chin at a haughty angle, pulled out, and passed his rig without a single glance. She could just picture his hazel eyes dancing with mischief as he laughed at her feminine ruffle.

Her hands shook so she could hardly drive as she continued toward her destination. She checked the time. Only thirty minutes had passed since his truck had pulled to a stop yet it felt like a lifetime. His actions had been unforgivable and she could hardly wait to give her Aunt Margaret a detailed report.

With strong determination she tried to exclude his brutish behavior from her mind. She had a month's vacation ahead of her and wasn't intending to let any backwoods truck driver interfere with its pleasure.

Rubbing the back of her hand over her lips, she scrubbed ineffectively in hopes of erasing the taste of his mouth. There was no way she would admit his kiss had rocked her on her heels. The only reason she was hypersensitive to his embrace was that her temper was riled. The fact that he'd gotten the better of her undoubtedly helped make the imprint of his mouth linger so long too, she reflected seriously. No man had ever controlled her before or would again, she vowed with the beginning of a fine temper.

She floored the gas pedal, recklessly pulling around several cars she thought were going too slow. Intent on meeting her aunt on time, she refused to admit the stranger's kiss was the sweetest she'd ever experienced in twenty-eight years, the last twelve of which were spent kissing all the men she'd dated and usually many more times than once.

Steele laughed out loud, his husky amusement resounding in the cab when Sammi sped by in her old car with a fixity of purpose that left him in no doubt that she was unused to anyone curbing her spirited personality. What a delectable little wench she was.

With the powerful diesel motor humming, he eased his rig out into the right-hand lane. One hand reached for his citizen's band mike as he maneuvered smoothly up the highway.

"Breaker, breaker, one-nine. This is Steele Man. How about any of you runners northbound on one-oh-one in San Jose just past the Tully Road off ramp doing a fellow trucker a favor?"

"You got one, Steele Man. This is Flower Power. Go ahead," a high-pitched male voice answered instantly.

"I'll give a C note to the first truck jockey that gives me the end location of a 1970 blue Datsun two-door sedan with a yellow daisy on the antenna and a ebony-haired female inside."

"You got yourself a bird dog, buddy, long as she's staying on the same ribbon I'm on." He asked for and received the license number.

"An extra hundred's in it if you get me her handle too. I'll be cruising one quarter mile behind. I'm on a stood by. Thank you much, good buddy. Keep your rubber side down."

Steele relaxed, settling down for a smooth ride as he kept his eyes on Sammi's car. A smile tugged the corners of his mouth when he observed a florist's van switch lanes and pull in behind her. Evidently Flower Power was going to do a good job of bird-dogging.

Within five miles a small produce truck had eased in back of the florist's van while the Datsun continued up the freeway.

Out of the corner of his eye Steele watched a pickup truck hauling a boat speed by. A gray-haired old woman was motioning for the driver to hurry. Obviously CBer's, he thought, reading their handle stuck on the camper shell window in bright red letters. Big Daddy Bill and Sweet Momma. She sure as hell didn't look like any sweet momma he'd ever known.

At the same time Steele decided he had three bird dogs tailing Sammi, he caught a glimpse in his side-view mirror of a highway patrol car coming up fast with its headlights flashing on and off. It paused to cruise alongside his rig a moment then pulled ahead in a burst of speed.

Evidently his good friend Denny had been listening to channel one-nine when he put out his request.

Amused as four lanes of traffic suddenly slowed to exactly fifty-five miles per hour, Steele listened as his handle was called.

"Steele Man, this is Dennis the Menace. You'd better call off the hounds, 'cause you're getting a convoy going for your y/l. There's a trio riding hot on her trail now."

"This is Steele Man, Dennis. You're just the man I need. How about doing a rolling DMV for me then rendezvous at the San Francisco Produce Market?" Steele asked evenly.

"You know I can't do a ten-twenty-eight for you, Steele Man," Dennis the Menace replied with faked censure.

"I read you, good buddy," Steele acknowledged, knowing good and well his friend would have the name and address of the car's registered owner when they met. "One more thing," he requested with some concern. "I want to verify a fellow Smokey with a handle of Whit Smith working this same beat."

The glossy-haired wench had damn well better have been lying about being engaged. *No man* was going to stand between him and the only female who had affected him like a bolt out of the blue from the first sight of her gorgeous, sassy face. Damned if she hadn't thought her frosty glance would intimidate him into groveling subserviency while he changed her tire.

The saucy little beauty was lucky he hadn't hauled her into his cab and done every lustful thing that had crossed his mind when he glimpsed her near-naked body and delectable, tender-looking fanny as she leaned over into her car for his dollar tip. God, what a sight that was. It took all his control not to reach up and sink his teeth into the rounded flesh. Come to think of it, there wasn't an inch on her he wouldn't like to place his mouth on, he admitted without embarrassment as heat flooded his taut loins.

"There's no Smokey with that handle assigned here, Steele Man," the patrolman told him, breaking into his lascivious plans for Sammi. "I'll check further then meet you in forty-five minutes unless I get a call. Remember, good buddy, you're buying the coffee this time."

Steele agreed readily. He had many good friends employed in law enforcement throughout the United States and never envied any the dangerous job they had to do.

He lost sight of Sammi as a tall rig pulled in front of his near the airport. It made no difference now. The three CBer's bird-dogging his tantalizing siren should be reporting back soon.

"Seduction time is near," he concluded. She'd be surprised

when he showed up at her door later. A shave, shower, and wardrobe change should offset her first impression of him as a dirty, uncouth brute.

"Thank God she's not going to Canada," he commented out loud into the luxurious interior of his custom cab. He'd hate to haul a full trailer two states past its destination just to make out with a raven-haired beauty with flashing blue eyes and the luscious shape of a woman just made for a man to love. The tension between them had been electrifying. Much too unique not to pursue farther.

His heart started to thud unsteadily. Hell, he was ready to give her pleasure now, he groaned in frustration. His body was hard just envisioning her beneath him, unclothed, and pushing up tight against his nakedness. He ached with unexpected urgency to take her wildly at first, and the fervent desire to leave his mark of possession immediately. Next would be slower, exquisitely prolonged and with a leisurely tenderness that would totally fulfill them both. A man would kill to feel those long, silken thighs wrapped around his hips while thrusting deep into the heavenly warmth between.

Sammi slowed down, unaware three motorists had to reduce their speed also as she checked the overhead freeway signs. This was her fourth trip to San Francisco in the last three years, but there was always new construction and unfamiliar detours to maneuver through safely. She frowned, her dark, narrow brows furrowing as she concentrated on changing lanes to take the one going toward the Golden Gate Bridge.

Twenty minutes later Sammi pulled into the motel's parking lot. Her aunt had wanted to stay at the prestigious Sir Francis Drake, the Fairmont, or Westin St. Francis Hotel, but she'd talked her into reserving a room where she'd stayed during her last visit. With the downtown streets torn up for cable car repair, she knew she'd find it much easier getting in and out of a Lombard Street motel. Besides, she always seemed to end up on the wrong one-way street in those areas anyway.

A sigh of relief escaped her lips as she made a left turn, drove right past the gaudy office, and pulled to a stop in the assigned space for room seventy-eight. Intent on greeting her aunt, who opened the door the moment she saw her niece park, she was oblivious to the two trucks and pickup pulling a trailer that drove in directly behind her and braked behind large palm trees overlooking the paved parking lot.

"Aunt Margaret!" Sammi cried out with joy, clambering up to greet her relative with open arms.

They hugged each other affectionately. It had been nearly a year since they had visited in person.

"You look great," she enthused with excitement. She thought Margaret the most intelligent woman executive in the world. Being president of a prominent Denver savings and loan bank was quite a feat for any female.

The older woman pulled back, her eyes running over Sammi's skimpy attire with dismay. "Good heavens, Samantha, isn't that rather a revealing outfit to travel in?" Youth certainly had its advantages, she mused, aware her niece's flawless skin wouldn't have a wrinkle to mar its perfection for years to come.

Sammi frowned. "Don't you start, auntie dear. I'm still furious over the last derogatory comment on my mode of dress."

She went to the trunk of her car, then opened it, balanced her purse strap over one shoulder, reached to take a Pullman case in each hand, and walked the few steps to the door of the room her aunt had reserved after she flew in the night before.

A brief glance took in the sterile atmosphere of the double-size room with its two queen beds, small circular table with two chairs, and a color TV mounted on the wall shelf over a long dresser.

"The bed by the wall's yours, Samantha," her aunt pointed out, carting in the cosmetic case and tote. "I see you came prepared to knock 'em dead." She laughed. "You must have enough clothes to fill the biggest wardrobe in the world."

"Most of them outdated," Sammi called out, going back to the car to gather up the final item, a garment bag stuffed with new dresses purchased especially for her vacation. With her back turned, she leaned over to lay the zippered bag on the bed.

"Samantha!" Margaret cried out. "What have you been up to now? You have a large handprint directly over the fullest part of your derriere."

Sammi straightened, moving to the large mirror over one end of the dresser. Looking over her shoulder, she stared at the dark imprint. Each finger was outlined along with the masculine palm print in dirty gray, vivid against the impeccable white of her shorts.

"I'll kill him!" Sammi screamed, her temper mounting to think the red-haired brute had left his mark on her brand-new shorts.

"Who, dear?" her aunt asked calmly. She was used to her niece's fiery temper and uncanny knack for being in the middle of one tempest after another.

"It's a long story," Sammi grumbled irritably as she unzipped the largest Pullman case and garment bag to search for a different outfit suitable for exploring the city.

"Let's hear it later then, dear," Margaret suggested, noticing it was almost noon.

They were interrupted by a loud knock, and she asked Sammi to answer the door while she freshened her makeup and recombed her simple hairdo.

Surprised to see a funny-looking young man holding a bouquet out in front of his narrow chest, Sammi was prepared to tell him he had the wrong room when he thrust it into her hands.

Automatically taking hold of the calla lilies, she looked at them with distaste. They always reminded her of funerals, and she hated them, from the monstrous funnel-shaped flower to the fleshy yellow center spike. They had no smell and weren't even in a vase, much less decorated with leaves to give them a semblance of beauty. It was the least professional floral arrangement she'd ever seen.

"Sign here, miss," the young man demanded in a soprano voice so high it brought the arrogant trucker's pleasant low tones to mind.

"What the hell," Sammi whispered, taking the sheet of paper and signing a name. Before she could leave to get a tip from her purse, he had scurried off toward the front of the motel.

Wrinkling her slender nose in aversion, she walked into the bathroom. "Who would send you this ugly bunch of flowers, Aunt Margaret?"

Her relative stared at the smooth white blossoms and answered, "None of *my* gentlemen friends would dare. They're not for me, honey."

"Me either," Sammi told her, returning to lay them on the dresser.

"What did the card say?" Margaret asked.

"There wasn't any. A weird little man just stuck them in my hands, had me sign my name, and left."

"You'd better call the front office. They must have been delivered to the wrong room."

As Sammi dialed 0 for the office, there was another knock on the motel door. She hung up and walked forward, opening it to see what the wimpy little guy wanted now.

A husky dark-complexioned man in gray coveralls stood before her, holding out a small net sack filled with bright red Washington Delicious apples. At least she liked apples, she thought, waiting for him to speak.

"Welcome to San Francisco, lady," he greeted her in a heavily accented voice.

"What's this for?" Sammi asked. She'd never received a single thing during any of her previous visits, and now two gifts in ten minutes was getting ridiculous.

"For you," he replied nervously. "Sign here." He pointed it out, placing a crumpled sheet of paper in her hand.

"What the hell," she said again, took the paper and stubby pencil, and scribbled a name for the second time.

Just as Sammi slammed the door shut, Aunt Margaret walked into the room. She hadn't even bothered to search for a tip this time, deciding she had never asked for the stuff anyway.

Holding out the bag of apples to show her aunt, she commented curiously. "I guess the local chamber of commerce is busy today. I've heard tourism has decreased dramatically, but these token gratuities border on the absurd."

"I agree this is getting to be silly, but we don't have time to question the reason now." Margaret looked at the bag's label and asked thoughtfully, "Why would anyone from San Francisco give free apples from the State of Washington away?"

"Who cares?" Sammi chuckled. "I'll eat 'em."

They were interrupted for the third time by a loud banging on the brightly painted door.

"I might as well answer it," Sammi said, shrugging her shoulders. "I'm getting used to accepting weird gifts."

This time a homely old man with a pitiful, home-styled haircut, pot belly covered by a worn plaid shirt and wearing faded denims, stood before her. He refused to acknowledge her inquiring look as a short, obese woman with mean eyes poked him in the side.

Before he could speak, the woman blurted out. "We're from the California Parks and Recreation Department and would like to ask you a few questions."

Some representatives, Sammi thought sarcastically. She knew the state was short of funds, but sending this couple as spokespeople was a bit much.

"What?" she asked impudently, figuring she might as well get it over with. Things were becoming stranger all the time. She looked back to see Margaret's brows raised. Obviously her aunt thought something unusual was going on too.

"Do you have a fishing license?" the woman wheezed, her frizzy gray hair as offensive as her voice.

"No," Sammi replied.

"Do you intend to get one?" the woman continued, moving to stand in front of her husband, who seemed pleased to let her take over.

"No," Sammi continued rashly, hating the way the woman stared.

"Why not?"

"Because I don't fish!" Sammi shot back, turning away as Margaret spoke in her clear, authoritative voice.

"We have a reservation at Nick's at one o'clock, dear, and you still haven't dressed," her aunt prompted.

"Excuse me," Sammi turned back, giving the odd couple a cool look. Why should anyone, especially the Parks Department, care whether she fished or not? Didn't the Fish and Game Bureau handle that?

"That's all we needed, anyway," the woman managed to blurt out. "If you'll just sign your name and address here, we'll leave you to continue with your previous plans." Her fervor was unnatural.

Sammi raised one shoulder, took the note pad, and scribbled a name and address for the third time. With a forced smile, she handed the paper back and slammed the door shut.

"Hurry and change, Samantha. We don't want to be late for lunch. Knowing you, you'll be starved no matter how many times you stopped on the way here."

Sammi kicked off her sandals, slipped her blouse and shorts off, and glared. The beast ruined them, she thought, looking at his big paw print. Standing in wispy briefs and bra, she withdrew a simple oyster-white dress with navy trim that cost her a week's salary and deliberately forced the stranger to the back of her mind.

Margaret straightened her skirt, slipped into different pumps with a lower heel, and remarked with all seriousness, "I don't think it's a good idea to give any stranger your name or address."

"No problem," Sammi explained, her speech muffled as she slipped a lace-trimmed slip over her head, smoothed it, and put on her dress. She smiled mischievously. "I never use my real name or address."

She undid the band holding her thick hair in its braid, fluffing the ends with pink-tinted fingernails as she shook it out. "I didn't get to this age without learning a few basic survival skills."

"I should have known." Margaret chuckled. "You've always been a devious little devil."

"A trait I inherited from *your* side of the family," she teased, reaching into her cosmetic case. She brushed her hair until it lay in natural riotous curls that spread around her shoulders in a raven-black glossy mane that entranced all the men she met.

Noticing with much chagrin that she had no lipstick on, she felt a tremor deep in her abdomen—a sensual stirring she couldn't ignore. Her mouth was totally devoid of any color other than its natural one. *Damn him*, she moaned inwardly. The memory of his hungry kiss still lingered, and she was more angry by the minute.

Applying lip gloss with expertise that came from years of practice, she blotted it with a tissue and put the tube neatly back. She stared at her shining eyes in the mirror, hypocritically blaming their brightness on the overhead light. She knew full well it was the remaining physical sensitivity to a mouth that had played havoc with hers from the very first.

Bawdy, brazen brute! She hated everything about him.

She tightened the navy belt until it emphasized her narrow waist even further, gave a final glance at her reflection, inhaled deeply, then walked into the living area. Slipping into high-heeled pumps, she gathered a matching purse, carelessly crammed her billfold and necessary items inside, and stood back. *The hell with you, trucker!*

"Let's hit the road, Aunt Margaret. I've eaten at Nick's before and can hardly wait to dine there again." Her smile was sincere.

Happy laughter filled the air as they walked to Sammi's Datsun.

Her aunt's features were filled with doubt when she gave it a thorough inspection. "You really should buy a new car, dear."

"I can't afford one," Sammi returned, not the least embarrassed by her aged vehicle.

"Not with that wardrobe, you can't," Margaret pointed out.

"I guess I like clothes better than cars," Sammi replied matter-of-factly. "Besides, all my dates have super wheels." She cautiously slid behind the steering wheel, careful not to scuff her shiny pumps or wrinkle her stylish dress.

Amused by her aunt's doubtful expression as she glanced at the dented right fender, Sammi reassured her softly, "Don't worry, Margaret. It'll get us there and that's all that matters."

CHAPTER TWO

"Samantha Thatcher, resident of Burbank, California," Steele repeated, liking the sound of her name. "Thanks, Denny. I owe you a big favor for getting the stats on my young lady from the Department of Motor Vehicles."

He was in a hurry and appreciated his friend's speed in sharing the privileged information. It hadn't been the least surprising to find out there was no Officer Whit Smith wearing the khaki-colored uniform of the California Highway Patrol.

Damn the lying little minx, he reflected silently. With one long swallow he emptied a cup of coffee, set the heavy pottery mug back on its saucer, laid money down to pay their bill, tipped the waitress, and excused himself.

Walking to the borrowed car, he thought back over the busy last half hour. He had talked with his bird dogs—all three of them—showered and changed clothes in the private rest room of the produce market owner, Vic, and gulped a lukewarm drink in between writing down the name and address of a woman immensely important to his future plans.

"Thanks, Vic," he said, returning the pressure as he shook hands good-bye. "I'll get your Italian chariot back to you later and guarantee it to be in one sleek piece of metal with all its fifteen coats of silver paint intact."

"You'd better, Steele," his long-time business friend warned. "There's magic under that hood. It's never failed me yet."

"With your blatant womanizing, I presume." Steele laughed.

"*Che sarà, sarà.*" Vic shrugged, refusing to comment further on his current life-style.

"I admit I'll probably need all the help I can handling this one," Steele told him, accepting the car key.

"Take care," his friend advised in a voice tinged with amusement. "That expensive ego booster took a big chunk out of a month's profit."

"Maybe I'm in the wrong business," Steele teased as he slid his long length into the low-slung Lamborghini Countach sports car.

"Don't cry poor trucker to me," Vic chided. "I know what income-tax bracket you're in." He frowned, suddenly serious. "How come you're driving a rig anyway instead of running the head office?"

"One of my drivers had a severe coronary coming through Ventura. His family's in Georgia, so I flew down to assure him he needn't worry about a thing until his wife arrived. It's been a pretty hectic three days, and to unwind I decided to finish his run myself."

"Is he okay now?"

"The doctors say he's on the way to a quick recovery," Steele said, smoothing a casual knit shirt into comfortable slacks that outlined his strong limbs. "Thanks for letting me use your dressing room. My first appearance was an obvious turn off, and I'm hoping my next impression will be better received. You should have heard her light into me." He laughed. "With all that energy channeled in the right direction she'll be something else!"

"I sure hope so," Vic scoffed. "A one-night stand's hardly worth the kind of cash you're putting out."

"She's no one-nighter, Vic," Steele assured him with a note of displeasure in his voice for even hinting such a thing. "No further questions now or your hot Italian blood will start stirring and you'll try to convince her a commission merchant is a better catch than a trucker."

As Vic waved farewell, his index finger and thumb joined to

offer wishes for victory in his friend's pursuit of feminine pleasure.

Steele eased across the wide streets, weaving through numerous trucks finishing the day's loading and unloading of vast quantities of fruits and vegetables necessary to keep the city of San Francisco and the surrounding areas supplied.

He was eager to get to the Lombard Street corner Jack in the Box, the agreed rendezvous point, and pay his bird dogs for the same information Dennis had given him for free. He'd learned the name of the motel she was staying at when they'd reported her destination earlier.

Within minutes he had swung the low-riding automobile into an empty space and parked. He'd told them what make of car he would be driving. As expected, they were impatiently awaiting his arrival. He easily recognized the trio of CBer's and sympathized with their need to make a fast buck. It hadn't been too many years since he'd been after a quick dollar too.

Steel eased out from under the wheel and stood up. He watched the florist walk forward, aware the man's glance swung nervously up and down his stylishly clad torso with the same thoroughness that his own had traveled over Samantha's.

God, it was nice to know her name. It seemed to fit her strong personality. Sassy and unique. He'd never known anyone called that before.

"Flower Power?" he asked, giving the outstretched hand a firm shake. The contrast between his tanned, work-calloused palm and the pale, cared-for hand in his was almost as startling as that of his own and the woman he was pursuing.

"Yes, Steele Man," the younger man answered. "I've got your woman's handle as you requested."

"Great," Steele told him in a friendly manner. He reached into his hip pocket, withdrew a fine leather wallet, and opened it to remove two one-hundred-dollar bills.

"Thanks, good buddy," Steele called out as the youth rushed to his employee's van to continue his deliveries.

His eyes lowered, expecting to see Samantha Thatcher on the invoice.

"Betty Boop!" he exclaimed beneath his breath, barely having time to get angered over her continued prevarication. What the hell kind of liar was he getting involved with?

His brief introspection ended when he reached up to shake the huge, dirt-stained hand of a truck farmer he'd occasionally seen either selling artichokes at Vic's or buying produce for his roadside stand.

They exchanged paper. Two one-hundred-dollar bills for a crumpled note with a penciled name in the same feminine scrawl.

"My God, the damned wench," he growled with increased fury. His eyes took in the words Jane Doe in disbelief. This one was definitely out of control. The sooner he formulated his plans to curb her impudence, the sooner the whole world would be better off. No telling what havoc she raised in the city of Burbank.

"Steele Man?"

"Yes, ma'am," he answered politely. This was definitely no sweet momma facing him. The florid-faced homely woman standing before a gentle-looking old man was going to see she wrung every dollar out of him possible. He'd seen that look before and wasn't fooled for a second.

"You owe me two hundred dollars."

"I know and here it is, ma'am," he told her, reaching into his wallet for the third time. It was fortunate he always carried a large sum of money as he was depleting it fast.

Taking the bills greedily, she shoved them down the front of her blouse after turning briefly away so he couldn't see her bosom.

God, he thought with sarcasm, *no one* in their right mind would want to look at those fat, saggy breasts.

She turned back to him, unaware her husband had given him a resigned look of apology for his wife's coy actions and poor manners.

"How much is it worth to you to know where she's going to have lunch?"

"Do you know?" Steele asked with mounting curiosity. It would be interesting to see Samantha's face if he was waiting at the restaurant when she walked in.

"I could or I couldn't," the woman sneered, batting eyes that were as faded as her husband's jeans at him.

"Depending on what?" Steele knew damn well what would revive her memory. The color green. The same green as on hundred-dollar bills.

"Depending on your generosity," she told him smugly.

Tired of playing games, Steele asked, "How much?" He'd give the old bat what she wanted, eager to get on with his sudden change of plans.

"Three hundred bucks."

"No deal," he told her, turning away to get in Vic's car. He decided to let her sweat a minute. He knew damn well she'd accept less and didn't want her to think him a complete fool.

"Give him the name of the café, sweetie," her husband interrupted. "The man's already paid you far more than he should have. It wasn't even out of our way to follow the young lass."

"Shut up, Bill. He can afford it," his wife shot back. She turned to glare at her husband, nagging in bitter condemnation. "If I hadn't married you, I'd be riding in an expensive sports car like his instead of bouncing cross-country in an aged pickup truck."

"Two hundred," she demanded, when Steele slammed the door in her face and started the motor.

"Fair enough," he conceded, handing out two more bills. "Where's she eating?"

"She and another lady have a reservation at Nick's at one o'clock."

Steele nodded to the woman, smiled sympathetically at the old man, and left without a backward glance. He hoped Samantha wasn't early, as he had another plan or two up his sleeve. He'd teach the minx to lie.

With a powerful roar he took off, knowing the shortest, fastest route possible to Fisherman's Wharf. Being a long-time acquaintance of Nick and his host, Luigi, would be a definite advantage.

He parked in one of several spaces reserved for friends of the owner and prepared to step out. For the first time he glanced at the name and address handed him by the obnoxious woman. Prepared this time, he laughed out loud.

This was one young woman who needed special handling for certain. Imagine having the gall to write Petunia—*God, where'd she think that one up?*—Petunia Smith. Apparently she had a fixation on the last name of Smith. His fury came suddenly as he recalled the lie about her *very jealous fiancé* with the same surname.

She'd pay for her impudence all right. He'd just blown eight hundred dollars for finding out he had the hots for a Ms. Samantha *Betty Boop Jane Doe Petunia Smith* Thatcher!

True to sweet momma's word they were parked on Fisherman's Wharf, had walked to the lobby, and were being escorted to an upstairs seat in Nick's at the stroke of one.

"I like Nick's decor with its high booths," Margaret mentioned, her eyes keen as they glanced around the room then returned to the compelling display outside the window. "I've never cared about staring across a table and locking eyes with a stranger."

"I agree," Sammi responded with a warm smile. "How was the conference?" Her aunt was on her way home from a weeklong meeting in Hawaii. "I'm glad you decided to join me for a few days rest and recreation before returning to Colorado high finance."

"So am I," Margaret concurred, giving a weary sigh.

"Did you have a good time?" Sammi's interest was genuine. Other than a few second cousins scattered across the Midwest, the older woman was her only living relative. They'd always been close, more like sisters than aunt and niece two decades apart in age.

She eyed Margaret's slender figure clad in a stylish navy blue suit that would have been severe had it not been for the pretty silk blouse in deep coral. Her straight hair was glossy, coiffed in a short, easy-care style, and professionally streaked to cover the appearance of gray among the medium-brown strands. She was elegant, intelligent, warm, and the finest woman she knew.

"Attending two or three financial conferences a year lessens the excitement considerably," Margaret answered briskly. "*This* is fun."

"I hope so," Sammi replied. "I'm rather excited about the men you've lined up. Double-dating with you should be a blast."

"You'd better behave for once. I said you were adorably sweet."

"That should test my acting ability." Sammi laughed.

Their conversation was checked by the waiter's low voice greeting them as he placed glasses of ice water, chilled butter, and a basket of napkin-wrapped warm bread on the table before handing each a large menu that had been tucked under his arm.

When he left, Sammi told her aunt with exaggerated enthusiasm, "Cute, isn't he? Italians have a reputation for being really great in the sack. Excellent, innovative lovers, I hear. Too bad he's a waiter. They earn abominable wages."

"Samantha dear, please shush," her aunt scolded. "Your talk is shameless sometimes. You're supposed to be reading the menu not speculating on the young boy's sexual prowess."

"I've already decided," Sammi explained, laying down the menu to stare at the impeccably dressed waiter in his black and white uniform. She observed his warm brown eyes light up as he returned to take their order. They swept over her features with the same fervor that the brute's had. A wide smile raised her pink-glossed lips with impudence. It was always fun to return look for look with a man. It invariably made them all ill at ease and the first to look away. This young flirt was no exception and it gave her feminine ego another boost. Men were so easy to handle if you just took the time to psych them out. *All except the beast*, she meditated.

Sammi ordered the luncheon special, asked Margaret if she'd like to share an antipasto with her, and requested a large glass of iced tea as soon as the waiter had time to bring it to their table. The way he was staring, she knew he'd return within moments.

Concentrating on spreading butter in a thick yellow swathe on squishy, soft sourdough bread surrounded by a chewy browned crust, she wasn't aware her aunt was studying her closely.

"Dare I ask how you got that hand print on your bottom, dear?"

"A redheaded brute did it," Sammi told her, chewing the delicious crust with obvious pleasure. She was starved. It had been far too long since she'd tasted such delectable French bread.

"Why?" Margaret asked, tearing a dainty piece off a slice and applying a thin layer of butter. She constantly had to watch her diet to keep a slender figure and envied her niece's high metabolism that appeared to burn up calories as fast as she could replenish them.

"Just a typical example of excessive male hormones and the need to dominate."

"What had you done to make this necessary, Samantha?" Margaret knew there was bound to be much more to the story than she'd heard so far. Her niece's sassy tongue and boldness had worried her parents long before their death when Samantha was twenty-two.

"Not much," Sammi explained, chewing the last bit of crust. She looked at her aunt, a deep frown puckering her brows. "I had a flat tire this morning and some damn hick trucker changed it. He got insulted because I offered to pay him so he put his hand on my butt."

"That's such an unladylike term," her aunt scolded.

"Okay, Margaret." Sammi chuckled. "But his big paw was resting on my backside and I have evidence to prove it. The cleaners will never be able to get his grimy hand print out and they're brand-new shorts. Pretty sexy ones too, if his darkened hazel eyes were any indication of his heightened libido. His look was downright lewd."

"I think you asked for it," Margaret told her, smiling at their waiter as he placed the meal on the table. He couldn't take his eyes off her niece, and if their shimmering warmth was any indication, his libido was heightened too. "You really did, you know?"

"I did not!" Sammi disagreed loudly. She poked her fork through the rich concoction of crab, prawns, and lobster mixed with noodles simmered in heavy cream and seasoned butter. It was thick, luscious, and loaded with tons of fattening calories, and she didn't intend to leave a single bit of it in the casserole dish.

"I disagree. Any woman wearing the revealing outfit you had on is subject to advances from men. It clung to your body like a second skin."

"Maybe so, but no male has the right to put his hands on any female without her permission, no matter what she is or isn't wearing."

"That's true," Margaret concurred, dipping a piece of broiled Petrale sole into a side dish of tartar sauce. "Unfortunately, your tall, voluptuous, leggy figure is lush, and exposed as it was in those skimpy shorts and brief blouse, any man with his sight intact would consider it his duty to see if you were available."

"The merchandise was for display only. No man gets to handle the goods without my prior consent," she blurted out angrily. The thought of how bold the trucker had been sent a shiver up her spine. She couldn't imagine that brute ever asking a woman for approval no matter what liberty he sought. He was all action and few words. Her stomach somersaulted just thinking of him. It was his red hair. Had to be. She'd completely erased his kiss from her mind hours ago. Almost anyway.

"Did he ask?" Margaret inquired.

"What?" Sammi asked. Her temper was rising and she'd forgotten her aunt's question.

"Did he ask to touch the, er, merchandise, as you so *in*delicately put it."

"God no! That trucker wouldn't ask permission to do anything," Sammi fumed. "He was the most arrogant, impossible man I've ever come in contact with."

She leaned over the table, her blue eyes shooting sapphire sparks that drew attention to the perfection of her classic features.

"He had red hair!" she burst out. "A redheaded giant of a brute. Now do you see why I hate him so?"

Margaret's soft laughter brought out the tiny lines by her eyes. "Samantha Thatcher, you're crazy. No one in their right mind would condemn a man for the color of his hair."

"Why not?" Sammi demanded. "You know I've always hated the species and always will."

"Have you ever considered it might be because that *species* could have a temper equal to yours and the strength to curb some of the bold recklessness you carry like a shield?"

Margaret's curiosity was aroused. Samantha was acting differently. Surely her thoughts weren't on the trucker who'd helped her out? If so, she'd like to see the man. Her niece had walked over every male she'd met since she'd first learned how to handle her natural beauty. Years of practice bantering unsought advances had honed her technique down to such a science she should be teaching classes in how to parry with the opposite sex and keep them happy at the same time. She had more men friends than any woman she'd ever known.

"Are you still a virgin, dear?" Margaret asked curiously.

"Yes, damn it," Sammi told her, expelling her breath at the thought. She leaned forward, explaining dramatically "I just can't find the right man. I've made a study on where to meet rich, eligible bachelors. I've attended so many sports functions, financial symposiums, and computer science assemblies I could scream. I've read *The Wall Street Journal,* studied the stock market until I damn near began to understand it, and paid one hundred and twenty-five dollars for Peter Finkbeiner-Zellman's book, *In World Guide,* figuring if anything could help me find out where the millionaires are, that would."

Sammi threw her hands up in disgust, leaned against the back of the booth, and moaned. "For all the good it did me I should have stayed the hell at home and learned to knit!"

"You shouldn't curse so much, Samantha. It's not feminine."

"My God, Auntie, you sound just like the beast today," Sammi said. "He told me he didn't like women who swear either. As if I give a damn. I only do it when I'm irritated anyway."

"Which is often," Margaret teased.

"True," Sammi admitted, more aware of her tempestuous personality than anyone.

"Maybe it's frustration instead of irritation that causes it," her aunt suggested. "You seem to have a lot of excess energy all the time."

"If it's frustration, I've had it for ten years," Sammi told her, vigorously stirring sugar into her second glass of tea.

"You're such a passionate-acting and -looking woman, I'm amazed you haven't succumbed to at least one of the men who've been chasing you since you were a mature fifteen years old."

"If those men knew I was so innocent as a teen-ager that I had to buy a *Playgirl* magazine just to see what a naked adult male looked like, they'd never believe it."

"That comes from being raised as a single child with no brothers, honey," her aunt mentioned sympathetically. "In many ways you led a sheltered life during puberty, but now"—her voice rose—"you've had your own apartment and been on your own so long, surely being propositioned by men is a way of life."

"That hasn't been a problem since I was eighteen." Sammi chuckled.

"Why not?" It amazed her that her niece had remained virtuous. She knew her many friends lived a free life-style.

"Easy." Sammi chuckled. "One of my lawyer boyfriends drew up a contract at my request that has cooled the ardor of my most persistent dates. Even he wouldn't sign it and he was passionate as hell."

"A contract?" She could imagine what it said if her niece had anything to do with it.

"It's legal too," Sammi told her. "When a date comes on too strong and won't take no for an answer, I dig it out of my purse, and by the time I've read all the wherefores and whereases, he's much less in the mood to make love. Read it and see what you think."

Sammi rooted through her purse and pulled out a long envelope. She handed it to Margaret, watching as she unfolded the legal-size papers.

Her aunt scanned the professionally typed sheets with astute thoroughness attained from years of practice reading intricate monetary contracts. She flipped the page, making no comment until she clearly understood each word of the contractual statement.

Margaret's eyes lifted, filled with derision as she observed her niece's intense expression.

"Samantha Thatcher," she said clearly. "I find this arrangement unbelievable even considering you had it drawn up."

"I don't know why," Sammi told her seriously. "It's merely a no-holds-barred gentlemen's agreement."

"Hardly that, my dear," her aunt pointed out, resting a manicured fingernail on the first condition and reading each word verbatim, " 'I, the undersigned, agree that on this date [blank space provided] I had sexual relations with Ms. Samantha Thatcher.' "

"What's so bad about that?" Sammi asked, perturbed by the open expression of dismay.

Margaret ignored the question, going right to condition number two. " 'I, being of sound mind, also agree that if any children born of this intimate relationship shall result, I bear full responsibility for its conception.'"

"There's nothing wrong with that either," Sammi persisted. "It's no different than a prenuptial agreement for the division of property in case of a subsequent divorce."

"Shame on you, Samantha," her aunt scoffed. "There's hardly a comparison between financial assets and physical ones."

"Not necessarily. I'm merely guaranteeing any, er, physical repercussion be the responsibility of his or her natural father."

Sammi swirled the crushed ice in her glass, took a sip of the aromatic tea, and continued unabashed. "Frankly, I should market these contracts worldwide. I'd probably make a fortune," she said with conviction. "I might even receive a Nobel peace prize for my brilliant contribution to women's causes."

She chuckled softly, her radiant eyes alight with mischief. Leaning forward, she rested both elbows on the edge of the table, remembering with sudden annoyance the attitude of some of her less-desirable men friends.

"You know as well as I do there'd be damn fewer fatherless kids running around if the male of the species had to sign an agreement admitting full responsibility for his part in the conception and giving a promise to pay for all expenses until the child reaches legal age."

"The entire idea's preposterous," Margaret told her. "I can certainly understand why it cools your dates' ardor. You list a total of expenses that comes to three hundred and fifty thousand dollars!"

"All carefully researched," Sammi added truthfully. She picked up an olive from the dish of antipasto between them, plopped it into her mouth, and chewed. Reaching for another, she laughed as her aunt listed one by one the stipulations Sammi had thought necessary for the care of a child.

"Good heavens," Margaret continued, her consternation rising as she perused the list for the second time. "Exclusive prenatal care and extended hospitalization for you. Why a private room? They're frightfully expensive. Plus live-in help for five years?"

"I figure to give my first and subsequent lovers the best I have to offer, so why shouldn't they shell out plenty too?" Sammi explained, crunching a crispy slice of iced celery.

"Fair enough," Margaret answered matter-of-factly. There was no need to censure her niece. She had obviously used the contract many times to put off overly ardent suitors. If it worked to quell their passion, why should she complain? Apparently it had stopped the men she dated thus far from using her for their own pleasures.

Finished with the celery, Sammi pulled the dish toward her, searching through the attractive appetizers for the foods she liked best. She speared a pickled mushroom, tasted a small bite, and put the remaining piece in her mouth. It was delicious.

"How'd you like the clause about using a pediatrician of my choice, dental care, hospital insurance, clothes, food, and housing for both of us?" She chewed a slice of mild provolone cheese, took another drink of iced tea, and set the glass down.

"Those conditions are understandable," her aunt granted between sips of steaming coffee. She watched Samantha daintily pick out each morsel and eat it with obvious enjoyment.

"Why private schooling? You went to public schools and it sufficed very nicely."

"I know it." Sammi chuckled, reaching for a deviled egg half; its bright yellow yolk had been swirled artistically and garnished with teeny bits of pimiento and chopped fresh chives.

"That's just for show. I figure if a man assumes he has to foot the bill for private schools and four years at the most expensive college in the country, he'll cool down all the faster. It's worked too," she teased, eating the egg and pushing the plate aside.

She motioned for the waiter, asking in her sweetest voice, "I'd like to order dessert now, Antonio." She rolled his name off her tongue expertly, just as if she spoke his native language.

Being called by his first name made his eyes turn to liquid fire.

He shifted uncomfortably, awestruck by the most kissable lips he'd ever seen.

"I'd like cherries jubilee." Sammi ordered in her huskiest voice, enjoying the brief interplay. She lowered her lashes demurely in a pretense of shy innocence.

Antonio's soft brown eyes filled with dismay. They didn't have that on their menu, and he hated to turn down anything this particular customer wanted. *Dio!* She was a beauty!

"Don't worry about it, Tony," she told him softly, aware he was about to ask her what her second choice would be. "What else do you have that's decadently sweet and terribly fattening?"

"The zabaglione, spumoni, and chocolate mousse are all delicious," he advised, his eyes lingering on the riot of ebony curls framing her lovely face.

"Chocolate mousse will be fine," she told him, adding as an afterthought, "a double serving of whipped cream on top, please."

Deciding to indulge also, Margaret had him double the order. She could diet tomorrow. Still curious about her niece's contract, she leaned against the back of the booth and queried, "How did you arrive at the staggering sum listed?"

"I added the cost of raising a child to legal age and extras for me," Sammi explained. She looked at her aunt and smiled. "The figure's been updated as the cost-of-living index rises."

Before Margaret could comment, Sammi added with saucy insistence, "In the past ten years the price—for me—has more than doubled."

"I can't believe this is a fail-safe contract," Margaret directed doubtfully. "Given the same situation, people invariably react differently."

"True," Sammi concurred. "The adverse backlash has been several marriage proposals from men I wasn't the least interested in." She shrugged one silk-clad shoulder and shook her head as she contemplated their reasons. "They must have figured they might as well support me full-time than be financially responsible for a child that was the result of a one-night stand."

"Your language borders on the crude sometimes, dear," Margaret rebuked calmly.

"What would you call it, Auntie dear? A single night making out? Getting it on? A hot, rowdy romp in the sack?" She chuckled as her relative's fine brows drew together in reproof. "Sex by any other name is still the same. Besides, it's all hypothetical anyway."

"Time for a change of subject, niece," Margaret scolded. "No man will ever sign his life away to the tune of that kind of money even to be first in bed with you."

"And *that*, my loving aunt, is the whole purpose of the contract!" Sammi laughed, not the least perturbed by Margaret's remark.

She looked away, watching as their waiter walked forward carrying two fluted parfait dishes on a silver tray. He set their dessert before them with all the flamboyance of a page serving his queen.

"Thanks, Tony." Sammi smiled, her eyes sparkling the deepest blue he'd ever seen.

When he left them, Sammi asked bluntly, "Tell me who you've got lined up for me to charm the next few nights?" She was especially curious since Margaret was well aware of the type of man who interested her.

"I think you need a rest from men more than additional dates, but first," Margaret said, studying her with personal interest in her future happiness, "a special friend of mine is bringing his younger brother for you."

"Is he wealthy?" Sammi immediately asked. She saw no reason to set her sights on a man who couldn't provide her with the kind of life-style she'd aspired to over the last ten years.

"Very," her aunt told her. "He's divorced, has no children, but does have a fine house in Marin County."

"Great!" Sammi's eyes widened appreciatively. "He probably has a hot tub and a Mercedes-Benz too."

"Doesn't everyone there?" Margaret teased back. "I've read a few books on the area myself."

"Where are they taking us?"

"La Bourgogne. It's very expensive with classic French cuisine."

"Fantastic! First class all the way. Just as I prefer." Sammi took a spoonful of the delectable mousse, savored the smooth taste, and swallowed slowly. It was the perfect end to a fine meal.

"Don't you even want to know what the first man looks like?" Margaret asked softly.

"Who cares?" Sammi shot back. "As long as he's no hick truck driver he'll suit me fine." Her stomach muscles clenched and she could feel a shiver run the length of her spine when his image filled her mind. She'd never forget his brazen attack.

"Would you see him again?" Margaret asked casually.

"God no!" Sammi stormed back. "How could I anyway? He doesn't have the foggiest idea who I am or even where I am."

"Didn't you exchange names?"

"Heavens no!" Sammi's eyes sparkled like precious jewels as she leaned over the table and gave an exasperated retort. "We were just beauty and the beast."

Sammi laughed, continuing in a clear voice, "That's a perfect description. You should have seen him, Margaret. He's a hick! A great big uncouth brute. A real airhead! A hillbilly eighteen-wheeler!"

"Enough! Enough!" Margaret stated sharply. "You really have it in for your knight of the road, don't you?"

"Need you ask?" Sammi gave a moan of irritation. "I can't even bear to think of the grimy man. He was terrible from the very first. The *last* man ever to interest me would be a down-and-out, domineering trucker who put me in, er, *tried* to put me in my place first."

"He sounds more intriguing all the time," Margaret tossed

back. Any man who could get the better of her niece she'd love to meet.

"For who?" Sammi snorted. Not giving her aunt time to reply, she continued with disgust. "The thought of what a date with that lout would be like is unbearable." She raised her eyes toward the ceiling in emphasis. "Warm beer, cold popcorn, and an X-rated movie followed by a wrestling match in the cab of his huge truck!

"Tell me about the second guy," Sammi prompted, deliberately forcing the brawny monster from her mind. If her aunt had three men lined up to meet, one should be a Prince Charming. She was darned tired of paying for her own clothes. Settling her charge cards was getting harder and harder each month. A direct ratio to the rising quality of her purchases.

"He's younger," Margaret enthused, pleased to see Samantha's temper subside. "His father's the wealthy one now, but when he finishes classes at Stanford he intends to specialize in internal medicine."

"They're getting better," Sammi applauded. "Doctors earn scads of money, the wives live in gorgeous homes and have unlimited charge cards. I'd have my own Porsche, fur coats to wear in winter, and a swimming pool to lounge by in the summer."

"Samantha!" Margaret scolded. "Doesn't their personality count at all?"

"Money improves everything about a man. His personality. His looks. His intelligence."

"Shush!" her aunt admonished, hoping no one had overheard her niece's foolish repartee. She was getting more out of hand each year.

"Tell me about number three," Sammi coaxed, amused by Margaret's puckered brow as she tried to decide if she was serious or not.

"He might be the best one," Margaret sighed. "His father's a sweetheart. One of the nicest men I've met in fact. Paul's a very prominent attorney. His son, Alan Anderson, is a partner in the firm."

"I love him already," Sammi crooned. "His name's beautiful. What's he look like?"

"From what I've seen of his photos he's your ideal. He's handsome, a perfect age for you, and has blond hair and baby-blue eyes, plus he drives a brand-new bright red Corvette."

"Sounds perfect. I'm glad he's last. It adds to the excitement to savor the best for the tail end," Sammi insisted. "How come he's not married if he's so great?" Perfect men were in high demand anywhere.

"His father told me he was deeply in love with a young woman who married a renowned contractor. In fact, he was the owner-builder of Hidden Coves Estates, where you stayed last year during your trip up the coast."

"My God, I wish I'd known that *he* was single. I'd have hung around the development until I hooked him."

"Alan's father told me he's firmly committed to his wife."

"Too bad, but Alan should be a cinch. Hooking a man on the rebound's the easiest catch of all," Sammi replied. She'd had plenty of experience with them, and they'd all been ripe for plucking if she'd been so inclined. All were positive pushovers in fact.

"Not hardly the rebound, honey," Margaret explained. "It's been a couple years now since they split up and he's been involved in one romantic liaison after another since then. She was a beautiful young woman, Paul told me. He seemed as despondent as his son that they hadn't married."

"It sounds like we have a terrific three nights ahead." Sammi sighed. "Having an attractive single aunt is a definite asset."

"It should be interesting," Margaret agreed pleasantly. "Though I think you're wrong to place so much importance on a man's bank balance."

"That's surprising coming from the president of a savings and loan company," Sammi pointed out. "You're surrounded by tons of the green stuff all day long. All I seek is enough of it to keep me in the style I want to become accustomed to."

She reached inside her purse for money to settle their bill. With three eligible bachelors lined up she was more than happy to pay for the excellent lunch. Placing a generous tip on the table for Tony, she looked up when her aunt chided her.

"You're becoming more impossible each year, Samantha," Margaret warned her.

"My dear, naive aunt, that's because it took me a while to find out that I prefer silk instead of polyester next to my skin, satin instead of cotton on my bed, leather instead of vinyl on my feet, and mink instead of rabbit next to my face."

"You sound just like a gold digger!" Margaret exclaimed.

"I know it and so what? It should be as easy to fall in love with a rich man as a poor one." Sammi's brows rose; she was not cowed by her aunt's derogatory comment. She saw nothing to be ashamed of.

"What will you offer in return? There has to be some giving on your side when and if you find the man of your choice."

"No problem there," Sammi insisted, having a ready answer for each question Margaret asked. "I'm an excellent cook, keep a neat house, am well-read, personable, and give great parties. In addition, I'll be a faithful, though not necessarily an exciting lover as a wife."

Her eyes closed, face innocently rapt, as she contemplated. "So far no man's turned me on enough to guarantee I'll ever act like a call girl in his bed. God knows I've kissed enough that one should have lit a spark!"

"Here you go again," her aunt scolded. "Your talk is so brazen."

"No, Margaret, it's not. I'm being honest now."

Sammi's thoughts returned to the earlier encounter in San Jose. A gnawing sensation curled in the depth of her abdomen, causing a tremor to run up her spine. The broad clutching palm with fingers splayed over the swell of her bottom hadn't been the least offensive. She could still feel the pressure of being drawn against his body. A taut, explicitly male form, to be exact.

They had touched from breast to thigh. His denim jeans had been rough against her bare legs. A hard, sensual roughness that wasn't unpleasurable, merely emphasizing the contrast in their gender. His lean, muscular strength was unyielding. Her feminine curves were soft and easily melded to complement their difference.

She'd never been kissed by anyone that much taller, that strong, and especially that experienced. The entire situation had taken her by surprise. That had to be the only reason the embrace lingered in her mind.

Her eyes closed in a vain attempt to blot out the touch of his mouth. She'd never had a man take her breath away—literally! The interchange was the most intimate she'd ever experienced. To think it was at the side of a busy freeway made it even more absurd. What on earth would he be like in the privacy of a bedroom?

"If you won't share those profound fantasies with me, then let's leave. I want to inhale some of this gorgeous ocean air."

Margaret gathered her purse and stood up, turning to wait for Sammi to do likewise. Her niece was acting unusual. The faraway expression had softened but was still remote and innocent. Yet passionate too.

Graceful as a model, Sammi slid from the booth and walked with unconscious sensuality to the door. She was proud of her height. With head held high and back straight, she left the dining room with her aunt to walk outside.

They strolled to the wooden railing, enjoying the shared silence of watching scenic private boats bobbing in the wake left by a large ship passing by.

Sympathetic to her aunt's sudden look of fatigue, Sammi suggested forgoing the anticipated foray into the local department stores and returning to their motel after an unhurried stroll around the wharf.

"If you don't mind, Margaret, I think I'll buy a book and retire early tonight."

With a look of acute pleasure, her aunt agreed that a full night's sleep would be wonderful. "Nothing sounds better to me than a long, leisurely bubble bath and a soft bed."

"It won't hurt me either to catch up on my rest." Sammi yawned. "I've been to a constant round of parties these last few weeks. I can't remember a single night I've hit the sack before one o'clock in the morning."

She hoped Margaret didn't realize she was lying. Energy surged through her body. It was impossible to remember when she felt better. Pretending lethargy the rest of the afternoon and evening would take all her acting ability if she was to perpetrate the lie.

At eight in the evening Sammi sat in the middle of her bed, munching on a crisp apple. She smiled compassionately at her aunt's figure curled in the center of the other bed. True to her wishes, she'd soaked in fragrant bubble bath and barely crawled between the crisply laundered sheets before she was sound asleep.

Hoping a luxuriant soak in perfumed suds would relax her taut nerves, Sammi filled the deep tub with warm water. She hung her clothes up neatly, rinsed out her underwear and draped them over a towel rack, and eased into the comfortable tub.

The room was unnaturally quiet and it heightened her senses. She couldn't watch TV or listen to the bedside radio for fear of waking her aunt. The unaccustomed silence acted in reverse. Instead of making her drowsy, it sharpened her awareness of the absurdity of going to bed before most people had eaten their dinner.

Finished much too soon, Sammi released the water. She stood up and reached for the white terry cloth towel. Wrapped around her damp curves, it revealed the perfection of flawless skin tinged with the rose-colored blush left by her recent bath.

She padded barefoot into the bedroom to root through the

smallest Pullman case for a satin camisole and tap-pant set she had purchased last month but never worn. They looked like the perfect sleep wear. Soft, shimmery, and decidedly sensuous.

With one hand clutching the towel to her breast, the other searched through the overflowing case in the darkened room lighted only by the glare from the bathroom.

"Damn!" she muttered, letting the towel drop. The thing was too short to cover her decently anyway.

"Ah, here they are," she whispered. Picking up the skimpy nightclothes, she flopped the lid down and took one step toward the bathroom when the phone rang. The unexpected shrill sound shattered her nerves. With ill humor at the possibility of disturbing her aunt, she reached out.

A quick glance proved the sharp ring hadn't disturbed Margaret's deep sleep. Sammi sighed with relief, lifted the receiver, and cradled the mouthpiece in both hands to muffle her voice as she prepared to answer.

CHAPTER THREE

"Sam?"

Instantly recognizing the deep-voiced caller, Sammi trembled uncontrollably. It was the beast! The arrogant stranger who had disturbed her thoughts throughout the afternoon.

"You've got the wrong number," she shot back in a harsh whisper.

"The hell I do . . . *Samantha Thatcher*! Get your sassy little rear in gear, woman, 'cause we're going out."

"Go to hell . . . *Red*!"

Sammi slammed the receiver down with fingers that shook so badly she barely hit the cradle. She snatched up the discarded towel and securely wrapped it around her naked body. It wouldn't surprise her a bit if he could see through the phone wires.

How could *he* have possibly found out her true name, much less the name of the motel and the number of the room she was staying in? The entire day had fallen apart since he'd stopped to change her flat tire. It had been impossible, no matter how hard she tried, to blot him from her mind for more than a few minutes at a time.

Her shaking fingers hovered over the phone when its ring shattered the silence of the darkened room for the second time. It was totally expected. She knew beyond a doubt he would redial.

She lifted it cautiously, prepared to slam it back down and

break the connection immediately. This time she was wiser and would leave it off the hook. No trucker was going to outsmart her tonight.

"If you hang up or leave the phone off the hook, *Sam*, I'll break down the door in exactly one minute."

Sammi listened to his threat in silence. Her knees were quivering so badly at his warning that she sank onto the bed, took a deep breath, and hissed as quietly as her rising temper would allow, "Where are you?"

"At the pay phone beside your motel office," Steele explained in such a calm voice he knew she would be livid. Obviously she couldn't speak in her normal tone or she'd have verbally torn his hide off the moment she recognized his voice.

"Go away!"

Her mind whirled, trying to think of something that would make the man leave her alone. What on earth did he want anyway? He'd made it darn plain he wasn't interested in her any more than she was him.

"You weren't listening too good, woman. I said we have a date in"—he paused, as if he were checking his watch—"ten minutes."

Sammi eyed her aunt, afraid she had awakened her when the older woman murmured incoherently and rolled onto her side. Thank God, she was still sound asleep. She didn't want a witness to the words churning in her mind.

"Nine and a half minutes now."

"Shut up, trucker," Sammi snapped. "The last thing I'd ever want in my life is a date with you!"

"Nine minutes left," Steele drawled in a husky voice that showed her he meant what he said.

"You dare come here and I'll call the police," Sammi stormed in a futile threat. Did nothing bother the man?

"Settle down, honey." He laughed before explaining in his most seductive tone. "I've gone to a lot of trouble and expense to show you a good time tonight. I've purchased new clothes, rented a vehicle, and made reservations for dinner and the theater."

Sammi's eyes widened in sudden excitement. His sexy voice did send a thrill up her spine and cause her heart to beat erratically.

Maybe she had been too hasty in her condemnation. She was restless and the rumbling of her stomach reminded her she hadn't eaten dinner. A bag of apples didn't sound nearly as good as dining in a plush restaurant.

And the theater. She hadn't been to a play in weeks. Perhaps he had purchased tickets to the Orpheum Theater, the American Conservatory Theater, the Palace of Fine Arts Theater, or even to hear a concert at Davies Symphony Hall.

"Six minutes or down comes the door of room seventy-eight."

"Damn you, *Red*," she snapped, shaking with the effort of keeping her voice to a whisper. "I'm not even dressed."

"Five minutes," he warned, laughing at her desperate indecision.

"You monster!" she hissed back. "I'll need twenty minutes, and if you dare bother me in the meantime I'll have you arrested."

"Twenty minutes it is, doll face," he allowed. "Meet me in front of the office for a night on the town you'll never forget."

"Conceited ass," Sammi stormed rudely before breaking off the connection with a pink-tinted fingernail. She left the phone off the hook and rushed into the bathroom. She'd really be rushed to dress in the length of time he allotted. Fortunately she was bathed, her teeth were brushed, and she'd only need to apply fresh makeup and pull together something to wear.

With speed that bordered on reckless abandon, she sorted through a myriad of clothes crammed in the motel closet. She reached for a new, chic outfit sewn of a glittering white lamé material with sapphire-blue threads running through it lengthwise.

Her normally deft fingers were clumsy as she fastened the

front hook on a wispy lace bra, stepped into matching panties, then eased on sheer panty hose over a rounded bottom that drew men's eyes whatever she covered it with.

The scoop-neck blouse was elegantly simple, and its elastic waistband flattered the rapid rise and fall of her bosom as she hastily put it on. Next came knickers that emphasized her shapely calves and fragile ankles.

Reaching into the largest Pullman case, she deliberately withdrew the highest-heeled shoes she owned. They were dainty ankle-strapped sandals that had cost a mint considering there wasn't a handful of leather in them.

She brushed her curly hair until it shone like polished ebony around her shoulders. Adding a subtle mist of perfume guaranteed by the saleswoman to bring any man to his knees, she set the crystal container down, picked up a sapphire-blue three-quarter-length velvet cape, threw it over her shoulders, grabbed a small evening bag, and walked into the living area.

Her mind had been so engrossed with thoughts of *Red* she'd completely forgotten about Margaret. With trembling fingers she wrote a note on motel stationery explaining briefly that she had received a phone call from an old friend.

An acquaintance of only ten hours could be considered a long-time friend if you stretched your imagination to the fullest, she argued with her conscience in a vain attempt to justify the lie to her aunt.

Hoping Margaret wouldn't awaken before she returned from her date, Sammi added a postscript not to worry and signed it with a flourish.

All the time she was dressing an inner voice had been asking, why? Why had she allowed the man to coerce her into a date? Why had she trembled at the sound of his voice? Why had she even recognized it after their brief encounter on the freeway shoulder late that morning? Most of all, she asked, why had she remembered his kisses above all others?

It rocked you on your heels . . . that's why! her inherent honesty insisted. It was the most sensually exciting caress she had ever experienced and unique enough for her to want to know if *her* anger or *his* expertise had caused the flare of electricity that ran through her body from the moment his mouth hungrily possessed her lips.

Searching for the motel key, Sammi dropped it into her purse and slipped from the room on tiptoe. She eased the door closed until it clicked shut before walking with eager steps toward the front office.

Her spike heels clicked loudly on the concrete walkway as her eyes searched the well-lighted busy office area for her escort.

"My God!" she spoke her thoughts aloud. "I don't even know the beast's name."

"Steele." He stepped from the shadows and calmly introduced himself. "Steele Whitfield to be exact."

Sammi spun around, her eyes wide pools of shock as she looked at her knight of the road for the first time since that morning. She could feel a bright flush stain her high cheekbones while she fought to control the outrage of seeing her partner for the evening. She swallowed back the words that threatened to spill from her throat—a slender throat that was suddenly dry as she let her glance travel from his head to toe.

"Ready, Sam?" he questioned, his brown-flecked eyes filled with devilment equal to the bright blue frost in hers.

Aware that his muscles tensed, she stood stock-still as one hand reached up to hold onto her forearm and securely prevent any idea she might have of lunging away. The strength of those fingers pressing into her soft flesh removed all thought of returning to the privacy of her room. He waited, filled with admiration as she bit back the bitter words that she visibly ached to spill forth in an angry tirade.

"You sure know how to package the goods, woman," Steele told her sincerely. His eyes narrowed, hiding his sudden desire to end the charade and tell her she was the most beautiful woman he'd ever seen. For him, there could be no other right from the first.

"You do too, Red," Sammi answered in her sweetest voice, though she had to clench all ten fingers to keep from smacking his confident face.

"Steele, Sam," he prompted, leading her toward the shadows and his rented transportation. "Call me Steele."

"Why not, Steele?" she agreed pleasantly.

Damned if she'd give him the satisfaction of saying a single derogatory word about his outfit. Not one damn thing if it killed her. Not a flicker of an eyelash, a sly remark, or the slightest rise in her voice would indicate just how furious she was.

Besides, venting her feelings would detract from the vengeance she intended to invoke for his future comeuppance. And, she vowed furiously, if it took her until her dying day, she would see he was paid back for this evening.

Sammi stood aside, not the least surprised when Steele escorted her to a beat-up, mud-splattered old pickup with a rusted metal stock rack around the truck bed.

Her nostrils flared daintly as she waited for him to step forward and open the passenger door. *What was that terrible smell?*

"Probably goat," he answered her unspoken thoughts in a voice that was filled with laughter. "Maybe even pig too. The farmer I rented it from says he uses it to haul some type of animal to the auction once or twice each week."

She made no comment when he picked up a rag that had been lying on the cluttered floor, quickly wiped the torn Naugahyde seat twice, and made an endeavor to rid it of a layer of dust. At least she hoped it was only dust.

Sammi counted to ten, smiled sweetly, never raised her voice above a soft, breathless whisper, and crooned, "Thank you, Steele."

She raised her head proudly, prepared to climb into the wrecked truck as if it was a chauffeured limousine, and gingerly settled herself on the seat as far away from the driver as possible.

She inhaled in silence as his hand glided from her waist to her hip in a soft caress she might have imagined until she saw the exaggerated innocence on his face.

She settled into the truck, placed her sixty-dollar sandals among ropes, tow chains, and two unidentified objects, then sighed.

Steele shut the door with a slam that rattled the cracked side window and ran up her spine like the scraping of fingernails across a grammar school blackboard.

I'll kill him! she vowed as he walked around the dented hood, fully illuminated in the overhead parking lot lights. *I'll get even for this if it's the last thing I do!*

She didn't know how yet, but somewhere, sometime, she swore to revenge this evening and extract a slow, agonizing payment in full for his nerve.

Her stormy eyes had taken in his *new outfit* from the thick-soled, ankle-high laced boots, up the legs of navy denim bib overalls. They barely touched the tops of his work boots. *Too-short overalls yet!* No one wore overalls anymore but dirt-poor farmers. Stretched across his wide shoulders was a plaid shirt with rolled-up sleeves in pale yellow, gray, and orange. She couldn't stand any one of those insipid colors.

Worst of all, the brute was enjoying himself. She hadn't missed the deepened laugh lines, the fluttering lashes too dark and thick to be wasted on a man, or the prankish glimmer in his keen eyes.

Steele swung his lithe frame into the front seat, closed the door with a gentle swish, and placed a key in the ignition. Before starting the motor, he reached across her lap into the open hole of the glove compartment and pulled out an eight-track tape. He paused before inserting it into the stereo to challenge in a voice whose sweetness echoed hers.

"Hope you like country music, Sam."

"Love it, Steele," she lied. She ground her even white teeth together while she attempted to control the urge to wipe the smug look off his face with the palm of her hand. She had always hated her name shortened to Sam. But never in her entire lifetime had it irritated her as it did now. *He knew it too! Damn him!* She could tell by the way he drew it out and emphasized it with such a husky intonation.

"Merle Haggard okay?"

"My favorite." Her voice was as expressionless as her features.

"Great," he answered enthusiastically. "I have three hours of his tapes. If you get tired of him we'll switch to Willie Nelson."

"Lovely," Sammi said smoothly. She turned her head, gave him a forced smile, and counted to twenty—ten wasn't enough tonight—and wondered what time the nightmare would be over. Darned if she'd let him get her goat . . . or pig! Ugh, what a horrible odor that had been. At least in the cab with the windows closed it wasn't noticeable.

"Hang on, honey," he told her, shifting the stick gears with tanned fingers that came threateningly close to her left knee as they sped forward, paused at the motel entrance a second, then lurched out onto the highway with the motor backfiring like cannon shots.

She moved her legs, trying to find a comfortable position that wouldn't scuff up her shoes. Before the devil was through her entire wardrobe would be ruined.

"Just kick the hay hooks aside if they're in your way," he told her sedately. A twinge of conscience made him reach down and shove all the farmer's tools under the seat. Her clothes were obviously expensive.

Steele admired her poise. He could feel the force of her volatile temper held in tight check. It was a living thing that enveloped him with its force. The sweet, innocent smiles and low, trembling voice didn't hide the sparks that flew at him from eyes as bright blue as the gem their color matched.

She was gorgeous, utterly surprising, and never in the world would he have dreamed she'd act like this. He expected a ball of fury to light into him—a human tigress with claws out, teeth flashing, and mouth screaming revenge.

No man in the world could have this one. Sam was his! Every last, impertinent, lovely inch.

"Dare I guess where we're going to dine? Trader Vic's? Mark? Four Seasons?" Sammi asked in dulcet tones. It had taken her a full five minutes to stop the epithets that still lingered on the tip of her tongue. She'd love to see their maitre d's give him the boot.

"You'll be astonished," Steele remarked nonchalantly. "It's all part of tonight's surprise." He glanced at her out of the corner of his eye while waiting for a traffic light to change, repeating verbatim from her conversation at Nick's, "It adds to the excitement to savor the best for the tail end."

"I don't doubt that in the least," she told him, turning to stare at the passing scenery as he eased the loud, rumbling truck through the well-lit streets of California's most sophisticated city.

While Merle Haggard extolled the virtues of being an "Okie from Muskogee" in his deep, melodic voice, Sammi resisted the urge to slink down into the seat for fear someone would actually see her sitting in such a filthy wreck. Instead she sat up, raised her chin proudly, and waited.

"That's one of my favorite songs," Steele taunted, beginning to miss her fiery temper and the impertinent retorts that had kept flying off her tongue. Actually Merle was one of his best-liked country western singers. Sam would be surprised to know how varied his tastes were. His collection of country music was no more vast than that of the classics, big band, and soft rock.

"Will I be surprised at the theater too?"

"Probably," he remarked stoically. "I tried to get tickets to the San Francisco Ballet, but tonight's performance was sold out."

"What's playing?" Sammi asked with a straight face. *No* ballet company in the world would allow in anyone dressed as her date was.

"Lew Christensen and Michael Smuin are directing *Beauty and the Beast.*" His face was expressionless, the well-chiseled profile as strong and masculine as the forearms and hands raised to grip the steering wheel. "Familiar with the story?"

Sammi nodded her head, stared through lowered lashes, and began to wonder what was happening. How could he have such privileged information about her? She knew for certain he wasn't at Nick's when she remarked about them being beauty and the beast. No one was even close when she made that remark to Margaret.

"That would have been nice." She paused, took a breath, and asked in a breathless feminine whisper, "How did you find out my name and where I was staying?"

"I learned long ago never to disclose my sources of information," Steele explained matter-of-factly.

Sammi didn't press the issue. She knew he wouldn't tell her anyway. His stubborn-looking chin was raised at much too intimidating an angle. Deciding it best to change the subject, she asked pleasantly, "Will it be long now?"

"Almost there, honey." He drove onto a freeway off ramp and braked to a stop before turning right.

Sammi looked around in dismay. They were well out of the center of town and she doubted anything she wanted to eat or see would be in this area of the city.

In a few blocks Steele eased the truck into a drive-in theater near the Cow Palace.

Sammi watched speechlessly as he paid the attendant in the booth, took the ticket stubs, and drove on in. *I should have known!* she swore, figuring it served her right for daring to expect more from a trucker.

Steele slowed the truck to a crawl as he checked intently for a parking area at the back. With expert precision he pulled to a stop in the last row directly behind the snack bar, shut off the motor, and turned toward her.

"Pull in the speaker and hook it over your windowsill, Sam. We don't want to miss out on a word of tonight's movies."

Sammi rolled the cracked window down cautiously for fear it

would shatter all over her lap. She was fuming again. He never asked, always demanded, commanded, or rudely insisted. The chauvinist!

Determined not to argue no matter how provoked she became, she reached out, grabbed the speaker, and set it over the window ledge. The show was just starting and she listened to the movie titles with dismay. *Zombie* and *The Last American Virgin*. Both expressed exactly how she felt. She was acting like a zombie by putting up with his ludicrous plans, and at twenty-eight she often thought she must be the last American virgin in the States.

Steele turned to smile at her shadowed profile. She looked so elegant, he knew he'd spend many hours taking her to the finest restaurants and theaters in the world. Tonight, though, was his—his coup de grace for all the insults and misnomers about his character she either spouted to his face or regaled her aunt with during their long lunch.

He couldn't believe what he'd heard while seated in the adjoining booth to hers at Nick's. Her previous dates must have been a disgrace to his sex to put up with such claptrap. No blackhaired beauty would ever see him tolerate such foolishness. The little devil asked for everything he could think of to dish out tonight. Her uncalled-for insults had roused a temper equal to hers.

Instead of taking her to the Mark for cocktails and dinner at the Fairmont Crown followed by a tour of the city she'd never forget, he'd spent the afternoon planning a different type of entertainment. Shopping for the perfect *hillbilly, hick, airhead, uncouth* outfit had taken hours. Scouting around for the ideal transportation had taken even longer. A quick stop at a corner market had supplied the rest.

"Care for a Colorado Kool-Aid?" he asked smoothly, figuring he might as well be hanged for a whole series of put-downs as well as one.

"A Coors beer, I presume you mean?" She'd been around enough men to have heard that nickname before.

"You betcha," he drawled back. He let his hand deliberately brush across her knee as he placed back the tape. She acted as skittish as the virgin she admitted to her aunt that she was. That news had floored him as much as hearing about the contract she had drawn up to keep her that way. Both, he thought with escalating appreciation, he would take care of in the not-too-distant future.

"Is it warm?"

"What?" he asked. If she meant him, she was wrong. He wasn't warm. He was hot. Boiling, fiery hot for the woman beside him.

"Is the *beer* warm?" Sammi repeated. She could feel tension in the air. The cab of the truck suddenly seemed too intimate. His breath had been drawn in sharply and she could feel without seeing that his eyes were surveying her, with the same lazy thoroughness they had that morning.

She let the cape slide from her shoulders to lie across her lap. She wished it wasn't so warm in the truck so she could hide within its soft folds completely. Tonight was going to be the longest night of her life.

"Yes," Steele answered with all the guiltlessness of a man who hadn't done everything he could to duplicate each part of the angry uncalled-for put-down he'd eavesdropped on during lunch.

"I don't drink," Sammi told him primly, expecting him to pressure her to try it. A little, just to make her relax, was the usual line.

"Glad to hear that," he replied. "That's why I picked up a couple cans of cola. Diet okay?"

"I detest all diet colas," she told him.

"I thought all women watched their weight," he remarked seriously.

"I don't!"

"Good," he teased. "I'd hate to see one inch"—his eyes

scanned her high breasts, concealed enticingly beneath the thin evening blouse—"er, ounce, I mean, less of you."

"How about a pretzel then?" he continued, removing a package from a sack on the floor and popping the bag open with his strong fingers. "I figured you for a woman that likes popcorn, but the store was all out so I bought these instead. Hope you don't mind."

"Of course not." She smiled without guile. She was determined to be agreeable even if it nauseated her to do so. "If you'll excuse me, though, I think I'll go to the snack bar and buy a hot dog. Warm beer and pretzels aren't my idea of a meal."

"Whatever you say, honey, though you'll miss the start of *Zombie*." He knew she'd hoped to embarrass him, but it hadn't worked. He was prepared for anything she could dish out tonight. "Sure you want to miss any of the movie? I hear it's really great."

"I don't doubt that it is, but I think I can bear up," she told him with an innocent look on her face. She hadn't seen a zombie movie since she was ten years old and hadn't missed them either!

She turned to reach for the door handle when she noticed the speaker prevented her from getting out on her side.

"This way, woman," Steele prompted agreeably. "I could use something more substantial myself. No telling how much energy I'll need later tonight. We're parked in necker's row back here, aren't we?"

A brief smile tugged the corner of his mouth when he saw the wary look she gave him. It changed from wary to furious in one brief flicker. Her look just dared him to try anything funny with her later. Apparently she needed another reminder about how sensual and soft she'd been in his arms earlier. Her response had definitely not been a figment of his imagination.

"How old are you?" Sammi stormed. He sounded like a high school teen-ager whose hormones were out of control.

"Old enough to know better but young enough to try." He could damn well match her flippant remarks word for word.

"Maybe I'd better get two hot dogs. As I recall, you were quite something alongside the freeway."

"Save your money!" Sammi snapped. "I'm not interested in swapping kisses with a stranger in payment for *warm* beer, pretzels, and one frank on a bun!"

"You're forgetting the movie, Sam. It set me back eight bucks."

Without demeaning herself to answer that remark, she waited until he opened the door and stepped out before scooting across the seat to follow.

With all the courtesy of a gentleman, he placed his hands on her narrow waist and helped her down. He steadied her for a moment longer than necessary, took her fingers and tucked them in his own, slowed his longer steps to match hers, and walked to the dimly outlined snack bar.

Each step was a trial on the uneven pavement. If she broke a sandal heel or twisted her ankle, she'd sue him for everything he was worth. Which was obviously not too much, she presumed peevishly, considering everything she knew of him so far.

Sammi gave a sigh of relief that no one was inside but a bored-looking young man and a female attendant. She ignored their curious looks and waited for Steele to order. If she hadn't been so mad at Red, she could have enjoyed their shocked expressions.

"Give us two of your biggest hot dogs. Those quarter-pounders look good," Steele told them politely. He turned to Sammi and asked mischievously, "Want chopped onion on it, honey?"

"Of course," she replied innocently. "An extra large amount, please."

That should get out of his head any further ideas that he'd get to kiss her either during the show or later when they said good night, she fumed in silence.

"Make that the same with mine," he laughed, seeing through her ploy. "Mustard and pickle relish too, please. Oh, better add a couple large Pepsis, a tub of hot buttered popcorn, and two giant Hershey bars with almonds."

Steele turned to look at Sammi standing like a bright light in the glare of the snack bar. Her velvet cape was the same color as her dark-rimmed beautiful eyes. Intriguing eyes that had filled his thoughts all day. They expressed each mood change, and he could hardly wait to see them shine with love for him. They would in the near future. He was confident she'd submit to his continued courtship despite their scarcely concealed fury now. Three more days of mischief and then he'd be ready to give her the world if she wanted it.

"Nothing better than a good hot dog," Steele teased, taking their cardboard tray of hot dogs and drinks after paying at the cash register. He handed the popcorn and candy to Sammi without a word.

"This will really be eating high off the hog," Sammi agreed, applauding herself for thinking of such a witty remark as she cradled the food gingerly.

"Glad to see you're not dieting," Steele told her. "My other women are picky eaters." That should bring a spark to her eyes. He didn't imagine she'd ever had to compete with other women for a man's attention. No man in his right mind could even think of other feminine interests with her next to him. He couldn't, and he'd had plenty.

"Your . . . *other women* probably had reason to be picky if this is the type of dining out you include in your plans for an evening on the town. If you enjoy *this* in sophisticated, cosmopolitan San Francisco, I'd hate to imagine what an evening with you in the town of Burbank would be like."

"Aren't you having fun, Sam?" Steele asked with feigned innocence.

"It's a blast, Steele," she returned, ignoring the made-to-order opportunity to explain just what she thought of him. It had been obvious from the very first he was as determined to get back at her for calling him a hick as she was at not letting him realize he had succeeded.

Sammi clambered back into the truck, scooted to the far side, and waited for Steele to get inside. Why was it so damn dark? She waited, letting her eyes adjust to the dimness after he shut the truck door.

Steele stuck a straw in her Pepsi, wrapped a napkin around a hot dog, and handed them both to her. She waited until he did the same for himself, raised the sandwich to her lips, and took a dainty bite.

My God, she told herself while chewing thoughtfully, she was calmly sitting in a wrecked vehicle, eating a three-dollar meal with a far-from-perfect stranger while dressed in two hundred and fifty dollars worth of fancy clothes. She couldn't believe it! The only people who went to drive-in theaters were oversexed teen-agers and harassed parents with a backseat full of tiny kids.

She took a second bite then a third, sipped some iced cola, ate some popcorn, and found to her dismay they were delicious. It was incredible. Despite her anger she wasn't the least uncomfortable with the beast. It had to be the pleasant thought she'd never have to endure a second date that made the first bearable.

Taking a last bite of hot dog, she felt a blob of mustard drop. She knew without checking it would be centered directly between her breasts on the white lamé. Another damn thing to take to the cleaners.

She held her breath, ready to let fly, when Steele reached across and carefully wiped the spilled condiment from her blouse. His touch was impersonal, deft and brief. Did the beast never do what was expected? She'd have sworn he'd attempt to fondle her breasts. Instead he'd touched her as platonically as a brother might.

"Careful, Sam," he warned huskily. "Your outfit's elegant enough for a millionaire. Be a shame to ruin it before you find one."

"I already have!" she shot back, unable to keep herself from letting him know her life had more to offer in it than a poor trucker.

"No kidding?" he remarked in a bored voice filled with disbelief.

"Three of them!" She reached into her purse, removed a breath mint, and surreptitiously placed it in her mouth.

"Really?" One palm raised to suppress openly a wide yawn.

"Really!" she shouted back, forgetting her vow to speak softly.

Steele suspiciously hid the urge to laugh, reached across, gently touched her shoulder, and asked with melodramatic seriousness, "Why don't you marry me, you bad-tempered little witch?"

Insulted by his effrontery, she faced him with chin raised and replied haughtily, "Sorry, Steele. I'm only interested in wealthy men."

"You're an impudent brat, Sam," he chided. "You need a firm hand on your delectable backside more than you need a meek, well-heeled male."

"You arrogant beast!" It took concentrated effort to control her explosive temper. She had pledged to act sweet, and she'd do it again if it caused an ulcer. "I wouldn't be interested in you if you owned a . . . bank. Er, er, thanks anyway," she added between clenched teeth.

"I'm considered quite a catch, Sam," he taunted, taking a package of mints from his pocket and boldly putting two in his mouth.

"I don't doubt that at all, Steele," she openly lied. She stared through the windshield when the credits for *The Last American Virgin* rolled across the screen and wondered what sane female would have him.

"Interesting title for a movie, don't you think?" he asked, picking up on her thoughts and deciding to exploit them.

Sammi shrugged a shapely shoulder and refused to answer. She wasn't about to get caught up in his further opinion of that title.

"Are you a virgin, Sam?" he asked bluntly. He was curious to see what she would say after listening to her open answer to her aunt.

"Are you?" she challenged with equal boldness. He was too much!

"Not hardly," he laughed, not the least embarrassed by his answer.

"Well, then don't cross-examine me about my past as it's none of your damned business." His gall was staggering.

"It was silly asking. Obviously at your age you're not," he prodded.

"What modern woman is?" she scoffed. "As you say, it's silly asking."

Steele suppressed chiding her bold lie, removed the remains of their meal, placed the trash, the uneaten popcorn, and the candy bars beneath his legs, and turned to face her. Accustomed to the dark, he could observe her stormy features clearly.

"Since you've managed to enthrall three affluent gentlemen, I guess I'd better give you something to remember in the future. A comparison between the haves and the have-nots, so to speak."

"How would *you* know the difference?" Sammi sassed. She frowned, trying hard to imagine anything further apart than Steele's life-style and those of the men Margaret had arranged for her to meet.

"I'm well read for one," he replied with a self-satisfied smirk. "In another, er, manly way, I'm probably as experienced as they are. Maybe even more so," he expounded, leaving her with no doubt about what he meant.

"In what way?" she asked, feigning innocence to exasperate him.

"This way," he told her, letting one hand reach up to touch her shoulder when she prepared to pull farther away. "Hold it, kid!"

"Now what?" Sammi stormed. She detested being called kid. She was a fully mature woman and expected to be treated as such. Kid was a put-down to any female.

"Er, what now, Steele?" she asked with a touch of naiveté when she realized she'd forgotten to subdue her sharp tongue for the umpteenth time.

"You've got something on your mouth I want to get off."

Sammi took the tip of her tongue and licked her lips. Darned if she could feel anything on them.

"What is it?" she asked, turning her face up to him.

"Your lipstick!" he teased, taking her completely by surprise.

Before she could counter his mischievous repartee, her face was cupped in both masculine palms. She was held still as death as he lowered his head. Expecting a swift, hard kiss as hungry and fiercely demanding as the one earlier in the day, she received another shock.

Instead of rushing her, he paused. He waited for both verbal and physical objections while savoring the luminescent shimmer in her eyes. Now that the moment of possessing her sweet mouth was at hand, he was in no hurry. They had all the time in the world.

Tension mounted in the cab of the truck. It surrounded them with a force that blotted out the sound of the movie and erased the fact they could be seen by anyone who happened to be looking their way from the cars that were parked close by on either side.

"Don't," Sammi whispered, swallowing nervously yet wanting him to quit teasing and to give her a proper kiss.

"Don't what?" Steele murmured back, his breath fanning her parted lips intimately—a sweet, clean breath that belied the fact he'd eaten onions earlier.

"Don't, er, don't kiss me . . . Steele," Sammi stuttered in a helpless plea for him to stop. What was the matter with her? She barely had time to question this silently before her hands came up of their own accord and held on to his broad shoulders. She felt as if she was drowning, and he hadn't even touched her mouth. She was sinking. Sinking slowly into an abyss of desire.

"I'm not, Sam," Steele crooned in a soft drawl that ran along the nerves of her spine like an electric charge.

It was odd, but she was beginning to think he had the sexiest voice in the world. Despite the darkened interior, she could see naked desire shimmering in the depths of his eyes, and was horrified to think after all their differences he might just see that same emotion reflected in hers.

A sigh escaped her lips as she let her head rest on the back of the seat. What was the matter with her? Her eyes closed, the lashes all of a sudden seemed weighted. Her limbs felt boneless, her body heavy and languid, and if he didn't kiss her soon, she'd assuredly pull his arrogant head down and kiss him herself.

Her response was a delight to watch. "I'm not kissing you," he repeated. God in heaven, he wanted her tonight!

"You're almost," she insisted breathlessly, aware that his muscles tensed.

His head was lowered, pausing a fraction of an inch away from her passionately shaped mouth. Wide shoulders inclined protectively above.

"*This* is almost, Sam," he told her, staying intimately close, though still not touching her upraised face.

His sensual teasing was becoming impossible to bear. It made her quiver inside just having the warmth of his body close to her. She thought the touch of his palms cupping her cheeks was the most erotic sensation she'd ever experienced until he began to move the pads of his thumbs in a slow circle across the smoothness of her skin.

Oh, God, she cried inwardly. *I'm being seduced by a man I abhor, in a vehicle I hate, while parked in a public place I detest and I haven't even been kissed yet.*

"Now, Sam, *this* is kissing," Steele explained, ready to show her how great the difference really was. His control was wearing as thin as the delicate skin beneath his circling thumbs.

His lips touched hers with more gentleness than those of any man she'd known, yet any similarity abruptly ended there. Steele played with her lips, first with his own then with his tongue. As he outlined the shape of her mouth, the moist warmth curled straight into her abdomen. No man had ever traced her mouth with his tongue. It was rough yet smooth, sensually bold and unbelievably erotic at the same time.

Sammi squirmed to get closer, unable to subdue the aching need to press her sensitive breasts against his chest. Her fingers clasped his nape, spreading out through the healthy waves of hair. Red hair, but . . . God help her, right now she didn't care. Nothing mattered but that he increase the pressure of his mouth.

She bit back a verbal objection when he raised his head and asked with pointed curiosity, "How many men have you kissed, Sam?"

"Hundreds, Steele," she whispered. She lay quiescent with her eyes closed. It was too much effort to do any more than murmur a soft-spoken plea for him to continue.

"I mean have *you* kissed," he persisted. "Not *who* kissed you."

He ignored her exciting implorings, all the time nibbling his way across her eyelids and along her slender nose.

"Don't you know you're supposed to kiss a man back?"

"I . . . I did." She sighed confidently. No man had ever complained before.

"Like you're doing to me, honey?" he asked bluntly.

"No," she told him truthfully. "I'm, er, er, more receptive to you." He smelled so good. Clean and intoxicatingly male.

"Then you need more experience," he told her. His voice was husky and mesmerized her into complete acquiescence. "Let me show you what to do?"

"Fine, Steele." Sammi sighed languidly. Her fingers were surprisingly strong as they pulled his head back down to her face. At the moment he could give her lessons in anything he wanted. She had spent too many years waiting for a man to come along who could excite her as Steele was doing. She wasn't about to let him go until she was thoroughly certain she had nothing else to learn.

"First, Sam," he murmured against her face. "Part your lips farther."

She did as he said.

"Now do everything to me that I do to you," he prompted, touching her teeth with his tongue.

She let the pink tip of her tongue trace the hard enamel of his strong teeth, first the top then the bottom, finding the slight imperfection of the lower endearing for some reason—a blemish that in its own way made him seem more flawless.

"How am I doing, Steele?" she asked softly, deciding to add a tiny nibble on his lower lip just to prove she wasn't completely helpless as a pupil.

"Pretty good for a beginner, Sam," he whispered, knowing the ache in his loins was going to assure that he had a restless night ahead. He cursed the uncomfortable overalls. They were worse than a chastity belt with their high-bibbed one-piece design.

Sammi sighed wistfully, her fingers working from his hair to his nape, across his shoulders and back to retrace their journey.

"Let your lips soften, honey," he prompted lazily.

As if they could, he thought. It seemed impossible any human being could bring so much pleasure to another by the touch of skin against skin. Making love to her—total love with their bodies pressed unclothed from head to toe—could hardly be imagined, it would be so erotically perfect.

"Like this?" Sammi asked, doing as he wanted without hesitation.

"Yes, sweetheart," he exhaled. "Just like that."

Steele had to be a male witch, she thought listlessly. She was totally under his spell. There wasn't even a hazy recess of her mind that wasn't taken over by his touch.

Steele removed his hand from her face, slid it under the silken mane of hair to cradle her nape, then moved the other beneath her chin to draw her mouth up. She needed no further tutoring. Not tonight.

"Lesson time's over, honey," Steele decreed hoarsely.

His voice was more gruff than he intended. He couldn't stand the torment of not drowning in the oral gratification offered so sweetly. She was responding so perfectly he couldn't bear any more.

"Follow my lead, then use your imagination from now on," he moaned.

Sammi's breasts rose and fell rapidly in time with each beating of her pulse. The interior of the old truck became their world. A private paradise just made for each to learn what pleased the other.

It was heaven. Sammi had never felt so indolent before. Could those soft, pleading whimpers that floated in and out of her mind actually be coming from the depth of her throat?

Steele's lips took control, possessing hers in a hungry caress that left them both reeling. His tongue explored the ridge of her teeth, then moved between them to explore voraciously the moist interior. He was greedy and wanted to drink of her as a man dying of thirst wants water. It went on and on. Each second was more perfect than the last. With a herculean effort he drew back his tongue. She felt so soft and responsive he feared he might frighten her with his pent-up passions—passions that were obviously still a mystery to her.

Not satisfied, Sammi squirmed beneath him, her mouth as eager as his.

"Oh, God, do it again!" he moaned when her dainty pink tongue followed his. He couldn't believe what was happening. She was repeating the same erotic exploration of his mouth as he had to hers.

"Hmm, that's good. My God, that's heaven," he managed to murmur between each intimate caress. She was stroking his tongue in a way guaranteed to get her into serious trouble fast!

He shuddered. His body was hard with excitement building close to the point of convulsive release. How could a kiss cause such trauma? He was experienced. Very. Had been for more years than he could remember. He never dreamed any woman could be so stimulating. He couldn't stand any more, yet he found it impossible to stop.

"No more, Sam." His body was on fire and he hadn't even caressed her with fingers that yearned to learn the shape of the curves pressed so tight beneath his chest.

He straightened from his half-reclining position across the seat. Without giving her an explanation he told her to put the speaker back, waited until it was in place, drew her unresisting body along his side, started the motor, and pulled from the parking space with tires spinning.

The return trip to her motel was made without music or conversation. Sammi was glad. She didn't want anything to break the spell of Steele's embrace. It was too profound to talk about.

Steele smiled at the exquisite profile alongside his shoulder. Her glossy hair was mussed, and he could feel the weight of it brush his neck as she bent into him with a gesture of affection that would have startled her had she been aware she did it.

Wiser to the ways of her sex than even she, he knew as soon as she was alone and had time to think about how she had acted, she would be back to her normal fiery-tempered self.

It would take more than one bout of kissing to quell her impudence or convince her she wasn't averse to redheaded truckers. He eased to a stop in front of her room, assisted her to the door, kissed her passionate mouth briefly, opened the door, returned her key, and said good night.

Sammi floated past Margaret's sleeping form. She was so mesmerized her preparations for bed were completed automatically. Her one intention was getting to sleep as soon as possible. Maybe, just maybe, if she was lucky enough, she'd dream about her red-haired brute.

CHAPTER FOUR

"Wake up, sleepy head," Margaret prompted with a rising voice. She held her niece's note in one hand, having read the words in amazement. Who could her enticing young relative have been out with her first night in a city over four hundred miles from her hometown?

Sammi murmured, "Go away," pulled the sheet over her head for a moment, then turned over and sat up as if she hadn't been sound asleep seconds before. Her face was softly flushed, eyes bright and hair tumbled in seductive disarray. She'd never looked more beautiful or vital in her life.

"Did you really go out while I slept? If so, with whom?" Margaret asked curiously. Her niece's popularity was phenomenal.

"Actually," Sammi told her, pushing the covers back in preparation for getting out of bed. "I went out with Steele Whitfield." She stared at Margaret shamelessly, waiting for her next question.

"I've never heard of him. Who is he?" Samantha had numerous men friends in the greater Los Angeles area, but she wasn't aware her circle of admirers spread this far north.

"The beast." Sammi laughed softly. "My red-haired, as you say, knight of the road."

"I thought you hated the man."

"I do!" Sammi retorted. "Even more so after last night."

A frown temporarily drew her winged black brows closer

together as she contemplated her evening with Steele. She was determined her uninhibited actions and passionate response would stay in the far recesses of her mind until she was in the mood to analyze carefully her unaccustomed receptivity.

Foremost in her thoughts now was his boldness. Her desire to get even for the blatant daring and roguish behavior that continued during their entire evening was renewed with escalating resolution. The proper revenge for his audacity would take serious concentration, and today she was determined to purchase a stylish new outfit.

"What happened?" Margaret asked, breaking in on Samantha's thoughts. She was filled with curiosity. After her niece's angry outpouring about the man, she had every reason to assume the last thing she'd do would be to go on a date with him.

"Plenty happened and all of it bad," Sammi scoffed.

"How did he even find you? You said he never asked you your name or where you were going."

"I haven't the faintest idea in the world," she replied. "Maybe the beast is psychic? He knew my full name, the name of this motel, and our room number too!"

"Start talking, as I expect to hear every single thing that occurred," Margaret teased. Samantha's affairs of the heart had always intrigued her. There was never a time in her relative's adult life she wasn't tormenting some man with her provocative figure and tempestuous ways. Usually it was many more than one man at a time. The remarkable thing about it was they all loved her and she succeeded in keeping most happy when she no longer saw them.

"It's a long, long story." Sammi spoke out, swinging her long limbs over the side of the bed. "A nightmare would be the most realistic description of our evening," she lied, mad at herself for the clear image of her hands pulling his handsome face down for a lingering caress. Had they really been as devastating as she remembered? *God, yes, they had,* she answered honestly. The most mind-blowing kisses of her life. Each one more perfect than the last.

"That's too bad," Margaret sympathized. "He sounded interesting."

"Ugh!" Sammi frowned, then gave her aunt an impish smile. "It was a total disaster, but I should have expected as much."

Margaret eyed Samantha's skimpy nightwear as her niece walked into the bathroom. Following behind, she watched as she removed a toothbrush from her makeup case, applied a curl of mint-flavored toothpaste, and brushed her even teeth to a polished brightness.

"Apparently"—Sammi spoke in a muffled voice—"he resented my calling him a hick and set out to prove he could put me in my place."

Sammi washed off the foamy brush, vigorously scrubbed her teeth free of the paste, rinsed her mouth twice, then turned to tell Margaret, "It was either a put-down or he really is a country hayseed and doesn't know any better. Whichever it was, I had an abominable evening. He even made me ruin another new outfit."

Sammi picked up her white lamé evening blouse and pointed out the ugly yellow mustard stain to her aunt. Dropping it back on the bench she returned to the bathroom and splashed her face with cold water, patted it dry, and returned to sit on the edge of the tumbled bedcovers to brush her mane of hair until it gleamed in riotous curls around her face.

"Start from the first and don't leave out a thing," Margaret coaxed. She was eager to learn more about Steele Whitfield. He was the first man she'd ever heard of who hadn't been overwhelmed by Samantha's impetuous personality. She was anxious to meet the only man able to curb her niece's slightest action, since she'd started winding men around her little finger as a child. First she easily captivated her adoring father, her youthful playmates, her grammar and high school boyfriends, then college classmates before enthralling more experienced men as well.

"Okay, Margaret," Sammi told her. Her eyes sparkled as she reached for another brand-new ensemble she felt appropriate for their day's anticipated shopping spree.

"Here goes," she warned the older woman, adding with a smile, "Just remember, I warned you it would take a long time."

And it did. She recounted it all day long and explicitly. Sammi repeated each detail over and over to make certain not a single prank was left out.

She continued during breakfast, while shopping in the morning, all through lunch, while shopping in the afternoon, and now while they both got ready for their evening's entertainment.

The only part not itemized in total detail was her response to Steele's caresses. Her aunt wouldn't believe it anyway. She found it hard to believe it had happened herself. *No man* could have actually seduced her into behaving as she had with kisses alone. Apparently she must have been more weary than she thought. Really weary! She'd driven from San Luis Obispo, leaving before daylight, and the journey had undoubtedly depleted all her energy. Years of independence had surely given her enough poise not to let any hick get to her.

It was physically impossible to be seduced by a man you didn't like a single thing about. Everyone knew that, she reflected in silence while relaxing in a warm bath filled with her favorite scented oil.

One hand reached up to touch her lips. A freshly manicured nail delicately outlined the shape of her mouth as he had with his tongue. She shivered despite the warmth of the water, remembering with precise clarity the exact feel of his mouth.

Lord, his kisses were so good! The familiar gnawing in her stomach began again—the deep sensual stirring she experienced when they were together—or she let her mind linger on the memory of his bold embrace.

Why she had returned his erotic explorations with equal fervor she decided it best to think over another time. The strain of the long trip and his unexpected appearance after their confrontation beside the freeway had apparently thrown her off balance for a while. Normally her responses to a man were merely affectionate. Mildly so.

With Steele, Sammi admitted reluctantly, her sensitivity had been as heated as the passionate dreams that had caused her to toss and turn in frustration before finally drifting into a deep sleep shortly before dawn.

Deliberately forcing the man from her mind, she finished dressing. Spinning around, she let the wide flow of deep blue knife-edged pleats swirl from the tightly belted waist of her cocktail gown.

"How do I look?" she asked her aunt in a lilting voice.

"Gorgeous and you know it," Margaret told her without envy. She eyed the naked shoulders glistening in the halter neckline and the enticing glimpse of cleavage visible in the ruffle-edged straps that covered her niece's beautifully shaped bosom. "As usual, you'll knock him dead."

"I hope not," Sammi chuckled. "I only want to dazzle the man long enough to find out if we're sufficiently compatible to make a match of it."

"What about the other two?" Margaret laughed, thinking she appeared achromatic next to her vibrant niece.

"They'll get their share of dazzling too," Sammi explained while tilting her head to put on one shimmering crystal earring then the other. Each matched the single-strand necklace encircling the smooth beauty of her slender throat.

Sammi sprayed her wrists and throat with perfume and stood back to survey her aunt's dress with a thoughtful expression. Glossy pink lips pursed in concentration as she rooted through her tote bag before removing makeup from her case.

"Let's see how this looks, Margaret." She spoke solicitously. Handing her a colorful designer sash to tie around her aunt's slender waist, she watched, admiring the difference the touch of vivid color made to the plain coral dress.

"Great. A perfect match. Try these evening sandals now."

Sammi urged Margaret to slip them on. "Here's the matching purse also."

Looking at her reflection in the dresser mirror, her aunt agreed it was a definite improvement. The dainty shoes made her legs more attractive. Samantha really had a flair for fashion.

"They're yours," Sammi told her generously. "Now hold still and let me add a touch of shadow to your eyes. You have beautiful eyes and long lashes but need to highlight them with mascara and liner."

Margaret sat down and let Sammi skillfully apply additional makeup. She made no protest when her niece took a brush and flipped her hair into soft waves around her face instead of the smooth bangs. With the flattering hairstyle and darker makeup she felt ten years younger. She stood up, kissed her niece on the cheek affectionately, and walked to the door. Samantha had always been lavishly considerate to those she liked. Male or female.

"Right on time," Sammi expressed when they saw the taxi pull to a squealing stop in front of their room. Their escorts had arranged for ready transportation to the restaurant, planning to meet them as soon as a business meeting ended.

Sammi was filled with eager anticipation as the cab pulled down a brick alley just across from the stage entrance to the Geary Theater and stopped.

Her jewel-toned eyes widened as the maitre d' escorted her and her aunt to a choice table and seated them graciously. It was going to be a perfect evening. She just knew it as she surveyed the room. The decor was muted, the linen rich, the silver impeccable, and the roses fresh. She felt pampered already and hadn't yet met her date.

Sipping a white wine as silky smooth as her flawless skin, Sammi swept her glance around the room. She was an intrepid people watcher, and tonight her fellow diners were the kind she preferred to study.

A twinge of ill humor touched her features as she compared

her surroundings with those of the previous night. This was how she always anticipated her future life-style to be—dining in elegant surroundings with cultured, refined people softly conversing about the arts and equally stimulating topics before going on to the symphony or opera.

Her frown changed to a humorous smile as she leaned over to tell Margaret, "I'd like to see the beast in this rarified atmosphere. He'd stand out like a sore thumb." Her eyes were alight with a devilish gleam while expounding on what a provincial he'd been. "The big brute would really draw everyone's eyes here."

"Like that gorgeous hunk of manhood coming in the door?" Margaret pointed out in a whisper as she stared at the couple entering the dining room.

Sammi's raven hair shimmered in the light when she turned her head to look. Her face blanched. She stared in disbelief. No man could change so drastically in one night. Not even the red-haired trucker.

Staring open-mouthed, she glowered as Steele walked past her table as if he owned the place. Clinging to his black evening-suited arm was a lovely, petite—she would be, Sammi grimaced peevishly—fair-haired woman with fashionable streaks of russet in her glistening blond locks.

They went on by Sammi as if she wasn't even there. He had to have seen her. It was impossible not to when they had been close enough to touch. A flush of fury stole into her face, causing her heart to beat with the beginning of her usual quick temper. Steele had been so enthralled with his companion he hadn't noticed her.

She'd get even now for certain. How dared he treat her to a country bumpkin night out and then have the nerve to show up the following evening where she was dining, dressed in an expensive suit and escorting a sensual-looking female who smiled as smugly as the cat who swallowed the canary.

"What's the matter, Samantha?" Margaret asked when the

couple were seated, and she forced herself to look back at her niece. "What's wrong?"

"What's wrong?" Sammi stormed between clenched teeth. "That's what's wrong!" She pointed to Steele's bright head as he leaned attentively toward his date and appeared to be asking her what she wanted to drink.

"*That's the damned beast!*" Sammi hissed, barely able to keep her voice to a decent level so that no one else would overhear.

"*That's* your red-haired trucker?" Margaret questioned in amazement.

"Yes," Sammi agreed furiously. She couldn't believe her eyes when a waiter rushed over with a silver cooler, set it by their table, and went through the ritual of serving Dom Pérignon in crystal glasses.

"*I* get a damned seventy-five-cent cola in a paper cup, and *she* gets a seventy-five-dollar bottle of champagne in an ice bucket," Sammi fumed bitterly.

Margaret chuckled. She'd never seen anything so amusing as Samantha's face when she pouted, complaining jealously about Steele. It was obvious the trucker had gained one up on her volatile-tempered niece.

"I doubt if that woman will have to eat a hot dog for dinner," Margaret predicted, unable to resist teasing her young relative after the terrible things she'd heard about the man all day.

"Whatever she eats I hope she chokes on it," Sammi grumbled. "God, I hope our dates arrive soon. I don't think I can bear to watch the redheaded beast shower that bitch with attention after what he did to me last night."

"For one, you undoubtedly deserved it, my dear," her aunt told her. "You admitted calling him such insulting names; any man with an ounce of pride would feel compelled to set you in your place. Another thing, my not-so-sweet-talking relative, that gorgeous trucker's hair is most definitely not red. It's the most vibrant, beautiful, burnished bronze I've ever seen on man or woman."

"Quit nit-picking, Margaret," Sammi stormed back. "That's red and you know it!"

Nervously pouring herself another glass of wine, Sammi emptied it in one long swallow, trying ineffectively to curb her trembling fingers. She'd burst a blood vessel if he hovered attentively over the blond-haired witch any longer. He was practically eating her with his eyes. In fact, he was so damned engrossed with the woman's comfort he hadn't even glanced across the room at her and her aunt.

"That does it," Sammi told Margaret in a forced whisper. "Now I'm more determined than ever to get back at the brute for last night. Only this time I owe him two nights' revenge, not one!"

"Why?" Margaret replied softly. "You have no claim on the man. It's hardly fair to retaliate for dating another woman. Because the man turns from a bumpkin to a prince overnight is also no reason to continue trying to attract his attention by shooting frosty glances across the room." Her niece was more livid by the minute.

A third glass of wine didn't help Sammi's temper one bit. She never remembered being more irate.

"She's a real beauty, isn't she?" Margaret asked honestly.

"She's terrible," Sammi pouted, not liking a single thing about the elegant woman smiling with passionate-shaped lips back at her handsome escort.

God help me, Sammi reluctantly admitted, Steele was the most stirring, physically appealing man she'd ever met.

"Hardly terrible," Margaret replied in a censuring voice. "She's a lovely woman. I've never seen a female with more class."

"Yes and all of it low!" Sammi added with unconcealed sarcasm.

"Here's Bob and John now," Margaret interrupted, smiling at the two impeccably groomed men walking toward them. She'd known Bob for years and met John once or twice a few years back.

Sammi looked up, hiding the twinge of dismay when she saw the two men nearing their table. They were both far older than she had expected. Even the younger brother had to be at least twenty years older than she was. Maybe even twenty-five or thirty.

Here goes anyway, she reflected silently, determined to have her escort eating out of her hand in minutes. Attracting the man should be a cinch, and she boldly resolved to use him to forget the beast. *If* Steele ever removed his sharp eyes from the sensuous shape of his date and gazed across the room, it would boost her battered ego to be the recipient of equal attention from her date.

"Hello, John," Sammi greeted the older man in her most sensual voice. She raised one smooth hand out in greeting. Her wide smile was as innocent as a baby's as she shyly lowered her lashes. Concealed beneath the fluttering dark fringe, her eyes sparkled with wrath. She'd get back at Red if it was the last thing she did.

"Hello, Samantha," John replied in a well-modulated voice. His eyes were alight with pleasure. He'd never expected such a fine-looking woman. It would be a delight to grant her anything she wished tonight.

While John imagined her gracing his prestigious home with her youthful beauty, Sammi wished she could stand up, storm across the room, and slap the smug look off Steele's face. He was ruining everything.

She compared John's soft hands with the masculine toughness of Steele's, noticed his narrow shoulders next to Steele's broad muscular fitness, listened unhappily to John's higher-pitched serious voice while reminded of Steele's teasing husky-toned words. Worst of all, John's lips looked soft and feminine, and she knew without touching them they'd never rouse her in the least.

She hated soft lips on a man unless they softened beneath the touch of hers as Steele's had.

Sammi's thoughts became harder to hide. She'd darn well quit making unfavorable comparisons, remember instead her brazen put-down by the trucker, and devote all her energy to charming John.

She sparkled, winning both men over within seconds. She was friendly to each, attentive to her escort, and practiced in her soft questioning about their work. It never failed to put a man at ease. John was no exception and followed her previous men friend's reactions with boring regularity.

"Are you in the savings and loan business also, Samantha?" John asked with sincere interest in knowing more about her.

"Heavens no," Sammi told him truthfully and laughed. "Math is my weakest point. I'm lucky if I can keep my checkbook balanced. Aunt Margaret was the only one in our entire family brilliant enough to major in economics."

"Perhaps you need a financially secure man to remove the annoyance of a meager checking account, Samantha?" John suggested, hopeful. "You're much too lovely to worry about supporting yourself." He stared with intense brown eyes. "Most mature men would relish the idea of sharing their wealth, I'm certain. For starters, let's order our meal and indulge your appetite for fine cuisine."

"That sounds wonderful, John," Sammi agreed, scanning the menu with keen interest as the conversation flowed across the table.

Trying to be attentive to John, Sammi listened, though she had to force herself not to stare continuously across the room. The côtelette de veau aux morilles was exquisitely prepared and like the other courses a gourmet delight that could have been sawdust she was so agitated.

Steele never looked up. Not once. He never even knew she was there, Sammi fumed. At least he could have glanced over their way when she was served Dom Pérignon too!

Sammi ordered cherries jubilee, watching rapturously as the waiter flamed the luscious-looking dessert before placing it before her. She was smugly placing a bite in her mouth when Steele stared at her for the first time.

One arrogant brow rose as his eyes went back and forth between the two men. His hand lifted, covering a yawn that blatantly implied how boring her escort looked.

While she spooned the second bite of dark bing cherry and creamy vanilla ice cream into her mouth, a mischievous smile tugged his lips and one eyelid lowered in a broad, exaggerated wink.

Sammi returned his silent communication with a fierce glare. His wink had told her more than anything could that he'd known all along she was there. And that he'd deliberately ignored her, knowing that by doing so it would raise her ire with continuous acceleration.

Her mood had definitely dampened. The idiot was taunting until her stomach was clenched in knots. She watched through lowered lashes as he actually raised the voluptuous, *overbloomed* woman's hand to his mouth. *Oh, my God,* Sammi screamed to herself, he was kissing the back of her hand as if he were some knight from the round table. While his lips were still pressed to the hand, he stared at her with bold amusement. The mischief in his eyes was visible across the room!

She turned away, vowing no man—especially that one—could do that to her.

Flirting outrageously, she gave John her brightest smile, took a third bite of jubilee, and felt with detached aplomb every bit slip off her spoon and land directly between her breasts.

John's, Bob's, and Margaret's startled glances were matched by surprise as Sammi placed a fine cloth napkin over her bosom and left the table. She walked with haughty insouciance to the ladies' room.

Sammi sighed with relief to find the room empty. At last she could vent her indignation with bitter epithets. Blaming Steele, she expressed her desire for him to burn in eternal flames in the not-too-distant future.

The wine-colored cherries had spilled onto the crepe de chine and stained it. Would there be no end to her cleaning bills? She'd never been clumsy in her life. The beast was a jinx. Had to be. Once or twice each day she'd ruined a brand-new, expensive garment.

"Damn you, Red!" She spilled out her wrath. "I hate—" she stopped in mid-sentence as the rest room door opened.

Watching in disbelief, she saw Steele enter and lean against the door to assure no one intruded on their privacy.

"Having problems, Sam?" he asked calmly.

"Get out!" she hissed.

"Shush, Sam. Don't you know women should be *obscene* and not heard?"

"Get the hell out of here, you barnyard comedian!" Sammi stormed furiously while trying ineffectively to remove the sticky dessert from her heaving bosom. She could feel the ice cream oozing deep in the valley between her breasts. It was a ghastly sensation.

"This is a ladies' room, you blasted pervert," she cried out, so angry her dainty nostrils flared as she clutched the napkin to her breasts.

"Then we should both leave," Steele insisted. "Your language is worse than a trucker's. I could hear you cursing before I came in."

"It's all your fault. *As usual*!" Sammi shouted back. She was so mad she didn't care if the owner, his help, and all his patrons heard.

Her frosty glance locked with Steele's. He dwarfed the room, his overt masculinity suddenly a living thing. She inhaled, momentarily breathless and as weak as a kitten as his look rapidly changed to one of deep desire. His arms opened, enfolding her with strength and warmth.

Steele's lips—so sweetly familiar now—took hers with a

thoroughness she knew she'd yearn for the rest of her life. It was happening again; she moaned as he crushed her the length of his body. She was out of control around the man. Had been from the first.

Held tight to his long torso, she inhaled the identical scent that had mesmerized her the day before. His clean skin had a heady male fragrance she found enticingly sensual. She parted her lips and clung to his neck as if she could never get enough of his caresses.

Steele played with her lips, hungrily kissing her until she rose on tiptoe to increase the pressure. He toyed seductively, nibbling his way across her face as she closed her eyes and let the exquisite sensation of his touch overshadow anything else. It was heaven to be in this man's arms again. Unheeded, the napkin dropped.

Sammi arched her throat and leaned back. His mouth trailed over each inch of her face and down her neck, where he lingered on the rapidly beating pulse centered beneath her necklace before moving slowly lower. He blew his warm breath ardently onto her perfumed skin.

Her fingers convulsively clenched the hair on his nape, both knees threatened to buckle, and her breath escaped in short gasps as his mouth probed deeper into the cleavage of her full, upthrust breasts.

She was hypnotized, sexually mesmerized by the man. Her mature, sensitive bosom swelled to meet his touch. She clung to his shoulders for balance, not believing what she allowed him to do to her body. His warm tongue was licking her heaving breasts clean of the sticky dessert, laving her in the most intimate experience of her life.

On and on, in no apparent hurry, he stroked the creamy flesh, licking and caressing the satin skin exposed in her décolleté gown until there wasn't a trace of ice cream or cherry.

"Oh God, no!" she cried out rapturously, aching for his tormenting mouth to take the sensually erect nipples into its warmth and tongue the tips with the same motions he was using to explore her breasts.

Steele's broad palm cupped one lush breast tenderly. He circled the hardened tip with open mouth over the thin material and then slowly did the same to the other. His lips closed to nibble the taut bud.

"No, Steele, please . . . no!" Sammi pleaded in a broken whisper.

It was impossible, she told herself silently, to continue with this erotic madness. It was also equally impossible to regain her senses and pull away.

This time she was being seduced in a ladies' room of an exclusive restaurant by a man who had ignored her all evening while his date and her escort were calmly waiting for them to return to the tables.

It could have been a passionate dream, except the deep pleasure going from her breasts to her lower abdomen was real—totally, erotically true. She whimpered as his mouth trailed up the cleavage, back across her throat and chin to possess her lips in a hungry kiss that was far too brief.

"That should do it, Sam," Steele told her, withdrawing her hands and placing them back at her sides.

"Do . . . do . . . what?" Sammi whispered breathlessly. Her eyes were dazed, mouth soft and moist as she waited for his reply.

"Two things," Steele explained in a husky voice that proved he was as aroused as she was. "Renew the difference between the haves and the have-nots in case your *old* escort decides to brave your haughty exterior and find out how kissable your lips really are, for one."

"And?" Sammi questioned softly, waiting for strength to return to her limbs so she could draw away.

"Second, it should have cleaned up all the spilled cherries jubilee," he returned in a teasing voice. "You're quite sloppy,

Sam. Quite delicious too. Vanilla ice cream's never tasted better!"

The sensual spell was broken as quickly as it started by his roguish words. She stamped her foot and hissed out an order.

"Damn you, Steele. Get out of here and back to your—your woman!"

"Do you mean Monique?" he asked with feigned innocence. "She's gorgeous, isn't she?" Not waiting for an answer, he added matter-of-factly, "She's French. They have a reputation for being really great in the sack. Excellent, innovative lovers I hear."

Sammi stared at Steele in shock. Wasn't that what she'd said about the waiter at Nick's? Her lashes lowered in confusion. Was the man a mind reader? Her speculation was broken when she heard a firm knock on the door.

With chin raised, she forced a look of nonchalance on her face and stepped out as Steele opened the door. With a brief nod of his arrogant head he followed close behind.

The elegant older woman was stunned speechless when Sammi and Steele walked from the ladies' room and returned to the dining room without saying a word about their unorthodox behavior.

Steele ran his hand in a bold caress down Sammi's spine, spread his fingers and traced the swell of her bottom, then walked on by. Sammi stumbled, regained a modicum of composure, and returned to the table, praying feverishly that no one had seen his intimate caress.

She ignored Margaret's dumbfounded look, apologized for her clumsiness, and agreed with enthusiasm when John and Bob suggested they all go to a nightclub.

Anything . . . anyplace . . . just as long as she didn't have to remain in the vicinity of Steele and Monique.

Monique, she repeated the name in her thoughts. She'd always thought it was a lovely name until tonight. Now she hated it more than any other.

Hours later Sammi glanced out the side window at the partially deserted street on the way to her motel. It seemed unfair, but she was pleased her evening was ending. Her glance returned to the interior of the car, taking in the soft dove-gray velour seats. John's Mercedes—she had guessed correctly what he would drive—was as elegant and proper as their entire date had been.

Margaret had hustled Bob off earlier after giving Sammi a sly wink. It was entirely unnecessary. She had known from the first glance that John would never be important to her future.

The poor man had seemed determined to prove he was as fit as a youth. They had danced, conversed, and went in and out of the finest clubs at an accelerated pace.

Yet her evening lacked a certain spark. Arguing with Steele had been more exciting than the silent accord of her tranquil time with John. Maybe she needed a psychiatrist. No one, she mused, *no one in their right mind anyway,* would receive more enjoyment with an arrogant beast in a filthy truck at a fifth-rate drive-in movie than being pampered by a gentlemen who indulged your slightest whim with chivalrous attentiveness. John hadn't raised his voice to argue once.

Sammi faced him when he pulled to a smooth stop in the darkened area beside her room. She gave him a sweet smile, waiting to see what he would do next.

He turned to her, gulped like an awkward youth, and ran one finger around his collar as if he was suddenly too warm, totally unaware Sammi was biting back the urge to laugh at his sudden embarrassment.

"I'd like to kiss you good night, Samantha," he whispered in a voice that changed tone. "But no gentleman would ever ask for such liberties on the first date. Later maybe, when you know me better and realize that I'm trustworthy of your respect, I'll ask again."

"Sure, John," Sammi told him softly. "Later will be fine. I'll look forward to it," she lied with such conviction his ego soared. She wished Steele could have heard that speech!

There would be no later for this man, Sammi assured herself in silence. The way John clicked his teeth—real ones or otherwise—during their meal and while staring at her throughout the night had driven her up the wall.

"Thank you for a lovely, lovely evening, John." She owed the poor man that much praise. He had tried so hard to please her.

Sammi took his hand, watching in dismay as he raised it to his mouth and kissed her fingertips with soft, pale lips that made her skin crawl. Irritated at her own stiffness, she wondered why she was unusually picky tonight.

John was wealthy, cultured, impeccably neat, and obviously enthralled, nevertheless she could hardly wait to go inside the motel room, tell Margaret everything that had happened after she left, and enjoy a crisp red apple while sitting in the middle of her bed.

As he waved good-bye, after escorting her to the door as if she was made of Dresden china, Sammi shrugged one exposed shoulder and spoke out loud.

"One down and two to go."

CHAPTER FIVE

"Well?" Margaret asked the moment Sammi entered the room. "Is he the one man you intend to forsake all others for for the rest of your life?"

"Not hardly," Sammi answered, throwing her purse on the bed and sitting down to unbuckle the ankle straps on her dainty shoes.

"What's wrong with John? He seems like a nice man and he was utterly captivated with you from the first glimpse."

"Nothing's wrong with John." She slipped off her sandals, stood up, and walked barefoot into the bathroom to remove her dress. Her voice rose as she called out to her aunt. "Nothing other than he bored me to death, he wears clear nail polish, and he clicks his teeth. Can you believe he never objected to a single thing I wanted to do all night? His solicitous behavior drove me out of my mind before our meal was finished."

"You always said you were looking for a wealthy man to indulge your slightest whim," Margaret reminded. "I thought John would be just what you wanted."

"So did I," Sammi sighed, throwing her soiled dress on the rapidly increasing pile of clothes to be cleaned. She removed her half slip, bra, and panties and pulled on sleeping attire.

She returned to the bedroom with two freshly washed apples in her hand, handed one to her aunt, and plopped on her bed.

"John seemed so old somehow."

"In comparison with your dates in L.A. or in contrast with Steele?"

Sammi, chewing the crisp apple while deep in thought, looked at Margaret. Had her meditation been obvious to her relative? She did spend a lot of time noting the differences in the two men, and poor old John came out second best in every way. Even his wealth and indulgence lost their appeal after acute apathy set in before she ordered dessert.

Margaret's laughter broke in on Sammi's deep concentration. "I seriously doubted John would appeal to you after I saw Steele. That man is the most gorgeous male I've ever seen."

"My dear Aunt Margaret," Sammi reminded jokingly. "Steele is at least fifteen years younger than you."

"So what?" Margaret returned with conviction. "If you think a forty-nine-year-old woman can't think how great a thirty-four- or thirty-five-year-old man would be in bed, then you're showing how immature you are."

"I didn't think you'd feel that way about a man nearly young enough to be your son!" Sammi remarked in awe. To think her aunt was attracted to Red really floored her. "That's almost . . . almost incestuous!"

"Hardly, Samantha," Margaret added calmly. She was propped against the headboard of her bed, dressed in a prim cotton nightgown that nearly covered her entire figure—a direct contrast to her niece's brief two-piece nightie and her sensuous aura.

Continuing matter-of-factly, Margaret questioned, "Didn't you realize that women my age and older can give a man passion that you, at your own admission, have yet to learn?"

Sammi glared across the short distance between the two beds. Her mood had definitely diminished at the thought that her own aunt considered Steele a hunk. Was she really serious?

Seeing the kindness in Margaret's eyes, Sammi's normal good humor returned. Who knows, maybe when she was fifty-one—she was certain Margaret had lied at least two years about her age—she would see someone like Steele and wish he'd take her to bed too!

Sammi gave her aunt a gracious smile, then stared at the partially eaten apple in her hand as if it was the most intriguing piece of fruit in the world. She reflected back to everything that Steele had done at La Bourgogne, and it brought a flush to her face—a touch of rose on each cheekbone for the embarrassment of allowing him to tongue her breasts so intimately and a spot of pink for the jealous anger she'd been consumed with when he raised Monique's hand to his lips.

Despite their incompatibility, she admitted she wanted exclusive rights to his caresses. Was it possible to loathe a man and want the sole privilege of receiving his touch? It must be, or why else would it have gone beyond anger to pain when he paid attention to another of her sex?

Margaret intruded on the sudden silence in her soft voice. "Some men prefer older women, Samantha."

"Older, *rich* women," Sammi added pointedly.

"Not necessarily, my innocent niece."

"What do you mean?" Sammi asked curiously.

Margaret continued in a clear voice. "They think, or have heard, we're more experienced than women their own age. We're better in bed to put it bluntly."

"Oh!" Her aunt's words stunned her. Her normally inhibited personality had changed. She had a bright, warm gleam in her eyes that bothered Samantha somehow.

"Actually"—the older woman laughed—"I think our reputed prowess comes more from desperation than super ability. A woman without a man, who wants one, can get exceedingly frustrated if she's had a normal sex life in the past."

"Like you and Uncle Dan?" Sammi asked softly. She knew her aunt had been happily married for ten years and had often wondered if she still grieved over his death four years ago.

"Exactly, Samantha," Margaret whispered. A cloudy, pained look came over her eyes for a brief moment before she continued with her thoughts about Steele. "I've lived a celibate existence since your uncle died, but many hours have been filled with the torment of needing a man's affection. There is no replacement."

"I didn't realize," Sammi returned sympathetically. "I can easily understand how frustration itself can release all of a woman's inhibitions when an exciting partner is found."

It had with her. She had never allowed any man liberties with her body no matter how attracted she was to him. With Steele she held back nothing.

"I imagine Steele's an absolute gem in the bedroom. Those keen eyes look as if they could see right into a woman's innermost thoughts."

"My bold-speaking aunt, you're too much. Thank gosh you're only pretending an interest in *my* trucker."

Sammi put a definite emphasis on *my*. It was bad enough watching Monique fawn over the man without having her aunt show interest too.

"Think what you like, Samantha. That honed-down physique has to be fit enough to make the man a veritable love machine." Margaret's lashes lowered and a smile rose her pretty mouth at the corners as she whispered in a subdued voice, "His date's dreamy, satisfied expression proved I'm right."

"Knock it off, Margaret," Sammi reprimanded. She couldn't stand to hear another word about Steele. "He's an aggressive beast and you know it."

"All the better," her aunt enthused. "Aggressive men are known to have strong sex drives. Their excessive physical energy makes them successful in their work as well as their intimate lives."

"Phooey," Sammi retorted. "Steele's not a successful anything. He's nothing but a poor trucker who's probably out of work more often than not."

"His evening suit looked ultra-expensive and tailored to fit his magnificent-looking physique."

"Undoubtedly rented." With much chagrin she was reminded

of the outfit he had worn on their date. Bib overalls sure didn't cost much, nor did the hideous plaid shirt.

"Maybe he did rent it. Maybe he didn't," Margaret rebutted. "But if you want him, you'd better get your act together and go after the man. There's an abundance of beauties willing to share the love banquet before his appetite for feminine flesh is satiated. Every woman in the dining room was giving him the eye."

"I'm going to sleep," Sammi said, throwing the apple core into the wastebasket and turning out the lamp between their beds. Damned if she was going to listen to one more remark about Steele's sexual charisma.

She curled onto her side after a brief good night and lay awake for hours wondering if Margaret was sincere in her admiration for Steele. It would never have occurred to her that her closest relative would fantasize about his athletic capabilities in bed. Damn it, she swore to herself just before falling asleep, she might not want him, but she didn't want any other woman to have him either.

Sammi's mood had definitely brightened after a second day of shopping and sight-seeing. She and Margaret chatted happily as they prepared for another evening out.

She tightened a wide black belt around the waist of a crisp white collarless six-button jacket, smoothed the pencil-slim skirt, and slipped on spike-heeled black pumps. A trio of ebony bracelets clicked as she patted an upswept hairstyle that framed the perfection of her face. She felt chic and comfortable in the soft cashmere wool suit.

Sammi chuckled, raising a tube of Chanel's Les Fantastiques lipstick from her purse. "At least I have one purchase from Neiman-Marcus."

"I admit I was stunned to see a fifteen-hundred-dollar price tag on the simple summer dress that caught my eye," Margaret called out from the bathroom, where she was adding eye makeup at Sammi's prompting.

"Me too," Sammi agreed readily. "The long-sleeved dress I

liked was *twenty-five* hundred dollars. That's a hell of a lot more to pay to cover your arms."

"I hear the men now," Margaret told her niece when she walked to the table to gather her purse and motel key.

"Good," Sammi replied with a teasing smile. "I'm anxious to see what Benjamin looks like."

Benjamin looked like trouble, Sammi told herself when the door was opened to reveal a kind-looking older man and a cocky longish-haired youth peering in with wide eyes that glowed instant approval in a way she hadn't seen since college. A nurse friend had told her male interns were in a perpetual state of sexual desire, and his gleaming dark eyes proved her assumption true.

"Hi, Benny," Sammi greeted him, hoping that by shortening his name to a childhood nickname it would ease him off a bit. He was already rubbing his palms together as if she was a feast.

Thank gosh she'd worn spike heels. It put her at least five inches above his brown locks. She swept past his startled face and into the backseat of the car before he could reach out to help.

Sammi watched him slide in beside her with a broad, confident smile on his face. His ego was bigger than he was, and she knew darn well he could hardly wait to prove he was the world's greatest lover.

She could understand what Benny was thinking as if he'd said the words aloud. Mutely planning his overused line, he expected a quick conquest followed by a speedy return to brag to his buddies about the older woman he'd made out with. She'd been out with his type before, but not for years, thank God.

"You're a knockout, Sammi," Benjamin told her, leaning sideways in an attempt to inhale more deeply of her perfume.

"Thank you, Junior." Sammi smiled, easing a fraction away. "It is Benny, Junior, isn't it?" That should tone him down.

"Er, yes," he admitted reluctantly. "Call me Ben, Sammi."

"Certainly, Benny," Sammi told him, emphasizing the last syllable. "I'm afraid you heard my name wrong. It's Samantha, not Sammi." Her voice left no doubt he'd better do as she said. Flashing him a false smile, she brought her aunt into the casual conversation while they drove downtown.

As Cyril pulled his luxurious Cadillac beneath the covered drive at the restaurant entrance, he had to pause while the owner of a silver sports car ahead of them exited.

Sammi peered out the front windshield, leaning forward in disbelief as Steele unwound his long length from an Italian-made car she knew cost one-hundred and seventy-five thousand dollars. It must be borrowed, she thought to herself.

He swept around the low hood to open the passenger door. With one hand he took the outstretched feminine palm.

Sammi's eyes were riveted on the distressing sight of long, slender legs swiveling around as a silver-blond woman gracefully stood up. Her full red lips were visible as she faced Sammi's direction and smiled at Steele, whose broad-shouldered, narrow-hipped, long-legged body was turned away from them.

With a toss of glistening hair, the sophisticated woman took his arm and strolled with elegance into the restaurant.

Margaret turned to face her niece. A look of dismay crossed her features, followed by one of sympathy. Sammi returned her glance with feigned disinterest and decided Junior appeared more appealing all the time.

The Cadillac moved forward and they stepped out. Sammi made no objection when Benjamin took her arm and threw his shoulders back as if he was a king. A small king with a big ego, she thought peevishly. The little twirp concluded she'd be a cinch to seduce.

Sammi strode into the dining room directly behind the maitre d' with her chin raised and spine stiff. She looked neither right nor left, sweeping by Steele's table without acknowledging his presence as he had arrogantly walked by hers the night before.

She slid into the low booth, gave Benny her brightest smile, and hoped Steele *and* his blond companion choked on their dinner.

For a poor trucker he certainly seemed to be able to partake of expensive meals—when inclined—she mused, thinking again of her date with him. Maybe he robbed banks on the side, she contemplated petulantly. If so, she'd delight in seeing him arrested at his table before they left.

Sammi glared straight across the room, hoping to catch his eye and give him an indication of her anger. How could he have possibly known she would be here? She didn't know where they were dining until they pulled into the driveway.

Margaret and Cyril continued their conversation after ordering dinner. It left Sammi to keep Benny at arm's length. He was coming on strong, and she knew she'd have to put him in his place before the meal was finished.

As she slid a fork into feather-light feuilleté leger with fresh California asparagus and anticipated the delicate mousse of salmon her body tensed. She could feel Benjamin's leg move alongside hers. When he dropped his napkin on the floor and placed his hand beneath the table to retrieve it, she was prepared.

One spiked heel rose, and when his fingers groped for her thigh, she slammed it down on his instep. It was a maneuver she had used for years. His sharp yelp turned into a cough as he tried to cover up his discomfort.

Sammi gave Margaret and Cyril a sweet, innocent smile before turning to shoot Benny a frosty glance through lowered lashes that warned him to keep his roving hands to himself.

She looked up to see Steele laughing. He'd seen what Benny did and her quick attack back. His eyes were alight with amusement as he turned back to his lovely date.

Sammi ate carefully, raising each bite to her mouth with slow precision. There was no way she was going to drop any food on her white suit tonight, no matter how disconcerted the beast made her.

"Why don't you try some Navarro Vineyard gewurztraminer juice?" Benny urged, taking a sip of his drink.

"What is it?" Sammi asked curiously.

"The *in* drink now," he told her. "It's squeezed from unfermented Mendocino County wine grapes. A trendy favorite of the fashionable people who've discovered varietal grape juices. Would you like some?"

"Why not," Sammi agreed. "It sounds delicious."

Benny waved for their waiter, was openly peeved to find they were out, and ordered Sammi a glass of concord grape juice instead. He leaned back, slid his left arm behind her back, and let his fingers tentatively touch her shoulder.

Apparently the pain in his foot had lessened, Sammi presumed correctly when his hand became bolder and started to fondle the soft material of her suit jacket.

Ready to remind Benny to keep his hands to himself, Sammi glanced at Steele. One burnished brow rose as he scrutinized everything she did. In ill humor over his continued observation she reached to take her drink from the waiter at the same time Benny did. Their hands collided and the glass dropped to the table.

She watched without saying a word as the bright purple juice splashed onto the tablecloth before her and was absorbed by the white suit sleeve she protectively put out to keep the liquid from spilling on her lap.

That does it, Sammi thought and frowned, clenching her teeth to keep from yelling at Benny. It wasn't his fault any more than hers. Tomorrow she'd wear combat fatigues in camouflage colors. Then she would be prepared for anything that happened.

"Oh, dear," Margaret said.

"Too bad, Samantha," Cyril commiserated.

"Sorry about the clumsy waiter," Benny added rudely as the poor man mopped ineffectively at the ruined cloth.

"Excuse me, please," Sammi told them all.

With one eye on Steele to make certain he didn't follow, she swept into the ladies' room. She gave a sigh of relief to see an attendant seated in the corner.

"What happened, miss?" The older woman addressed her as she rose to help.

"An awkward accident," Sammi told her, barely able to hide her bitter thoughts. She and Benny might have caused the drink to spill, but it was all Steele's fault. She blamed him for every bad thing that had happened since he'd stopped to change her tire. And there had been enough to keep her in a perpetual state of wrath.

The attendant took cold water and a soapy cleaning solution, wiping the stained sleeve until the deep purple stain was a faint lavender.

"Sorry, miss, but that's the best I can do," she apologized. Her capable hands patted the material, trying to dry it between two pieces of cloth.

"That's fine." Sammi thanked her. She eased from the ladies' room, looked cautiously around, and started back to the dining room, nervously glancing behind her she walked on, expecting to see Steele loom up from behind every potted plant lining the wall.

With a relieved sigh she continued down the broad carpeted hallway, determined there would be no repeat of her uninhibited actions of the previous night. Thank heavens he was nowhere in sight.

As she passed the opened door of a small cloakroom, Steele reached one long arm out and drew her behind a row of fur jackets hanging on a long metal rack.

Sammi recognized his touch immediately and tugged vainly to free her arm imprisoned in his steel-hard grip.

"What the hell kind of a pervert are you?" Sammi hissed.

"You want the finer things of life, so I thought you'd enjoy talking with me surrounded by expensive mink coats." Steele laughed.

"You're nuts, trucker," she stormed. "A real sicko who gets his kicks lurking in weird places and pouncing on innocent victims."

"Only since I met *you*," he told her with emphasis on the last word.

"What do you want this time?" She was furious at his nerve.

"If I told you, I'd probably get my face slapped," he teased.

"And you'd no doubt deserve it too!" she returned, twisting to get away.

"Hold still, Sam," he ordered. "I want to give you some advice."

"You're the last person I'd take advice from," she snapped back.

"Shut up and listen or I'll kiss you quiet," he warned.

"Your sexual threats don't bother me," she assured him. Her eyes shimmered a vivid blue in the muted overhead light.

"They should, Sam," Steele insisted, his pupils suddenly darkening with a sensual glimmer that forewarned her his desire was being held in tight check.

"Tell me what you have to say then get back to your date," Sammi demanded.

"How much are you getting paid?" he questioned innocently.

"For what?" She faced him squarely, wondering what he was talking about now.

"For baby-sitting."

"Who?" she insisted, filled with sudden vexation that he had the nerve to question her about anything in her life.

"The horny little creep that tried to feel your leg under the table. He's at least five years younger than you are." He cupped her slender shoulders with both palms, holding her still while she stared into his narrowed eyes.

"So what? I happen to like young men."

"He's five inches shorter too."

"I don't care how tall a man is, only how much money he has."

"It won't work at all, sweetheart. It will take a man of experience to control your raging temper and tolerate your moodiness, much less satisfy your sexual needs. You're too passionate ever to be contented with an awkward, inexperienced youth. Try him and see."

"I think I will." She definitely gagged on that lie. The thought of being in bed with Benny, Junior, was totally revolting.

"You'd be better off marrying the older man you enslaved last night. After he kicks off you can afford to hire all the short, young, experienced studs you need to satisfy your kinky tastes."

"*My* kinky tastes! Your girlfriends look like you rent them by the hour."

"You mean lovely Kay?" he asked calmly. "She's a beauty, isn't she? I've always adored tall, *slender* women."

"She's built like a whippet," Sammi shot back.

"Meow," Steele teased. "I think you're jealous, Sam, because Kay's several luscious pounds lighter than you."

He was incredible. Nothing she said or did pricked his tough hide. He wasn't the least vulnerable. She refused to talk further about his dates. She hated them both.

Tugging her arm free, she spun around to leave. One thing she didn't need was a country Dear Abby to tell her how to run her life.

"Hold it, Sam," Steele commanded in a low voice. "I'm taking one kiss then I'll let you return to Junior."

"Like hell you are," Sammi moaned, raising on tiptoes with parted lips to meet his hungry mouth. Did she have no willpower? She was obsessed by the man. Apparently all he had to do was enfold her in his strong arms as he was doing and she was lost.

"Oh, Steele," she whispered tenderly. "That feels soooo good."

He hugged her tightly to his chest and murmured back. "Don't you think I know that, Sam?" He kissed her again. Over and over.

She removed her fingertips from their customary place on his nape and allowed them to explore his shirt front. Her throat arched, offering him easy access to the throbbing pulse that beat like a wild thing when he was near. Entrapped against his chest, she thought it the safest haven in the world.

His fingers were tangled in her hair, holding her still while he nibbled his way over the scented skin. No part exposed went untouched—her neck, cheekbones, chin, ear, eyelids, and forehead.

"Does it bother you to know how good we'd be together in bed, Sam?" he teased against the corner of her luscious mouth.

"I never gave it a thought," she whispered in a choked voice.

She was lying through her teeth and he knew it.

"You'd better," he warned, still kissing her everywhere but on her aching mouth. He'd thought of nothing else all night.

"Samantha. Where are you?"

She moaned, hearing her name called by Benny—the most disturbing sound in the world. And the most unwelcome at the moment.

"Here's lover boy now," Steele whispered into her dainty ear, exposed by the upswept hairdo. "Better watch him tonight. He's got the look of a man on the make."

"It takes one to know one," she murmured in a hushed tone.

"Have I ever asked you to go to bed with me?"

"Not yet."

"Disappointed?"

Sammi trembled in his arms, shook her head no, and leaned into his heaving chest. She was desperately unhappy he hadn't asked at the moment.

"Samantha!" Her name was called louder.

She tore herself from Steele's arms and exited the darkened room without a backward glance. She gave Benny a wide smile and took his arm, deciding it best to ignore his bewildered look as he stared at her flushed face and pulsating mouth kissed free of lipstick.

"What were you doing in there, Samantha? You didn't bring a coat with you?" he insisted, peering into the shadowed room.

"I ducked inside to repair a run in my hose," she explained, not caring in the least if she was telling a lie. She was so muddled by Steele's caresses she didn't know what she said anyway.

"I got rid of old Cyril and your Aunt Margaret," Benny gloated. "They took the Caddy but we can use a taxi. That way both my hands will be free just in case you get cold on the way back to your motel."

"Don't count on it, Junior." Sammi glowered. "I'm very warm-blooded."

"I'd hoped so." He leered, his forehead breaking out in a nervous sweat at the image of making love to her.

She gave him a look that would have frozen anyone with an ounce of sense. "I have a sudden headache, Benny . . . a migraine . . . and want to go to my room now."

"Did you forget I'm a doctor, Samantha? I have the perfect drug in my apartment. We'll go there now and I guarantee that in fifteen minutes you'll be feeling mellow."

"Sorry. I'm allergic to both drugs and doctors."

"You must be frigid," he complained petulantly. "Your headache's probably a psychological rejection of my overt manhood."

"No doubt!" she agreed in disbelief. His conceit was staggering. One hand went to her head. Now it did hurt. The main thing that made her feel ill was the vision of Kay's willowy blond beauty and the amount of time she'd have to spend riding with Benny before they got back to her room.

They walked outside, hailed a waiting taxi, and stepped into the darkened interior of the smoke-scented backseat.

Sammi eased to the far side, clasping her purse in her lap like a shield. She stared warily at Benny as he scooted closer. Before they had left the circular driveway, she was pushed against the corner and he was clumsily leaning across her with his wet mouth groping for hers.

"Bug off, Benny!" she admonished severely. Raising her purse with one hand, she turned her head to avoid his disgusting touch. The little creep was stronger than she had imagined.

"Kiss me, Samantha," he pleaded. He ignored her censure and

awkwardly fumbled for her passionate-shaped lips. "It's not healthy to suppress your normal needs."

"How do you know I do?" she stormed back, pushing so hard to keep him from coming in contact with her body that he fell away.

"Come on," he begged with a sullen look on his face. "Sex is good for a woman."

"Not with you it isn't," she informed him sharply.

His face expressed shock that she resisted him. Gathering his nerve, he lunged back with hands outstretched, only to be met by a barrage of words that stopped his second fervent advance before it started.

"If you don't want your voice raised to a permanent soprano, Junior, you'd better shut your mouth, remove your damn roving fingers from my shoulders, and stay as far in your corner as possible!"

"Come on, Samantha," he implored. His blood was pounding with excitement and his breath came in short gasps as he maneuvered to avoid her suddenly upraised knee. "You'll like it."

"The only thing I'll like is an end to this abominable evening," she snapped. Aunt Margaret's friend had really picked a bummer of an escort. "You have all the finesse of a teen-age sailor on leave after a year at sea."

"You'll regret turning me down," he bragged, undecided if she was serious or only playing hard to get.

"My only regret is going out with you at all!" God, would the taxi never get there.

As it squealed to a stop in front of the motel office, Sammi jumped out and ran down the walkway to her room. The damned wimp had her shaking she was so mad. She hadn't wrestled in the backseat like that for years.

"Two down and one to go," she fumed as she reached her room.

Searching for the door key with shaking fingers, she paused to look up at the sound of a car braking to a stop beside her. Its powerful motor hummed as the driver stepped out and took her elbow in his strong grip.

"Get in the car, Sam."

Steele led her around to the passenger door, opened it, and gently assisted her inside.

Sammi made no protest until she was seated in the low bucket seat with her long limbs stretched out before her.

"What do you want now, Steele?" she asked as he made a wide turn and zoomed out of the parking area.

"You, Sam. Forever you," he responded in a low, serious voice.

"Me?" Sammi whispered. The way he rolled, *forever you*, off his tongue sent a shiver from her fingertips to her toes.

"Yes," he reiterated slowly. "I decided a platonic kiss in a cloakroom wouldn't be enough to see me through the night."

"Platonic?" she questioned. "Nothing you've done to me so far indicates you've suppressed a sexual relationship between us."

"Oh, honey, how naive you are," he corrected her softly. "I haven't begin to touch your body in the ways I've wanted to since you raised your saucy little face to me on the freeway."

The lovely faces of Monique and Kay crossed her mind. What was his relationship with the two women? What had happened with the blonde tonight? In no time the beast would have a harem, she thought, vowing not to be its newest member.

"Go touch Kay," she suggested in a voice filled with jealousy.

"Kay has a heavy schedule tomorrow morning and had to get back to her condo for a few hours sleep. Modeling's a hard job and uses up a lot of energy."

"I wouldn't know," Sammi commented, not caring to talk another moment about her. In fact, she hoped the woman's work was so tiring she didn't have the strength to date the rest of her life.

She watched in silence as Steele wound through side streets, going higher all the time. He stopped next to the curb on a deserted hilltop overlooking the city. It was like a fairyland—a place of delicate beauty and magical charm.

She could see rich sparkling lights of the distant Golden Gate Bridge and silvery buildings towering in the downtown area. She watched entranced for a long, long time.

"Was he bad?" Steele inquired softly.

"The worst," Sammi answered. She knew he was asking about Benny.

"I warned you, honey."

"I know." Her eyes never left the view below her as she calmly replied to each comment. It was always that way when they were together. Periods, like now, of complete accord or—*could she be responsible?*—moments of verbal dissension. All were more pleasurable somehow than time spent with any other man she knew.

Steele leaned over the gear shift, adjusted his hip for maximum comfort, and drew Sammi into his arms.

"Maybe this will help, sweetheart."

As in the past she made no protest. If he wanted to caress her, she was more than willing. The revolting memory of Benny's mouth on her neck needed erasing—remedied with the intoxicating sensation of Steele's firm lips against her skin.

"Now, Sam," he drawled. "Let's get the hell on with some loving."

"You're awful," she told him, parting her lips in expectation as he nuzzled her neck.

"Aren't I though?" he agreed, taking her ear lobe in his teeth and tugging it gently.

She could feel his warm breath fan the sensitive area behind her ear. It sent currents of pleasure through her languorous form. Did nothing the man do to her body feel bad?

"You're really a . . . a terrible . . . terrible beast," Sammi stuttered when he traced the shape of her ear with his tongue before delving inside with such intimacy she felt she'd faint. Both hands rose to cradle his head. The clean wavy hair beneath her caressing fingertips was as vital as the man. "You're arrogant too."

"I know, Sam," he murmured, withdrawing from the tantalizing pink cavity of her ear. He could feel her body quiver when he ended the erotic exploration. "How did that make you feel?"

"Like swooning," she answered honestly. Her breath came in short gasps more uneven than Benny's had ever been.

Steele nipped the side of her neck, his words muffled against the heady scent of her satin-smooth skin. "Women don't swoon anymore, honey," he laughed. "That went out with whale-bone corsets."

"What do you call it, Mr. Know-It-All?" Sammi insisted. She squirmed closer, scooting down so she could press beneath his hip.

"A fit of the vapors." He laughed. His mouth never left her skin.

"That's worse than my explanation," she scolded, trying desperately to retain a semblance of sanity. "There must be something more modern."

"There is," he murmured, moving to her closed eyelids. "You're as aroused as I am. You're turned on. And you want me to make love to you as eagerly as I want to do so."

He nibbled the corner of her parted lips, inhaling the fresh, sweet scent of her rapidly exhaled breath.

"Are you sure?" Was that why she wanted to experience their naked bodies pressed close together on a bed in a private room rather than in a luxurious sports car? Of course it was, she admitted truthfully.

"I'm sure," he complained. "Now shut your sexy mouth because I'm going to kiss the sweet hell out of you."

With eyes closed, she lay her head against the leather seat back. Her soft, ecstatic sigh was swallowed by his mouth as he took her lips in a searching, hungry kiss that proved he enjoyed their passionate interchange as much as she did.

She inhaled the fragrance of his after-shave while returning the ardor of his mouth with fervent kisses of her own. His tongue moved sensuously against hers, speaking its own message. She answered an endless erotic summons with a frustrated moan before pulling away.

"Don't," she cried, twisting her head helplessly. "No more, please!"

Tears slid unbidden beneath her clenched eyelids. The man's sexual expertise had never been in doubt, but his deep, exploring kisses were more than she could handle.

Steele had pulled up the moment she resisted, crooning tenderly to her as he rested his face along the scented skin of her neck. He could feel her body tremble beneath him. Her breasts rose and fell and were irresistibly soft.

Taking one dainty hand from his nape, he bent his head into the palm. "Relax, honey." He attempted to soothe her. "I only want to touch you like this." He circled his tongue in the hollow of her hand. "And this." His mouth moved to her pulse, where he placed a soft, lingering kiss before licking the skin around her wrist. "And this." He moved the ebony bracelets with his tongue, alternately licking and blowing his warm breath against the smooth skin.

"I think I'm being seduced," she told him as tears continued to roll down her cheeks.

"Not here, Sam," he assured her. "Not in a car. When I seduce you it will be in the finest suite I can find. You deserve no less."

He replaced her hand on his nape, gently taking the salty drops of moisture from her cheeks into his mouth before placing a long, lingering kiss on her quivering lips.

"Do you trust me?" His eyes were dark and compelling.

"Why?" Her voice was barely audible, her eyes closed. She wasn't emotionally ready to meet his look of naked desire clearly visible in the moonlit interior.

"I'm going to caress your breasts, Sam," he warned. "Their feminine beauty has haunted me from the first."

All the time he was telling her his intentions his fingers worked deftly to unbutton her jacket. She heard a low gasp like the one the night before when his knuckles brushed the straining flesh. Her breasts were barely contained in low-cut cups of a bra so fragile the material threatened to tear.

Taking his other hand he unclipped the jeweled fastener between her breasts. He was quiet, worshipping her in silence. With great tenderness he cupped the satiny fullness and raised it to meet his lowering head. He kissed the tip with such reverence she cried out.

"I shouldn't allow this," she protested as his tongue stroked the hardened tip and sent waves of pleasure deep into her abdomen. His fingers kneaded the burgeoning flesh while he teased the rigid tip with the edge of his teeth until she involuntarily arched her hips.

"Can you feel my desire for you, Sam?" he asked bluntly.

"I—I—" She broke off. She wasn't that naive.

"Can you feel it!" he insisted, lying more fully across her.

"God yes!" She was aware of every inch of his fully aroused body. It was hard, explicitly male, and a reminder his passions would never be satiated by making gentle love in a car.

"Why do you ask?" A faint rose touched her face. Never would any of her men friends have asked such a blunt question.

"Because," he whispered into the deep cleavage of her heaving breasts. "I want you to know I could die happy with my face cradled to your breasts and my body—the part of me you say you feel—buried deep inside you."

She couldn't answer. She didn't think he expected her to. It was enough to absorb the bluntness of his impassioned comment. No man she'd ever met would have dared express his needs so honestly.

He drew back, easing away from her feminine softness. "Open your eyes and let me look at you. Let me see the passion you can never hide."

Sammi complied, not caring Steele could detect a reflection of his desires echoed in their depths.

"You're gorgeous, Sam."

She felt gorgeous. Everything he said and did made her think she was the most beautiful woman alive. His trembling palms gave her a sense of power over him for the first time. It was the only moment they'd been together when she had some control.

With a sigh she drew his head down to offer a kiss.

Accepting the invitation, he appeased her need with such hunger she whimpered and drew away. His suit was pressing against her naked breasts, and she ached to tear it from his body and push into the muscled strength she had yet to see.

His lips slid the length of her arched throat, trailing down to the thrusting perfection of full breasts gleaming with an ivory sheen. The erect tips enticed, demanding attention. His mouth obliged, leaving its warmth on every portion of her exposed bosom.

His tongue was driving her wild. She hadn't known a loving touch could be so devastating. He'd never dream he was the first man she had allowed to fondle her so intimately.

Steele placed a lingering kiss on each hardened tip, then fastened her brassiere with fingers that weren't nearly as deft as they had been minutes before.

"Time to take you back home."

Sammi raised her eyes to watch as he settled back into his seat and reached up to start the ignition.

"Home?"

"Your motel," he corrected himself. "For now."

He started the car, turned on the defroster, waited until the windshield was free of moisture generated by their bodies' heat, then eased down the winding road back to town.

"How's the millionaire hunt going?"

"Why should you care?" She was still breathless from the most passionate experience of her entire life and he was curious about her interest in other men. Contemplating his sudden nonchalance, she gripped her hands together in her lap and stared straight ahead.

"I've thought about what you said you wanted in a man and decided tonight to see you marry a wealthy one."

"How nice, Steele," she told him through clenched teeth. Of all the nerve. He'd kissed her as if he couldn't get enough, caressed her breasts like a long-time lover, insisted she acknowledge his desire, and minutes later calmly remarked he was going to help her find a man of means.

"Don't bother matchmaking," she warned, hoping her face didn't look as stricken as she felt.

"Why?"

"I have a date tomorrow, er, tonight, with my ideal."

"What's that, Sam?" he asked as if he hadn't overheard everything she had told her aunt at Nick's.

"A blond, blue-eyed professional man."

"Is he wealthy?"

"Very!"

"Sounds good. I like blue-eyed blondes myself. I hope it works out."

"It will," she bragged. What was the matter with the man? Had he forgotten already that he'd told her earlier he wanted her forever?

"I'm glad," he said with feigned pleasure. He wasn't going to be cheated out of one more night of chasing her around town. Her belligerent face and continued consternation would settle the high score for her unjustified insults that first day.

"Why?" she questioned. Her snappy reply was blurted out without thinking. Why should he care one way or the other?

"I'm getting tired of you following me around town." He ignored her flaring nostrils and continued unabated. "Your frosty glances constantly darting my way are upsetting my dates."

"Following you? You have more conceit than any man I've met!" She avoided talking about his women, but the next time she saw him she'd put a crimp in his love life a hot iron couldn't smooth out.

"Settle down, Sam. You're getting mad again."

"For good reason, *Red*." How could she have ever forgotten she hated all men with that color hair?

Steele stopped the Lamborghini, kissed her pouting lips, got out, assisted her to the door, opened it, returned the key to her clenched fingers, kissed her again, and walked away without saying good-bye.

"I hope I never see you again!" she shouted to the brilliant red taillights as he sped away. "Another thing," she continued beneath her breath, "if you think I'd ever allow a redheaded trucker to seduce me, forget it!" His promise of a *fine suite* was probably a pile of hay anyway.

CHAPTER SIX

Sammi dressed for her evening out with a sense of certainty. She was absolutely convinced her third date would be the charm. Everything Margaret told her about Alan made him sound like the ideal person to drive thoughts of Steele from her mind. She was through allowing him to mock her one moment, then make love to her the next. If he wanted to play games, he could go to an amusement park.

"You're even more stunning tonight, Samantha," her aunt complimented her when she walked into the living area to gather a beaded evening bag.

"Thanks. You look lovely yourself," Sammi told her truthfully. Vivid makeup and new accessories had made a remarkable difference in the older woman's appearance.

"I like the dark print of your dress, dear."

"It's the closest thing to a camouflage outfit I brought with me." Sammi laughed. "The navy and wine design should conceal anything the beast causes me to spill."

"How do you know Steele will be where we are?" Margaret asked.

"It's inevitable." Sammi grimaced. "No matter where we go he'll be there wreaking havoc with my nerves and causing me to ruin another brand-new garment. I just feel it."

"You can't blame him for all your mishaps," Margaret pointed out. "The poor man—"

"Poor man is right," Sammi interrupted. "He probably doesn't have a cent to his name."

"The poor man," Margaret continued, "wasn't even close to you when the accidents happened, other than the mark he made on your shorts."

"It makes no difference where he was," Sammi said, fuming. "Everything is his fault. Every bad thing that's happened since I came to San Francisco he caused."

"I don't see how he could have known where you'd be unless you told him. Did you?" Margaret asked curiously.

"How could I? Other than the first night with John, I didn't know where we were going, nor did you."

"That proves it's just coincidence that Steele and his beautiful dates—"

"I don't want to hear about his women, Margaret." Sammi checked her comments. "Hearing you say the beast's name is bad enough."

"Okay, honey," Margaret answered agreeably. "But his arrival had to be accidental. It's the only explanation possible for seeing him where we dined two nights in a row."

"Three, Margaret," Sammi insisted. "I guarantee it will be three after tonight. There will be a big difference in tonight's outcome, though, as I intend to fall head over heels in love."

"With Steele?" Margaret asked, agape.

"God no, my suddenly dense aunt," Sammi scolded. "With Alan! Tomorrow I intend to start shopping for a trousseau."

Margaret's amused laughter brought a glare from Sammi as they walked forward to answer an impatient knock on the motel door.

Margaret opened it, took Paul's hand in greeting, smiled at Alan, and introduced both men to her niece.

"Hello, Alan." Sammi welcomed with a sincere smile. Her eyes sparkled with pleasure. Margaret was right. He was her ideal. His glorious hair was a shiny golden blond, his face was handsome, and the eyes that met hers just barely a fraction higher were robin's egg blue. His navy-blue suit was impeccable, silk tie a pattern she liked, and shoes polished to a high gloss. An urbane man in every way.

Sammi could hardly wait to show Alan off to Steele. There would be no pretended interest tonight. Her escort was perfect and the beast was nearly a forgotten irritation of the past. Within a half hour she'd forget his kisses, and in an hour she'd probably have a hard time remembering the name Steele Whitfield.

"Samantha," Alan said in a pleasant voice, "you're very beautiful, and it will be my pleasure to see you have an unforgettable evening. We'll go in my new Corvette, if you don't mind?"

"I can hardly wait," Sammi answered with an eye-catching smile. She looked at both men, touched Paul's hand, and instantly enchanted him as well as his son. "I adore riding in sports cars."

"Bright red ones?" he questioned courteously.

"Especially that color," she returned, thinking how polite he was. First he complimented her then he asked her preference in transportation. He was the epitome of her ideal and she couldn't be more thankful.

"What do you do for a living, Samantha?" Alan asked during the drive to the restaurant.

"I'm a qualified tenth-grade history teacher, which I did the first four years after college."

"And now?"

"I assist the owner of an ultra-exclusive gift shop in Hollywood."

"Why the change in careers?" Alan questioned. "Did the male students insist you were more interesting than what happened in the past?"

"The students were easy to handle," Sammi explained. A sudden frown marred her brow at the memory of her last year teaching. "It was the principal who was bothersome."

"I can understand why," Alan enthused. "There were no

women teachers where I attended school who were nearly as lovely as you. What was the problem?"

Explaining with a shrug, Sammi told him in a flat voice, "The principal was single but his wife wasn't. When the atmosphere became too uncomfortable, I decided the heck with it."

She gave Alan a tantalizing smile as he pulled into the parking lot. "I much prefer working with pretty things that don't sass back."

Sammi swept her glance around the paved area, trying surreptitiously to see if Steele's Lamborghini was in the lot. Perhaps he was already seated inside, which would be perfect.

Taking Alan's arm, she walked proudly into the foyer. God, she hoped Steele was watching. Alan's handsome blond looks were an excellent foil for her ebony hair. If she had to say so herself, she thought they made an absolutely smashing-looking couple.

Sitting down gracefully, with Alan's hand assuring she didn't stumble, she lay the purse beside her in the plush booth. With lashes lowered, she casually scanned the softly lit interior of the dining room, refusing to admit she felt a sharp twinge of disappointment that Steele was nowhere in sight. Her grand entry was made in vain.

Determined to blot Steele from her mind, Sammi concentrated on finding out more about her date while waiting for Margaret and Paul to arrive.

Sammi chuckled softly as Alan told her an amusing story about a recent court case he had handled for a client whose golden Pekingese-look-alike little mongrel dog kept getting into the neighbor's yard and impregnating a valuable pedigreed Irish wolfhound.

"It seems the judge was convinced the little male could never father a litter of pups with a bitch that was five times his size."

"What convinced him otherwise?" Sammi asked.

"Nine furry pups with pushed-in faces the identical color of their sire." Alan laughed. "The bitch's owner seemed more upset that her elegant animal would condescend to let the tiny male breed her than over the fact that she was stuck with a valueless litter of mutts rather than ultra-expensive registered pups."

Sammi looked up, smiling as Paul assisted Margaret into the empty seat across from her and Alan. She winked as her aunt smoothed her skirt while trying surreptitiously to communicate her interest in learning her niece's opinion of this night's date.

"Have you ordered yet?" Margaret questioned, obviously pleased that Sammi seemed extremely happy.

"No," Alan answered. "We've been discussing my work while waiting for you two. What took so long, Dad?"

"Obeying the speed limit," Paul answered in a serious voice, well aware how recklessly his son usually drove. His number of speeding tickets since the age of sixteen was solid evidence of his carelessness.

"Touché, Dad." Alan laughed, unperturbed. He saw no reason to own a sports car that could travel over a hundred miles an hour and not use all the horsepower beneath the hood whenever traffic allowed it.

"Are you girls hungry?" Paul asked politely.

Margaret beamed, enjoying being called a girl for a change. It wasn't often she was included in that category.

"I know Samantha will be," she explained with a soft laugh. "Am I right, niece?"

"Definitely," Sammi answered. "Especially after scanning this menu."

"Would you like me to order for you?" Alan asked with masculine courtesy.

Sammi thought a moment, set the menu down, turned her head, and gave Alan a wide smile. "That sounds delightful. There's not a thing listed I wouldn't enjoy."

Alan was a dream come true. She felt so pampered. He was striking to look at, courteous to a fault, and determined to see she was enjoying herself. A cultured, educated professional man of means had always been the kind of man she preferred.

Sammi reluctantly acknowledged her constant searching of the room's interior and that not seeing Steele bothered her. Even when the beast wasn't in the same room, he managed to annoy her, she complained in silence. What was keeping him away tonight?

She sipped a smooth white wine that was the most delicious she had ever tasted, convinced that her escort's presence made it so. Accepting a crystal ice-filled plate with pink, succulent prawns surrounding an inner dish of spicy-looking seafood sauce, she thought of her date with Steele. There would be no franks and popcorn with Alan. Picking up the tiny cocktail fork, she speared a prawn and dipped it daintily before raising it to her lips. The seafood was sweet, tender, and delicious. It was wonderful dining in such luxurious surroundings for the third night in a row.

By the time Sammi had finished her first taste of pheasant under glass, she was convinced Alan was Mr. Perfect. The succulent meat was flavored somewhere between poultry and venison and was a tender, delectable symbol of the opulent living she aspired to.

She sipped her fourth glass of vintage wine while waiting with keen anticipation for the soufflé Grand Marnier au chocolat.

Sammi's eyes raised when Margaret gave a suspicious-sounding cough. She watched her aunt's eyebrows arch as she stared over her niece's shoulder to signal what was happening.

Sammi's back stiffened. She knew what was coming without turning around. The fine hairs on her nape rose as she sensed that Steele was behind her. It was such a strong feeling that she'd have known he was in the room if her aunt hadn't drawn her attention to it first.

Deliberately leaning into Alan's shoulder, Sammi raised her eyes to give him her most seductive look. She smiled with such passion that she could see the instant darkening of his pupils as they enlarged with his rising desire. His quick intake of breath made her hope she wasn't overdoing her come-on when she placed her fingers over his on the table.

Eager to touch her, Alan responded by lifting her hand to his lips and brushing his mouth across her fingertips at the same moment Steele passed their table.

My God! Sammi cried out in silent disgust as her hand suddenly lay limp in Alan's clasp. The beast swaggered into the room with Monique clinging to one arm and Kay attached to the other. Both women were dressed to their eye teeth in long gowns that made Sammi cringe at the cost. They were coiffed and clad as elegantly as any women she'd ever seen. Tonight both looked like they'd captured a grand prize.

"God, what beautiful women," Alan exclaimed as he caught a glimpse when they passed the table. "Anyone would envy that man."

"I don't!" Sammi told him peevishly.

"Any man," Alan corrected, turning to smile at her lovely face. "Other than me, of course," he added. "Neither woman holds a candle to you, my gorgeous Samantha."

"Thank you, Alan," Sammi said, preening. Her ego took a sharp jump at his sincere voice and enthralled expression.

Sammi watched beneath lowered lashes as Steele seated the women with a flourish so they faced Samantha's way. She was furious when he sat down with his back toward her. Apparently he wanted to observe both smooth, carefully made up faces and pouting lips raised in identical glossy red smiles. She fumed inwardly, knowing it wouldn't do a bit of good to shoot frosty glances across the room. He couldn't even see her.

She glared anyway. It made her feel better, since she hated him all the more tonight. With a rush she remembered her vow to pay Steele back for his insults of the night before and set to work on a plan.

During the next twenty minutes Sammi excused herself to go to the ladies' room three times. Not once did Steele acknowledge her presence, though she walked out of her way to pass his table.

"Excuse me, everyone. I need to use the ladies' room again," she told Margaret, Paul, and Alan after removing a handkerchief from her purse.

"Perhaps you need to see a doctor, my dear," Mr. Anderson suggested helpfully.

"A doctor, hell," Alan snorted, temporarily forgetting to control his quick temper. "Samantha needs a plumber."

Alan couldn't help but grumble. Each time he gained Sammi's undivided attention, she hopped up and took off. It was beginning to be damned irritating. She was so passionate-looking he didn't want to waste time on idle conversation and was counting the hours until they could be alone. Those soft pink lips and sensual body were made to be explored, and his apartment was just the place to do it.

With chin raised, Sammi ignored Alan's peevish remark and walked with a predetermined plan toward Steele's table. It was the long way around, but necessary since she was resolute in her desire to make trouble. The beast deserved any mischief she could come up with. Any bit of embarrassment she could cause would be worth the interruption of her meal and intrigue with Alan. She owed Steele plenty, and tonight would be a good time to start paying off her debt by putting a permanent crimp in his love life.

Sammi deliberately dropped her hankie beside Steele's table and paused, waiting impatiently for him to pick it up.

Steele ignored her, continued to talk attentively to both women, and acted as if he didn't hear her fabricated cough. He was far too astute not to recognize her purpose.

Sammi was furious. She could tell by the upraised corner of his twitching mouth that he knew she was there, and she darned well intended to stand by his table until he turned her way if it took all night!

"Excuse me, sir," Sammi interjected in her most innocent voice to the back of his shimmering red hair when agitation overcame her vow to wait by silently.

"What's the matter, kid?" Steele asked without turning his head.

The way he said kid made her feel about four feet tall with pigtails, bare feet, and one tooth missing. It also added to her fury.

"I appear to have dropped my handkerchief and it fluttered under your table. Would you mind handing it to me?"

With one nylon-clad toe bared by her wispy evening sandals, Sammi kicked the hankie beside Steele's large Gucci-clad feet, thinking he had probably rented his shoes as well as his suits.

One tanned hand reached beneath the table while his conversation with the two women continued unabated.

"My goodness, if it isn't Steele Whitfield," Sammi exclaimed in a soft, angelic voice as she leaned between them to break up the entranced threesome.

"My goodness, if it isn't Samantha Thatcher," Steele echoed. He looked her lazily up and down before turning to Monique and Kay to add with irritating nonchalance, "Sam's a new friend."

"New friend!" Sammi exploded, her voice an angry hiss. "Hardly new, my dear, after last night." She smiled indulgently at Steele, then glanced meaningfully at Kay. "Yes, he was with me *after* he dropped *you* off." Sammi's vivid eyes were bright with devilry and she enjoyed every word.

Placing her hand on Steele's shoulder, she gave him a coy look through fluttering lashes before glancing back across the table. Thoroughly relishing her impudence, Sammi added with suggestive emphasis, "Last night till dawn . . . and the night before . . . I guess when a man like Steele finally finds a woman who can satisfy him . . ."

"Please excuse Sam, ladies," Steele cut in. "Her atrocious manners are only exceeded by her overactive imagination."

As Sammi fumed, uncertain how to answer his blatant retort, Steele reached up, took her hand in his, and with one sharp tug forced her to sit alongside him.

She stiffened as she felt his touch from thigh to waist. Beneath the table his hard grip assured she wasn't going to get away until he had his say also.

"Kay and Monique, I'd like you to meet Sam, that eighteen-wheeling groupie I told you about. We met alongside the freeway the first of the week and she's been pursuing me ever since."

"How troublesome for you, Steele," Kay pointed out with sweet sarcasm that equaled Sammi's, "to have her following you around."

"Yes, it must be tiring at the very least," Monique added matter-of-factly. "Especially since you're a man who likes to do the chasing."

"Don't forget to mention how much fun for Steele though," Sammi added with barely concealed fury while raising her heel. She was intent on seeing Steele's foot suffer the same fate as Benny's. When her foot slammed down it hit nothing but the carpeting.

Steele had moved his feet aside and sat grinning at her furious face when she found her old trick hadn't worked with him.

Sammi stared in silence at the women while tugging with all her might beneath the cover of the impeccable white linen tablecloth.

Steele ignored her mutinous expression, smiled at his dates, and controlled Sammi's grip with an ease that was all the more infuriating as she squirmed alongside him. He held her palms in place over the silk of her dress and pressed down on her lap with such intimacy that it brought a soft flush to her face.

She moved her hips over, managed to push his hands on top of her thigh, and counted to ten as his index finger straightened out and trailed a daring path from her knee to her hip while easily dragging both her hands within his grip.

The lecherous beast! she fumed in silence. How dare he fondle her body while across from two of his aging consorts? She'd fix him for certain now. Kay and Monique hadn't said another thing after the one derogatory comment when he introduced her as a truck-stop groupie. That was one more thing the beast deserved being paid back for, Sammi reflected.

She turned to stare at Steele with luminous eyes, moistened her parted lips with the tip of her tongue, and leaned into his muscled shoulder. She hoped her final words would embarrass all of them so much they'd rush out of the room and she could concentrate solely on Alan.

"Don't come by tonight after you take your, er, old friends home, Steele. I'll be entertaining my gentleman friend Alan until morning. He's a prominent attorney. Lawyers have so much more finesse in the bedroom compared to gear-jammers. I find the contrast quite stimulating."

She gave the two women a wide innocent smile and received a sharp retaliatory pinch from Steele for that bit of sarcasm, but it didn't matter. The shocked expression on both women's faces at her bluntness was worth it. That should end the beast's nightly orgies. No woman with any pride would put up with a man using another woman to appease his sexual needs after each date.

Finding her hands free, Sammi stood up and walked from Steele's table to the ladies' room with a straight back. Shiny ebony curls were tossed back with such spirit they bounced across her shoulder blades as she stormed away. She made a loop through the hall and returned to her table.

When she slid into the booth, Alan concealed his chagrin to ask curiously, "Who was that man, Samantha?"

Alan hadn't liked the man's looks any more than he had those of his ex-girlfriend's husband Derek. Both men were larger than him and ruggedly fit-looking. Thank God he knew self-defense that didn't depend on muscles. No man would ever leave him in his car and cart his date off as if he was a ninety-eight-pound weakling and they were Charles Atlas.

"He was a casual acquaintance, Alan. Not even a friend, but he felt it was polite to introduce me to his, er . . . cousins," Sammi lied while assuring him with a squeeze of her hand that she was sincere.

"Oh good, our dessert's ready," Sammi said happily. She stared at the luscious-looking chocolate soufflé in its fluted dish. "This looks well worth the long wait."

Margaret watched in amazement as Sammi calmly took a spoon and prepared to taste the rich dessert. She couldn't believe her niece's feigned trip to the rest room just to pass by Steele's table. It was obvious, despite her apparent interest in Alan, that the trucker was constantly on her mind. It was also apparent the man continually bested her in verbal and physical confrontations.

"I don't like that man, Samantha," Alan whispered in her ear after moving closer so he could enjoy the touch of her long limbs and soft hip against his.

Sammi swallowed a spoonful of velvet-smooth soufflé, wiped her lips with the napkin, and smiled at his concerned face.

"You're an excellent judge of character. I barely know the man and hate him too. It was hate at first sight actually."

The words were barely out of Sammi's mouth when Steele appeared at their table. He gave Margaret a wide smile that caused her heart to lurch, introduced himself with suave poise, and shook hands with Paul, who stood up briefly, then settled back beside Margaret. The two men had sized each other up in an instant and liked what they saw.

With Paul's son it was a different matter. Steele glared down at Alan's suddenly petulant lips and stretched his hand out until the man was forced to shake it. He laughed inwardly, knowing their instant dislike was mutual.

"You must be Whit Smith," Steele said. The words flowed out of his mouth in mischief.

Sammi glared upward, admitted Steele looked devastating in another custom-tailored evening suit, and counted to ten for the second time in thirty minutes. They had never discussed it, but she knew damn well the beast was aware there wasn't—that there never had been—a Whit Smith. In fact, she knew she had just mentioned Alan's name moments earlier.

"The name's Alan. Alan Anderson," the blond-haired man answered with obvious irritation.

"Oh, sorry. I thought you were Sam's fiancé." Steele apologized with such conviction the man believed him.

"Samantha's engaged?" Alan blurted out, looking from one to the other for an explanation while Margaret and Paul watched what was happening in silence.

"I am not!" Sammi snapped, staring up at Steele with flushed anger-filled features before turning to Alan to assure him it wasn't the truth.

"You were four days ago," Steele reminded her calmly. His commanding appearance and deep voice filled Alan with doubt.

Steele looked at Sammi for a long moment. "Sorry it didn't work out, Sam," he commiserated with feigned sympathy.

He patted Alan on the shoulder in a condescending way he knew would infuriate the man instantly.

"Well, pleased to meet you anyway . . . Adam," Steele said.

"Alan!" Sammi's escort corrected him, though his even teeth were gritting with resentment at the man's intrusion.

"Sorry about that, Alan. How careless of me to forget so soon."

Steele shrugged his broad shoulders, looked around the table at the foursome as innocently as possible, then turned to leave after telling each good-bye.

He stopped before taking a step away, spun around, and returned to lean toward Sammi and whisper.

"By the way, Sam, this jewel fell off your brassiere fastener last night. Careless of you not to notice it missing, honey."

Steele gave Alan a resigned smile. "A man could get the wrong idea, couldn't he?" He glanced back at Sammi's stunned face with his hand outstretched. "Be a shame to ruin your reputation, Sam."

Sammi's hand instinctively reached up and accepted a round metal object, which made her look as guilty as Steele intended.

"Good luck . . . Adam," he told Paul's son. "You'll need it

132

with this one. Sam's quite a handful." His eyes took in Sammi's rounded breasts outlined in the clinging silk of her dress. "A very satiny handful though."

At the start of Steele's blunt conversation, Margaret loudly engaged Paul in an intense though stilted discussion. It was a vain effort to drown out Steele's comments about her niece. An unsuccessful attempt, since she was well aware that Paul was listening, as dumbfounded as she was, and was as thankful when Steele returned to his own table.

To think she had actually told each man her niece was adorably sweet. The minx had obviously been doing more than making idle conversation while out with Steele, and as soon as the evening ended she intended to find out just what they'd been up to.

Sammi ignored Margaret, smiled at Paul, and refused to glance at Alan. If he believed anything the lying beast said, then it was too bad. She spooned the last few bites of soufflé into her mouth, relaxed in the booth, and gave herself an imaginary pat on the back for not getting one bit of food on her clothes. That proved more than anything that the trucker's spell over her was broken. It was the first meal out she hadn't spilled something on a new outfit.

When she and Alan were alone, she'd be extra nice and explain that Steele was a pathological liar, which should soothe his ruffled feelings. She had enough confidence in her acting ability to know that she could convince him Steele was nuts and had come to their table intent on causing trouble. No hick was going to interfere with her desire to see that the man beside her was thoroughly enchanted before the evening was over.

Giving Alan a sugary smile, Sammi planned her strategy for the rest of the evening and thought about shopping for lingerie the next day. She would need to buy lots of new clothes in the next few weeks since she intended to have her date so smitten he'd want to marry her immediately. At twenty-eight she didn't see any need in wasting time on a long courtship.

Sammi slipped the piece of cheap jewelry into her purse, deciding to look at it later. It was obviously from a Cracker Jack box if Steele had it. She regretted not ignoring his outstretched hand. It would have been interesting to let him stand there like an awkward oaf and see what he would do, but he'd taken her by surprise and she was slow reacting.

"That was an excellent meal," Sammi said, thanking Paul as he laid a credit card on the tab.

"I'm glad you're finished." Alan spoke up, still ired by the stranger's interruption of their meal. "Would you like to go to a disco and dance?"

He wanted to hold Sammi in his arms. Maybe touching her full length would erase the jealous thoughts that kept crossing his mind. Only an idiot would have missed the electricity that flew between Samantha and Steele as they exchanged glances. He wasn't used to a woman's divided attention and was determined to make her forget the man before they said good night.

"I'd love it," Sammi enthused. She touched Alan's hand in gratitude for a brief moment before gathering up her purse.

Paul signed for the bill, then took Margaret's arm as he walked behind Sammi and his son toward the entrance door.

Sammi gave Steele one last furtive glance. She was pleased to see he was was just starting to eat his meal. At least she wouldn't be bothered with him any more tonight. She'd make certain Alan escorted her directly to her door, then would slam it shut before he left. That way, even if Steele was waiting there when she returned to the motel, it wouldn't do him any good. No way, absolutely no way, would she go anywhere with him again.

As the valet left to get Paul's car, Alan suggested the couples go their separate ways.

"I know you won't like the clubs I intend to take Samantha to, Dad." He was eager to be alone with the most passionate-looking woman he'd met in years.

"Fine with me," Paul told his son. "How about you, Margaret? Do you want to tag along to loud, smoky discos or retire to a quiet lounge where the music's as mellow as the drinks?"

Margaret took Paul's arm. "I'm in total agreement with your favored form of entertainment. Enjoy yourselves," she told Samantha and Alan before stepping inside Paul's gleaming Rolls-Royce.

Sammi slid into the car waiting behind Paul's and leaned her head against the black leather seats of the low-slung Corvette as Alan sped onto the busy boulevard. She hated to criticize anything about the man but his father was correct. He was rash and agitated behind the wheel. Steele had been impatient with her but was an excellent driver with never the slightest sign of annoyance if someone in front of him drove poorly.

Sammi immediately forgot her brief pique over Alan's erratic driving. His behavior the rest of the evening was as flawless as his handsome features. He was the most superb dancer she had partnered and time flew by.

After four hours of club hopping Sammi felt there wasn't an interesting place in San Francisco she hadn't visited. Walking arm in arm to Alan's car in the early morning hours she inhaled the crisp air. Fog had settled lightly over the city, adding to the comfortable intimacy she felt with her escort.

Seated in his car, she waited as he walked around to get into the driver's seat and wondered where he would take her next.

"It's much colder than I anticipated, Samantha. Do you mind if we stop by my apartment to pick up a jacket before we wind up the evening at an after-hours spot I know you'll enjoy visiting?"

"That's fine with me, Alan," Sammi told him agreeably.

She was curious to see where he lived anyway and speculated it would be to her liking. They had shared the same likes and dislikes all evening. It was uncanny how compatible they were. They enjoyed the same kind of music, danced the same steps, shared identical tastes in food, and were interested in travel.

She had rarely—almost anyway—thought of Steele the entire night except to compare his demanding bossiness with Alan's concern for her pleasure. Alan was one of the most considerate men she'd ever dated and she trusted him implicitly.

"Here we are," Alan told her, easing to a stop in front of a new, multi-storied condominium she presumed would be even more plush inside than the polished marble exterior with its professional landscaping.

Sammi's breath caught in her throat when Alan shut off the ignition but failed to remove the key before turning toward her. She glanced at his face in the darkened interior. His eyes had a sensual gleam and she knew he intended to kiss her.

"May I kiss you, my beauty?" Alan asked with forced politeness. It was becoming more difficult to control his desires. Stopping at his condo was a ploy to get Sammi inside. He found it impossible to wait until he took her lips and touched her full breasts.

Sammi's hands rose to clasp Alan's shoulders, much more narrow than Steele's but in proportion to his slender frame. She closed her eyes and waited. Her softened lips were all the answer he needed.

Deluded by the amount of wine she had consumed and Alan's soft-spoken request to caress her, Sammi relaxed. His lips touching hers were somewhat feminine, much softer than Steele's, but the beast had never asked once before possessing her mouth. Probably never thought of it, she fumed.

Sammi cursed inwardly, furious that visions of Steele entered her consciousness when she was being kissed by the man she just might spend the rest of her life with.

With Steele's image in her mind, she squirmed, unable to concentrate fully on the man whose breathing was becoming more labored by the moment.

Alan's lips, which had been gentle and smooth, hardened and pressed over hers with uncomfortable insistence. Sammi's eyes opened. She could see beads of perspiration on his forehead. Instead of holding his shoulders, she began to push him away. When he tried to explore forcefully the interior of her mouth with his tongue, she was instantly repelled. It was a vile invasion and turned her off as fast as Steele's had aroused her.

Suddenly she stiffened her back, wanting to leave. All feeling for Alan left in a rush when he changed from a gentlemen to a male animal out of control. She twisted her body to avoid his insistent kiss, appalled as she felt one hand lower to fondle her breasts. His fingers were rough as they trailed from her neck to the front of her dress and ignited a temper she no longer tried to control.

"Quit it, Alan! Get your damned hands off me!" Sammi demanded.

Abruptly alarmed as he easily avoided her upraised knee and showed no sign of heeding her demand, she cried out again.

"Let me go, you beast!" Where was her perfect gentleman now?

"No!" he moaned against her neck as she attempted to push him off. "I can't stop! You're too soft, too sexy, and I want you now!"

One hand tightened around Sammi's nape, pressing into a nerve and temporarily stunning her with a numbing pain.

Taking advantage of Sammi's sudden motionlessness, Alan groped beneath the neckline of her dress for the rounded beauty of her breasts that had enticed him all night. He ached to fondle their nakedness.

Sammi's temper exploded to its fullest. No man had ever been allowed to touch her against her will, and she wasn't going to start with Alan. How could she have misjudged him so?

She thrashed out with hands that ached to leave their imprint on his smooth face. As she struck out, she pulled her body away from beneath his, reached for the inset door handle, and stumbled out.

She was frantic as much with anger at her misconception of his nature as with fear. His hand on her neck had damned near paralyzed her. What kind of hold had he used?

Deep whimpers of anger were torn from her throat as she tried to gather her senses and run. A breathless cry escaped her lips when she wrenched her ankle on the uneven paved walk and caused one slender shoe heel to break as if it was made of glass.

The screeching brakes of a large Lincoln Continental pulling to a halt beside her added to her fear. Clasping her purse to her breasts, she stopped, braced against the side of the building, and tried to gather her senses while deciding what to do next.

Her frightened scream turned to sobs of relief when Steele rushed from the driver's side to hold her in his arms. His brief hug assured her as no other could that he was the man—*the only man*—she could ever love.

"Get in the car, Sam!" Steele commanded, opening the passenger door and gently thrusting her inside.

"O—okay," she stuttered.

"And stay there until I take care of Alan."

"Be careful," Sammi cried with tears streaming down her face. "Alan's an expert in martial arts."

"Good!" Steele growled. "I enjoy a fair fight."

Afraid Steele would be hurt and might need her help, Sammi disobeyed his demand to stay put and hobbled after him. She arrived in time to see Steele pull Alan by his neck from the Corvette with one hand and shove the other hard fist into his face with a resounding crack before the smaller man could raise his hands to strike back.

Dusting his palms together, Steele left Alan slumped and cowering in the front seat of his car. He returned with a glimmer in his eyes that bode ill will for the retreating Sammi.

He took her arm, not caring that she had to hobble to follow him back to the car. For the second time he shoved her in the front seat, this time on his side and markedly less gently. He slid beside her, keeping her close to his hip as he started the motor.

Pulling from the curb with a roar, he drove straight to her motel without saying a single word. It was obvious by the set of his strong chin she should remain silent too.

After Steele stopped in the shadowed area behind the motel,

he turned to Sammi and spoke for the first time since fracturing Alan's chin.

"Before I find out what the creep did, we'd better get one thing straight, Sam. When," he growled with anger equal to any she'd ever seen. "When," he reiterated, "I tell you to stay put . . . *do it*!"

Sammi's hands rose helplessly. Her voice was barely above a whisper as she tried to explain her fears.

"Alan told me he'd taken self-defense classes and I was afraid he would hurt you."

"Afraid Alan would hurt me!" Steele scowled in disbelief. "That namby-pamby wasn't raised in the streets like I was. I grew up fighting for survival as a youth, honey. A black belt in karate and my unsavory past will overpower any classroom martial arts graduate."

Sammi turned away. She had a sudden headache and felt none too steady. Raising her fingertips, she cradled her bowed forehead and closed her eyes.

"I thought you didn't drink, Sam?" Steele admonished her.

"I don't!" Sammi snapped without looking up. First she had to put up with Alan's unexpected change of personality, and now she was forced to listen as Steele chastised her.

"You're soused," he said in disgust.

"You didn't let me finish the other night. I don't drink *warm beer*. Cold wine and expensive champagne are something else again."

"My God, you little devil, you really do need controlling."

Suddenly Sammi couldn't stand any more of Steele's anger. She raised her face to his, stared at him with pleading eyes that were deep blue and filled with the need for understanding over her recent trauma. With a gratified sigh she fell into his arms as he reached to enfold her.

Cradled to his broad chest, she lay silently, receiving immediate comfort from his tender embrace.

Hugging Sammi close in the comfortable interior of his luxurious automobile, Steele's lips placed gentle caress after caress on the top of her tousled, sweet-scented hair.

"How could my perception of Alan's personality have been so grossly wrong?" Sammi asked, hoping Steele could explain.

"You're mixed up in your expectations of a man's worth, honey," he told her truthfully. "You judge a man by his job, his appearance, and his wealth. That's not a true indication of his inner character."

"I . . . I realize that now," Sammi stuttered. She pressed her face into the warmth of Steele's chest, seeking the haven of his strength and understanding.

"Alan seemed to have everything I've always dreamed of in a man. He had impeccable manners, extreme wealth, and an engaging wit. I even thought him sensitive, yet he was nothing but a crass boor."

Sammi looked up at Steele. Her lips parted unconsciously when he lowered his head to touch them with a mouth that was the sweetest, most gentle she'd ever felt. The excitement of his touch filled her body with contentment. His tenderness made her choke with the effort of not telling him how much she cared.

"How was I to know the damned bastard—"

"Watch it, Sam," Steele interrupted, admonishing her on her language.

"The damned bastard," Sammi continued unabated, "was an expert in defensive holds." She was totally unperturbed by Steele's frown.

"Watch your tongue, woman," Steele warned.

"Alan is a *bastard*! Any beast like him with a father that nice has to be illegitimate. The creep tore my new dress and made me break a heel on my sixty-dollar shoes. Besides," she continued in a fine temper, "he damned near paralyzed me with his slimy hand on my neck."

Steele raised Sammi's chin with fingers that were rough-tender on her skin. His lips took hers with such reverence she wanted to cry. She was getting positively weepy over the man.

When they were finished with a long caress that left them both breathless despite the fact he never parted her lips or attempted to deepen it with the intimacy of his tongue, Steele told her, "Forget Alan. Forget every man but me, sweetheart. You're mine, Sam. You have been from the very first."

Remembering Monique and Kay, she pulled away and scolded him with adamant boldness. "I'm damned if I'll be part of any harem."

Hugging Sammi to his chest, Steele laughed. "Honey, I could handle three women with no problem at all. But one like you will suit me just fine," he whispered into her ear.

Sammi listened to the deep rumble in his chest when his amusement over her ill humor continued. Deciding she had had enough of everything for one night she pulled away again and stared at his entertained expression. He looked positively rakish, and she didn't doubt for one minute he could make good his threat of taking care of a harem if he so desired.

"I'm going to bed."

"A good idea, Sam."

"Alone!" she pointed out in case he had other ideas in mind.

"I wouldn't have it any other way for now," he told her huskily. "You'll need lots of rest because later today and tonight we've got a date, and we're going to do it up right. Get your fanciest dress ready."

"Sorry, Steele," Sammi told him seriously. "I've seen all the shows at the local drive-in theaters."

"Forget that, witch. You deserved that set-down for calling me such insulting names. This time it will be you and me and a night on the town."

Sammi shrugged her shoulders and scooted out from the plush seat as he stepped to the ground. She clung to his arm after removing her one good shoe. The pavement was cold against her stockinged feet as he walked her to the door.

Feeling small beside him without high heels on, she turned into his arms before the motel door. Lifted up by the strength of Steele's hands, Sammi clung to his muscled shoulders while he kissed her with such passion she thought she'd die. His lips were no longer gentle. They were the searching, hardened lips of a man who hungers for the one woman he knows can bring him satisfaction.

After long moments of intense intimacy he released her mouth but retained his hold on her body. He cradled her tight to his chest, and his hands shook as the fingers stroked over and over through her tumbled curls while he caught his breath after the explosive good night kiss.

"Where's the Lamborghini?" Sammi whispered into his jacket.

"My God, woman, how you dissemble," Steele moaned. "I'm trying desperately to curb my desire to make love to you this very minute and all you're concerned about is a damned sports car."

"Well," Sammi persisted. "What happened to it?"

"It wasn't mine. Since it was too small to hold both Monique and Kay, I returned it to its owner and picked up the Lincoln."

"I knew from the first it was borrowed," Sammi told him, not wanting to hear another thing about his other women. That verified the fact that he was as poor as she had always suspected.

"Why did you think that?" Steele queried.

"It was much too expensive for a trucker."

Without further comment Steele opened the door to the darkened room, gently pushed Sammi inside, and closed it securely behind him. He'd explain later how far off her misconception of his financial assets were, he reflected silently on the way to his car.

Tiptoeing across the carpet to undress, Sammi told herself in a low, confident voice, "Three down and Steele to go."

In the wee hours of the morning she concluded, as she slipped into bed, the beast seemed to be the best catch of all.

CHAPTER SEVEN

Unable to fall asleep, Sammi called softly, "Wake up, Margaret."

"What's the matter, Samantha?" her aunt asked in a strained voice.

"I'm in love, that's what's the matter," Sammi told her smugly.

Margaret turned on the beside lamp and sat up to stare at her niece with a look of disbelief reflected in her intelligent brown eyes.

"With Alan?"

"Of course not, my silly aunt." Sammi pulled herself to a sitting position to remark with a touch of chagrin, "I'm in love with Steele!"

"My gosh, Samantha." The older woman blinked, trying to understand her young relative's sudden change of heart. She glanced at her watch and moaned. "Eight hours ago you told me you were going to shop for a trousseau to honeymoon with Alan."

"I am. Only now it's Red!" Sammi replied quickly. A touch of soft, feminine happiness tinged her voice as she envisioned yards of chiffons, silks, and satins in dainty peignoir sets that she intended to purchase. Each, she vowed, would captivate Steele.

"A new day and a different man," Margaret reminded. "What happened? When Paul and I left you last night, Alan seemed to be your ideal."

"He was until he stopped his car!" Sammi stormed, remembering his crude behavior with a rush of anger.

"Don't tell me Alan acted like Benny?" her aunt questioned. Paul's son had seemed the essence of courtesy during their dinner.

"He was worse. I definitely won't talk about it tonight," Sammi fumed. "Nor will he! His sore jaw will keep him silent for days."

"What did you do to him?" her aunt asked, while wondering if she'd ever fully understand Samantha's complex love life.

"I think Red broke his jaw."

"Oh, no!" Margaret cried out. Paul was such a dear, she hated for there to be trouble between them over his only son.

"Oh, *yes*." Sammi smiled, delighting in the thought of Alan in extreme pain. He deserved maximum discomfort for his brutish behavior as well as ruining an expensive dress and her most costly pair of shoes.

"What happened?" Margaret asked with a resigned sigh, thinking it too early to hear a blow-by-blow description of her niece's problems with the third escort she had procured.

"The creep wanted to make out and I didn't," Sammi explained in a disgruntled tone.

"Why didn't you hand him your sex contract?"

"I didn't have time," Sammi admitted reluctantly. "Besides it isn't a hundred percent effective against young sex maniacs or older men with too much to drink and a definite mean streak. End of story."

"Good." Margaret yawned. "It's four o'clock in the morning and I'm returning home on a flight at nine."

"You're leaving?" Sammi asked in a disappointed cry. "What came up?"

"A problem at the office. My assistant manager thinks I'm the only one who can handle it, so I told him I'd return this morning."

A twinge of sadness filled Sammi. She would miss her aunt's

company. Realizing the older woman needed all the sleep she could get, Sammi pretended a wide yawn.

"I suggest we turn out the light and go to sleep," Sammi proposed.

"Good idea," Margaret echoed before scooting down and going right back to sleep.

Sammi lay awake thinking over the long evening and her sudden realization that she was in love with Steele. How could it have transpired when she had spent as much time detesting the man as she had loving him? Had it really been hate at first sight or her inner self rebelling at his strong, sensual appeal and dominant personality?

When Margaret's breathing became even and Sammi was assured the older woman was sound asleep, she eased from the bed, grabbed her purse from the end table, and walked into the bathroom.

With the door shut, she searched through the cluttered bag for the metal object Steele had pressed into her hand at the restaurant. Suddenly a cheap Cracker Jack ring didn't seem too bad if it was given to her by the man she now thought the most wonderful in the world.

Beneath the illumination of the bright overhead light Sammi caught the gleam of yellow. Her mouth opened as she looked wide-eyed at the shimmering beauty of a new wedding band made of rich gold. On the inside of the golden circle she caught a glimpse of engraving. Barely able to read the delicate script, she felt tears slip from her eyes as she made out three words. Three very special words.

You're forever mine.

Wiping her blurred eyes with the back of her hand, Sammi tried the ring on. It was a perfect fit on the third finger of her left hand.

Uncertain of Steele's intent, she took her jewelry case out of the makeup kit resting on the sink and searched until she found a gold chain. With unsteady fingers she removed a pearl pendant and replaced it with a much more highly valued piece of jewelry.

Slipping the long chain over her hair, she let the cool metal rest against her skin. The token symbol of love lay snug in the hollow between her full breasts. In minutes she was back in bed, curled on her side with one hand touching Steele's ring and sound asleep.

Awakened barely three hours later by the phone's jarring ring, she grumbled in ill humor. She resented any intrusion while she was dreaming about a blissful future with her bronze-haired lover. Margaret was right, she thought, lifting the receiver off the cradle and dragging it to her ear.

"Sam?" Steele's deep voice intruded into her meditation.

"Hmm," Sammi murmured dreamily. He had a way of saying her name that was almost as arousing as a caress. "Did you realize your hair's not red at all? It's a beautiful, gorgeous, burnished coppery bronze just as my aunt said it was."

"Well, I'll be damned," Steele burst out with unconcealed pleasure. "Don't tell me you've come to your senses, Sam? You sound as if you finally realized that I'm your man—redheaded, eighteen-wheeling, gear-jamming country lout and all."

"Forget I ever called you those names," Sammi crooned into the phone. Her eyes were bright and she was as alert as if she'd had a full eight hours' sleep. One hand fingered the gold ring while she smiled in response to his teasing voice.

"I've decided you have definite possibilities after all," Sammi flirted. She could hear the shower running and knew Margaret couldn't overhear her sassy remarks.

"In comparison with your last three dates or on my own?" Steele questioned in mock seriousness.

"Both." Sammi chuckled. "What do you want so early in the morning?"

"You," Steele told her, making no attempt to hide the desire in his voice.

"Now that sounds worth thinking about," Sammi taunted

mischievously, knowing full well she was safe while they were talking with some distance between them.

"Send your aunt on a day-long errand and I'll be there in ten minutes," he suggested with sensual teasing equal to hers. "What happened to warrant this change of face?"

"Don't all damsels in distress get turned on by their knights in shining armor?"

"Am I your knight?"

"This morning you are. This afternoon might be a different matter," she sassed impudently.

"That reminds me of a joke I heard once about a king and a knight."

"Don't tell me," Sammi groaned, "if it's the one I'm thinking of. Once a king always a king but once a night is enough."

"You're a bawdy young broad, Sam. I thought only men heard those kind of jokes . . . *and remembered them,*" he added with sharp emphasis to make his point.

"You've a lot to learn about today's liberated women, Steele." She giggled. "What time are you coming to get me?"

"I'll be by in an hour. Better wear comfortable clothes today."

"Will slacks and a sweater be okay?"

"Fine."

"Dare I ask where we're going?"

"Nope. It's another surprise."

"I thought I was going to get a fancy night out on the town?"

"You are later. Today we relax. Hopefully you'll tell me all about your childhood. The last ten years I think I prefer you keep a secret."

Thinking of her strong denial that she was virtuous, Sammi smiled to herself. Steele would be surprised when he found out she was totally innocent of all the sensual pleasures between a man and woman.

"Scared to find out how many men I've entertained in my decadent past?" Sammi chided boldly.

"Have there been many, Sam?" Steele demanded, knowing she was lying if she agreed with him.

"I lost track years ago," she told him in a voice that barely concealed her playful banter. "How about you?"

"The same," he agreed readily, amused when he heard her sharp intake of breath.

Margaret entered the room, wearing a comfortable pants suit. She could tell by her niece's softly flushed cheeks and sparkling eyes it was Steele on the other end of the line.

"Oh, my gosh," Sammi exclaimed, returning her aunt's smile. "I have to get Margaret to the airport by eight thirty. She's leaving this morning for Denver. We'll have to meet here at ten, I guess."

"No problem," Steele assured her. "I'll pick you both up at seven forty-five. That way I can get acquainted with your aunt while we drive to the airport."

"That will be great," Sammi told him, pleased she would see him earlier than anticipated. Besides she always hated driving in early-morning commuter traffic. "Hang up now so I can hunt through my suitcases for some old faded denim pants and a stained sweat shirt."

"Good-bye, minx," Steele told her. A broad grin touched his mouth. He doubted very much if she had such clothes in her wardrobe if her other outfits were any indication. Every time he saw her she was wearing something different.

Sammi jumped out of bed and tore into the bathroom to shower. She'd need every minute to assure she looked her best.

"Steele's coming to pick us up in a few minutes," she called out to Margaret while adjusting the temperature of the splashing water. "He wants to talk with you on the way to the airport."

"That I'll enjoy very much," Margaret enthused in a raised voice.

"After your flight leaves we're going to spend a long, lovely day fooling around."

"Fooling around?" Margaret questioned in a doubtful voice.

"Not literally, my dear prudish aunt." Sammi chuckled, turning beneath the sharp spray to rinse off the perfumed suds from a bar of her favorite soap. "That's only an expression for not having any particular plans."

Margaret walked into the bathroom, watching as Sammi ran the towel over her glistening wet body with careless speed.

"After what the man said about you last night, my dear liberated niece, I certainly have a right to be concerned. He talked like a man overly familiar with you. In a physical sense as well as a mental one."

"All lies," Sammi protested. With a towel wrapped sarong fashion around her powdered body, she carefully applied mascara and lipstick before brushing her hair into a semblance of control. The silky strands were lustrous, seemed to have a mind of their own, and rarely conformed to lie smooth. She gave up, letting the curls bounce around her shoulders and frame her face as they wished.

"*All* Steele's words were a figment of his imagination?" Margaret insisted on knowing in a tone that was filled with suspicion.

"*Almost* all of them," Sammi added. "Since I'm still as pure and innocent as the driven snow, you can relax." Adding a spray of heady perfume, she warned, "What I'll be after today's date is another matter."

"Samantha!" Margaret cried out in outrage. Her niece was absolutely shocking sometimes.

"My dear priggish relative, I'm twenty-eight years old and damned tired of sleeping alone! Before the night's over I intend to tear up my contract to keep me virginal and find out what most of my girl friends have been raving about for the last ten to twelve years."

Margaret zipped her suitcases and buckled the wide strap over the middle before looking up to see if Sammi was serious or not. Eyeing her niece's voluptuous figure as she paraded around the room in a lacy black bra and teeny panties that clung to her body like a second skin, she was openly skeptical that she was joking. Her brief underwear was almost indecent it was so delicate.

Sammi noticed her aunt's shocked face and laughed. "This isn't the most daring underwear I own, Margaret. I have a vivid blue set that reveals much more than it conceals."

"Good heavens, Samantha," Margaret protested. "When on earth do you wear them?"

"I haven't yet," Sammi teased, holding up the vividly colored skimpy lace undies so Margaret could see how erotic they were. "Tonight might be a good time to see how they affect an easily aroused male like Steele."

"Maybe I should cancel my flight and chaperon you two," Margaret said with a touch of seriousness that made Sammi give her a deep glare.

"Forget that, Auntie dear. I haven't spent an entire day yet in Steele's company, and the last thing I want is strict supervision from an overwrought relative. I'm well past the age of consent!"

"Agreed," Margaret told her with a worried frown marring her neat brow. "Call me tonight, please. I don't think I could stand the thought of wondering if you were all right or not."

"I intend to, my darling relative." Sammi laughed. "Not to tell you what mischief I've been up to, but to assure myself that you arrived safe at home in the high mountains of Colorado."

Sammi eased her rounded hips into a skin-tight pair of designer jeans the same ebony color as her hair before buttoning the front closure on a luxurious long-sleeved cashmere sweater in sapphire blue that gently hugged her high breasts with an alluring fit.

Tying the shoelaces of black tennis shoes, Sammi looked up to see Margaret scanning her figure with a troubled glance.

"Don't worry," she assured her aunt. "The days of scarlet women are over. I'll be careful, discreet, and so utterly captivating Red won't be able to think of life from now on without me by his side."

"I certainly hope so, Samantha," Margaret said thoughtfully.

"It's the woman who always pays for any little, er . . . indiscretions."

"There speaketh a lady from a different generation," Sammi reminded with a smile. "I intend to see Steele is the one who pays plenty from now on."

"You do!" Margaret blurted out agape, misunderstanding her meaning.

"Yes," Sammi said nonchalantly. "He'll pay for my clothes, my lodging, and my upkeep if everything works out as I intend to see it does."

"That should cost him a fortune the way you shop," Margaret shot back.

"Since Steele's a poor trucker, I'll probably have to re-evaluate my life-style immediately. As I suspected the Lamborghini was borrowed, and he's probably up to his eyeteeth in debt over the rental of the evening suits and charges for his three nights' dining out."

Ignoring Sammi's ramblings about Steele's finances, Margaret couldn't help but point out, "I can't picture you shopping for clothes at K mart."

"It won't be as much fun as browsing through Saks and I. Magnin." Sammi's eyes turned dreamy as she contemplated her future. "To think I had aspired to move up to Neiman-Marcus in the near future. Oh, well"—she shrugged, dumping dark glasses, makeup, and a wallet into a black canvas bag whose casual look belied its price tag—"I'll just have to learn to adjust my standards to a lower level."

"What do you know about Steele?" Margaret asked with rising concern. Her niece sounded deadly serious about the man who was still a stranger.

"Nothing much now," Sammi told her truthfully. "Tonight I resolve to know every single detail about the man from the moment of his birth until this date."

"Good luck, honey. Steele looks like a private person, and I imagine he'll tell you what he wants you to hear and only that."

"Phooey," Sammi scorned. "I've been worming men's pasts from them for years. Once one starts talking you can't shut him up. In twelve hours I'll have learned Steele's life history. There won't be any information I haven't cleverly wheedled out of the man about his past, his present, and my future."

"Your confidence is staggering, Samantha. I hope you're right. As I recall, you haven't had much success with conning the man so far."

"That was while I was fighting him. I intend to spend today showing him the angelic side of my personality. I'm through arguing. From now on life will be all honey and roses or whatever they say when the future looks perfect."

"You're hallucinating," Margaret scoffed, knowing it would be impossible for her niece to act that sweet for any extended length of time.

Ignoring Margaret's derogatory words, Sammi continued without pause, "I'll never shout or raise my voice again. I won't get the least angered, act impudent, or show a temper. My disposition has completely changed."

Sammi glared at Margaret's raised eyes and perplexed expression. Her own relative had no faith in her reformed character. With a toss of her unruly curls, she went to the door, making certain to erase the chagrin over her aunt's lack of trust from her face.

She pulled it open at the second impatient knock, gave Steele a devastating smile, and rushed into his opened arms with smug satisfaction. Enfolded in his embrace, she raised her face to take his stirring kiss with eager enthusiasm. This should show Margaret she was sincere.

Holding Steele's neck with strong arms, Sammi squirmed to get as close as possible. Her lips parted to deepen the heady kiss. It seemed like years since he had held her tight to his strong body.

Steele eased away from Sammi's passionate mouth and

laughed as she gave him a fierce frown in complaint. He looked over her shoulder to greet her aunt.

"Good morning, Margaret. Like I said last night, this niece of yours is quite a handful. Fortunately I can easily curb her daring impetuosity."

He took Sammi's arms, removed them from his shoulders, and ignored her sudden intake of breath at his words. Holding her hand with tender affection, he walked inside the motel room.

"Tell me which bags go and I'll load them in my trunk."

"Fine, Steele," Margaret agreed readily. She stepped aside as he easily picked up one large Pullman, tucked the smaller one over it, and took the makeup kit in his free hand.

Moving forward, Steele eased sideways through the door and walked to his nearby car. He placed Margaret's cases in the opened trunk, slammed it shut, and motioned for Sammi to get in on the driver's side while he held the passenger door open for her aunt.

Margaret smiled, scanning his strong body and good-looking face. He really was a confident, imposing-appearing man.

"Thank you, Steele." She didn't doubt for a minute that her sexually inexperienced niece would lack the willpower to say no if the man decided to seduce her tonight. He was the most virile-looking male she had seen in her life, and she doubted any woman could resist him if he intentionally pursued her.

Margaret conversed with Steele during the drive while Sammi enjoyed being at his side. His relaxed attitude and easy, intelligent manner assured the older woman that her niece had made the right choice.

She still didn't understand what had happened with Alan. Sammi had seemed so enthralled at the start of their date. It was apparent now that the only man with enough strength of character to control Samantha's tempestuous impulsiveness was Steele. She admitted in all sincerity that there were many, many times her niece needed someone with his dominant nature to curb her more outrageous ideas.

Steele parked on the upper level, took Margaret's cases to the check-in counter, and picked up her boarding pass with innate chivalry. He had her luggage tagged, handed her a box of Godiva chocolates to enjoy on her flight home, then walked away so she and Sammi could say good-bye in private.

As they hugged each other, Margaret said in a low voice, "I adore Steele already."

"Me too," Sammi whispered back.

"Take care, honey. Steele's nobody's fool."

"I will, Margaret," Sammi bragged. "I'm in complete control now."

"Of you or him?"

"Both!" Sammi chuckled. "Have a safe trip."

Tears shimmered in Sammi's eyes as she watched her aunt leave to board the plane. She knew the motel room would seem empty without Margaret's cheerful companionship.

She turned back to Steele, seeking his company with the same fervor she had usually avoided it.

"Now, sweetheart," Steele told her with a smile that matched hers. "You and I have the entire day to ourselves."

They walked hand in hand to his car as he warned her, "I want you to know from the start that I won't tolerate any impudence on your part."

Sammi swallowed twice, took a deep breath to contain her normally tart reply, and leaned into his shoulder.

"No need to waste your breath." She chuckled softly. "I'm a completely reformed woman. Today you are in the presence of a truly sweet celestial spirit."

Steele's loud laughter tested her new personality with considerable force. She stared at his mocking face and wondered if she was really capable of turning over a new leaf even for him.

"I intend to spend the entire day learning what goes on in that lovely head of yours," Steele persisted, well aware of her fight to control her hot temper. "We will have no arguments, no battles, and no sassiness."

"You've a hell of a lot of nerve giving me such an admonition," Sammi burst out, fuming that she should be the one who did all the changing to meet his desires.

As he bent to kiss her neck when she tried to tug her hand free of his grip, she asked, "What about controlling your damned temper too? I don't see a halo around your head."

Steele gathered Sammi into his arms, stopped her sharp tongue with a lingering kiss, then gave her a devilish reprimand. "No swearing either, my, er . . . celestial spirit."

As she prepared to reply, he kissed her pouting pink-tinted lips until she was clinging to his shoulders to keep from collapsing at his feet.

"Oh, Steele," she moaned, resting against his broad chest. "I tried to be sweet. I really did. We might as well part right now."

She raised her chin and stared at the tiny laugh lines on each side of his twinkling hazel eyes. Laughter filled her voice as she admitted, "I've never been as good as you expect in my entire life though I vowed earlier to be an angel all day."

"No need to get an ulcer, my enticing witch." Steele chuckled. He ran his hands up and down her spine, enjoying the feel of her soft wool sweater. "I'll let you get in one or two mischievous taunts during the day."

"That's probably best." Sammi laughed, looking away from the brown flecks in his keen eyes to stare at his well-shaped mouth instead.

God, it wreaked havoc with her nerves every time it touched her lips or even when it didn't, she contemplated. She could feel a tremor run over her sensitive skin at the anticipation of future kisses.

"We'll never leave the airport if you look at me like that."

Steele held open the driver's door and watched as she scooted her delectable body across the leather seat.

"I didn't doubt for one moment that your faded denims and sweat shirt would look brand new. You're going to bankrupt your husband by either adding on wardrobe closets to his house or by filling them with gorgeous clothes."

"That sounds like a fair exchange to me," Sammi teased as Steele started the motor and pulled away from the parking lot.

"Fair exchange? What's the poor man get in payment?" Steele quizzed.

"Me."

"You?" he returned, contemplating her answer. "That does have definite possibilities of being a worthwhile business venture. You did say you were experienced."

"Er, naturally," Sammi hedged, hoping she didn't get herself into trouble with that lie.

Sudden thoughts of Steele's ring nestled between her breasts brought the image of them making love as man and wife. Her lashes fluttered closed. It was too profound a subject to brood over this early in the day.

"You're thinking of being in bed with me, aren't you, Sam?" Steele interrupted her silent contemplation.

"How could you tell?" Sammi asked. There was no need to deny her bold vision.

"Your eyes turned a deep midnight blue, a soft flush tinged both cheekbones, and your breasts rose and fell as your breathing increased."

"Was I that obvious?" Sammi asked in a soft whisper.

"You looked as eager as I am."

"Is that bad?"

"Nothing could please me more." Steele eased through the heavy traffic in a northwest direction.

"We'll be good together, Sam," he warned her. "As good as any man or woman in the world could possibly be. I guarantee it."

"That sounds intriguing, but I think I should have some say in the matter."

"Neither you nor anyone else will be able to alter my intentions when I feel the timing is right to seduce you, Sam," Steele advised her. "When the moment comes and I decide to make love to you—total explicit love—*nothing* will stop me."

Sammi looked at Steele's determined chin and strong profile as he maneuvered through the heart of town.

"Nothing?" she asked in a barely audible voice.

"*Absolutely nothing.*" His eyes met hers with no embarrassment.

His voice was so serious it sent a shiver from her head to her toes. She didn't question his truthfulness for one minute.

"Won't what I want make any difference to you?"

"What you want—when I start making love to you—will be exactly the same as what I want, honey," he promised in a somber voice.

Steele turned his head to give Sammi a loving glance that melted her heart. It was filled with complete confidence he could overcome any protest she might make, and she knew it to be true. Around him she was as helpless as a baby once he touched her.

"You're an arrogant, conceited man."

"I've never denied it," Steele mocked, giving Sammi a quick kiss on her upraised lips as she snuggled closer to his side. "I should also alert you I'll explicitly detail each despicable deed I intend to do to your body beforehand, and I'm making up my erotic list right now."

"You'd better curb your fantasies and tell me where we're going," Sammi insisted breathlessly. His warning alone had her heart beating wildly. She clasped her fingers together in her lap to still their trembling. Was she really going to lose her virginity tonight?

"Tell me where you're taking me." Sammi spoke again in an attempt to dampen the sensual tension between them.

"It's all part of today's surprise," Steele informed her.

"Oh, God," Sammi moaned. "Not another one of those evenings."

"You sassy brat." Steele chuckled. "You deserved everything I did, though I never expected you to accept it calmly."

"Actually," Sammi explained in a sudden burst of honesty, "later I rather enjoyed that night despite my anger. You made me furious. I've never been so mad at a man in my life."

"You hid it well except for the daggers that pierced my body each time you glanced my way. I thought I was pretty good that night."

"The hot dog and popcorn were good," Sammi pointed out. "You weren't!"

A sudden vision of their lovemaking in the cab of the old truck was as clear as the sky outside the front windshield.

"I enjoyed necking with you too." Steele laughed, interrupting her thoughts with his constant ability to read her mind.

"Necking is such a gross word for something as romantic as kissing. Do they really still call the back parking area necker's row?"

"How the hell would I know?" Steele questioned with one eyebrow raised as he shot her an amused glance. "I hadn't been to a drive-in for fifteen years or more."

"Why, you beast," Sammi cried out. "That entire evening was a put-on just so you could make a fool of me."

"Not all of it," Steele admitted. "Part was an uncontrollable urge to see if you kissed as well at night as you did in the daytime."

"Did I?"

"Better."

"Really?" Sammi asked, pleased that he thought she was exciting as a sensual playmate.

"Really," Steele agreed with a wide smile. He reached down to cup her knee in his broad palm. "At least you were after I taught you how to pucker up."

Sammi shot him a scathing glance, placed her fingers over his hand, picked it up, and placed it back on the steering wheel.

"You really are a vain man."

"Don't forget I'm also the world's best instructor."

"Why?"

"Each time I kiss your passionate mouth you seem to improve."

Steele ignored Sammi's silent reproval to add with deliberate devilry, "By the day's end you'll probably be an expert osculater."

As their glances merged, one a sparkling icy blue and the other a warm deeply flecked hazel, it was impossible to control their ready humor.

"You are also an incorrigible maniac." Sammi chuckled. She leaned her head into Steele's wide shoulder.

"We make a good pair, then, Sam," Steele told her. He turned sideways to place a kiss against her brow.

"How?"

"Because you're an unalterable mouthy little minx."

Sammi refused to comment further on Steele's ridiculous comparison. Instead she stared out the passenger window as he waited for a signal to turn green. Realizing she hadn't eaten breakfast, she reached out to touch his arm.

"Will you stop at my motel?"

"You bet," Steele consented eagerly. "Have you decided you want to seduce me instead of the other way around?"

"Good lord no," Sammi rebuked him. "I'm starving and suddenly remembered there are three apples left."

"Two for me and one for you." Steele voiced his thoughts aloud. He hadn't eaten breakfast either and they sounded good.

"Sorry, fella. They're my apples so it's the other way around."

"Let's compromise," he suggested hopefully. "We'll each eat one whole apple and share the third."

"Okay," Sammi agreed reluctantly. She jumped out of the car when Steele pulled to a stop before her motel door.

"Need any help?" he called out of his opened window.

"Not on your life," she shouted over her shoulder as she opened the door. "Margaret said she should stay and chaperon us today, and after your many brash comments I think she was wise."

"Okay, honey." Steele grinned. "I'll just sit here then and add some more deeds to my erotic list. Think I'll title it . . . the seduction of Sam."

Sammi slammed the door behind her with a sharp bang in hopes of drowning out the sound of Steele's deep, teasing laughter. He was getting worse by the minute.

Returning in seconds with the apples in her hand, she gracefully eased in on the passenger side.

"Get over here, woman," Steele commanded. He reached his hand toward her shoulder to assist her as she slid across the seat.

"Do you want me or something to eat?"

"What would you say if I said I wanted to eat you?" His voice deepened, as dark and seductive as the pupils in his eyes.

Sammi flushed, uncertain how to reply to the barely concealed innuendo in his speech. She was well aware what he meant. It constantly surprised her that nothing he said or implied offended her. Somehow any physical act with him seemed right.

"Too bashful to comment?"

"No," Sammi told him truthfully.

"Afraid to answer?" Steele persisted.

"With your appetite . . . yes!" Sammi retorted. He could take that reply any way he wanted.

Sammi placed a shiny apple in Steele's outstretched fingers and watched as his mouth opened and he sank his white teeth into the crisp fruit with obvious relish.

"This was an excellent idea," he told her. "And it should sustain us both until lunch."

"If we don't eat too late it will," she warned him while chewing each dainty bite with enjoyment equal to his.

It was going to be a wonderful day and Sammi could never remember being happier.

CHAPTER EIGHT

Steele drove his Lincoln Continental across the Golden Gate Bridge, took the route west, and began a steep winding drive up Mount Tamalpais.

Sammi watched with increasing excitement. She had traveled throughout the United States but thought Highway One ran along the most breathtaking shoreline in America. It would be a thrilling change to relax and enjoy the view as a passenger instead of watching to make certain she didn't miss a turn on the tortuous road chiseled and sliced from the steep mountainside.

"Are we really going for a drive along the coast?"

"Yes," Steele affirmed. "I figured it would be nice to get away from the city and relax in the solitude of a special place I found years ago."

"What a wonderful idea," Sammi enthused.

She regarded Steele for a long time. He took her breath away dressed in black Levi's jeans that hugged his strong legs, a rust-colored close-fitting knit shirt, and casual suede loafers.

"Where is this particular spot?"

Her eyes continued their scrutiny of his body. He was a very powerful-looking man but proportioned so athletically that he gave an impression of fitness not bulk.

"North of Jenner," he interrupted her thorough examination. One hand reached to touch her knee affectionately. "Have you been there?"

Steele's question intervened as she studied his arms, bared

below the short-sleeved shirt. They were covered with fine dark hair, and she had been contemplating how sensual they would feel wrapped around her naked back.

"I stayed at Hidden Coves last year but didn't stop between San Francisco and there on the drive up."

Sammi observed Steele ease around the bends. He was an expert driver, yet she could feel her stomach churn with rising awareness. It was impossible to take her mind off his compelling physical attraction.

"Do you have a hairy chest?" Sammi blurted out without thinking.

Steele's sudden laughter filled the car. He could often read her mind, but never knew what remarks would spill off her impetuous tongue.

"Reach under my shirt and find out," he challenged.

She looked away, staring out the side window, though not focusing on any of the passing scenery. *Damn it!* she chided herself for speaking her thoughts aloud.

"Afraid to, Sam?" Steele prompted.

"On this road, yes," Sammi explained. She looked warily down the cliff as they approached Stinson Beach. "If you're ticklish, we might go over the edge."

"I'm not," Steele told her seriously. "Besides the next sixty or so miles most of our travel will be inland."

"I know," she answered in a whisper. She clasped her fingers together in her lap to assure they wouldn't reach forward as he suggested.

"Do you like hair on a man's chest?"

"Yes," Sammi told him honestly. "At least I think I'd like it on yours."

"Well, then, until you feel enough at ease to touch my naked torso, you'll have to wonder, won't you?"

"Oh, Steele, look at the gorgeous blue lupine," Sammi cried out, pointing along the road ahead. "And fiery orange poppies too."

"You're changing the subject again, aren't you, Sam?"

"Yes," Sammi agreed. "You're also too astute not to know why."

"You hope to calm the sexual tension between us," Steele told her. He leveled a glance at her bowed head. The riot of curls shimmered with an obsidian glint. She had the most sensual hair of any woman he'd known.

"Yes."

"It won't work."

"It will," Sammi insisted.

Steele extended his hand to clasp her knee, moved it to take her hand, and raised the fingers to his lips.

Sammi's stomach clenched. She could feel his strong white teeth nibble the manicured nails of her fingers before turning her hand over to place a burning kiss against the sensitive palm. He was right, she mused. Nothing could dampen the physical excitement generated when they were together—neither anger nor an attempt at indifference.

His brown-flecked hazel eyes smiled into her vivid sapphire blue ones, which softened as her passionate mouth curved into a sweet smile.

"I'm right, am I not, sweetheart?" Steele persisted. He gave her a wide grin when her lashes fluttered to conceal the fact that she was in total agreement. "The sparks passing between us are electric."

"It's only because we're strangers," Sammi lied. "By the end of the day, when we're better acquainted, we'll be relaxed . . ."

"Relaxed!" Steele scoffed. "By tonight the sparks will have started such a conflagration it will only be put out when we make love."

"Hush," Sammi reprimanded. "I don't believe you one bit."

"You should, Sam. You admit being experienced, so don't act

as if you don't know what I'm talking about. We've been skirting around each other from the moment we met."

"I haven't," Sammi rebuked him.

"The hell you haven't, woman," Steele scolded back. "Until we satisfy our desires—yours as well as mine—*in the bedroom,* our minds will never relinquish the problem."

"At night maybe," Sammi admitted with reluctance. "Right now my only thought is how beautiful this time of year is. Winter is finally over and the fragile wild flowers are blossoming with tenacious regularity in the spring sunshine. I've never seen them so profuse."

"You're dissembling again," Steele admonished. "As well as lying to me. The emotional upheaval between us isn't bound by hours, season, or sunlight. My feeling's as strong now in broad daylight as it is at night, and I think yours is too."

Steele's forceful honesty made Sammi tremble. She was far more vulnerable to his sensuality than she cared to acknowledge. She turned her head and let her deep blue eyes scan his strong profile. Her heart was suddenly full, overflowing with love for the strength of the commanding man beside her.

"Aren't you honest enough to admit that you've been as curious as I to find out whether the act of love we share will be the ultimate sexual experience in both our lives?" he asked softly.

Steele waited patiently for Sammi's answer. He wondered if she would confess her sexual naiveté. His lips curved into a tender smile as he gazed at the multitude of expressions crossing her face.

Sammi remained quiet. She didn't know how to answer Steele's blunt statement. He thought her experienced. Lord help me, she begged, feeling more inadequate than she ever had in her adult life. She had never even seen a naked man other than in photos, nor did she have the slightest idea how a skilled lover would act in the bedroom. How could she ever hope to bring a man of his admitted virility satisfaction with her untutored body?

Reaching for her hand, he gave it a gentle squeeze, assuring her with his deep voice. "Don't worry about what's ahead for us, Sam. I already guaranteed you when we make love it will be the very best it can be. I'm neither an inexperienced youth without knowledge of how to please a woman nor a selfish lover who lacks the control necessary to make certain his partner receives satisfaction also."

"It's not your sexual prowess or ability to seduce me that worries me as much as when you will," Sammi told him nervously.

"Soon, my beautiful lady, *soon!*" Steele warned her with serious emphasis on the last word.

Sammi's heart thudded against her ribs at the vivid image of their naked bodies entwined. She could almost feel the touch of his lean hands exploring her sensitive body, the warmth of his skin pressed tightly over her soft, yielding form, and the urgency of his hungry mouth. Her willingness was never in doubt. All he had to do was touch her and she was lost.

"Look over there, honey," Steele told her, pointing across a pasture to a young foal running and bucking in small circles around its dam as she rolled in the high grass of a vast pasture.

Sammi looked up, her eyes wide with pleasure when he pulled to a stop so she could observe the animals' actions. As the mare lurched to her hooves and shook her satiny body, the foal stopped by its dam's flanks, put his head beneath her belly, and butted against her bag to nurse his fill of the warm milk.

"He's precious," Sammi sighed in a tender voice. "What a lucky little fellow to have such a large area to run and play in."

She watched in silence, leaning upon Steele's sturdy chest as he placed an arm around her shoulder in a gentle hug. A herd of black Angus cattle grazed with the horses. The rolling pasture was green and lush against its background of pine-covered hills, which were cooled by a soft ocean breeze. It was a picturesque, idyllic scene.

Sammi sighed as Steele started the engine and eased back on

the narrow highway. She watched, entranced, as they passed through tall groves of pungent eucalyptus, traversed the edge of Tomales Bay with its salty-smelling commercial oyster beds, and passed unique century-old farm homes and tumbled-down barns.

"Hungry?" Steele asked as they approached Bodega Bay.

"Yes, but I wouldn't be if you hadn't eaten more than your share of the third apple."

"I had three bites, the same as you," he reminded her with a wide grin.

"Your three bites were so big they barely left me a fourth of the apple!" Sammi chastised in an unsuccessful attempt at acting gruff.

"I guess that answers my question." Steele laughed. He pulled his car into a parking space before a market, shut off the motor, and opened his door.

"Move it, woman," he commanded, reaching to grab her fingers. "We're going grocery shopping, and I want to see if you're going to make some man a thrifty wife."

Sammi took his hand, eased gracefully out of the car, and raised her chin to answer in an impudent voice, "I'm hoping my husband-to-be is so wealthy he won't care!"

"No poor trucker will do, huh?" Steele questioned, pushing open the door and stepping aside so Sammi could enter the market.

"Depends just how poor," Sammi teased, passing him with a toss of her shimmering black curls.

"Sassy little gold digger," he murmured beneath his breath. He took a small metal grocery cart from the front of the store, headed for the nearest aisle, and turned to tell her, "I'll push and you fill it up."

"Okay, but remember I'm a compulsive shopper and also a starving one."

"Pity my poor pocketbook," he moaned in an exaggerated manner. "I distinctly recall hearing a person should never shop when they're hungry as they always spend more than they budget for."

Sammi laughed at his troubled face when he stopped before the deli items, thinking he would make an excellent actor.

"Sliced corned beef okay?" she inquired with a wide smile.

"Nope. I want boiled ham," Steele disagreed, reaching around her to place a package of each in the cart.

Sammi gave him a sassy glance and asked in her sweetest falsetto voice, "Cheddar or swiss to go with it?"

"Both," Steele shot back.

Sammi picked up two packages of sliced cheese and walked on down the aisle. Reaching for a small jar of mayonnaise, she grimaced at the price. As she debated whether or not to get it, he took it from her hand.

Steele added a jar of mustard with horseradish and placed each next to the lunch meat and cheese before turning his head to scold her.

"Quit worrying about the prices, Sam. I'm buying."

He took a jar of pimiento-stuffed green olives from the shelf, added a jar of sweet midget pickles, and moved toward the potato chips.

"I prefer home-style cucumber pickles." Sammi admonished him for not asking.

Steele backed up without saying a word, searched the shelf, found what she wanted, and placed them with his other purchases.

"Okay, Sam?"

"Fine, Steele."

He picked out a loaf of dark rye bread without slowing down and laughed as Sammi added a package of onion rolls.

Before they were finished the cart contained crispy red lettuce, exorbitantly priced imported peaches and nectarines, pretzels for Steele and potato chips for Sammi, a package of coconut macaroon bars, and a carton of ready-prepared coleslaw. Adding paper plates, tablecloth, napkins, plastic forks, and a metal paring knife, they next examined the beverages.

Sammi was quiet as Steele picked up two bottles of gewurztraminer juice, two crystal drinking glasses, and a bag of ice. Surely he didn't know it was the same drink that Benny had ordered?

"This time I assure you you'll get to find out what it tastes like."

"How could you possibly know about a drink the restaurant was out of?"

"I make it my business to learn all there is to know about the things that interest me."

He stopped, gave her a long, hard look, and spoke. His rich baritone voice vibrated with intense awareness. "Everything about you interests me, Sam."

Sammi dropped her gaze, tried hard to ignore the depth of feeling in his voice, and stammered, "You . . . er, you have enough now to feed a family of five for a week."

"I'm a pretty hungry man," Steele drawled. His darkened eyes lazily ran up and down her tight jeans and clinging sweater, leaving her in no doubt he was talking about something other than his appetite for food.

"It's time to start curbing your appetite then." Sammi laughed with feigned indifference. "In all ways!"

"Minx!" Steele rebuked.

He looked at the boxes tightly stacked around the checkout area, picked up a jar of macadamia nuts and two Hershey bars, put one back and replaced it with an Almond Joy, and explained matter-of-factly, "Just in case you decide to argue about my choice of candy."

Sammi ignored his censorious comment and asked, "What happened to my Hershey bar that you bought me at the drive-in?"

"I ate it," Steele told her, unperturbed by her deep frown.

"Pig!" she scolded. "You could have saved it for me."

"I didn't want it to get stale."

Sammi ignored him, remembered her aunt's gift, and said, "It was nice of you to get Aunt Margaret a box of Godiva chocolates. They're so expensive though."

"Yes they are," Steele agreed, laughing inwardly as she looked worried, wondering whether or not he could afford them.

As the clerk totaled up their purchases, he placed his hand under her chin, held it still, and placed a lingering kiss on her soft lips. Totally unperturbed by the covert glances of the clerk, he turned to him and raised one shoulder in a nonchalant shrug.

"My woman needs lots of convincing I'm her man," he told the long-haired youth. "Lots!" he added, giving Sammi another lengthy kiss on her parted lips to emphasize his point.

Sammi pulled free, shot Steele a flustered look, walked outside, and waited on the sidewalk as her aggravating escort paid for the picnic supplies, pocketed his change, and carried the two large bags outside.

He placed them in the trunk, slammed it shut, and called out, "Get a move on, Sam. I want to spend as much time as possible on my hill."

"Your hill?" Sammi asked. She raised one narrow brow in a doubting delicate arch. She was well aware of the price of oceanfront land.

"Possession is nine-tenths of the law, and when I'm on it I'm damned well in control of all the soil beneath me."

"You're too much," she scoffed.

"Not today!" he leered, backing out of the parking spot and easing north. "Now tonight might be another thing."

"Are you bragging again?" Sammi chuckled at his audacious nerve.

"Just telling it like it is."

Sammi ignored Steele's blatant comment and watched the road ahead as he drove closer to his destination.

Steele passed through Jenner and wound higher and higher up the curving mountainside. Sammi glanced at the ocean, pleased to be back in view of it. The horizon was clear and a vivid teal blue.

Steele knew right where he was going and pulled to a stop in a small lay-by that was barely big enough to get his luxurious automobile completely off the road.

Sammi scooted out right behind him, raised her arms heavenward, and inhaled the brisk air as she stared at the ocean far below them.

As she started to walk down the grassy hill, Steele scolded, "Stay close, Sam."

She glanced at the waves crashing against the rocky shore hundreds of feet below, then back across the road at the mountain that rose just as steep and far above them.

Sammi faced Steele with both hands on her hips, raised her chin, and boldly informed him, "I'm not afraid of heights."

"Well, I am, so don't go skipping off. I might need you to hold my hand."

Sammi chuckled at the vision of Steele cowering and afraid of anything, offered to take one of the grocery sacks, and walked ahead when he refused. She scrambled nimbly down until she reached a broad level spot.

Hidden from view by the curve of the road, it was completely private and the only flat surface she could see on the entire mountain. The sharp drop was breathtaking.

"This is it," Steele told her unnecessarily. He set the groceries down and stepped behind her. With both hands crossed in front of her waist he hugged her close.

Sammi could feel his broad chest expand as he breathed in the invigorating air. A shudder ran through her body when a jaunty breeze tugged her hair and ruffled it across his chin as she looked at the view.

"It's, er, lovely," she whispered when he placed a kiss on the back of her neck.

Steele's hands spread and gently drew her back until they were touching from shoulder to thigh. He wanted her to know that his body was instantly aroused by her touch. It was important she be conscious of how volatile and easily ignited their passions were. He trembled with the effort of not placing her on the soft grass to claim her then.

"Neither as lovely or profound a sight as you, Sam," he murmured.

Tormented by the desire to push back against him, Sammi eased away. She was awakened to his heightened mood and knew he wanted to make love to her. She avoided his eyes, afraid he'd read her willingness to go to him with opened arms, and stood alongside him instead.

Arm in arm they stared at the view. For long moments they mutely watched, too inspired to break the special tranquillity with further words. As far as each could see nature had formed the land to obstruct man's invasion. The hillside sloped at a seventy-five-degree angle before dropping straight to the sea. Covered with lush, delicate green grass, it was scarred by narrow trails winding horizontally along the edge of the landmass, one over the other.

"Steele, look!" Sammi squealed when she spotted sheep ambling around the corner. They grazed on the steep slopes without concern.

"Did they make all those trails?"

"You bet. This is sheep land, honey," Steele explained. He bent sideways and planted a kiss on her cool brow. "They roam back and forth across the highway at will."

"What keeps them from going to San Francisco or Fort Bragg?"

"Cattle guards across the road, you unobservant female."

Sammi stood enthralled as more sheep appeared. It seemed unreal after her life in the city to find an area that animals still grazed freely on each side of a major highway.

"Look up the mountain," Steele told her, turning her around so she could see behind them.

"My gosh, they're all over the place," Sammi exclaimed as she began to pick out the grayish-white bodies scattered on the rugged upper slopes.

"How do the owners ever round them up without getting killed?"

"They use dogs." Steele laughed. "It would be impossible any other way on these hills."

"I believe it," Sammi agreed readily. "We must be at least a thousand feet above the ocean."

"At least," Steele concurred. "Let's eat."

He followed his suggestion with a sharp tug on Sammi's hand as he moved over to sit down.

Sammi kneeled beside him as he stretched out on his side in the sweet-smelling grass.

"My God, don't tell me you're going to relax while I wait on you?"

"Feeding the male of the species is woman's work," he teased. His warm brownish eyes twinkled with mirth as he watched her expressive face. "Man provides the groceries and his woman prepares the meal."

"You're a real chauvinist, aren't you?" Sammi scoffed.

"They're the best kind," Steele shot back in a voice that broke with laughter.

Sammi gave him a fierce glare, broke into a soft giggle, and began to remove items from the sack. She spread out the red-checked tablecloth, set each article in an orderly fashion on it, and concentrated on making sandwiches.

Steele watched every graceful movement with deep pleasure. She was the loveliest, most enticing woman he'd ever known. Her ever-changing personality was a constant delight. It seemed impossible that he had ever been happy with anyone else in his life.

"Add a couple slices of the ham and some more cheese, Sam," he prompted. "I couldn't survive on what you're making."

"How could you get your mouth around the sandwich if I

did?" Sammi scolded. "It's already two inches thick and I haven't put the lettuce on yet."

"Better make me two while you're at it also. One on rye and one on an onion roll."

Sammi grumbled beneath her breath, making certain she did exactly as he asked, and couldn't summon up the memory of a single time in her life when she'd felt more enchanted.

"Too bad we didn't buy some grapes," Sammi cooed sweetly, handing him a heaping plate overflowing with sandwiches, coleslaw, and sweet pickles.

"Why?" Steele asked, popping open the chips and pretzels with his tanned fingers. Placing a pickle between his strong white teeth he crunched its tart sweetness while waiting for her to answer.

"I could peel and remove the seeds from each and feed you while the ocean breeze fanned your face as you reclined on your grassy throne."

"You're learning, Sam." Steele grinned with annoying superiority.

"Arrogant beast," Sammi shot back. She sat beside him, crossing her legs Indian fashion and placing her plate across her lap.

"I'm improving," Steele reminded her between mouthfuls of sandwich.

"How, pray tell?" Sammi asked. He was still the same commanding brute she'd met the first of the week.

"I'm usually an arrogant *redheaded* beast."

Sammi stared at the sunshine caught in Steele's thick wavy hair. It glimmered with bright coppery streaks in the bronze curls. She hated to admit that it really was more brown than red.

"Forget it and eat your lunch before I throw it to the sheep," Sammi threatened.

"Sheep are grazing animals and wouldn't care for ham and swiss on rye."

Steele rose to a sitting position, reached across her, and pulled a sack forward. He reached inside, withdrew a tall slender bottle, the partially melted ice cubes, and two glasses. Wiping the glasses with a paper napkin, he balanced each carefully, filled them with ice, and made a melodramatic show of opening the bottle.

"Watch me, kid," he told her with preposterous seriousness. "I'll show you the proper way to drink fine unfermented juices."

He tore off the gold foil, removed the cap, withdrew a corkscrew from his pocket, pulled out the cork, made a loud pop with his mouth, then smelled the end with a thoughtful expression on his face.

"An excellent bouquet, which advances me to the next ritual."

He poured a small amount in the large glass, swirled it around, then raised it to his nose. He inhaled, coughed twice, then lifted it to his lips. Taking a small sip, he swished it around his mouth, swallowed, coughed again, and frowned as she giggled.

"Passes every test a connoisseur of vintage juices has devised to assure a palatable drink." He handed her a glass filled with the clear golden liquid. "A toast to you, my gorgeous wench."

"You're crazy," Sammi insisted, raising her glass to clink it with his.

"Crazy about you, Sam," Steele returned, still holding the edge of his glass to hers, his voice lowered, each word spoken with sincere meaning.

"To you, Sam. You're forever mine."

Not removing his eyes from hers, he raised the glass to his lips, took a long swallow, passed it across to her, exchanged it for hers, placed his lips where hers had been and licked the edge before taking another long swallow from her glass.

It was done in total silence and was so erotically suggestive she felt her stomach muscles clench. He hadn't said a word, yet she could read every sensual thought in his mind. He was warning her he would taste of her body as he tasted her drink. His mouth would ply her figure with explicit pleasure before his tongue explored each curve with extended intimacy.

Sammi's hand began to shake. Before she could set her drink

down, several drops spilled onto her wrist. She inhaled as Steele reached out, took her hand to his mouth, and licked her skin free of the tangy juice.

"Cleaning you up is beginning to be my favorite pastime," Steele teased, smacking his lips together with exaggerated enjoyment.

"You're kinky," Sammi retorted, jerking her wrist away. She wiped it on her pant leg as he laughed.

"Do you like the juice?"

"It's delicious." She imitated his actions, swirled the liquid, took a sip, and with eyes alight with mimicry told him, "Exquisitely full-bodied, yet has the essence of grape flavor without being alcoholic plus it tastes much, much better than cola."

"I figured you'd prefer gewurztraminer juice," Steele grumbled.

"Why?" Sammi asked before emptying her glass in one long satisfying drink.

"Because it cost almost five bucks a bottle."

"Oh, dear." Sammi looked crestfallen to think Steele had spent so much. "You should have bought a couple sodas instead."

"Now you tell me," Steele moaned, throwing up his hands in simulated disgust.

Sammi finished her sandwich, set the plate aside, and cupped her glass in both hands. She sat with her knees up and stared at the waves crashing with continuous force against the rugged shoreline. It was time to start interrogating Steele about his life. He was full, acting contented, and unusually amiable.

"Where do you live?" she casually inquired. Her voice was soft and she made certain her eyes never wavered from the ocean.

"Over the hill," Steele answered with equal nonchalance.

"I'm surprised," Sammi told him. "I thought you'd live by the ocean."

"Can't."

"Why not?"

"It would rust my truck."

Damn him, Sammi fumed inwardly. It would take weeks to find out anything about him if he answered all her questions in one- or two-word sentences.

"I like your Lincoln Continental."

"That's a company car."

"Oh," Sammi commented foolishly, unable to think of a sensible reply. She'd hoped talking about his automobile would get the stilted exchange going. Instead, as suspected, the damned thing wasn't even his.

"You must have a nice boss," she said between clenched teeth.

"The best. Generous too." Steele watched her profile with amusement. It was obvious she was furious, yet she controlled her temper in an effort to delve into his life story.

"How long have you worked for the company and its generous owner?"

"From the first day."

Sammi fumed. Steele was becoming more impossible by the second. Giving him a surreptitious glance through lowered lashes, she could tell he was enjoying himself. He was reclining on his side, staring at her with a wide, smug grin. It was clear he was deliberately not volunteering any information about his past, present, or future. Did the man ever do anything the same as her past escorts?

"Tell me about your work?" Sammi asked in a honey-sweet voice. She gave him a pleading look, hoping her expressive, shimmering blue irises would succeed where words had failed. Appearing eager to hear an in-depth report on a man's work was fail proof.

"Long hours. Short pay."

Sammi waited for Steele to continue. When she couldn't stand to hold his glance without him continuing the conversation, she turned away. She ignored him, gathered up the empty plates, and placed them with the trash in an empty sack. He probably had an unsavory past anyway.

"Do you want some more gewurztraminer, Sam?"

"Can you afford it?" she asked with feigned sweetness. He could irritate her more than any man she'd ever known. The closemouthed beast!

"Just barely," he told her with a devilish smile.

Sammi stood up and tried to count the grazing sheep in a provoking, unsuccessful attempt to take her mind off the first thwarted interview of her life. How could any woman love a man like him? *Especially her.*

Steele popped open the second bottle, added more ice, and called out in a voice so solicitous she ached to smack him, "Here's your drink, my darling Sam."

When she failed to take it, he grabbed her slender ankle and tugged.

Sammi glanced down at his hand, which was starting to fondle her ankle with intense interest, then looked at his face and decided not to argue. She sat back down, accepted the glass, thanked him, and clasped her hands around her bent knees.

"Why did you give up teaching without taking Mr. Purcelle before the school board or hiring an attorney to bring suit?"

Sammi nearly dropped her glass she was so stunned. She faced Steele with a shocked expression on her face. Where had he heard about that part of her life?

"How did you know I used to teach school?"

"You're bossy."

"I'm not!"

"All teachers are bossy."

"They aren't!" she argued defensively.

"All mine were," Steele told her matter-of-factly. He reached out to touch her arm gently. "Why didn't you make trouble for the principal? He had no right to get off scot-free for sexually harassing you at work."

Sammi observed Steele's concerned expression with wonder. He was visibly bothered about her losing her job, while Alan, an attorney, had never questioned her decision not to fight for her rights.

"I felt sorry for his wife," Sammi explained. Steele was the first to hear her real reason for quitting so suddenly. "If I had pressed the issue with Mr. Purcelle, it would have broken up their marriage, and I didn't want that on my conscience."

"I can understand that," Steele agreed sympathetically. "A private school is like a small closely knit world of its own."

"Your perception astounds me," Sammi told him in a soft whisper.

"Why, Sam?" Steele solicited her answer.

"You're so, er, forceful I thought you'd be unconcerned about women's rights."

"That's a surprisingly narrow view," Steele rebuked softly. "I'm interested in everyone's rights. Every human and animal, but especially about yours, honey."

"How did you find out that about my past? It was kept very, very private. I never even told Aunt Margaret my reason for changing jobs."

"I told you before I made it my business to learn everything about you."

"That still puzzles me." Sammi cocked him a curious look.

"What?"

"How you found out my name, where I was staying, and the room number of my motel." A deep frown creased her forehead.

"That was easy." Steele grinned, remembering the three bird dogs following her unawares for forty some miles. "The latest information was a little harder to come by."

"What . . . er, what information?" Sammi stammered. What else could he possibly know about her?

In answer to her unspoken thoughts, Steele added, "I know your current address, birthplace and date, the schools you attended . . . and the grades—" He broke off laughing as he taunted, "You were terrible in math."

"Worse than that," Sammi admitted. Her eyes sparkled as

they locked with his. "Aunt Margaret is a genius at it, which makes me even more of a family disgrace."

"Don't worry about it, sweetheart. Since your sights are set on a rich man he, can hire someone to keep your charge cards and checkbook in order."

"What else do you know about me?" Sammi asked, wanting to avoid any further discussion about her marrying a rich man. Wearing the latest fashion didn't sound nearly as appealing as spending her life with an arrogant trucker who was the most tantalizing, magnificent male she'd ever met. Besides she could always learn to sew her own clothes if she had to.

"What else do I know about you?" Steele repeated with a broad smile. He drew her back until they were both lying on the soft grass. He tucked her head on his shoulder and stroked her shoulder as he related further details.

Sammi was so intrigued, she completely forgot she had originally started the discussion to find out about him and moments ago had been peeved.

"You had a happy childhood with parents who adored you as well as each other," Steele continued with his revelations. "They were both tragically killed during your first year teaching tenth-graders. Also your entire life has been spent residing in the city of Burbank."

Sammi turned sideways to get closer, listening in awe. She raised one hand to lay it on his chest and turned her face up as he spoke. She could see the taut skin of his throat and his strong jaw. Even the tiny laugh lines at the corners of his keen eyes were visible. He had lovely eyes for a man. Clear and beautiful and shadowed by thick dark lashes. Watching him was far more intriguing than hearing her story.

"You even organized a feminine revolt in the second grade." Steele broke into her deep contemplation of his features.

"Oh, God," Sammi cried out in disbelief. "No one—*absolutely no one*—knew about that but my teacher and classmates."

"And me," Steele told her, quoting verbatim from the report

he'd been given. "Little Miss Samantha Thatcher, with the long black pigtails, decided the boys in her class had more freedom during recess wearing blue jeans, so she pestered old, straitlaced spinster Ms. Tuttles, until she consented to allow the girls to wear them to school."

"Did you also unearth the results?" Sammi quizzed. She could still remember how embarrassed she had been.

"Yes." Steele chuckled. "On the day set aside for women's lib to rise up. Little Miss Sam was the only girl in her class dressed like a boy. Your female classmates all backed out. Ms. Tuttles then added to the insult by making you sit with the boys during lunch and playing on the boys' team during recess."

"I can't understand how you know this. It was so long ago." Sammi chuckled. "You have to be psychic."

"Not really," Steele disagreed. "You were homecoming queen in high school and college. You dated the sports heroes as well as the intellectuals. Your reputation was impeccable, your outspokenness renowned, and generosity unmatched."

"Stop . . . please!" Sammi silenced him by touching his mouth with her fingertips. "I sound too good to be true."

Steele lifted her hand, held her fingers still, and kissed each one with attentive thoroughness.

"No," he teased. "Your temper was also renowned, as well as your impetuosity in championing every cause you thought worthwhile. Most of which weren't."

"True," Sammi acknowledged. Her enthusiasm and desire to help the underdog had placed her right in the middle of many weird situations.

"Now," Steele continued in a husky, disbelieving voice, "you help out each Sunday at a local pet shelter. You clean cages, bottle feed baby kittens and puppies, and don't get paid one cent."

"I like it," Sammi blurted out.

"Shush, woman," Steele reprimanded with a firm hug, and placed his fingers over her lips.

Sammi kissed his fingertips as he had hers while she listened in awe. He knew more about her than her closest relative did.

"On Saturday mornings you go to a local rest home and shampoo the residents' hair. You also bring them pretty presents that you pay for and home-baked cakes and cookies. They love you more than their own children, who often ignore them."

"I love them too," Sammi whispered. "Will you go with me sometime?" The question slipped out before she thought how impossible that would be to arrange.

"I would be honored, Sam," Steele assured her with such conviction she knew he meant what he said.

"Now stop interrupting me," he scolded. "One night a week you do volunteer work at the local hospital, another you tutor special children in history, and on Thursdays you attend night classes. This term you're taking advanced electronics. Advanced?" Steele queried.

"I figured it might be a great place to meet a prospective millionaire," Sammi told him, unperturbed. "Unfortunately the teacher suggested the proper procedure was to start at the beginner's level and work up. I was going to quit anyway because there weren't any men in the class that appealed to me."

Steele rolled her over him, shaking his head in disbelief as she explained why she went to night school. He slid both hands down her back and spread his fingers over her hip pockets to hold her body still. A broad grin widened his mouth as a soft pink flush colored her cheekbones when she realized how intimate her position was.

"What I want to know, Sam," he insisted, "is how the hell you have time to date some lucky fool . . . *almost every night* of your life?"

"Good planning," she sassed, squirming her hips as she stretched her limbs between his.

"Careful, sweetheart," Steele cautioned when she moved against him. "My control is good but not infallible."

Sammi could feel Steele's body harden beneath her and

yearned to continue with the tutoring he had started at the drive-in. There were far more intimate things to learn than how to kiss a man.

Braced above him, she traced his features with her eyes, waiting entranced as he trailed his hands up her back to cup her head gently.

With little effort he drew her face down until their lips met with such sweet tenderness she had no apprehension he would ever do anything she didn't want. He was nothing like Benny or Alan.

"I like that," Sammi murmured into his mouth when he rubbed her nape.

"You're supposed to," Steele whispered back between hungry kisses.

When he released her lips, she sighed, lay her head on his shoulder, and tried to regain her senses. Her head was spinning from the trauma of his mouth possessing hers with such probing intimacy she forgot everything but the man holding her.

"Was that kiss on your erotic list?" Sammi asked breathlessly. She loved the protection of his strong arms and long, powerful torso.

"Heavens no!" Steele scorned, kissing her forehead in emphasis. "My erotic list is for your complete seduction. The kiss I just took was only a little afternoon ad-libbing."

Sammi squealed when Steele rolled her over, and she found herself pinned beneath his powerful body bearing his definitely male—decidedly aroused—imprint.

"It's too soon after lunch to ad-lib lovemaking," Sammi boldly admonished him. His darkened pupils had an extremely sensual gleam.

"The hell you say!" Steele shot back. To emphasize his point he held both her hands above her head and gave her a long kiss before burying his face in the curve of her neck.

As he nibbled the smooth skin, Sammi squirmed in a vain

attempt to stop his probing lips before he found the gold chain with his ring hidden beneath the soft cashmere wool.

"What's this?" Steele murmured against her throat. He released her hands, rested on his knees while straddling her hips, and reached to open the top of her sweater.

"Er, nothing," Sammi stammered. Her breasts rose and fell rapidly as his fingers touched them in his effort to undo the tiny buttons.

"Nothing!" He scowled, when he exposed the gold circle lying in the enticing cleavage of her full bosom. "Like hell it's nothing, Sam. This was made especially for you. Didn't you read the inscription?"

"Yes," she admitted breathlessly. Her pulse was beating so fast she could hardly breathe. The touch of his fingers slowly stroking the skin exposed above her skimpy bra had ignited the need to feel his hands on all her flesh, not just that heated by his bemused gaze.

"Well then, you know damned well that it's much more than nothing!"

Steele replaced the ring between her breasts and let both hands cup their flawless beauty as he sat above her.

Sammi's hair was tumbled and lay around her face in silken curls as she stared at his narrowed eyes. The sexual desire expressed was almost as arousing as the continued surging pressure of his palms and the weight of his hips pushing her down.

With great tenderness he undid the fastener, letting the burgeoning flesh spill free. He stared at her dainty pink nipples, entranced as they became erect beneath his torrid gaze and lingering touch.

Surrounding the sensitive aureole with widespread, gentle fingers, he lowered his body until he was stretched between her limbs low enough so that his mouth was in a perfect position to take the entire bud into its warmth. He teased her with his tongue, slowly working it in erotic circles round and round the tip before flicking more rapidly back and forth. His head rose, allowing his teeth to nibble a gentle circular path.

"Do you enjoy this, Sam?" Steele inquired as his breath feathered across her skin with stirring warmth.

"It . . . and everything you do . . . is perfect," Sammi confessed, drawing out each word with the effort of speaking.

She tossed her head back and forth as he went from one breast to the other with identical attentiveness. Arching her back, she yearned to press her flesh farther into his mouth. Each delicious sensation surged straight to her lower abdomen with alarming intensity.

"I . . . I think you'd better . . . *quit,*" she started to say, but the last word never passed her parted lips.

Steele raised his head, cupped her breasts together, then pressed his face into the soft mounds of flesh. Inhaling her sweet, perfumed scent, he moaned in a harsh voice. "I'd better what, Sam?"

"Quit," she finally blurted out, despite wriggling her hips upward in an instinctive invitation to fill her aching body with his. Her slacks-clad legs rose, intuitively clinging to his lean hips.

Steele shuddered, straightened to a sitting position over Sammi, and lowered his hands to cup her bottom hard against the strained material of his slacks. He held her still until his tensed muscles quivered with the effort of not stripping her clothes off and taking her virginity on the soft grass. If she hadn't been chaste, he would have made love to her until the moon rose. Damn, he protested in solemn anguish, knowing that taking her innocence deserved a more appropriate setting. He wanted her so much it was driving him wild.

"I think I love you, Steele," Sammi admitted softly as her hands reached up to cling to his taut biceps. She moved her shoulders, aware her full breasts were totally exposed and swayed with alluring appeal to the man above her.

"You think?" Steele groaned, using his hands to draw her body back and forth against his with explicit sensuality.

"No, heavens no!" Sammi cried out. His sexual teasing was becoming too much. "I'm absolutely, totally, completely devoted to you."

Steele looked down at Sammi's eyes shimmering with the love he had ached to see from the first. They were alight with slumberous, incredibly honest passion simmering in their deep blue depths.

"You'd better be, Sam," he warned in a harsh outburst.

Releasing his intimate hold on her rounded bottom, he shivered. One more moment with her legs wrapped around his hips and her crotch pressed against his and he'd forget his good intention of taking her virginity elsewhere. With the strength of his powerful arm muscles he drew her forward until she was kneeling before him.

"You have the most gorgeous breasts of any woman in the world, Sam." He moaned at the thought of covering them up.

His fingers shook as he fastened the hook on her bra. He lifted his gold ring, kissed it before laying it back, and buttoned her sweater.

"I . . . I do?" Sammi asked, unashamed that she had let Steele fondle her as he wished. He was so assured and touched her with such tender reverence that he could have done anything he wanted without a single word of protest leaving her lips.

"Yes, you do, sweetheart," he confirmed huskily. "It's not surprising since you're the most beautiful woman in the world to me."

Sammi leaned forward, threw her arms around Steele's neck, and kissed his lips with lingering passion as tears of emotion slipped beneath her closed eyelids. She had never felt more feminine or desirable in her life.

Steele cradled Sammi's face in his palms and returned caress for caress. He took charge as they clung to each other on the cushiony grass-covered earth. His tongue searched the interior of her soft mouth, slowly rubbing her tongue tip before moving in and out with such precise erotic suggestiveness he could feel a shudder run up her spine.

Sammi hugged him with strong arms, not wanting the stirring kiss ever to end. She instinctively knew he was using his tongue to express his desire to thrust his body into hers with the same continuous motion.

As her kness threatened to give out and she swayed with the urge to lie back down, Steele released her mouth. His hands were as unsteady as his voice as he blurted out, "What's your favorite position to make love, Sam?"

"Er, the, er, normal one," Sammi stuttered. Her lie was getting her in grave trouble. She lowered her lashes and gave him a disarming smile.

"You're a little missionary minx, huh?" he asked. His voice was deceptively soft as he solemnly pledged her bold claim would be a reality soon.

Sammi avoided Steele's penetrating gaze and suggested, "Shouldn't we be going soon?"

"I guess it's time to gather up the sacks, you subject-changing wench."

"Are you hungry already?" Sammi asked, ignoring his other comment.

She made no protest when he stood up, briefly hovered above her with his legs spread, hands on hips in a dominant male position, and watched her in silence. He smiled, pulled her up until she was gently enfolded in his arms, and gave her a prolonged embrace.

"I'm hungry for you, Sam. Always and only for you." His eyes bored into hers with indulgent tenderness as she leaned back.

"Shush," Sammi murmured, turning away from the sensual tone of his profound words. "Every comment implies lust the way you word it."

"It's meant to, sweetheart. There are many ways, other than the missionary position you prefer, to make love to your woman.

With words and hugs, or as before by nibbling, tasting, and slowly stroking each exposed inch of her body."

"Stop it, Steele," Sammi scolded, trying to gain a little composure by pulling away to pick up one of the sacks.

"Okay, Sam," he agreed in a surprisingly quick mood change. "I guess I'll have to be satisfied with this instead."

Steele rooted through the sack on the grass, took out the coconut bars, opened them and removed one, and found a large peach and took a bite of the fruit while Sammi protested impudently.

"You rude male! Everyone knows a man is supposed to offer a woman the first bite."

"Some woman's idea no doubt?" he teased, holding the fruit out of reach as she tried to take it from his hand.

As Sammi grabbed at Steele's upraised arm, he lowered it and placed the peach so she could take the second bite.

"Here you are then," he grumbled, giving her the fruit and the coconut bar before reaching into the sack for another.

"That's better." Sammi smiled smugly. She took a second mouthful of the sweet peach and chewed it thoughtfully. "It appears you need some training also."

"Me?" Steele asked with a shocked expression on his face as he raised his chin in mock arrogance. "In what way?"

"In manners, that's what way," Sammi chided. She took a last, lingering look at the natural beauty spread before her, knowing she had never enjoyed an impromptu picnic or afternoon as much in her life.

"We'll come back sometime," Steele promised, aware of her thoughts. "And I promise when we do, I'll make love to you all day long."

"In front of the sheep?" Sammi laughed as they started arm in arm back up the hill to his car.

"In front of God and *all* his creatures," Steele vowed seriously.

As Sammi struggled on the steep climb, he tugged her hand, urging her to hurry as they had a long drive ahead.

Winding their way back down the mountain on the return trip, Sammi laid her head on Steele's shoulder in complete contentment. She let her hand rest on his thigh with total confidence he was as in love as she was.

"Where are we going now?"

"Back to your motel."

"For what reason?" Sammi asked suspiciously.

"I'm going to drop you off so you can get out of your raggedy jeans and sloppy old sweater."

"These are brand-new clothes!" Sammi rebuked him firmly.

"Really?" Steele teased. "Well, they aren't nice enough for where I'm going to take you tonight. I want you to enthrall me with your sexiest dress for an unforgettable evening."

"And what will you do while I'm preparing to dazzle you?" Sammi insisted with coy sweetness.

"I'll go to a phone booth and change into my super-escort outfit."

"That sounds like an excellent idea." Sammi chuckled.

"I thought it would," Steele told her softly. He pressed his hand over hers. "You seem to approve of all my ideas today."

"Arrogant, *redheaded* brute!" Sammi slammed back, pulling her fingers out from under his hand.

"I'm back to square one again." Steele laughed, easing through Guerneville on a different route back to the city. "For a woman who claims to be in love, you certainly have some derogatory names for your man."

"Shove the throttle down, you double-clutching gear-jammer, 'cause you ain't heard nothing yet!" Sammi sassed in a deep Southern drawl.

"My God, you little eighteen-wheeling groupie!" Steele exclaimed in disbelief. "Where did you pick up that trucker talk?"

"I learned long ago," Sammi told him smugly, "never to disclose my sources of information."

She had thought the time would never come when she could argue back with the same irritating cliché he used when he didn't want her to know anything.

"Touché, Sam. Touché." Steele laughed in good humor.

CHAPTER NINE

With Steele's "See you in two hours" ringing in her ears, Sammi entered the motel. She glanced at the neatly made-up beds. The room seemed so empty without Margaret's pleasant company.

Carelessly throwing her purse on the bed, she kicked off her tennis shoes and prepared to remove her clothes. There wasn't time to worry about her aunt's absence. It would take every minute of the time allotted if she was to dazzle her man as she wished.

"I love you, Steele Whitfield." Sammi spoke her thoughts aloud.

Planning each move, she let the bathtub fill to the brim with foamy warm water redolent of her favorite bath oil while rummaging through an unpacked Pullman case for black lace underwear. They were so wispy and brief that she could imagine Steele's eyes alight with the darkened sensual gleam she'd come to learn was his first outward sign of rising desire.

Minutes passed as Sammi concentrated on each beauty ritual. With her mind divided between thoughts of Steele and assuring she was impeccably groomed, she glanced at the dainty gold watch strapped to her left wrist. She had just enough time left to straighten up the room and decide which accessories looked the most flattering.

An impatient pounding interrupted her attempt to join the clasp of an ebony crystal necklace. A welcoming smile raised the corners of her mouth as she placed the jewelry on the dresser. She knew instinctively it was Steele.

Without saying a word, she pulled open the door, stood back, and twirled around to show off her slinky black halter dress.

Steele stared transfixed. His hands trembled against the smooth skin of her naked back when he stopped her movement to enfold her in his arms.

"Where's the rest of it, Sam?" His eyes grew darker, nearing the color of his lashes, as he looked at her lovely face. "My God, woman, but you're really something special when you set out to entrance a man. My damned knees are shaking you're so beautiful."

"They're just weak from hunger," Sammi contradicted in a low, throaty voice. She clung to his neck with hands as smooth as her bared arms and leaned back to give him her most enticing smile.

"It's a hunger for you, not food," Steele insisted. "You're too too much!"

He watched enthralled as Sammi's eyes sparkled, shimmering the most vivid blue he'd ever seen. The color of her dress matched the sheen of her raven-black hair and hugged the full curves of her breasts and her narrow waist with alluring appeal.

"Do you like my dress?" Sammi implored.

As Steele prepared to answer, she took in his appearance with equal appreciation. Excitement pulsated through her veins. He was such a tremendously stunning man. She could feel the now-familiar quivering begin deep in the pit of her stomach. This was her body's first warning sign of deep arousal.

His black evening suit fit the width of his shoulders and lean hips with such perfection that it was obvious it was custom tailored. A ruffled evening shirt, which would look feminine on most men, only accented his masculinity.

She had never seen a man as devastatingly handsome or been this proud of an escort in her life. Love welled up in her breast so strongly she was temporarily speechless. His dark bronze-toned hair was now her favorite color, making her wonder how she'd ever thought it the bright red she loathed in the past.

"Well, Mr. Whitfield," Sammi repeated. "Do you?"

"Do I like your dress?" Steele echoed her question. "It's absolutely gorgeous, though it resembles a sensual nightgown more than a cocktail dress."

"Hardly," Sammi scoffed. "I'm perfectly respectable."

"You may be faultlessly proper, but your attire's an erotic dream. There isn't a man alive who will see you tonight who won't fantasize about taking you to bed."

"Including you?" Sammi taunted impishly.

"Especially me," Steele told her with assuring emphasis.

He ran his widespread fingers around her rib cage, cupped the side of each full breast, then slowly slid his hands lower to linger around her waist. Lifting her up, he planted a fierce kiss on her responsive lips before reluctantly allowing her to pull away.

"You forgot something, Sam?" Steele reminded as his hands fondled the curve of her hip before falling with knuckles clenched along his hips.

"What?" Sammi inquired, reaching out to pick up her crystal beads.

As she fumbled with the clasp, Steele turned her around, separated the shimmering curls of hair, and concentrated on securing the necklace.

"What, er, what did I forget?" Sammi asked breathlessly as she felt his mouth touching her nape in a warm caress that shook her to the soles of her spike-heeled sandals.

"Your underwear," Steele returned in a husky voice that proved he was as moved by her presence as she was by his.

"I'm wearing the complete works," Sammi assured him softly.

"I swear I didn't feel a thing beneath that arousing piece of man-catching material you're clad in."

"I admit it's pretty brief." Sammi chuckled, drawing away to cock him a mischievous glance. "You're far too knowledgeable about women's attire for a bachelor trucker."

"We're not on the road all the time, honey," Steele pointed out. Watching as Sammi gathered up a chic, ultra-feminine velvet coat and coordinated evening bag, he complained, "Your outfit has shortened the self-indulgence promised during the start of my seduction-of-Sam list."

"What was that?" Sammi inquired, giving him a lingering smile as she took his arm while he shut the door behind them.

"My first pleasure was to be undressing you slowly piece by delicate piece," Steele told her in a solemn voice. He watched with delight as a length of nylon-covered thigh was exposed when her skirt was hiked up as she scooted across the glove-soft leather seat from the driver's side.

"Tonight's skimpy gown has reduced my much-anticipated long minutes of bliss to a couple of pieces of clothing and brief seconds of enjoyment."

As Steele started the motor and eased his automobile into the heavy evening traffic, Sammi hastened to remind him, "I wondered when you would start alerting me to the evil deeds you have planned for my distant future."

Sammi watched with amusement as the humor curving Steele's lips upward disappeared with lightning swiftness.

"Distant, hell!" Steele disputed gruffly. "We'd better synchronize our watches because in hours you'll be . . . forever mine . . . body and soul."

"Maybe Margaret was right and I do need a chaperon," Sammi returned with an impish glance. "You're talking arrogantly again."

"Do you actually believe anyone could keep you safe from my plotted advances now that you have declared you love me?" Steele questioned seriously.

"That incriminating comment was made under duress," Sammi explained without giving him a direct answer. It was definitely time to change the subject. "Where are we dining?"

"In a cozy little hideaway guaranteed to make a man irresistible to any female who eats a meal in its seductive environment."

"The women probably weren't as strong in character as I am," Sammi reminded Steele boldly as she met his amused glance.

"I won't argue that point." Steele laughed. "You're the most impertinent, outspoken, independent minx I've ever met."

"A trait of eighteen-wheeling groupies, no doubt," Sammi chided, suddenly reminded of his put-down in front of Monique and Kay.

Ignoring her frosty glance as she thought of his previous dates, Steele questioned boldly, "Are you finally conceding this poor trucker wouldn't make a bad bed mate, Sam?"

"Not on your life!" Sammi scoffed. "Words alone don't prove any man's a great lover."

"Now you're asking for it," Steele growled. He pulled into the first empty parking space, slid the gear into park, and turned sideways. Without shutting the motor off, he reached for Sammi, held her head still, and took her parted lips in a kiss so passionate she thought she'd never come back to earth.

Sammi lay her head on the seat back, felt her hands rise to grip his neck, and responded without thought. It made no difference if her carefully applied makeup got smeared or her dress rumpled.

When they were both too breathless to continue, Steele drew away. "Does that convince you that my ability as a lover is more than mere words?" he whispered into her ear before returning to caress her parted lips with short, feverish kisses.

"Hmm . . ." Sammi murmured, making a desperate effort to act composed. She had a sudden yearning to slide under him and thrill to the weight of his body pressed tightly over her own.

Unsuccessfully trying to stop his wandering mouth with the grip of her fingertips on each side of his strong jaw, she sighed and let him nibble across her closed eyelids with complete contentment.

Her nostrils flared daintily the moment she inhaled the heady scent of his clean hair as he pressed a deep kiss into the hollow of her throat. She knew he could feel the pulse beating wildly beneath her sensitive skin as she cradled his head close.

"Hmm?" Steele chuckled, raising his head to hold her glance when her eyelashes fluttered open. "Is that all you can say when a man asks if you like his loving?"

"Hmm, er, oh, er . . . no," Sammi stuttered.

"No!" Steele exclaimed, leaning forward to place a single kiss on her cushiony mouth before smoothly easing into the flow of traffic.

"No . . . meaning I can say more and yes . . . you're undoubtedly a very good lover," Sammi hastened to explain. She stole a quick look at his profile. The tiny laugh lines beside his eyes and mouth were much too apparent to be ignored. Damned if he wasn't enjoying himself. The beast!

"That's more like it," Steele told her in an amused voice. "Now we can go on to our destination."

"Good," Sammi whispered, trying vainly to equal his unruffled state. She was really angry with herself for lacking the control to hide an immediate response each time he touched her.

"Next time," Steele warned her, "you want to taunt my abilities I might not stop with a few chaste kisses."

"You haven't given me a chaste kiss yet," Sammi reminded her arrogant escort in a firm voice. Rooting through her purse, she removed a lipstick, forced her fingers to stop shaking, and carefully applied lip gloss to her tingling mouth. When finished, she leaned into his shoulder. It was obviously a mistake to taunt the man's sexual prowess.

"A frosty pina colada drink sounds good," Sammi told him, suddenly feeling thirsty.

"A delectable Sam Thatcher sounds much better," Steele shot back, keeping his eyes on the road as he maneuvered his Lincoln around a car that was illegally double-parked.

"Hush, Steele," Sammi admonished firmly. "You're getting out of hand again."

"And you're sounding like a teacher again," Steele pointed

out. "No one else has that fixed way of telling someone to be quiet."

Sammi ignored Steele, watched the evening traffic, and unconsciously reached a hand over to touch his leg. Her fingers stroked the smooth material of his slacks. Entranced, she marveled at the feel of his hard thigh muscles tensing beneath their exploring tips. Her expression became dreamy as she envisioned his athletic body unclothed. Would she find out tonight if his chest was hairy?

Steele placed his palm over her hand, held it on his leg, and asked, "Is this blatant exploration part of your erotic list for me, Sam?"

"I don't have an erotic list for you!" Sammi shot back, pulling her fingers away in sudden embarrassment. Surely the man couldn't have read her mind?

"A woman of experience and you haven't been planning how you want to make love to me. Shame on you," he scolded in a serious voice, though she detected a devilish gleam in his eyes.

Steele found it hard to conceal his knowledge of her innocence as he witnessed her flustered reaction to his taunting words.

"I was looking forward to your expertise and assumed from the passionate response to my kisses that you would be able to teach me something I haven't tried yet."

Sammi turned away from Steele's keen eyes. A soft flush tinged each cheek as she tried to think of something to say that would end the interrogation about her supposed bedroom skills.

"The gewurztraminer juice was certainly delicious today."

Steele's deep laughter resounded through the car's interior as he pulled to a stop before his chosen restaurant.

"You have the most delightful way of concealing it when you get backed into a corner and don't want to answer a question."

He turned to give her an indulgent smile while his eyes traced each lovely feature. He would never tire of looking at her.

"I don't," she argued back, unable to hold his glance longer than a moment. The flaming warmth expressed in his hazel eyes was too profound this early in the evening.

"Speaking of avoiding queries, Mr. Whitfield." Sammi paused. Her voice was vibrant with censure. "We've been together all day and I still hardly know a thing about you."

Unperturbed, Steele explained in a steady tone, "You know I adore a short-tempered ebony-haired beauty with flashing sapphire-colored eyes, a sharp mind, a generous nature, and a sexy body."

"That's uncertain most of the time," Sammi scolded. "In between telling me I'm forever yours, you keep insisting I'm going to marry a rich man."

"What's so confusing about that?" Steele asked, leveling an innocent glance at her stormy features as he took her fingers to help her out of his car. He listened, entertained as she quickly responded.

"Since I have no desire to be a bigamist I apparently have to decide which I want—a poor trucker . . . or a wealthy husband."

Steele picked up her velvet evening coat and draped it around the creamy loveliness of her bared shoulders.

"Which sounds best?"

For a moment Sammi considered. Her dark brows arched as she prepared her answer. It wouldn't hurt to dampen his ego a little.

"This afternoon, on your hill, an indigent trucker did." Sammi's chin rose as she met his glance squarely. "Now that you're acting chauvinistic again, a rich husband—a rich, indulgent one—sounds much more appealing," she added with emphasis to show him being wealthy and pampered too was a double bonus.

"You delectable wench." Steele smiled, kissing her fingertips as he opened the hand-carved wood doors forming an oval entrance as intriguing as the dimly lit interior. "I'm all the man you'll ever need, rich or otherwise."

"You're bragging again, Mr. Whitfield." She leaned into his shoulder, enjoying each word of their playful banter.

As Sammi looked over the dramatic decor, Steele never took his eyes from her profile. His unguarded look was filled with love as he watched her turn her face to observe their host sweep forward with a long white burnous trailing away from his swarthy, hawk-nosed features.

Sammi's first thoughts were that it was like entering another world—a time and place she had read about but never visited. She felt transported in time back to the vast deserts where a sheik pursued the woman of his choice on a flowing-maned Arabian stallion. She gave Steele a surreptitious glance and imagined him in billowing robes like those of their host. He would make a devastating tribal chief.

Steele bent sideways, whispering into her ear as if he had read her thoughts, "Would you be a willing concubine in my harem if I was a sheik?"

Sammi stared at his vibrant hair, which looked dark auburn in the dim room, and sassed, "As I recall from past history, there were no red-haired sheiks."

"That didn't answer my question at all," Steele answered, moving Sammi forward with a hand on her waist as he watched the host sweep burgundy velvet drapes aside and motion for them to enter the privacy of their dining area.

"Oh, my gosh," Sammi enthused as she sank onto deep cushions forming a vast couch in front of their low circular table with its lavish silver inlay.

"Persian carpets, tented ceiling, and absolute isolation from the other diners make me feel decadent." She chuckled.

"I promise not to scream if you misbehave," Steele teased. He sank down onto the cushion along her side, rearranged his long legs so they would be the most comfortable, and looked around as curiously as Sammi. Leaning forward, he cupped her hand affectionately.

"It is rather blatantly erotic, isn't it?" One eyebrow rose as he whispered in a devilish manner.

"Deliciously so." Sammi smiled back. She ignored his roguish leer and continued, "I love it, and if the food's as tempting as the decor, it should be an unforgettable night."

"I intended from the first it would be a night you'll always remember," Steele reminded, bending over to place his lips over hers with the certainty they would be welcomed.

Sammi's hair swung away from her nape when she quickly pulled back as a waiter wearing an ornately embroidered black vest over white shirt and slacks entered. She watched intrigued as he placed a bowl on the table and indicated she should raise her hands to cleanse them in water he poured from a huge silver urn.

"Let me," Steele suggested. Gently taking one hand, he washed and dried it, then did the other. Unperturbed by their witness, he kissed each fingertip with lingering warmth before cleaning his own hands.

Sammi's breathing quickened. His motions were slow, deliberate, and as arousing as a caress. Her lashes lowered, unconsciously seductive as Steele ordered the Moroccan wedding feast.

Sammi frowned, jealously picturing Kay, and Monique, and no telling how many other of his women gloating as they lounged by his side in the posh Arabic atmosphere.

"This is the first time I've eaten here," Steele assured her with a knowing smile.

Brightened by his words, Sammi watched expectantly when the waiter returned with a silver tray lavishly laden with the first of an assortment of exotic dishes.

Laughter filled the room as Steele tried to emulate Sammi's finesse as she picked up the vegetables with her fingertips. With a confident shrug she daintily managed to consume the salade marocaine, pastella au poulet, pigeon rôti aux amandes, deftly roll the steamed wheat of the couscous aux brochettes, and smugly sip her first cup of tea without spilling a thing. She savored the foreign taste of each spicy rich course.

"Careful," Sammi prompted. "You dropped a bit of pastry." She wiped the speck of food from Steele's sleeve with self-satisfaction. After all the outfits he had caused her to ruin, turnabout was fair play.

"Just how many evening suits do you own?"

"Two," Steele told her, watching closely as she finished and returned the napkin to her lap.

"Two?" Sammi questioned. She was absolutely certain he had worn a different one each night she had seen him out. Could she have been so angered she'd made a mistake?

"Yes, two. This little old Oscar de la Renta and the new one I purchased for our first date."

"Don't remind me of that," Sammi rebuked. "Besides those bib overalls hardly compare with tonight's tux."

Steele shifted his legs, turned sideways, and enfolded Sammi in his arms. Before she could say she was willing, she found herself stretched out on the feather-soft cushions and squirming to get even closer to the man above her.

"Is this on your, er, list?" she whispered, offering her lips for his possession.

"Part of it," he answered against her enticing neck while one hand tenderly cupped her breast.

"Which part?" Sammi asked huskily, becoming more breathless by the moment.

"The good part!" Steele told her with a deep chuckle that warmly feathered across her skin.

"What if the waiter should come back in?" Sammi murmured between kisses.

Steele pulled a breath away, scanned her lovely face as she lay on an array of vivid, jewel-colored satin pillows, and told her in a deep voice, "If the waiter intrudes, he'll have to get his own girl. You're my lady, Sam."

Excitement was mirrored in Sammi's eyes as she softly laughed.

"That isn't what I meant and you know it."

Steele drew her up with him as he pulled back, nuzzled her bare shoulders, and spoke in an undertone against her scented skin.

"I don't share the things I care deeply for."

Sammi ignored the implication that Steele loved her and asked, "Were you selfish with your toys as a boy?"

"I never had any toys as a youth," he told her matter-of-factly.

This time it was Steele who changed the topic of conversation. He leaned over the table, picked up a sticky date and pistachio nut pastry heavy with syrup, and held the rich confection to her mouth.

Sammi steadied his wrist, took a bite, then guided his hand to his own mouth. Chewing the delicate dessert, she watched him place the remaining piece between his strong white teeth and thought of his words.

Margaret was right. She knew very little about the man she loved and it was time to find out more.

"Are your parents alive?"

"No," Steele told her in a monotone voice. He paused to pour each of them their third cup of mint tea.

"Were you ever or are you now married?"

Sammi accepted the cup of dark aromatic liquid, unconsciously holding her breath while waiting for him to answer.

"No to both," Steele answered, ending her sudden interrogation with surprising abruptness. He rarely thought of his past, and tonight his sole interest was entertaining the woman he loved.

Sammi watched through lowered lashes as he sipped the strong-tasting hot drink. Not finished, despite his serious expression, she persisted.

"Where were you raised?"

"I wasn't."

"That's ridiculous," Sammi scoffed. "Everyone grew up somewhere."

"I grew up in the East."

Finished with his drink, Steele set the empty cup on the table, then held her glance with eyes that had the power to make her bones feel as if they were made of putty.

Before Sammi could question him further, he told her, "Only the future's important, darling, and as soon as I've settled our bill, I have plans to hold you in my arms without interruption. First vertically, then horizontally."

"That's a rather provocative statement," she stated in a low, soft voice. She gave him her hand as he assisted her to a standing position. "Explanation, please?"

Finding out everything about the man she loved would take forever, but she had plenty of time. All the rest of her life if need be.

"I'll hold you vertically on the dance floor," Steele told her. "We're going to the only dark, intimate club I know that plays music you can hold your lover to."

"I'm not your lover," Sammi corrected softly.

Steele brought her hand to his lips, kissing first the back then the palm.

"Not yet," he mouthed against her palm. "That comes during the horizontal holding I mentioned."

Sammi pulled her fingers free of his intimate exploring. She had felt the tip of his tongue circle her palm and was undecided whether to sit back down on the pillows and pull him down with her, or to reach for her purse and prepare to leave.

"Since I couldn't eat another bite of food and I love to dance, we'd better leave," Sammi suggested with a tinge of regret in her voice.

"A much safer idea," Steele agreed, holding her coat as she slipped her arms inside the sleeves. "The total privacy and soft cushions look much too enticing all of a sudden. Are you certain you want to go?"

"With that gleam in your eyes"—Sammi chuckled—"we'd better leave immediately."

"Now you're reading my thoughts." Steele laughed back.

Steele removed a wallet from his jacket and placed several bills on the tray.

Sammi watched, wishing she had the nerve to grab it from his hand. At least she could find out his home address by reading his driver's license. She stared so hard that Steele noticed and handed it across to her without saying a word.

Fingering the fine leather, she held his look for a moment, then opened it. Inside were numerous credit cards and required identification, but no photos or a single personal item. She ignored the temptation to check the amount of money, though it felt surprisingly bulky. It was either filled with lots of dollar bills or he carried more cash than she knew he had.

Hastily memorizing his address, birth date, and trying to figure out his correct age, she hoped she wouldn't forget either before she was able to write them down.

"I had guessed you were thirty-five years old," Sammi said, returning his billfold to his outstretched hand.

"I'm not." Steele smiled, unperturbed. "You subtracted wrong. I'm thirty-four."

"As you found out earlier, math is my worst subject," she reminded him.

Taking Sammi's arm, he swept the drapes aside, thanked their waiter and the host for a delicious meal, and escorted her outside.

"Come on, sweetheart," Steele encouraged as he hailed the valet with an upraised hand and waited impatiently for the man to bring up the Lincoln.

"Why the hurry?" Sammi asked when the gleaming automobile was parked before them with the door held open for her to get in. She scooted across the seat, arranged her coat, and watched as Steele prepared to start the car.

"Dancing with you sounds much too enticing to prolong it any longer."

The glance he gave her brought a soft flush to each cheek. His eyes mirrored the desire to hold her close, clearly showing a rising need as exciting as hers.

Sammi lay her head on Steele's shoulder, closed her eyes, and relaxed as dreamy thoughts of the wonderful night ahead flitted in and out of her mind while he drove to their next destination.

Steele was right, she reflected in silence. This was certain to be a night she would long remember.

CHAPTER TEN

Sammi held her chin up with haughty insouciance. She was filled with satisfaction knowing she, not his other dates, was the woman holding on to Steele's arm as they entered the darkened club resounding with music from a different era.

After he returned from checking her coat, they were shown with obvious deference to a center booth.

Steele was filled with pride and mounting jealousy when every man's eyes in the shadowed room did a double take as they scanned Sammi's eye-catching beauty and tall, voluptuous figure.

"You always seem to get the best tables," Sammi pointed out as she sat down gracefully.

"The host is a friend of mine," Steele said matter-of-factly, scooting in to sit beside her.

Not knowing if Steele was teasing or not, Sammi ignored his comment, settled her hips comfortably on the plush velour, and looked around. The music was soft and romantic. It perfectly expressed her heightened mood.

Steele motioned for the waiter who was waiting attentively in the background.

"My lady would like a pina colada and I'd like a scotch and soda, please." He turned his head to ask, "Is that right, darling?"

"That's fine, Steele."

Sammi's voice was barely above a whisper, she was so awed by the way he referred to her as his lady, followed by the huskily worded endearment, darling.

She made no protest when he reached for her hand, placed it on the tabletop, and slowly stroked it with his index finger.

"Where's your ring, Sam?" His short clipped nail touched the bare third finger of her left hand which a wedding ring would encircle.

"In the motel room." Her lashes rose, no longer shadowing the emotions that were expressed with shimmering beauty. "It didn't seem proper to wear it on my finger since it looks so much like a wedding ring."

"It is a wedding ring," Steele informed her. "Your wedding ring, Sam."

"That's, er, that's ridiculous," Sammi stammered. "We're neither one married and certainly not to each other."

"We might as well be," Steele told her with arrogant assurance. "The inscription—You're Forever Mine—means just what it says."

"You're incredible," Sammi murmured beneath her breath.

"No, Sam," Steele argued. "I'm merely a man determined to have what he wants and I want you."

She was relieved that the waiter interrupted with their drinks. The topic of conversation was suddenly becoming too confusing. Did he always talk in riddles where her future was concerned? Imagine asking about a wedding ring but failing to mention either a ceremony or a license.

Pulling her fingers free of Steele's hold, Sammi reached for the pineapple slice adorning the top of her drink, took a bite, and offered him the rest.

"You're learning." Steele laughed as he took the fruit into his mouth. "Of course I should have had the first taste, not you."

"You're lucky I shared any with you at all." Sammi chuckled, sipping the delicious drink slowly.

She watched the dancers swaying together on the crowded floor as the band played nostalgic songs of the forties. Turning her face, she gave the man beside her a tender smile. He looked so breathtaking she could hardly wait to feel his arms around her.

"Drink up or leave it, honey," Steele warned her. "I'm in the mood to feel your lovely body close to mine."

"How close?" Sammi asked with a mischievous smile.

"As close as legally possible in a public room," Steele shot back.

He took the glass from her hands, placed it on the table, and stood up. His fingers reached forward, drew her up, and enfolded her within his arms before they had taken a step away from their booth.

Sammi's breath caught in her throat as she found herself cradled close to the powerful form of the man she loved. She lay her face against his chest, and for the first time admitted how much nicer it was to be dancing with a partner who was tall enough to make her feel protected and petite.

"Are you ready now, Sam?" Steele whispered the question into her ear.

"Ready for what?" Sammi returned breathlessly. If their feet hadn't been moving, what Steele was doing with his fingers and mouth would be called making love.

Circling slowly around the crowded floor, he boldly informed her, "Ready to hear my seduction-of-Sam list."

Steele splayed his fingers, letting them explore her bared back with leisurely movements that further ignited Sammi's heightened senses.

A shudder shook his shoulders as she pressed her soft breasts into his chest. Their full feminine roundness brought his body to instant arousal. It was impossible to curb his desire for the woman he had loved from the first moment she had dared try to put him in his place with her sassy, uncurbed tongue.

"I may never be ready for that," Sammi answered truthfully. There was no doubt in her mind he would express his feelings explicitly and without a bit of embarrassment.

"We've both been ready since we first touched, Sam. It's just taking you longer to admit it!"

Excitement welled in her breast, knowing their first reaction had been equally strong even if his was only trampled male pride and hers purely anger.

"Let's hear it then," Sammi suggested in a weak voice as her hands clung to his shoulders for support.

Steele nuzzled the silky curls away from her ear and whispered eloquently, "After I have the pleasure of undressing you—short though the time will be with the skimpy attire you wear—I'm going to lift you in my arms and, with my lips kissing yours, lower you to the bed."

"And—and, er, then?" Sammi asked, missing a step at the vision of being held naked in his arms.

"And then, my lovely lady, I'm going to place a reverent kiss on the pulse that beats wildly in your throat each time I touch you."

"Followed by?" Sammi asked in a stirring voice.

"A slow, thorough caress on the enticing pink tip of each lush breast and one in the delectable hollow of your navel."

"And, then what?" His plans for seduction were clearly visible in her mind.

"And then at an even more leisurely pace I'll bury my lips in the silken, hair-covered guardian of your heavenly femininity . . ."

"Shush!" Sammi demanded, burrowing her face against the smooth material of Steele's jacket.

She could feel heat color her cheeks at the fear that someone might have overheard his blatant declarations. No man had ever seen her unclothed, yet Steele boldly declared he was going to place a passionate kiss where her thighs joined. And to top it all off, was going to do so without haste.

"Shush, hell!" he complained against the sensitive skin below her ear. "I've hardly begun. After that I'll—"

Sammi pulled back, interrupting his next declaration. She met the shimmering boldness of his darkened eyes with stern censorship and frowned.

"I think your seduction-of-Sam list has come to an abrupt end for the night!"

"Why, Sam?" Steele questioned. He placed both hands behind her waist and clasped them together as she leaned back.

"You're not innocent to the ways of making love," he reminded her in a soft-spoken voice. She was unbelievably beautiful as she tried to match his taunting words with ones equally provocative.

"No, er . . ." Sammi faltered.

She avoided his keen, penetrating gaze by staring at his mouth. Surely that wasn't a twitch at the right corner? No man would be amused while his mind was consumed with thoughts of enticing a woman into his bed.

"No, er, what?" Steele prompted.

"No, meaning of course I'm not," she insisted with an audible crack in her voice.

"I thought it only fair I warn you ahead of time what to expect when I'm the honored recipient of your beautiful body."

"I prefer that you surprise me," Sammi blurted out, unable to think of anything else to say. His talk was putting images in her mind that were hard to blot out—images so potent her stomach quivered and both knees threatened to buckle if he didn't change the subject.

Steele ran his hand beneath the shimmering weight of her hair, held her nape tenderly until she was forced to look up, then placed his lips over hers in a gentle kiss. His feet stopped moving automatically as he deepened the caress until a dancer intruded by bumping against his back.

Sammi clung to his shoulders, not caring that they were in the middle of the dance floor. The man's kisses had always had the ability to blot out the entire world from the moment of first contact.

"Back to the table, Sam, or you'll be arrested for disturbing the peace," Steele warned. He glanced down at her with a rapt gaze. "Mine to be exact."

"I'll be arrested!" Sammi exclaimed as they walked to their table. "You're the suspect. I'm just a helpless victim."

"Helpless victim!" Steele chuckled in a deep voice. "The way you responded, Sam," he told her as they sat down, "I'd say kissing you is a victimless crime."

Sammi glared, refused to admit he was right, and asked, "I'll have another drink now, please."

"You're changing the subject again, honey." Steele smiled indulgently. He motioned for the waiter, ordered a bottle of Dom Pérignon champagne, and looked at Sammi curiously when he felt her foot nudge his ankle beneath the table.

"What's the matter, Sam?" One eyebrow rose in question as he reached out to hold her fingers.

"The champagne," Sammi whispered into his ear so the waiter wouldn't overhear.

"Dom Pérignon is excellent," Steele mouthed back.

"I know and it's also very expensive."

Steele smiled, assuring her with amused tolerance, "This is a special night and I intend you to have only the best." Did she really believe he couldn't afford to buy her anything she wanted?

Sammi leaned into his shoulder affectionately after he motioned for the waiter to proceed with his order. She wasn't going to protest after hearing that he thought their night noteworthy, even if she had to pay for part of the tab.

"You're a perfect escort, Steele, and since I'm thirsty, I won't argue with your choice of drink at all."

"Good. Now maybe we can continue with my former conversation." He gave her a meaningful look.

"As I recall it had something to do with which one of us was the victim and which the suspect." She smiled.

Sammi knew darn well he had been about to comment on her unease when he expressed his future intentions too bluntly. Did he like to see her blush?

"I was about to mention that I never thought you'd be bashful about our going to bed together."

Steele waited for what seemed a long time as she pondered how to answer. "Especially since you're a sexually liberated woman," he couldn't help but add.

"Actually," Sammi answered softly, while first contemplating the fine linen of their tablecloth then the brass lantern with its flickering candle. "I'm probably not quite as experienced as you think."

"Really?" Steele asked in an innocent voice that belied the fact that he knew she was a virgin "How many men have you, er, made out with, Sam?"

"Not too many, as a matter of fact," she told him.

Avoiding his eyes, she desperately wished the waiter would hurry up with the champagne. Her throat was suddenly dry and she needed something to do with her hands other than pleating the material of her skirt over and over.

"More than a dozen?" Steele persisted, though barely able to hold back his continued amusement at her evasive words.

"No."

"Less than six?"

"You're getting closer," Sammi muttered beneath her breath. "Oh, look, Steele. Isn't that a lovely silver ice bucket our champagne is arriving in."

"One of the loveliest I've seen." He laughed, ignoring her deep censurious frown as she watched to see if he was serious or simply making fun of her awkward attempt to avoid a direct answer to his personal questions.

Steele checked his watch, smiled at Sammi's anxious expression, and gently stated, "When we're through drinking our champagne, we'll dance another thirty minutes or so, and then it will be time to leave for more . . . serious entertainment."

"That's fine," Sammi enthused with mounting trepidation.

It would take an hour to finish their drinks if she deliberately dawdled and another half hour dancing. That should give her plenty of time to prepare herself mentally for losing her virginity. Physically she had been ready since his first kiss.

Sammi's heavily lashed eyes roved over Steele's appealing features and her voice lowered in a soft, throaty confession.

"I enjoyed our meal and don't think I've ever felt so pampered in my life as when you insisted on hand feeding me the cinnamon-seasoned meat in pastry."

"That's how it should always be," Steele returned.

He reached forward to clasp her hands on the tabletop. His eyes narrowed, dark as pitch in the dimly lit room, and held hers with compelling seriousness.

"You were made to be pampered by a man, Sam."

"A rich man, hopefully," Sammi joked in return.

"Would it bother you if I'm not?" Steele asked with sudden intensity. All humor left his face as he waited in silence for her answer.

"Not anymore," Sammi whispered back, totally serious.

She turned her palm up, giving his fingers an affectionate squeeze. He was far too intelligent not to realize it no longer mattered that she had expended time and energy on plans for meeting and marrying an eligible millionaire.

"When I first met you, I wouldn't have wanted a poor trucker on a bet," she admitted honestly.

Before she could take back her confession that she was hopelessly attracted to him, he elaborated further. "Not all truck drivers are poor, Sam."

"All the ones I know are," Sammi argued. "And most are out of work more often than not."

"My, er, company manages to keep hundreds of drivers working full-time year-round. Perhaps your friend's employers aren't as aggressive managers as they should be."

"Possibly so," Sammi agreed. "I'm grateful that I still have teaching credentials and a viable college degree that will allow me to share the financial burden of establishing a household if need be."

"Would you be willing to resume your former occupation if I should find myself out of work?"

"Yes," Sammi replied frankly. Her eyes went to Steele's face, which seemed curiously pleased.

"I adore you, Sam," he told her in a voice thickened with passion by her generosity.

Reaching for her hand he urged her to stand up. "I also have a sudden urge to hold you in my arms again and whisper sweet nothings in your ear until you're ready to get on with tonight's much anticipated pleasures."

Sammi swept into Steele's arms without protest. For the next half hour she was held spellbound as he tenderly seduced her by word and touch as they swayed in ever smaller circles to the rhythmic beat.

"It's time to leave, my darling," Steele murmured hoarsely into her ear.

Sammi could feel the urgency of his need flow between them as they clung together, touching intimately from breast to thigh.

"Whatever you want," Sammi returned softly. "For now and always, sweetheart."

The words came unbidden and straight from her heart. Using an endearment for the first time seemed as natural as anticipating them spending their first night together entwined in each other's arms.

Without a backward glance, Steele swept her from the dance floor and headed for the cloakroom after a brief detour to throw a handful of bills on their table.

Sammi smiled at his eager impatience, stopping him with a tug on his fingers to explain, "Excuse me a moment, please. I want to phone Aunt Margaret and freshen up in the ladies' room before we leave."

"Do you need any money for the call?" Steele asked, before reluctantly releasing her hand.

Sammi resisted the impulse to kiss him for being so thoughtful. Instead she gave him a dazzling smile and shook her head no.

"Just wait here until I return," she asked. "I'll probably be gone several minutes."

"Wild horses couldn't drag me away from this spot without you tonight." Steele chuckled in devilish sincerity.

He watched with tender amusement as she flushed at his thinly veiled meaning before disappearing around the corner on the way to the pay phones located in the plant-filled hallway.

"Aunt Margaret," Sammi greeted her aunt after reaching her on the first try. "How was the flight home?"

"Forget me, Samantha," Margaret declared forcefully. "How are you? And I do mean that in every sense of the word."

"I'm hopelessly in love," Sammi crooned into the receiver. "And still a virgin," she added with a knowing laugh before her overwrought relative could ask.

"Thank God, though the evening's still young yet. Tell me what you found out about Steele today."

"I learned he works long hours for a small amount of money driving a truck he doesn't want rusted."

"Is that all?" Margaret asked with disappointment. "What happened to your practiced conniving that would wheedle the man's entire life story out of him within hours?"

"I'm not certain," Sammi admitted truthfully. "Apparently I got sidetracked, but it's not important."

"What about your adamant intention of marrying a millionaire?"

"I changed my mind." Sammi snorted. She didn't want to be reminded of that one more time. "Now I'm willing to put up with a man gone weeks at a time while I return to teaching to help him get started and to keep me in clothes."

"I can't believe it!" Margaret exclaimed in a stunned voice.

"I don't know why not!" Sammi flared back, miffed by her relative's lack of faith. "I love Steele and he loves me and that's all that matters."

"Great!" Margaret told her niece. "When's the wedding?"

"I'll let you know," Sammi answered smugly. "Let me go now so we can get on with the honeymoon."

"Samantha!"

Sammi could hear Margaret's outraged cry as she hung up the phone and walked to the washroom. Her eyes were bright with devilment; she knew her aunt would be filled with curiosity until she heard from her niece again.

Feeling as if her entire life was perfect, Sammi rushed down the hall. She could hardly wait to give herself to the man she loved.

Stopping to wait until a group of gossiping women moved aside before she walked around the corner, Sammi picked up the distinct sound of Steele's voice as he talked to a male friend of apparent long standing.

Not intending to eavesdrop, Sammi strained to hear each comment the moment her name was mentioned. A fine rage begin to burn inside her as she listened to the revealing conversation. Her tender look changed to one of fury when the words began to make sense.

"Do you think you might have to marry Samantha?" the unseen stranger asked.

"Not until I've tried everything else first." Steele laughed. No way was he going to let Vic, or anyone else, in on his intentions before Sammi and he were firmly committed for the rest of their lives.

"Next time you see Monique and Kay thank them again for me, Vic," Steele asked. "They were great sports."

"They loved every minute of their part in your charade," Vic answered Steele candidly. "Considering you paid for their designer gowns, hairstyles, and makeup sessions plus lavish meals, I'm not surprised they volunteered their services to make your lady jealous anytime you want."

"I'd better end this act soon or I'll be in the poor house,"

Steele complained dryly. "I've spent more on seducing Samantha than all my other dates this year combined."

"You mean she's still unaware of your devious actions?" Vic asked, shaking his head in disbelief.

"My woman doesn't have a clue and I intend to make certain she never catches on to a single thing I've done."

"You'd have thought she would have at least observed three different vehicles following her forty miles from San Jose to her Lombard Street motel." Vic laughed with astonishment.

"It doesn't surprise me a bit. Samantha was so mad at me when she pulled back onto the freeway that I'm amazed she drove straight to her room without getting lost. Hell," he pointed out, "the little beauty's never once noticed the twenty-four-hour tail I've had on her since the three bird dogs told me where she was staying the first day we met."

"It still sounds like you've taken on a handful with this one, Steele."

"No problem, Vic," Steele assured his friend. "My woman's no problem at all."

"You think so, *mio amico?*" Vic refuted.

"I know so," Steele informed him firmly. "Samantha has acted just as I knew she would in almost every single thing she does."

"You're too smug, Steele," Vic warned him. "She's a female and everyone I've ever known has a trick or two up her sleeve. Your lady has plenty of spirit according to Kay and Monique. They said she was a spitfire and it wouldn't surprise me if she had a plan or two for you."

"If so, I'll thwart them as I have all the others. With my raven-haired beauty I'm in complete control and have been from the first."

Sammi gritted her teeth as she listened to Steele's prompt contradiction. She was livid. Absolutely seething to think any man, especially a redhead, could ever have the gall to think he could control her—a mature, independent, liberated woman—in any way, shape, or form. How could she ever have fallen in love with a brute like him? He was the most arrogant, despicable man she'd ever met!

"Not to change the subject, but isn't this about the time of year you take off for your annual mystery retreat?" Vic asked.

"Yes," Steele agreed in a solemn voice. "In a couple days I'll be on my way."

"Where is this place that draws you back each year?"

"No questions, Vic. It wouldn't be a mystery trip if anyone knew where I went."

"Hell, Steele, you can tell me," Vic urged. "Like our other friends, I suspect it involves women."

"No comment," Steele replied elusively.

"Now that you've met Samantha, are you still going?" Vic persisted curiously.

"It's too late to back out now," Steele replied matter-of-factly. "Samantha doesn't affect those plans anyhow."

"Does she know you're leaving her?"

"No."

"She may not like being deserted for that long now that your affair's running hot and heavy."

"I hope like hell she doesn't," Steele insisted with a deep laugh. "I want her missing me for now and ever."

"Like you will her?" Vic persisted. He was determined to find out all he could about his friend's latest romantic relationship.

"No further questions," Steele warned dryly. "I suspect this will be my last year doing it anyway."

"Hmm," Vic mused. "It sounds like you'll be busy breaking off other, er, exciting feminine interests. These yearly trips sound more intriguing all the time."

"They are," Steele told him in a thoughtful voice. "It's bad timing now, but my annual travel companions need love even more than Sam."

"What a way to go!" Vic enthused.

Steele ignored his friend's innuendo to check his watch. Surely Samantha should be finished talking to her aunt by now. He could feel his body respond with sudden urgency at the image of the evening ahead. Never a patient man, he felt as if he'd waited all his life to make love to her and wondered why she didn't return.

"When do you get back?" Vic asked, interrupting Steele's thoughts. "I'd like to set up a double date for a wild night on the town."

"My flight arrives back at twelve thirty on the afternoon of the fifteenth and my immediate plans are to hunt down Samantha." Steele laughed heartily. "It'll do the little minx good to wonder about me while I'm gone. She's much too sassy and confident of her devastating feminine power right now."

The damned arrogant beast! Sammi fumed inwardly. Various schemes ran through her mind at full speed as she prepared to make her presence known. He'd soon find out just how confident she really was. No impoverished trucker would ever get the better of her again.

"Good luck," Vic told Steele, offering his hand as they prepared to say good-bye. "I have a feeling you'll need all the help you can get and soon."

"Thanks, Vic, but keep it for yourself. As I said before, I have my lady in complete control, speaking of which, I wonder what's taking her so long?"

"You can go check while I head for the bar. It's been a long, long day and my throat's dry as a bone."

Afraid that Steele would come searching for her, Sammi forced her lips into a wide smile, unclenched her hands, and stepped forward with an angry toss of her ebony hair. She had a plan or two formed already, and the waiting to execute each would make her revenge all the sweeter.

"There you are, Sam," Steele greeted her. He watched her keenly as he held up her coat. "I've missed you, honey."

"I've missed you too, darling," Sammi crooned with false sweetness. Her stomach clenched, but this time it was caused by holding her anger in tight check and not by his stirring presence.

"Are you ready for some adult entertainment now?" Steele questioned in a teasing drawl.

"Ready, willing, and able," Sammi replied much too quickly.

Steele's eyes never left her face as she slipped into her coat and prepared to leave. Deep trouble was brewing and he knew with astute certainty that his plans for the night were going to change rapidly.

"Do you mind if we stop by my motel room before we, er, continue on with our plans?" Sammi asked in a sugar-sweet voice.

"Anything you want, my darling," Steele agreed readily. "Your every wish is my command."

"That news couldn't make me happier," Sammi blurted out quickly.

Before she could make any further comment, or form a plan to crimp his evening, to give herself the most satisfactory pleasure possible, he had swept her from the club and into the front seat of his waiting vehicle.

"To your room it is, my love," Steele told her with equal sweetness. "Any particular reason that you need to go there?"

"Yes," Sammi explained through lips that were forced into a false smile. "I have some papers to pick up."

"Papers?"

"Yes."

"That sounds serious, darling. Would you care to explain?"

"Not yet, dearest. But soon, I guarantee you. Very, very soon you'll find out why they're so important to me."

My God, Sammi groaned inwardly. How could she have been such a dupe? It was common knowledge that one's first instincts were nearly always correct. Her immediate feeling when the beast stepped down from the cab of his truck had been wrath that a red-haired yokel had been the first man to stop and offer to change her tire. Now it went beyond fury to open warfare!

Within minutes Steele had pulled to a stop before her motel room, shut off the motor, and turned sideways in the seat. His arm rose to curve around her slender shoulder. He knew without asking what papers she was going to get and had prepared his response on the silent ride over.

"Do you need my help?" Steele asked, knowing full well she didn't.

"Not this time," Sammi answered through clenched lips. It was almost impossible not to explode with the need for vengeance that had been building up inside her since she had first heard him talking to his friend Vic.

"One kiss before you get your . . . papers . . . and we continue on to my motel room to make love."

"Fine, but make it quick, dearest," Sammi urged. "I can hardly wait to be yours—body and soul—as you expressed so poetically earlier tonight."

Steele drew her into his arms tenderly, placed his mouth over her closed lips, and kissed her without letting on he had the slightest idea she wasn't as passionately responsive as normal. Vic was right. The little minx had apparently overheard their conversation and, without asking for his explanation, had drawn her own false conclusions and was determined to make him pay.

Sammi remained stiff and unyielding in his arms while trying to think of the most horrible job she'd ever done. Cleaning her bathroom! That was it. While Steele continued the caress, she pictured her hands deep in the toilet bowl scrubbing away at rusty water stains.

Aware of Sammi's subterfuge, Steele raised his face and gazed at her with eyes filled with such passion she did a double take.

"You take my breath away, darling. That was the most exciting kiss between us yet," he moaned hoarsely in a pretense of showing great excitement.

Steele forced back the urge to laugh out loud as she pulled back and scooted quickly over to storm out of the car as if he suddenly had the plague.

Sammi's hands shook so she could hardly insert the key and

enter her room. Making no pretense at politeness, she slammed the door shut.

"Damn! Damn! Damn!" she swore bitterly. How could any man, even a redhead, be so dense he couldn't tell the difference when a woman responded to his kisses or when she held herself rigid?

Gritting her teeth to stop further epithets from leaving her lips, she took her fail-safe contract out of the wastebasket, where she had flung it before their date.

"To think I felt so smug and assured the beast loved me after our afternoon together that I threw the damned thing away," Sammi blurted out to the empty room.

With a high-tempered toss of her lustrous hair, she returned to the car with a forced smile on her face as innocent and loving as the one he had given her when she rushed away. Deliberately, she moved close against him.

Putting a tight curb on her tongue, she reached with outstretched fingers to caress his taut jaw.

"I'm ready now," Sammi whispered breathlessly.

"Ready for my love, precious?" Steele questioned in a voice equally feigned.

Instead of scratching his face with nails that ached to sink into his tanned skin, she trailed them sideways until her fingers were threaded through the thick strands of red hair. How had she ever thought it a beautiful bronze? It was as vivid as her lipstick.

"I've never been more prepared for anything in my life, sweetheart," Sammi assured him, leaning forward to rest her cheek against his briefly.

"Well then, my eager little wanton, get off me and I'll floorboard this gas-eating chariot in order to hurry up our trip to ecstasy land."

Steele pushed her gently away and reached for the ignition key, wondering what she would do next.

Sammi reached for his hand, held it still, and lowered her

lashes to shadow the sapphire sparks that she knew would reveal the anger held in tight check.

"There is one other, er, small matter to take care of first," she mentioned innocently.

"What's that, Sam?" Steele asked, fully aware that the time had come for him to see her sexual contract.

Sammi withdrew to the passenger side of the front seat and handed him a worn envelope.

"Just a small condition I insist on before going to bed with my current lover."

Steele took the envelope, switched on the overhead light, and opened it. His eyes hurriedly scanned the contractual statement. He had been eager to see just what Sammi's lawyer friend had drawn up, and could hardly contain his amusement as he read it word for word.

"This is remarkable, Sam," he told her without looking up from the papers.

"I thought you'd say that," Sammi blurted out with unbridled impudence. He'd see who was in control now! "Since you have no intention of signing it, I guess our, er, little fling . . . is over."

She reached for the contract, intent on snatching it from his hands and rushing inside to the safety of her room.

"Did I say I wouldn't sign it?" Steele replied intensely as he held on to the papers with a firm grip. "I'm quite intrigued and admire your foresight in protecting yourself prior to a sexual encounter while you're still a single woman."

"You're what?" Sammi flared back, uncertain what to do next. Damn the beast anyway! Did he never do anything she expected him to?

"Give them back to me," she demanded, not caring now whether or not he knew she was mad.

Before the words had left Sammi's throat, Steele had reached inside his jacket pocket for a pen and was scrawling his signature boldly across the lines marked with an X.

The little devil needed a curb on her daring impetuosity even more than he had imagined, he thought with mounting humor.

"Are you ready now to go to my room, Sam?" he asked, resolutely holding her shocked glance as he returned the pen to his pocket. "It's getting late and I'm not a man who likes to be rushed when he's making love. The first time is especially lengthy, since we both have so many positions to try out before we find the four or five we like best."

Four or five! Sammi cried inwardly. While she fumbled for the door latch, she heard it click as Steele locked it with the electric controls on his side of the car.

"My God, you really are a pervert!" Sammi gasped, leaning against the side panel to brace herself in case he attacked. Maybe he really was as deranged as she had suspected on their first date.

"Not really," he teased. "Just a man intent on getting what he's signed his future away for."

"Well, you'll have to wait a day," Sammi returned bluntly. She had a sudden inspiration that would wreck his plans forever.

"Why the delay?" Steele questioned. "I'm an impatient lover, Sam."

"I have to run a credit check or the signed papers will be worthless." That should end his audacity. No impoverished trucker could ever qualify for her expensive demands.

"That's fine with me," Steele assured her with cool nonchalance. "I'll need one thing also."

"What?"

"A blood test and signed application for a marriage license."

"Why?"

"If you do get pregnant"—Steele hesitated as if it was a painful decision—"we'll get married immediately. A wife would be a better tax advantage than a mistress."

Steele could hardly contain his amusement at Sammi's petulant expression. It was obvious she was biting her tongue to keep from letting fly with a verbal blasting for his feigned insult.

"We'll see about that," Sammi muttered unintelligibly. One

unused marriage affidavit was only a worthless piece of paper anyway. She'd check it out later just to make certain. Damned if she was going to get married just to be some man's income-tax deduction!

While Sammi was trying to devise a way of leaving with her dignity intact, Steele stunned her even further.

"It's a good thing we're calling off our tryst tonight, Sam. I have a headache."

"You have a headache! Isn't that particular ailment a woman's most overworked excuse?" Sammi blurted out in complete shock. Steele never said or did a damned thing a normal man would do.

"The car door's unlocked now," he told her with a meaning that was perfectly clear.

Instead of her giving him the brush-off, he dared to suggest she should leave. Snatching the offensive contract from his outstretched hand, she rushed from the car without saying goodbye.

Even in that he had the last word, she thought, fumbling with her door key as his words lingered with irritating clarity.

"See you at nine o'clock tomorrow morning for our trip to the hall of records," Steele had yelled after her retreating figure.

"Also you'd better think about what I'm going to do to your sexy body when I finally get you alone, Sam! Imagine, if you dare, where I'm going to touch you with my hands, my mouth, and my tongue. In the meantime I'll plan our night from the very beginning to its, er, climactic end!"

CHAPTER ELEVEN

"Fat chance you'll ever have of getting me alone long enough to do anything to my body, you despicable red-haired lecher," Sammi flared out to the empty room.

With the need to expel the fury that had built up inside her breast like a raging volcano, she threw her purse down, dumped her evening coat on top, and drew on a full-length London Fog trench coat.

"Who ever heard of a damned man intent on seduction having a headache anyway?" Sammi swore with increasing ire over his unexpected physical withdrawal and abrupt departure.

Drawing the coat's hood over her head until each strand of hair was covered, she slipped into knee-high boots before cupping her wallet in fingers that shook.

With all the lights turned off in her room, she cautiously opened the door to peer outside. There was no redheaded man in the world sharp enough to outsmart her if she was aware of his subterfuge. Plans were forming in her mind as fast as her change of clothes, and she vowed each would leave Steele reeling with everlasting regret that he had stopped to change her tire.

Sammi carefully scrutinized the surrounding area. She had important telephone calls to make and wasn't taking any chances on her conversation being overheard. It wouldn't surprise her one bit if her room phone was bugged or the motel manager was on the take doing a little part-time detective work.

A glimmer of smug delight crossed Sammi's features as she

thought of the amount of money Steele would have to fork over for a romp in the sack that she pledged would never take place. She'd dated a private investigator once and knew they charged astronomical fees. Round-the-clock surveillance would bankrupt a trucker in no time. Especially a poor one!

Assured that no super-sleuth was lurking in the bushes, Sammi stealthily eased from the room, closed the door behind her, and without making a sound walked to the lighted phone booth by the front entrance. All was clear except for a pitiful-looking old bag lady sleeping on a nearby bench.

Sammi dialed her aunt's phone number and waited impatiently for her to answer.

"Hi, Margaret," Sammi answered the sleepy-voiced hello. "I'm sorry to wake you, but this is extremely important. I need your help desperately."

"Oh, good lord," her relative cried out. "Steele attacked you!" Not giving her niece time to correct her false assumption, she blurted out, "I warned you, Samantha. Your tempestuous ways have finally caught up with you. Where are you? Are you hurt? What happened?"

"Absolutely nothing, Margaret," Sammi interrupted. "Not tonight or any future nights as far as my sex life and that rake are concerned."

"Well then, why on earth are you calling me at this hour of the morning?" Margaret asked in a perplexed voice.

"I want you to run a credit check for me. A really thorough one that I can use to put Mr. Steele Whitfield in his place once and for all."

"Why should any woman—even you—want to get back at a man she's hopelessly in love with?" Margaret questioned between yawns. What would her niece do next?

"*Was* hopelessly in love with," Sammi contradicted in a raised voice. "Past tense as of now and always."

"Only hours ago you exalted the man," her aunt reminded in

a resigned voice. "Do you care to explain your sudden change of feeling?"

"Not in detail, but I will tell you our affair is off. Steele's been playing me for a fool. I found out about it, and now I'm going to return the favor."

Sammi turned to glance at the old woman, checking to make certain she hadn't disturbed her heavy sleep. Pleased to hear a deep, rhythmic snoring, she returned to the conversation with her aunt.

"Listen to me, Margaret," Sammi urged. "I'm checking out of here in the morning. I don't want Steele to know where I'm going, so I'll have to call you when I get settled into a downtown hotel which I guarantee will be so expensive they won't even let him in the lobby."

Sammi cupped her hand around the mouthpiece and hissed a final reminder. "In the meantime, I want you to get every bit of information possible that proves he's the poor credit risk I presumed from the first."

"Why bother if you don't intend to see Steele again?" Margaret asked sensibly.

"Why?" Sammi repeated the question. "Because the damned monster insists he's going to make love to me tomorrow night."

"You seemed as eager as he to start your, er, so-called honeymoon when you phoned earlier," her aunt reminded unnecessarily.

"Not after I eavesdropped and heard him tell a friend he's leaving right afterward for an . . . annual two-week orgy! When I handed the rogue my sex contract, hoping to cool his libido once and for all, he had the nerve to sign his signature calmly just as if he's financially able to honor the damned thing."

"Suppose he is?"

"Don't be naive, Auntie dear," Sammi exclaimed with disgust. "At thirty-four Steele's wardrobe consists of one Li'l Abner suit and a designer tux that's probably rented. He drives a borrowed company car, makes payments on his truck"—she assumed he did anyway—"and lives a credit-card existence that no doubt puts him deeper in debt each day of his profligate life."

"Maybe so, maybe not, Samantha," Margaret pointed out wearily. "As I've been warning you for years, you were destined to meet a man that wouldn't put up with all the—you know what I mean—that you've been dishing out. And believe me, niece, it's about time someone controlled your impetuosity."

"Control!" Sammi exclaimed. "I don't want ever to hear that word again. Steele had the nerve to tell a friend of his that I—do you hear me?—that I've been under his control from the very first."

"Good for Steele," her aunt said, liking the man more by the minute. "I'll see what I can come up with regarding his credit rating then wait for you to call me tomorrow evening. Good night, dear."

Sammi heard the receiver disconnect the call before she had time to say good-bye. She wasn't pleased at her aunt's good opinion of Steele, though it wasn't a surprise considering the fact that her aunt had admitted the first night she saw him that he looked as if he'd be an absolute gem in the bedroom.

With her plans in motion, Sammi phoned information, then made certain she dialed correctly. Thank gosh Carl didn't have an unlisted number. It had been nearly a decade since she'd spoken to the man.

"Carl Thompson? This is Samantha Thatcher."

"Samantha Thatcher! I can't believe it," the startled man answered. "You aren't in jail, are you? Do you need an attorney?"

"No to both," Sammi answered shortly. Even if it had been years since she'd talked with the man, it didn't seem right that he presumed she was leading a life of crime just because he had a law practice.

"I need legal advice before morning and you were the only lawyer I could think of."

"I'm flattered you remember," Carl replied clearly, despite being sound asleep when the phone rang.

"If I apply for a marriage license, am I committing an illegal act if I have no intention of going through with the ceremony?" Sammi asked in a serious voice.

"God, Samantha, only you could even think of doing something like that." Carl groaned. "Just put the poor guy down like you did to me. Either tell him to get lost, or dig out that old copy of the sex contract I drew up for you years ago. It worked for me, and it ought to work for any other male with his brains intact. Why bother getting a license anyway?"

"I don't have the time or the desire to explain," Sammi retorted. "Just tell me yes or no and then we can both go to bed and get some rest."

"No, my dear Samantha," Carl explained in a weary, resigned voice. "You can apply for all the licenses you want."

"Great! That's just what I suspected," Sammi answered enthusiastically. So far everything was working out perfectly for Steele's comedown.

"Remember," Carl called out before she could break the connection. "The minute you use just one of them you'll be as legally married as I am."

"There's not a chance in the world of me being that foolish." Sammi chuckled confidently. "Thanks, Carl, and say hello to your wife . . . whoever she is."

Sammi exited the phone booth so happy she went to the old lady and gently patted her shoulder. It was hard to believe how ugly the woman was when she glanced up to see who had disturbed her. The poor soul's bleary eyes peeked through wispy bangs of dirty gray hair under an old cloche.

"Here, honey," Sammi told her, generously placing two twenty-dollar bills in her shabby purse. "Go find yourself a safe place to sleep, eat a hearty breakfast in the morning, then go to the Salvation Army, Social Services, or the Welfare Department for assistance. It's not safe for a decent woman to be alone on the street this time of night."

Ignoring the old woman's startled expression, Sammi returned to her room without a backward glance. She had further plans to make before nine o'clock.

She was up early, had all her clothes and personal belongings packed, and was impatiently pacing the small room hours before Steele was due to arrive.

At the sound of the Lincoln braking to a stop, Sammi slipped out of the motel room and eased into his car before he could step out and open the door.

"Good morning, Sam." Steele greeted her with a smile as innocent and loving as if nothing untoward had happened the night before.

"I thought last night's dress would outshine any outfit you'd wear again, but you look equally gorgeous in your stylish white suit with the chic black accessories."

Steele's eyes were alight with appreciation as he lazily surveyed her figure. "I hope you don't mind that I have business to take care of this afternoon. Some necessary shopping before our evening tryst."

"Of course not, dearest," Sammi crooned in a voice so super-sweet it grated on her own nerves. "Though I'll miss you desperately."

It was apparent Steele had no idea she was mad or that she'd spent a restless night plotting her revenge.

"Come here, honey," Steele urged, reaching out to draw her alongside. "I want you close while I drive to the clinic for our blood tests. When they're ready we'll get our license."

Sammi couldn't believe it. Steele had been as busy making arrangements for the day as she had. "You must have been up for hours."

"Hours that I've spent counting until you're mine," Steele ground out. His voice was harsh, the words direct and totally sincere. "God, Sam, they've seemed long and lonely without you close."

"I, too, thought the night would never end," Sammi cooed. "Is your, er, headache better today."

"Funny about that," Steele answered quickly. "The discomfort left the second we parted." It was apparent the moment Samantha had slipped into his car she hadn't forgiven him for a single overheard remark.

"Maybe the pain was a subconscious reminder that you had signed an extremely binding financial contract."

"Do you think so?" Steele quizzed with humor that was well hidden. He drew his brows together and gave her a puzzled look. "I hope it doesn't affect my, er, abilities later tonight, if you, er, get my meaning."

"That would be a shame, wouldn't it?" Sammi told him blandly. "Any sexual difficulties would certainly curtail our finding which . . . four or five . . . positions we like best."

Sammi looked away. Steele was too astute not to notice by her facial expression that her words were spoken tongue in cheek.

"I've never had a problem of that kind before." Steele shook his head as if perplexed. "Quite the extreme opposite in fact."

"I don't doubt that in the least," she lied.

My God, Sammi groaned inwardly, raising both hands to her forehead in disbelief. What gall! How could any man have the nerve to brag about his excessive libido?

Sammi leaned into Steele's shoulder affectionately. She didn't want him to have the least suspicion that her mind was whirling with devious plans for his downfall.

The immediate reaction of her body to his closeness so angered her that she clenched her fingers tightly and slowly counted to one hundred. It didn't help one bit. The man's touch was magical and her traitorous feelings surged in response.

Sensing Sammi's unsuccessful efforts to curb her stimulated senses, Steele added to her discomfort by bending sideways at the first stop light and placing a tender caress on her cheek.

"Your hat's pretty cute, but the brim makes it hard for me to steal a kiss each time I want."

Sammi smiled and silently reached up to remove it from her gleaming upswept hair.

"Is this better?" she asked softly, lowering her lashes in a demure way that heightened her look of innocence.

Entranced by her loveliness, Steele's voice was husky as he whispered, "Anything that exposes more of my beautiful woman is preferable."

"Am I really your woman?" Sammi quizzed, all the time thinking how surprised he'd be when she failed to be around for their night's rendezvous.

"Need you ask, Sam?" Steele asked huskily. His quick glance was filled with rising excitement. "I thought I'd made it abundantly clear from the very first you were forever mine."

"That's a pretty broad commitment," Sammi warned. "What if we're not physically compatible?"

"Practice makes perfect," Steele retorted boldly. "Besides, with both of us experienced and willing, how could we not be as I told you days ago—the best in bed any man and woman have ever been before?"

Sammi looked out the passenger-side window. It was hard to keep from laughing at the thought of Steele's eagerness changing to chagrin when he came to pick her up and found an empty room instead of a passionate partner for a night of lovemaking. He'd be livid!

Steele reached his right hand down to grip her nylon-clad knee, exposed below the hem of a straight skirt. His fingers spread, lingering in a familiar caress before moving intimately over her soft thigh.

"Don't you agree we'll attain the ultimate heights of love tonight?" Steele persisted huskily.

Sammi gave him an ardent smile and shifted her limbs. She took his hand, squeezed it once, then placed it back on the steering wheel before answering. "How could we miss?"

Damn it, she thought furiously. His touch ran over her skin like an electric current and made her want his caresses so badly she felt weak as a kitten.

"We can't, Sam," Steele taunted with bold innuendo. "When it comes to getting it on, I never miss!"

Not until now, Sammi gloated in silence as he pulled to a stop before the clinic. He'd see who was in control before this day ended. And it wouldn't be an arrogant male!

Despite her anger, she couldn't help but regret that they would never come together in the act of love. She knew there would never be another male who kindled her sensuality like Steele. It was ironic that the only man she'd found physically appealing in her entire life had to have flaming red hair!

Later that afternoon Sammi was graciously seated in Steele's Lincoln Continental. A coolness in the air reminded her that it would soon be the last time she would be with him. She'd been stunned at his foresight in seeing nothing prevented them from applying for a marriage license.

Their VDRL blood tests were rushed through in record time, a rubella-free certificate from her Southern California doctor flown special delivery to the clinic, and the legal papers signed without a hitch.

All day he'd been as attentive as any man could be. In between the necessary requirements for getting a license he'd done everything he could to act the part of a chivalrous escort.

They had strolled around Ghirardelli Square, enjoyed the colorful street acts, eaten a leisurely meal at Nick's that had brought back memories of dining there with her aunt the first day she arrived, and, walking hand in hand, watched boats with vividly colored sails make their way across the bay.

"The day's passed fast, hasn't it?" Steele asked, turning the corner toward her motel. "It's unfortunate I have unavoidable business that keeps me from whisking you away right now to my room."

"Time has seemed short and it is too bad, but I have preparations to make also, dearest," Sammi pointed out with false sweetness.

She was really proud of herself. In only one day's time she had become an accomplished actress. Steele was completely duped, and she had enjoyed every minute of letting him think she was as anxious for their evening to begin as he was.

"God, Sam, I can hardly wait to feel you beneath me," he ground out, interrupting her complacent thoughts. Pulling to a stop before her room, he continued, "I feel more excited than I did the first time I made love. Is it the same with you?"

"Of course," Sammi returned softly, giving him her most practiced smile. Her lashes fluttered as she reached up a hand to stroke his cheek briefly.

"I'm glad, Sam. A man likes to think he's the best even if he isn't the first."

"I thought he might," Sammi agreed with feigned innocence. "Especially you. It's too bad then that I really don't remember my . . . initial experience . . . all that clearly, but it was a long time ago. I'll have to use my last partner for comparison, I guess."

She couldn't help but add that final mischievous taunt in hopes it would dampen his ego or at least give him something to wonder about.

"One of the . . . less than six?" Steele shot back in an equally devilish reminder.

Gathering her hat and purse, Sammi prepared to get out of the car. There was no need to parry words with Steele any longer. No matter what she said the man always had a comeback to match hers.

Her body stiffened, braced for his parting kiss. All afternoon he seemed unable to keep his hands from touching her at every opportunity. Only a woman with a strong personality or shrewd plans could have resisted such seductive actions. *Thank God, she had both!*

"Tonight I intend to stop the clock," Steele announced passionately. Ignoring her unyielding figure, he cupped her chin in one hand and continued in a husky drawl that ran along her spine like a soft caress.

"With your limbs wrapped around my hips and my body finally inside you, I'll stop time forever if possible."

Sammi's eyes widened at his blunt declaration, then were held by the rapid darkening of his pupils. She couldn't look away, whether drawn by the force of his warm, compelling glance or the strength of his fingers on her face she wasn't sure.

"Why don't you take a nap until it's time for me to pick you up this evening? I guarantee you won't get a wink of sleep tonight," Steele advised. He'd never forget her sudden wariness at his comment. It made him feel tender and protective at the same time.

"I, er, I won't?" Sammi asked in a breathless whisper. Surely even Steele couldn't last all night! One thing for certain, she'd never find out.

Her plans included spending the evening ensconced in a plush room watching TV alone while her would-be lover paced the floor or took cold showers nonstop until his blood had cooled enough to let him sleep.

"Not a wink," Steele warned, still holding her apprehensive glance with dark hazel eyes that narrowed dangerously. "By ten o'clock tonight you'll be mine in the fullest sense of the word."

Sammi gave a moan of disgust, scooted out of his car without saying good-bye, and rushed into her room. He could take his warning and stuff it.

"Steele down and none to go." She laughed miserably. Her entire San Francisco trip was fast turning into a bummer.

Long before sunset Sammi was registered in the city's most renowned hotel, had eaten a light dinner, taken a leisurely bath in a marble tub, and was dialing her aunt's number for the fourth time.

"At last," Sammi complained when Margaret answered. "I've

been trying to get you all evening. What did you find out about the beast?"

"Are you sitting down, Samantha?"

"Smack in the middle of a plush bed centered before a view window on the twenty-fifth floor of the most gorgeous hotel you ever saw. Why?"

"Because, my silly little niece, you blew it this time," Margaret informed her seriously.

"How?" Sammi asked. Her brows drew together in a deep frown. "All I did was ask you to check the credit rating of an indigent trucker."

"Indigent trucker!" her aunt exclaimed. "Steele Whitfield happens to be listed in Dun and Bradstreet, is the sole owner of Whitfield Interstate Trucking Company—a name that we were both foolish not to recognize—and has unlimited credit and assets that make John, Benny, and Alan's wealth combined seem minuscule!"

"I don't believe it!" Sammi gasped. "It's just not conceivable Steele's loaded. He can't be!"

If Sammi hadn't been sitting down, she would have collapsed she was so shocked. Her fingers were white as they gripped the receiver to her ear. It was totally impossible. Margaret must have meant some other Steele Whitfield.

"Are you certain? Absolutely, irrevocably, completely certain?" Sammi asked in a weak voice.

"When it comes to finances I don't make mistakes," Margaret reprimanded her niece. "As I said before, honey, you just ran away from the kind of wealth you've been searching for for the last ten years."

"Damn him!" Sammi swore, not the least perturbed she had let a millionaire slip through her fingers. She was still furious that he dared brag she had always been under his control. What bothered her even more was meekly offering to return to teaching to help him financially.

"Do you know, Margaret?" Sammi fumed. "I actually told the

devious monster he shouldn't spend so much money on champagne for me last night."

She could hear her aunt's laughter and wasn't the least bit entertained by it.

"According to a man I talked to who knows him personally, Steele has a gorgeous home and—"

"More likely a single pad with hot and cold running women," Sammi interrupted scornfully.

"Do I detect a note of jealousy?" Margaret quizzed.

"Not a note but an entire symphony," Sammi admitted with unexpected honesty. The thought of Steele with any woman other than herself still had the power to arouse uncontrollable possessiveness.

"Too bad, honey," Margaret offered sympathetically. "I was also informed Steele has no desire to take on a permanent female partner to share any of the aforementioned with."

"That's not surprising either, since he's so fond of playing games," Sammi flared back before several moments of silent introspection.

"Now what?" Margaret asked curiously. It was the first time she'd ever heard Sammi at a loss for words.

"Now what, what?" Sammi quizzed back.

"You have a signed contract from a man intent on possessing your body tonight, and that same man is clearly able to afford every ridiculous demand on your self-composed virginity protector," Margaret told her, adding bluntly, "I have a very definite feeling that your sex pact will soon be a sex act, Samantha Thatcher!"

"Think again, my dear aunt," Sammi bragged. "I've outsmarted the man from the moment I discovered he liked to play games. No one—not even you—knows what hotel I'm registered at, what room I'm staying in, or how I got my belongings here unseen."

"I thought you said last night that Steele had a private investigator following you around the clock?"

"I did," Sammi admitted. "My ex-boyfriend who was a detective gave me a few hints that would put James Bond to shame. I used a few of his ideas this afternoon, and here I am safe and sound, away from Steele's paid-for advances, and ready to enjoy my solitude. Tomorrow morning I'm checking out and returning to Burbank to book passage on a swinging singles' ocean cruise. They're supposed to be loaded with an equal number of wealthy old men and poor young studs. Right now I can't decide which sounds best!"

Sammi could hear Margaret scream, "Samantha!" as she hung up the phone. The last thing she needed was another lecture from her prudish relative.

Before she had time to let the thought that Steele was actually an excessively prosperous business executive sink into her mind, she was disturbed by the phone ringing.

She picked up the receiver, prepared to see what the office wanted. No one else in the world knew she was a registered guest in their plush establishment.

"Hello," Sammi answered in a bored voice. She hated to miss the start of the movie she had picked to be her evening's entertainment.

"Sam?"

Both hands gripped the telephone, or it would have fallen to her lap. It was impossible! If she hadn't recognized his umistakably amused voice, she would have thought she'd lost her mind. This just proved what she'd always suspected. The man was psychic!

Not bothering to ask how Steele had found her, Sammi answered in a voice that trembled as much her body, "W-what do y-you want?"

"You, Sam."

Feeling secure despite knowing the fact that he knew her room number, she retorted in a tone as sharp as her temper, "Tough!"

"Don't hang up," Steele ordered abruptly, boding ill for her if she disobeyed. "You have exactly a half hour left before I start making love to you."

"That's what you think, Red!"

This time Sammi was prepared. She had thoroughly checked the hall. There was no pay phone on the entire floor and her door had a dead-bolt lock along with a protective latch chain. His sexual threats were nothing but a bluff.

"I forewarned you that nothing would stop me when I decided to possess you," Steele insisted with icy calm. "Your time has run out, Sam. You have precisely thirty minutes left to countdown." He paused to add, "In the meantime you'll hear a knock on the door every five minutes. The first will be now."

Sammi's brows drew together in a puzzled frown. She couldn't believe it. At the exact moment Steele spoke, she heard a hard pounding on her door. Without saying good-bye, she hung up the phone and walked forward.

"Who is it?" she asked cautiously.

"Room service," replied a kindly voice that could never be Steele's no matter how good he was at mimicry.

Sammi opened the door, left the chain latched, and peered around the edge. Facing her without expression was a uniformed old gentleman holding a silver ice bucket cradling the biggest bottle of Dom Pérignon champagne she had ever seen.

Following on his heels was another hotel employee pushing a serving cart literally covered with serving dishes of hot and cold hors d'oeuvres.

With a nonchalant shrug Sammi slipped the chain and let the men enter. She still had the desire to bankrupt the beast. Because of his wealth it would just take longer, and this was an excellent start.

"Good heavens!" she exclaimed out loud, eyeing an iced dish of caviar plus savory appetizers that were the most delicious-looking she had ever seen. "These look delectable."

"They are," the two men agreed in unison.

"Thank you," Sammi enthused as one placed the posh bucket

in its three-legged stand beside a circular table set before her window and the other wheeled the serving cart alongside.

Inspecting the sparkling white wine's label while deciding whether to open it now or later, she heard the phone ring for the second time.

Chewing a flaky puff pastry filled with tiny bay shrimp, Sammi anxiously answered Steele's second call. Little did he know she was aware there were no phones in the hall. All she had to do was check who was outside her door, accept any additional gifts forthcoming, then make certain she bolted it securely each time the hotel clerk left.

"Sam." Steele spoke before she could say hello. "You have twenty-five minutes and five presents left. Go see what I have for you now."

"Fine with me," she sassed back. "By the way, the hors d'oeuvres are scrumptious. Too bad you won't get any."

Sammi chuckled impudently as she heard Steele hang up at the same moment there was a knock on her door.

Feeling totally safe, she asked for identification, received it, and accepted a small package curiously from the outstretched hand.

Wrapping paper and ribbon fell to the floor in her eagerness to check her latest gift. She gasped with pleasure when she saw a hand-blown glass vial filled with Joy perfume inside. A generous dab from the hurriedly opened jar was applied to each pulse point of her freshly bathed body.

"Twenty minutes now, Sam," Steele pointed out in a composed voice that equaled Sammi's mood when he rang the third time.

"Time does fly when you're having fun," she interrupted saucily. "I adore expensive French perfumes. Unfortunately you'll never get a whiff of its heady fragrance."

"I will and soon!" Steele growled back. He couldn't believe her confidence.

"What are you sending me next?" That should prove she was

unconcerned about his repeated threats to make love to her within the next few minutes.

"You'll see, you sassy little minx."

Waiting by the door, Sammi went through her safety routine again, then opened the door. This time she was overcome with the fragrance of two dozen roses that were the deepest velvety wine color she'd ever seen, plus a five-pound foil-wrapped box of Lindt chocolates she knew cost twenty-four dollars per pound.

Accepting the boxes, she placed them on the bed. She removed the flowers from the tissue paper, took one perfect bud and held it close to her face with a feeling of awe.

Sammi lifted the receiver up before the phone had stopped ringing and exclaimed exuberantly, "The roses are gorgeous! Thank you, Steele, for them and the luscious, decadently rich chocolates."

"You're welcome, Sam. In case you've forgotten, the countdown is now fifteen minutes."

Sammi lay the rose on the table and walked to the door. She loved receiving presents as well as giving them, and this was better than any Christmas would ever be. Anxious to see Steele's next gift, she was waiting with the door pulled aside when the hotel clerk returned with a box from Neiman-Marcus.

Sammi tore off the ribbon, eager to see what was enclosed. The box barely weighed a thing, and she was clumsy in her haste to view her first gift from the prestigious store.

A nightgown and peignoir of such delicate beauty were inside that she stood a moment just staring at them. Packaged separately were dainty slippers with high heels and puffs of silk over the toes.

With trembling fingers she let the ivory silk glide over her fingers then walked into the bathroom. In seconds she was preening before the full-length mirror in a slip-style gown whose lace bodice clung to her breasts in revealing splendor and hugged her hips like a second skin before draping her slipper-clad feet in soft folds.

"I can hardly wait to see you in it, Sam," Steele told her as she lifted the receiver for his next call.

"Too bad you won't," Sammi teased boldly.

"Ten minutes now, love," Steele reminded her unnecessarily. "Time's running out for you, Sam."

"That's what you think, Mr. Whitfield," Sammi said with deliberate emphasis. Steele should be learning rapidly that no man in the world could control her unless she wanted him to.

Sammi slammed the receiver down and returned to the bathroom to pose in front of the mirror in her gown and its matching peignoir, trimmed in ruffles and lace that made her feel all soft and feminine and, unfortunately, extremely affectionate too.

"Damn you, Red!"

If they hadn't been fighting, she just might be receptive enough to give him everything he sought in return for his unexpected generosity. Instead she accepted each gift greedily, hoping it would put him well on the road to financial bankruptcy.

This time Sammi was handed a slender box from Cartier. She held it to her breast a moment before opening it to expose a necklace that shimmered with the exquisite glimmer of a sapphire and diamond pendant on a fine gold chain. Sammi had never seen anything more delicate or beautiful in her life.

"Put it on, Sam," Steele told her when she answered his ring. "I want to imagine it around your lovely neck before I have the pleasure of removing it when we make love."

"Imagine our making love too, Mr. Whitfield!" Sammi chuckled mischievously. "Because that's the closest you'll ever get to fooling around with me."

Sammi hung up the phone just as Steele reminded her the time was near for him to claim his reward. She swore she could hear his "Five minutes is all that's left, Sam" long after she replaced the receiver.

Feeling like a queen Sammi sauntered to the door with head held high to receive her last gift. She had never looked more glamorous in her life.

Accepting a mammoth-sized ribbon-bedecked gold box, she thanked the man effusively. After a furtive glance right and left down the hall she shut the door behind him, replaced the chain, turned the dead bolt, pushed in the lock on the knob, and walked confidently to the bed.

Holding her breath, she tore off the ribbon. Tears filled the corners of her eyes when she lifted the lid back to reveal a pearl-gray chinchilla coat. With trembling fingers she removed the full-length fur, held it out for a quick peek, then found it an irresistible temptation.

With Steele's timetable erased from her mind by the shock of receiving such gorgeous clothes Sammi slipped out of her peignoir and pulled the satin-lined fur over her arms. It was a perfect fit, and the softest thing to touch her skin in her life.

Oblivious to anything but the pleasure of her exquisite gifts, she raised the capelike collar around her face and paraded around the room like a haute couture model until the phone's ringing disturbed her fantasy.

"Your time is up, Sam," Steele pointed out in a voice whose seriousness jarred her mind back to his explicit timetable.

"If you want a woman tonight, Mr. Steele Whitfield, renowned owner of the Whitfield Interstate Trucking Company," Sammi told him in an angelic feminine voice that quickly changed to one of anger, "you'll have to call Kay or Monique. I hear—rather overheard—they'll both be glad to oblige you anytime you want!"

"Ten . . . nine . . ." He started the countdown.

Sammi slammed the receiver down, breaking off Steele's ridiculous countdown. A smile raised the corner of her glossy mouth at the thought of finally getting the best of a red-haired man.

She walked over to the ice bucket. It was time to start the party. A party for one, but nonetheless sweeter because of it.

Struggling with the cork, she finally managed to remove it with a resounding pop. As the foamy liquid spilled over the top, she concentrated on pouring a glass to the brim, not caring if she wasted it or not. There was no need to conserve anything tonight.

Entranced by the brightly lighted view beyond her window, Sammi stared at the prominent arches of the Golden Gate Bridge shimmering in the distance. She had never felt so smug in her life.

Was it the heady scent of imported perfume, the feel of silk whispering over her skin, the satin-lined lustrous fur, or the weight of expensive jewelry around her throat? Undoubtedly it was all four, she thought with a confident smile.

She pushed the bottle of champagne deep into the crushed ice, raised her glass, and broke the silence of her room with a toast.

"To me, Samantha Thatcher." She stopped speaking to take a slow delicious sip that tickled her nose, then continued, "And the downfall of the arrogant Mr. Whitfield."

CHAPTER TWELVE

"Better pour another glass, Sam," Steele's firm voice interrupted. "My toast will be to the final, inevitable capitulation of that same Mr. Whitfield's new mistress!"

"How'd you get in here?" Sammi cried out, spinning around with the glass still held upright in her hand. She stared across the room in stunned disbelief.

"From my adjoining room." Steele indicated it, pausing with feet widespread in the opened doorway.

Sammi stared in silence as he calmly waited to see how she would react. She hadn't paid the least attention to that door, presuming it was nothing more than an extra closet. How could he have possibly found her?

The shock of seeing Steele was overshadowed by the instant realization that he was wearing nothing other than a short velour robe loosely tied around his narrow waist.

Her eyes widened as they slowly traveled over both bare feet, across bony ankles, and up sinewy muscled calves covered with dark hair. She hurriedly skimmed the rest of his powerful body to linger on his unyielding aristocratic face with its strong chin raised as impertinently as hers had ever been.

"Eight . . . seven . . ." Steele continued in her presence.

Sammi looked right and left, still holding the wineglass before her, while foolishly wishing there was a quick escape route or that somehow she could vanish in thin air.

"W-would you like something with your drink?" Sammi whispered in a shaken voice.

"Yes I would, Sam, and you damned well know what it is. Six . . . five . . ." he enumerated backward.

"Something to eat, I meant," Sammi countered, nervously turning her back to him as she desperately tried to think of something to block his intent.

"You'll do fine tonight in satisfying all my hungers. Four . . . three . . ." he resumed counting.

Steele moved forward, not the least surprised that Sammi spun around and moved backward step for step.

"There's no escape this time, Sam. I've warned you, I've signed for you and I've damned well paid for you, so let's quit skirting the bed and get into it."

"Why don't you leave me alone and start your"—Sammi stopped to place an emphasis on the next few words, a mutinous expression in her frosty glance—"annual two-week orgy a day or so early!"

"Orgy?" Steele spoke aghast. "My God but you drew erroneous conclusions from your eavesdropping. Next year instead of stopping my excursions I'll take you with me. I know you'd be welcomed joyously."

"Next year I'll undoubtedly be married to a normal man," Sammi informed him in a haughty voice.

"Of course you will," Steele agreed. "Now get the hell over here. You're wasting time much better spent between the sheets."

Sammi faced Steele undaunted. Her eyes widened as she hesitated, hopelessly wishing she could come up with a sensible reason that he should withdraw as suddenly as he arrived. She knew if he stayed much longer she'd weaken and go to him on any terms. A sensual current flowed between them that was too powerful to ignore.

"Won't it bother you that you're not the first man to have

me?" Sammi asked, vainly hoping that might make him change his mind. Her pulse was beating so fast she could hardly think.

"Being first isn't the most important thing in the world to me, Sam," Steele told her in explicit tones that shortened her hopes of getting out of the night unscathed. "But being last is!"

"What if I told you that you would be the first? That I'm a virgin. A totally inexperienced one to boot!"

"Are there any other kind?" Steele teased with deep amusement at the constant challenge of her quick tongue.

"Of course!" Sammi shot back, trying unsuccessfully to curtail his ready humor. "Some women are technical virgins only. If you were a true gentleman, my innocence would make a difference."

"It does, Sam," Steele assured her in a voice thickened with desire. "My God, how much it does."

By the fiery warmth of his eyes traveling over her body, she knew he put a different meaning on her words altogether. Nothing would stop the man tonight.

"Being both first and last to worship your precious body will be the ultimate treasure to me."

Stopping within arm's reach, Steele smiled. He had never seen a more beautiful woman in his life. Sammi's raven-black hair glistened in curly disarray around her shoulders. It was a vivid contrast to the pale gray fur that covered the soft, feminine curves he would soon know as intimately as the harsher planes of his own body.

"I love you, honey. I always have and I always will. Now quit all this foolishness and get over here."

"I—I won't!" Sammi defied him though her knees were quivering as much as her stomach. She had waited so long to hear him declare he loved her.

"Come here, Sam!" Steele persisted. "Step into my arms of your own free will and let me make love to you until we're both mindless with the wonder of it all."

Tears blurred Sammi's eyes as her fierce pride warred with the stirring desire that coursed through her body like a raging torrent.

"Two . . . one!" Steele warned with eloquent conviction. "Time's up, sweetheart."

He stared into her dramatic eyes, which poignantly revealed her inner turmoil. She was proud, aggravatingly independent, and totally determined to prove no man, especially him, could force his will on her.

Sammi hesitated briefly, raised her chin to defy him, then placed the glass on the table so fast it toppled over.

"Come to me, darling," Steele urged. "My countdown's over at last."

His eyes softened, filled with tender concern, as he surveyed her vacillating expression. Opening his arms wide, he admonished softly, "Move it quick, Sam. I'm a very anxious man when it comes to making love to the only woman I've ever adored."

At the same time Steele stepped forward to meet her halfway, Sammi gave a cry of delight and lunged into his outstretched arms.

With her heart beating wildly, she burrowed her face into the vee opening of his robe and scolded, "It's about time you lowered your arrogant chin and came after me. I was getting damned tired of standing in one position so long!"

Steele raised her chin with gentle fingers, looked into her twinkling eyes, and laughed, "My God, woman, how you do try a man's patience."

Pulling back, Sammi lowered her eyes to stare at the exposed portion of his naked chest, then looked up to meet his glance with an impish smile.

"You, Mr. Steele Whitfield, have a very decidedly hirsute chest."

"A what chest?" he teased, knowing full well what she meant.

"A hairy one."

She ran her fingers through the whorls of curly hair covering his muscled breastbone.

"Aren't redheads supposed to have red hair all over their body? This"—she tugged a patch—"is dark brown."

"Who gives a damn, woman?" Steele complained. "We'll talk about the entire spectrum of colors between bouts of bedroom calisthenics if you wish."

"Impatient, aren't you?" Sammi teased, arching him a daring smile. Her index finger continued to explore the contours of his chest as she delighted in the exciting touch of his hair-roughened skin.

"If you'd push your hips a little closer to mine you'd feel just how impatient I am, you teasing little wench," Steele warned with suggestive emphasis.

He shifted his limbs, joined his hands behind her fur-clad back, and drew her forward until he could tell by the sudden flush on her cheeks that she was aware of his obvious arousal.

"Good heavens," Sammi whispered boldly. "I hadn't suspected you were . . . that . . . much in need."

Holding her still, he regarded her passionately and murmured, "Foolish woman. I've been in agony with sexual frustration from the first day we met."

Sammi gave Steele a saucy smile. All animosity between them had disappeared the moment she was in his arms. It had been that way from the first. It still seemed impossible that only one man had the power to break through the barriers of her self-imposed innocence.

"That bad, huh?" Her eyes were alight with concern.

"Worse," Steele admitted with a low moan. "But right now my feelings aren't important. My only desire is to make you smile with deep satisfaction. I ache to see the languorous, adoring look of contentment a man receives when he's given extreme sexual pleasure to the woman he loves."

"Oh, dear," Sammi replied softly. "I suppose I should have paid more attention to your seduction-of-Sam list."

"No problem there." Steele smiled with tender regard. "I

memorized every dastardly, despicable deed so I can do them backward and forward."

Sammi threw both arms around Steele's neck and lay her head against his throat in a surge of affection she couldn't contain any longer.

"I think I'm in love," she whispered against the warmth of his neck.

"Think?" Steele moaned, burying his face into the fragrant strands of silk beneath his chin. "Why don't I see what I can do to convince you it's definite, Sam?"

"Hmm, that sounds nice." Sammi spoke softly, squirming to get closer to his protective strength.

"Good," Steele agreed hoarsely. "But first we have to get rid of this expensive piece of dyed rabbit fur."

"Don't you dare insult my chinchilla coat," Sammi rebuked with an uneasy laugh.

Aware that Steele's attitude had shifted, Sammi knew the time had come to stop all bantering. It was only a temporary foil he had allowed to help put her at ease.

She stepped back the moment he released his hold to remove her coat, withdrew her arms from the wide sleeves, and watched in silence as he carelessly threw the luxurious fur over the end of her bed.

Steele turned his head to look down at Sammi, slid his arms under her back and limbs, and effortlessly lifted her weight into his arms. Cradled close to the warmth of his scantily clad form, she clung to his neck with her face resting upon his throat.

"It's time to get down to some serious loving, Sam," Steele insisted in a voice thickened with desire.

"I k-know," she murmured against the jut of his strong jaw. The impact of his words surged straight to the pit of her stomach.

Instead of carrying her to her own bed, Steele walked through the opened doorway into the most lavish suite Sammi had ever seen.

Her widened eyes surveyed the elegant furnishings with curiosity as he strode straight through another opened doorway and into a vast bedroom chamber dominated by a raised center platform.

"Oh, my gosh," Sammi blurted out, staring at a king-size four-poster bed whose spread was turned back to expose satin sheets the same vivid blue as her eyes.

"This is quite some pad, isn't it?" She had never seen a bedroom so extravagantly decorated.

"I promised you days ago that we'd consummate our love in the finest suite available," Steele murmured into her ear. "This is the hotel's best, my darling."

Sammi could feel his calloused hands trembling as he pressed her to his heaving chest. Awed by his continued thoughtfulness, she knew the time had come to confess the truth about her innocence.

Taking a deep breath, she lowered her lashes and, expelling a throaty whisper into the hollow of his strong throat, admitted, "I've never b-been with a man before, Steele. Not even once."

"Oh God, honey," he moaned into her silken hair. "Don't you know I've been aware of that from the moment we met?"

Later he would explain about overhearing every revealing statement she made to Margaret at Nick's restaurant.

"If you hadn't been virtuous, Sam, I'd have taken you home with me the first day we met."

Steele let her silk-clad feet slide to the carpet as their glances locked. With her held close to his hips, he could feel the warmth of her body through the whisper-thin material of the nightgown he had purchased that afternoon.

"You always knew?" Sammi questioned, raising her heavily lashed eyes.

"Yes." His hands lifted to cradle her upturned face. "It was obvious during our first kiss. Your passion is incomparable, but given with such sweet innocence I had many sleepless nights hoping I wasn't rushing you just to satisfy my needs."

Sammi opened her mouth to scold Steele for his many taunts about her past lovers, felt his thumbs start to move in a circular caress, and stopped. An overwhelming urge to discover the sensual pleasures she had only imagined made any teasing exchanges in the past unimportant.

Sammi's arms raised to clasp Steele's strong neck.

"Kiss me . . . please." She couldn't continue. The sudden darkening of his eyes when he heard her soft-spoken plea left her too breathless to say another word.

"God, yes, I will," Steele moaned, needing no further urging. He lowered his head to accept the gratifying pleasure of lips that had driven him wild since he had experienced their sweetness the first day they met. Passion surged between them, igniting the instant their mouths joined.

Holding his hunger in tight check, Steele toyed with her lips, nibbling his way from side to side, until her legs eased between his with unconscious sensuality.

After long, restless nights of envisioning this moment he took great care not to rush her. They had all night. Each touch was beautiful, far exceeding his imagined expectations. The prolonging of each intimacy would only add to its anticipated pleasure.

"You won't believe how often I've imagined being inside you, Sam," Steele confessed in a poignant cry. "My heartbeat goes crazy every time I think of finally climaxing between your silken limbs."

Overwhelmed by the purport of Steele's blunt words, Sammi trembled, burrowing her face against his chest. It was wonderful to hear him express his mood so profoundly.

"It's time to remove this silk barrier between my hands and your beautiful body," Steele insisted into the strands of silken hair under his chin.

He pulled back to let his eyes linger on the beauty of her voluptuous figure, watching entranced as her high breasts rose and fell, straining to escape the clinging lace gown.

"God, Sam, I can hardly wait to see you naked," Steele declared fiercely.

"Really?" She raised her face and smiled. Her answer was absurd. She was well aware the shimmer in his eyes signified heightened curiosity.

"Really!" Steele laughed back. "Now hold still," he insisted when she hugged his waist and squirmed her body side to side to get closer.

"Why?" Sammi implored, giving him a bemused look.

"Because I'm going to remove everything between us but your perfume, and I don't want to be distracted by the sight of your sexy little behind wiggling back and forth."

"Everything?" Sammi questioned softly. "Can't I keep on my new necklace?" She raised her fingers to touch it. "It feels so elegant I hate to remove it."

"Okay," Steele agreed, reaching up to replace her hand with his. He could see the tiny vein in her throat pulsate as he lifted the necklace. "I'm pleased you like this little bauble because the jeweler talked me into buying the whole damned set."

"There's more?" Sammi gasped. Would she get them?

"One or two," Steele answered with a shrug.

He leaned forward and inhaled the heady aroma of perfume. "You smell delicious, but imported scent isn't nearly as intoxicating as your natural fragrance."

Sammi drew a shuddering breath. Steele's words had caused a tremor deep in her abdomen as she imagined his flared nostrils breathing deeply of her skin as his eager mouth explored her nakedness from head to toe.

"Do you really think so?" she asked softly.

"I know so . . ." Steele assured her, letting his deep voice trail away.

His fingers moved, briefly caressed the satiny skin of her shoulders, then eased under the stretchy lace to ease the straps down. Inch by inch he leisurely exposed her rounded breasts. Bared in the golden glow of muted bedside lamps, their flawless beauty left him breathless.

"There will be no darkness in this room tonight, Sam. I need the sight of you as much as I need your touch, your taste, and your intoxicating, unforgettably imprinted fragrance."

Her eyes widened, taking in each feature of his strong face as he slowly—too slowly—slid the bodice of her gown to her waist. She could see his darkened eyes reflect the reverence flowing from gentle hands that cupped the shape of each breast in their wide palms.

"Whatever you want is fine with me," Sammi promised in a soft murmur.

"My God, woman, you don't know what you're saying," Steele gasped. "I'd shock the hell out of you if I did all the things to your body tonight that I intend to seek in the future."

Sammi's breath caught in her throat, was held, then escaped in short gasps. Steele had been seducing her with words and actions from the moment they met. As always, in his presence she was powerless to resist.

She felt her knees tremble, matching the quivering fingertips that clung to his nape for support. It was a heady feeling to know the man she loved anticipated making love to her with such obvious excitement.

Arching her back, she thrilled to the pleasure of his sun-browned fingers kneading the burgeoning flesh. A sharp moan was torn from her throat when he caressed her soft nipples into erect buds that ached for the moist warmth of his mouth.

"You're stunningly beautiful, Sam," Steele told her gruffly. "I could never have waited another day to make you mine."

Sammi couldn't speak. She could no more comment on his throaty entreaty than she could move her limbs. She felt paralyzed—rooted to the deep carpeting by the exciting touch of masculine hands that were as gentle as a child's.

"I like you with your hair hanging loose and curly around

your shoulders. It looks so damned seductive in contrast to your creamy-pink breasts."

"I'm g-glad you're pleased," Sammi stuttered. Her heart was thudding against her ribs so fast it was a wonder she could talk at all.

She voluntarily raised her smooth arms, standing motionless as Steele lifted the whisper-thin silk over her head and discarded it with a toss as careless as the one that had dispensed with her fur coat earlier.

A pensive smile raised her lips as she posed in front of him without shame. It was gratifying to know she could give such pleasure to a vigorous, experienced male. She knew he could have almost any woman he wished. She'd witnessed their covetous looks, been jealous of them, and exalted in the thought she was now the recipient of his complete attention.

Steele's keen eyes slowly surveyed her feminine contours. He swallowed to relieve a throat suddenly gone dry as he continued to scrutinize her high breasts, narrow waist that flared to rounded, womanly hips, and the long, flawless limbs that had left him breathless the moment she stepped from her car in San Jose.

Steele moaned, slipped to his knees, and bowed down with reverence before her innocent body. Without saying a word, he encircled her hips in muscular arms, pressed his face into her soft abdomen and held her close.

Sammi looked down at his glistening auburn head. She reached to touch his hair, threading her fingers through the wavy thickness. His warm breath wafting across her stomach was so erotic she was afraid her wobbly legs would collapse.

Steele turned his head to place a series of hot, intimate kisses into the silken triangle of dark hair before reluctantly ending the intense moment. Standing up, he lifted her into his arms with such tender concern she felt tears slip unbidden from the corners of her shimmering eyes.

His head lowered, the sweetness of his warm mouth unerringly taking her parted lips in a kiss that would have buckled her knees if she hadn't been cradled securely to his broad chest.

Without releasing her mouth, Steele walked up the steps of the carpeted platform and laid her reverently on satin sheets he knew were no smoother than her skin.

Sammi's eyes were vivid, barely shadowed by their heavy fringe of dark lashes as she lay still, watching inquisitively as Steele stood beside the bed.

With one nonchalant shrug he shed the loosely belted robe that had concealed his athletic physique. She surveyed his torso openly. It was impossible to take her eyes from his body. The wide muscles of his chest were partially concealed beneath whorls of thick dark hair that veed downward in a sensual pattern. They crossed his concave navel in a narrow line before thickening around the hardened form rising from his loins.

Standing with his long legs splayed comfortably and hands resting alongside his hips, Steele looked down at her expressive features. He was amused by her wide-eyed stare as she boldly surveyed his nakedness. It was apparent his woman had never seen an unclothed man in a state of arousal.

Still keeping distance between their bodies, he leaned over the bed, braced his hands on each side of her lovely face, and placed a tender kiss on her mouth.

Sammi's tongue appeared, moistening her parted lips with unconscious sensuality. Stopped by Steele's harsh groan, she placed her fingers around his neck and pulled until he raised his legs to kneel alongside her hips.

Steele shuddered with the herculean effort of not sliding between her limbs immediately and joining their bodies in a rush of passion.

"If you weren't a virgin, I'd take you with a wild urgency that's haunted my dreams each night since we met," Steele admitted in an agonized outcry.

"I think it's time to continue with your seduction-of-Sam list then," Sammi prompted, giving him a dazzling smile.

"Ready, are you?" Steele teased softly, letting his tanned fingertips stroke a tousled black curl off her forehead.

"Ready..." Sammi gasped when his mouth trailed a path over her sensitive throat, interrupting her low reply.

"Willing..." She tried to continue, stopping when his nostrils flared to inhale the fragrance of her naked body as if he wanted to retain the scent forever.

"And able," he finished for her, staring at her heavy mane of hair tumbling across the satin pillow in seductive disarray. He watched entranced as a silken curl wrapped around his outstretched index finger. It was the most sensual hair he had seen or touched.

Cupping her face, he kissed her with such hunger she wasn't cognizant of time or place. It seemed he would never release her mouth. His tongue invaded, searching until he found hers to join in a deep kiss so devastating she was forced to pull away.

"Oh, Steele," Sammi cried out, overcome by his hungry touch as emotional tears spilled from her eyes. "I never dreamed how devouring a man's unreleased passion could be." Her heavy lashes fluttered, making crescent shadows on her smooth cheeks. "Or how enjoyable—" She broke off in sudden shyness.

"God, my innocent beauty," Steele moaned against the wildly beating pulse in her throat. "You haven't experienced anything yet."

"You're wrong, darling," Sammi gasped as his burnished head lowered to her throbbing breasts. "My sexual education has continued each time we meet, and I have a distinct feeling—" She broke off to exclaim, "Oh, darling, that feels wonderful!"

"It damned well better," Steele mouthed against an enticing nipple that hardened the moment his warm mouth surrounded the rosy bud.

Sammi clasped Steele's head with both hands. Arching her back into the tantalizing wonder of his mouth, she squirmed her hips restlessly. It was unbelievable that he knew how to bring her body to the peak of excitement the first time they made love.

"Please . . . oh, please . . ." Sammi broke off, making a vain attempt to sit up as his restless mouth moved from breast to breast.

"Hush, Sam," Steele groaned, his voice thickened with desire. He would never tire of closing his mouth around her nipples to extract the alluring sweetness offered so generously. With an urgent tongue that was restless in its demand to taste, he sucked each swollen tip until he began to question his own control.

"Steele . . . oh, S-Steele," Sammi stammered, helpless to stop the soft murmurs of contentment that escaped her throat. She had never experienced anything so pleasurable in her life as his insistent mouth giving ardent attention to her breasts.

"Don't speak, Sam," he ground out, trailing his tongue from the plump underside of her breast to the velvety skin surrounding her indented navel.

"Just relax, enjoy, and let me show you what loving's all about."

Sammi fell back, cradled luxuriously on top of the deep mattress, and let out a sigh that closely resembled a deeply contented purr as Steele's skilled ministrations continued with lazy thoroughness lower . . . ever lower.

His experienced touch left her breathless, her bones so weak they felt liquefied. Wanting to be intimate with the man she loved was the most natural, the most urgent, thing in her world.

There wasn't an area he didn't touch, playing her body like a fine instrument. Her head moved restlessly as his long fingers stroked her sensitive skin with extreme gentleness. His surging mouth was insistent as were his tongue and teeth in their passionate exploration.

She accepted his hands, moving luxuriously on the satin sheets as he investigated each curve and hollow over and over. He continued, up and down her limbs, across her breasts, around her waist, but always returned to linger on her most feminine part.

With gentle, persuasive fingers he probed, stroking warm and sure, each time a little deeper and for a longer period of time. When she began to move against his hand, arching her hips for his possession, he paused, then slowly repeated the same erotic rhythm.

"P-Please! Steele . . . p-please." Sammi's cry broke the silence of the room as she lay writhing sensually.

Steele raised his head, smiling with satisfaction when he observed the flushed beauty of her skin and the deeply aroused shimmer of her eyes barely visible beneath the half-closed lids.

"Not yet, Sam. You're not ready yet."

"I am!" Sammi cried out, reaching with trembling fingers to pull him between her limbs. The sudden ache in her lower abdomen was clamoring to be assuaged.

"Trust me to know, darling," Steele insisted. It was a command, not a question, and spoken in such a compelling whisper Sammi couldn't have answered if he had asked.

When her pelvic muscles quivered, begging for immediate release, and she thought she couldn't stand any more, he proved her wrong. Her introduction to sexual intimacy had barely begun.

"Now we start page two of my seduction-of-Sam list," Steele moaned, lowering his head directly over the tops of her thighs.

He kneeled comfortably, cupped her bottom in his broad palms, and continued ravishing Sam as he'd patiently planned. Every kiss, each erotic caress was more exciting, more passionate than the one before.

"That's so . . . Oh, do that again! Right there! So w-wonderful," Sammi cried out.

She could feel his tongue move against her greedily. Its firm tip gave her exquisite pleasure as he repeatedly stroked the most vulnerable erogenous zone of her entire body with intense enthusiasm.

Sammi's hands clenched Steele's shoulders, leaving marks with her fingernails. Without thinking, she continuously kneaded the taut muscles over his rib cage, convinced she'd faint from the bliss of his probing touch. She couldn't get enough, yet she couldn't stand any more.

When Sammi trembled convulsively, Steele raised his face and placed a long, tender kiss on her eager mouth. He moved between her limbs, pressing forward until the throbbing hardness of his aroused body touched her.

Sweeping a damp curl aside, he whispered in her ear, "Now, my sweet love, you're ready for the final paragraph."

"Show me how, Steele," Sammi pleaded. "Tell me what to do so I can please you too."

"Wrap your legs around my hips, honey. Let me feel their silken length hug me tight."

Braced on his knees, he reached out with both hands to caress her breasts gently, delighted that she pushed up into his palms. Slowly moving his fingers to her waist, he adjusted her soft feminine form closer to his well-defined, muscular body.

Sammi watched with adoring eyes. She had never seen anything as beautiful in her life as his bronzed shoulders and wide, hair-roughened chest tapering into strong masculine hips that fit so perfectly between her upraised legs.

When she couldn't stand the torment of not being his any longer, she reached her hand boldly out to assist him in entering her throbbing body. Holding a man's aroused hardness in her fingertips for the first time caused a flood of desire to spread throughout her veins. She trembled, envisioning giving his splendid body satisfaction as zealously as he had hers.

Steele clasped her fingers in his own, moving them with regret from his pulsating manliness to his glistening shoulders.

"That's much too dangerous," he groaned harshly. "I'm pretty close to losing control, and the touch of your soft hands at this stage is more than any man could handle."

Sammi thought she'd die she wanted Steele so much. She scooted down, shifting her hips until she heard him moan and could feel for the first time the touch of a man start to enter her receptive warmth.

Slowly, taking great care not to hurt her, he eased forward until she stretched enough to accommodate his great size. When she could receive him totally, he began to make steady thrusts, deeper and deeper. He felt as if all the sensory tissue in his heated body had collected in his loins. There was no magic in the world that could ever compare with being inside Sammi.

Tears slipped unnoticed from Sammi's eyes as she arched into the driving motions that continued on and on until all her nerve endings screamed out for relief.

"Oh, Sam," Steele rasped painfully. "You're so tight I can't last much longer."

"Steele... Steeeeele..." Sammi returned with equal yearning. "I love y-you." The throaty plea to release her from the unbearable ecstasy of his lovemaking was answered with a final, shuddering thrust.

Tremors shook her body when he drew her tight against his chest, mastering her mouth as he had her body. The mystical spell of his possession left her gasping and spent. Too overcome to move, they lay entwined. With tender fingers she cradled the burnished copper head that was still buried close to her neck.

"I love you, Sam." Steele's words brushed her ear. "Climaxing inside you is all the love I ever wanted, and knowing you are forever mine all the heaven I'll need."

Steele drew back, still embracing Sammi's body close. He was filled with power, knowing he had brought her the first fulfillment of her life. Her virginity was a precious gift, and one he never expected to receive. Offered with uninhibited passion from the only woman he had ever loved, it was a cherished reward beyond compare.

Steele rolled over, drew her onto his shoulder, and after long moments of bliss, asked in a devilish voice, "How'd I do, Sam?"

Sammi tossed her hair back, gave him a disconcerted glance, and complained, "Aren't men supposed to fall asleep right after sex?"

Steele pressed a kiss on her forehead while lazily stroking her arm. "Old men maybe, or ones with frigid women." His voice was arrogant as he added, "Neither factor applies to me."

"Aren't redheads supposed to have freckles?" She continued to question, lifting a hand up to explore his chest. His skin was evenly tanned all over. It was obvious that when he swam or suntanned he didn't wear a bathing suit.

"Aren't shy maidens supposed to be quiet after they've just been—"

"Shush!" Sammi reprimanded sharply, fearing what he might call their recent lovemaking.

"Awakened to the lustful pleasures of the flesh was what I was going to say when you rudely cut my words short," Steele admonished. He leaned forward to place a spontaneous kiss on her full mouth.

Responding eagerly, Sammi pressed close and asked, "Why don't you order me a sandwich while I shower? I'm starved."

"Good God, you expensive wench," Steele scolded. "I spent a fortune on hot and cold hors d'oeuvres. Why don't you eat them?"

Sammi slipped out of his arms, stood up without embarrassment in front of him, and sassed back, "Because I'm not hungry for them now. They'll be my breakfast."

Steele lay with his hands crossed beneath his head and let his eyes linger on Sammi's flawless figure. She had the most sensual shape of any woman he'd seen.

"You're a damned good-looking woman, Sam. You've got the best-looking"—his glance stopped on her full breasts—"tender little backside I've ever seen." He laughed loudly. "Fooled you, didn't I?"

Sammi observed his impudent stare and returned with one equally bold. She let her eyes run up and down his nude torso sprawled nonchalantly in the center of the massive bed and shot back, "Your, er . . . feet really are bigger than those I've seen in *Playgirl* magazine."

"Feet?" Steele laughed even louder.

"Among other things," Sammi replied with feigned innocence.

"I'm a big man, honey," Steele pointed out unnecessarily as he sat up and prepared to leave the bed. "That's why you're so perfect a match for me. You're tall, gorgeously endowed, and fit me perfect in every way. *In every way!*" he emphasized in case she didn't understand what he meant.

Sammi shot Steele a disapproving look and stormed down the two stairs and straight into her suite. By the looks of his body suggesting a cold shower for him wouldn't be a bad idea either.

At four thirty in the morning Sammi sat in the center of the rumpled bed cockily wearing nothing but an exquisite engagement ring, her necklace, and her chinchilla coat, with a silver tray balanced across her lap.

Steele sprawled alongside her with the top sheet draped over his hips and watched in disbelief as she took another bite of a hot, thick cheeseburger.

Giving him a mischievous smile, Sammi laid the delicious sandwich down and reached for her milkshake. "I learned tonight why I always wanted a wealthy man."

"Why?" Steele asked, running a finger up her leg. He had never touched such silky-smooth skin in his life.

She turned her head to look with twinkling eyes at his amused face, raised her ring finger proudly, and explained, "Because I'm hopelessly addicted to receiving elegant gifts. I adore swank hotels and the luxury of twenty-four-hour room service. But most of all I love an arrogant trucker who supplied me with all the above."

She took a spoonful of creamy chocolate drink too thick to sip through a straw and sighed with ecstasy.

"Do you think the waiter thought I was pregnant when I asked for a side dish of pickles?"

"Probably," Steele said with smug confidence. "You have four chances of being in that condition right now."

"Four?" Sammi questioned, licking the ice cream off her spoon with unconscious sensuality.

"One on this bed. One in the shower. One on your bed—" He broke off when Sammi reached to stop his words by placing a pickle slice in his mouth. He chewed the tart relish, neatly swallowed, and calmly resumed his explanation. "And one on the couch."

"I should have known you'd be keeping score," Sammi scolded, stifling a wide yawn.

She handed Steele the small portion of unfinished sandwich and the rest of her milkshake to finish and whispered in a sleepy voice, "If you don't need your rest, I do."

Sammi slipped off her fur coat, carefully placed it over the end of the bed, and snuggled naked into Steele's arms when he returned from placing the tray on the bedside table.

"Giving up so soon, Sam?" Steele murmured into her ear as he gently adjusted his hard body to her softer, feminine curves.

"Of course not!" she flared back, nuzzling his throat between kisses on a strong chin already bristly with dark whiskers. "It's just that I've never slept with a man before and want to see if I like it."

"By sleeping, I presume you mean literally, not figuratively, you wanton little wench," Steele countered, watching lovingly as her eyes fluttered shut and she relaxed, cuddling close as if she had slept in his arms every night for years.

"Whatever you say," Sammi agreed with good humor before adding an impertinent taunt. "For this one night only I concede you're the man in control, though I still owe you one for letting me believe you were a poor trucker."

"Shut up, Sam," Steele growled, pressing her face into his chest.

"Okay, Red," Sammi murmured sleepily. Enfolded in Steele's powerful arms, she had never felt so safe or contented in her life.

CHAPTER THIRTEEN

"Margaret," Sammi greeted her aunt rapturously. "You won't believe it, but your . . . experienced . . . niece is contentedly residing like a queen in the middle of the best three-room suite in town."

"Good heavens," her aunt cried. "Steele found you!"

"He sure did." Sammi chuckled. "Five times to be exact. Four before we went to sleep and once before he left on a, er, business trip."

"Samantha Thatcher, you have the most brazen speech of anyone I've ever known," Margaret scolded adamantly. "Apparently there's no need to ask about your virginity."

"Ex-virginity," Sammi pointed out in a lilting voice. "My innocence is a thing of the past, and now I wonder why I saved it so long. My gosh, I've never felt anything so good in my life and—"

"Enough!" Margaret exclaimed. "God forbid I hear all the details. Just tell me when there's going to be a wedding."

"In fourteen days," Sammi announced proudly. "As soon as Steele returns. He told me if I loved him despite thinking him poor, his having red hair, and his seducing me before a legal commitment, nothing could separate us after we're married."

"He's the first male friend of yours I've met with a strong enough personality to back that statement."

"You should see my engagement ring, Margaret," Sammi broke in.

She held up her left hand to view it. The huge diamond shimmered with fiery brilliance between dark sapphires Steele said were as vivid as her eyes. Her stomach muscles clenched at the memory of his burnished copper head bent reverently to her trembling hand when he slipped the ring on her finger and pledged his love.

Sammi's eyes were soft as she smiled. In two weeks she would be wearing the engraved wedding band as well.

"Oh, Margaret," she vowed in a dreamy voice. "When Steele returns I'm going to devote my life to making up for all the loving I sense he missed as a child. I'm going to do everything possible to see he has a warm and happy home." Tears of emotion spilled from her eyes. "It's going to be my biggest challenge and I can hardly wait."

"And what are you going to do in the interim?" her aunt asked, interrupting her sentimental thoughts.

"Everything I can get away with." Sammi laughed with sudden impish humor. "Steele left me the key to his house, his Lincoln Continental, and this suite if I want to stay here."

"He's insane," Margaret couldn't help but point out, knowing her niece's knack for spending money.

"You'll really think so when you realize he also told me I had carte blanche to shop for my trousseau, to plan the wedding, and to redecorate his house if I want."

"Oh, good lord," her aunt sighed in disbelief. "You'll bankrupt the man before you're legally married."

"No way, auntie dear," Sammi scolded. "I do have some sense of responsibility."

"I know, Samantha, but you've never had a full bank account at your unaccountable disposal before either."

"That's why I'm phoning during your lunch hour. I want you to come stay with me until Steele returns."

"Sorry," Margaret answered in a disappointed voice. "I can't get away now though I will fly out for the wedding."

"Okay," Sammi returned slowly. She was depressed to know

that Margaret couldn't share the fun of making preparations for the only wedding of her life.

"Well, I'd better say good-bye then. I'm in a hurry too. I'm dying to see Steele's house, and I want to look over Whitfield Interstate Trucking Company first. A fiancée should know what her husband-to-be's source of income looks like."

"How about beautiful Kay and Monique? Are you going to see that they get an invitation to your wedding?" Margaret asked innocently. She knew her temperamental niece would dislike their presence more then she would Benny's or Alan's.

"Of course," Sammi lied. Those two would be the last people on earth invited to anything she had a say in. The last thing she needed around were two gorgeous women fawning over her man! Especially if they wore the designer dresses he had paid for just so they'd be knockouts in his three attempts to make her jealous.

Sammi could feel her temper start to rise as she said, "Goodbye, Margaret. I'll let you know the exact date that I have plans to end Steele's bachelorhood!"

Sammi rechecked that she had everything packed, then rang for a porter to pick up her cases. She waited impatiently, too excited to sit still.

"Thank gosh I'm in cool San Francisco." She spoke out loud, slipping her arms into the sleeves of her fur coat. It would have been impossible to wear any kind of outer wear in Burbank's summer heat.

She was determined to exit the hotel as if she owned it. No one would know she was an ex-school teacher living from paycheck to paycheck when they saw her luxurious coat and expensive jewelry.

True to her wishes, all heads turned as she left the lobby with her chin held high and stepped outside. Steele continued to offer thoughtful surprises. Inside his gleaming automobile was a uniformed old man who looked as if he intended to stay behind the steering wheel.

"Mr. Whitfield asked me to drive you anywhere you wished today. He thought you might be tired after your long night."

"Long night?" Sammi questioned as she slipped into the backseat and adjusted her limbs to the shorter leg room.

"He explained when I took him to the airport that you had a bad attack of insomnia. In fact, he said it was around five this morning before you fell asleep."

"Mr. Whitfield talks too much," Sammi exclaimed through gritted teeth, giving the man a forced smile. Already Steele's distorted sense of humor was making her itch to get back at him.

"I said I'd like to go by his office before we go to his home, Mr. . . ." She lied in a clear voice, when the driver said he hadn't heard what she said.

"Burt Smithers," he replied politely with his name.

"Call me Samantha, Burt," Sammi told him. He was a nice-appearing old man, and she admired the calm way he maneuvered the large automobile through the heavy summer traffic.

Sammi relaxed, enjoying the unexpected pleasure of being chauffeured. She felt uncomfortable sitting alone in the backseat, but decided to wait until she had been by Steele's plant before moving forward.

Burt turned off the freeway on the southern edge of Santa Rosa and was soon pulling into a vast chain-link-fenced area.

Sammi smiled at the security guard's stunned expression when he observed her sitting in the backseat of his employer's car.

"Mr. Whitfield's fiancée needs something from the office," Burt told the man with a touch of arrogance.

Sammi's eyes widened, taking in the busy paved yard. Trucks of every size and description were parked about, all with Whitfield Interstate Trucking Company in bronze letters on their gleaming beige sides and backs.

It was the same lettering she had taken the name Whit Smith from. How could she have been so stupid not to have caught on sooner to Steele's ploy to make her think he was poor?

Burt stopped in a parking zone set before a modern office

building as impeccable as the surrounding landscaped yard. Everything so far indicated Steele could well afford to give her an entire store's worth of baubles without skipping a meal or having to budget for another night out on the town.

Sammi exited the backseat as proudly as she had the hotel. This time she decided it would look too pretentious to wear her fur wrap, so reluctantly she left it lying full length on the backseat.

"Watch my coat, Burt," Sammi reminded as she prepared to walk through the glass-doored entrance into a ceramic-tiled foyer.

Green plants, excellent artwork, soft stereo music, air conditioning, modern furniture, and expensive office equipment were in direct contrast to the noisy outer yard with its truck servicing and mammoth pickup and delivery warehouses.

Unobserved, Sammi sat down in a corner chair, deciding to apply fresh lip gloss before announcing her presence. The receptionist had apparently stepped out for a moment, which would give her plenty of time to assure she looked like a fitting companion for their arrogant employer.

Holding a small makeup mirror before her face, she caught the words Mr. Whitfield. My God, not again she thought, leaning forward to eavesdrop as she had at the restaurant when she overheard Vic and Steele talking. Listening to two secretaries gossip should be more revealing than two men.

"Do you think any woman will ever snag the boss, Hilari?"

"Who knows?" a sophisticated voice answered.

"Sandy told me Mr. Whitfield has a huge home with vast parklike grounds and that just he and one old man live there."

"He does," the sophisticated voice agreed with a touch of boredom.

"What a catch!"

Sammi could hear a youthful giggle and waited, unashamed, to overhear every word about Steele. Whatever she found out, good or bad, served him right for being so closemouthed each time she tried to interrogate him.

"Yes, but you won't get him nor will I. The man's definitely a loner."

"No one that sexy is a loner all the time, Iris. The boss must have lots of women holed up somewhere."

"None we'll ever know about," Iris drawled out. "He's too astute to select his playmates from his staff."

"How do you know?" Hilari demanded.

"From experience. I tried every feminine trick known to attract his attention the first two years I worked here."

"What happened?"

Sammi leaned forward, makeup forgotten, as she strained to hear Iris reply, "He bluntly told me he was only interested in my secretarial skills, then said lay off or find a new boss. The advice still stands."

"It sounds like it will take a sharp female to lead him to the altar."

"Agreed!" Iris answered seriously. "He believes in honeymoons, not weddings. We probably won't even know he has a woman in mind until she waltzes in and announces herself as the future Mrs. Whitfield."

With that, Sammi hurriedly stroked her mouth with color, stood up, straightened her dress, and making certain her ring finger was prominently displayed, walked, with high heels clicking loudly, to the counter.

"Is there anyone around?" she called out in her sweetest voice. She was especially interested in seeing what Iris looked like.

With a smug smile on her freshly glossed lips, she introduced herself to the startled women rushing out of the nearest office.

"Hello. I'm Samantha Thatcher. Mr. Whitfield's fiancée. I stopped by to introduce myself since Steele has spoken so highly about each of you."

He hadn't said a word, but they didn't need to know that. "And"—she made a spur of the moment decision—"to invite you to a party. We're holding it at the house on the fifteenth of June. If you'll give me a list of his Northern California employees and their home addresses, I'll see everyone receives an invitation within the week."

There was no need to tell them it was a wedding party since she hadn't had time to finalize those plans yet. It would be embarrassing anyway to have a group of people she didn't know arriving with presents.

Sammi played an employer's fiancée to the hilt. She was polite with just the right amount of reserve and loved every minute of their deference as they rushed to supply her with freshly brewed coffee and asked if there was anything—just anything—she wished.

She wandered around, glancing in and out of the offices, and wished more with each passing minute that she had worn her chinchilla coat. It would have added the perfect touch to her first attempt at being the only woman capable of bringing their . . . sexy boss to heel. They didn't need to know she had failed at every attempt to outsmart the man thus far.

With a bright smile, Sammi thanked them, gave Iris another thorough glance, then raised her chin to a haughty angle, and glided out of the office with grace that would have made a model proud.

"A job well done, Samantha," she congratulated herself beneath her breath before sliding into the front passenger seat for the upcoming drive to her future home.

Sammi's eyes were enormous as she took in the black wrought-iron gates and ornate overhead sign declaring she was entering Whitfield's Haven.

"This is a haven," she told Burt in an awed voice. A broad tree-lined driveway led through fenced pastures to a hilltop home commanding an unobstructed view of the rolling Sonoma County hillside.

Sammi stepped from the car the moment Burt parked. She was much too eager to wait for anyone to open her car door. Trying desperately to take in everything about Steele's home and surrounding acreage, she knew it would take weeks to explore all of the land and each nook and cranny of his sprawling residence.

Late the first night, searching through private papers concealed in Steele's office desk, she had found out many things that explained his hesitancy to speak of the past. Her heart bled as she read a yellowed sheet of paper reporting a redheaded infant boy found wrapped in newspaper and discarded like rubbish in an alley trash can.

An old copy of *Forbes* magazine gave a lengthy report of his poor background. Shuffled from foster home to foster home, he had started washing trucks at the age of twelve, greasing and parking them in the yards at thirteen, and working at every job available until he saved enough for a down payment. From then on his success had been phenomenal. He was a brilliant businessman despite his lack of advanced education, also a tireless worker who, the reporter said, had invested wisely.

Sammi's hands had trembled when she turned page after page of check stubs indicating his full support of a boy's home in his birth state. Obviously he was as generous as he was desirous of anonymity.

A week later Sammi felt as if she had lived in Steele's home all her life. Despite being busy all day, she missed him desperately. At night, snuggled in the middle of his oversized bed, she was so lonesome for his touch she found it difficult to sleep.

With the bedroom drapes drawn back, she could glance directly out at the lights of the distant city. She yearned for time to pass. In one night he had awakened her body to physical pleasures she wanted to experience again. And soon!

She glanced at the time. It wasn't too late to phone Margaret, and she just had to talk to someone or she'd explode.

"Hello, Samantha," her aunt answered on the first ring. "I've been hoping you would call. For some reason I have a hunch you're up to no good."

"Why would think that?" Sammi asked sweetly, wondering how her relative knew she wasn't planning a traditional wedding.

"Because the last time we talked you told me you had found—through snooping—an entire dossier on yourself in Steele's locked desk. You sounded decidedly perturbed to learn an old bag lady turned out to be a male private investigator in his employ."

"That old cross-dresser soaked me for forty bucks!" Sammi complained.

"You went so far as to mention you owed Steele retribution," Margaret prompted in case she'd forgotten.

"Why would that little bit of information make you think that I'd plan something unique just so I could pay my fiancé back on our wedding day?" Sammi chuckled impudently.

"My God, Samantha, you wouldn't do anything rash, would you?" Margaret admonished in her most cultured voice. "Weddings are a thing of solemn beauty. A time when dignity is the norm."

"You're forgetting I'm marrying a man who was the first to start playing games," Sammi reminded her, relating with chagrin the numerous ways Steele had led her on.

"Don't do it, niece," Margaret warned. "Whatever it is, forget it. Act like any normal woman would who's managed to snag a millionaire. Steele has bested you every time you tried to get back at him. Believe me, I know for a fact that marriage to you will settle all scores when he finds himself curbing one outrageous idea of yours after another."

"It's really a shame when one's only relative sides with a fiancé-in-law she hardly knows," Sammi chided.

She smiled, not the least upset about Margaret's lengthy criticism. She'd been subjected to it for years and always went on about her life as she wished.

"Don't worry about my plans. Just make sure that you're here in plenty of time to see me get hitched to my redheaded trucker."

"I knew it!" Margaret exclaimed. "Whenever you mention the color of Steele's hair you have mischief in mind."

"Good night, Margaret." Sammi laughed, hanging up the phone with a wide smile on her face.

Propped in the middle of Steele's comfortable bed, Sammi had papers and receipts spread all around her. Her arrangements were nearly complete for a wedding that would even up all scores and let them start their marriage without a single revenge owed.

On the morning of the fifteenth Sammi preened in front of a full-length mirror in the lavish dressing room adjoining the master suite.

"Perfect," she told her reflection, pulling each bright red beribboned pigtail forward. "I'm a perfect Daisy Mae."

With the sharpened tip of a brown eyeliner held in her fingers, she applied twelve exaggerated freckles over the bridge of her nose.

"A little added effect." She smiled with twinkling eyes full of devilish lights. The elastic neck of her red and white polka dot short-sleeved blouse was pulled down to expose smooth shoulders and tucked into a short black flared skirt that barely covered her ruffle-edged red cotton panties. White low-heeled sandals completed her carefully chosen outfit.

She could hear the sounds of workers busily adding the finishing touches to a reception her bridegroom would never forget. The day before sides of beef wrapped in damp gunny sacks were placed in a deep pit lined with hot stones and covered with earth. The chef had assured her it would be the most tender barbecued beef anyone had ever eaten.

Caterers supplied long tables spread with red-checked cloths that would be laden with vast tubs of coleslaw, potato salad, baked beans, relishes, cold fruit, and hot buttered loaves of garlic bread. Fresh lemonade plus beer and cola packed in metal washtubs covered with crushed ice were already waiting.

Sammi walked outside to check that her last-minute inspirations were comfortable. Crossing the bricked courtyard leading to the front door of Steele's elegant home, she stopped at the edge of lawns as smooth and green as a golf course.

"Hello, Esmerelda," she said, leaning over the makeshift pen to greet the biggest red sow she had ever seen in her life and to count her thirteen squealing piglets. "I see you're looking happy on your thick bed of straw, and well fed too," she added, noticing the trough filled with corn and wet mash.

Not receiving so much as a squeal or oink, she walked to the next corral, holding a half dozen multi-colored baby goats, all standing with front hooves on the highest rail to see if she was bringing them a treat.

"Spoiled you, didn't I?" She laughed, touching each inquisitive face. "You think because I brought you fresh alfalfa last night I should give you some now."

"Miss Thatcher," a young man dressed in Western wear interrupted. "Do you think it's too early to saddle the ponies for the kids to ride?"

"No, Jerry," Sammi answered. His eyes hadn't left the curves of her figure or her long legs since she had come outside. Today she didn't mind. The more male attention she received the better. When Steele arrived at two, she hoped to be surrounded by good-looking young men.

"The press and photographers, local dignitaries, and Mr. Whitfield's employees should start arriving at one, and I want the festivities in full swing when he drives in the gate."

"I hung the banner over the front entrance last night and tied balloons to each fence post along the drive this morning. They look real pretty too. How do you like the way I spread the bales of hay around for seats?" he asked.

"You did a great job," Sammi praised him. They had spent the last few days scouring local shops for antique milk cans, wagon wheels, harnesses, and old horse tack to set around that would give an authentic touch to the Western-style theme.

Sammi turned her head when she heard the sound of a large truck chugging up the hill to the house. "Here's the band now.

I was worried they wouldn't make it in time to set up. That's the most important part of my surprise."

"The carpenters did a good job on their bandstand," Jerry said, moving forward to point out where they should park.

Sammi took the hand of the band's leader. He was a handsome man and knew it. In fact, he looked so much like the photo she had seen of Merle Haggard she could hardly tell who was who. That, and the fact that he sounded like Merle too, was the only reason she was paying his astronomical fees for one afternoon's gig.

"Don't forget, Buck," she told the cocky young musician, "when you see a bronze-toned Lincoln Continental pull in the gate, start playing 'Okie from Muskogee' and keep it up until I motion to stop. That's Mr. Whitfield's favorite song."

"You betcha, honey," he drawled, ignoring her frown at his familiarity. "I'll be singin' so purty your intended won't know it ain't Merle himself."

"Fine," Sammi agreed, leaving as fast as possible to return to the house. She trembled with anticipation. Whether it was from knowing that she was finally getting back at Steele, or that she would soon see the man she loved, she wasn't certain. Whatever the reason, she had never been so excited in her life.

Later Sammi mingled among the guests, introducing herself and seeing each was comfortable as she watched nervously for Steele to appear. She couldn't believe how happy everyone seemed to be. They had entered into the spirit of the party with enthusiasm equal to hers. All, from the youngest to the oldest, were dressed in Western or hillbilly clothes.

The First Annual Whitfield Picnic was in full swing when she spotted Burt turn into the driveway.

"Heaven help me later," Sammi prayed, swallowing as her palms broke out with nervous perspiration. Suddenly she wished she had taken Margaret's advice and conducted herself as any normal woman would have.

Lifting her chin bravely, she motioned to Buck. The moment

he switched songs, each guest stopped what he or she was doing and applauded Steele's arrival. Press and photographers darted forward, prepared to focus their cameras and take notes for later news stories.

Sammi ducked behind the tree-shaded pigpen, watching with wide eyes as Steele stepped from his car wearing the most elegant gray three-piece suit she had ever seen. He smiled at everyone, waved hello, and turned to see that the line of cars following his parked close by.

She stood up, aghast as she observed first one group after another step out. Margaret was escorted from the backseat of the Lincoln by a nice-appearing middle-aged man. She was wearing a full-length blue-checked dress that fit in with what everyone except Steele had on. Where on earth had her aunt bought that and why? She hadn't told her a single thing about her Western party plans.

Next two handsome couples, the women gloriously pregnant, exited their cars. Immediately following were Monique and Kay dressed like high-priced saloon girls, clinging to the arms of a striking Italian man.

"Who invited them?" she complained jealously beneath her breath, admitting with reluctance that both women looked as pampered as ever.

Creeping around the edge of the tree, Sammi couldn't believe it when she saw, gently assisted out of sleek limousines by the drivers, several of the old women she visited each Saturday in Burbank.

Tears came to her eyes at the thought that Steele had gone to the trouble and vast expense to include them in the festivities. They looked so sweet in their long old-fashioned gowns.

Last to step out were a bus load of youths, staring with eyes as wide as hers at the gathering.

"Enjoying the First Annual Whitfield Interstate Trucking Company Picnic, Sam?" Steele questioned in her ear.

Sammi yelped with surprise as she was spun around into the

arms of her husband-to-be and kissed with such fierce hunger she thought she'd collapse on his elegant shoes.

She had been so engrossed in watching the entourage unload she had completely forgotten to keep her eyes on Steele. The sound of the band had completely drowned out his footsteps.

"My God, you little devil," Steele groaned. "You really do need twenty-four-hour care, don't you? It looks like Old McDonald's farm with pigs on my patio and goats near my garage. I said you could decorate the inside of my house, not open a zoo!"

"Don't you like your wedding reception?" Sammi asked with eyes as innocent as a child's.

"I damned well better like it," Steele growled, pulling her behind a huge oak tree so they couldn't be overheard. "By the looks of the crowd and the changes in my landscaped yard it's going to cost me a bundle."

"Not for a month or two it won't," Sammi replied with eyes as bright as the stones in her ring. "I charged everything. Besides, it's all tax deductible anyway, isn't it?"

"Who cares." Steele frowned, dragging her into the milling crowd. "As soon as I introduce you to my friends I'm going to run your little butt inside the house and kiss the hell out of you. And as ornery as you are, that will take some doing!"

Pleased by Steele's promised form of chastisement, Sammi took his arm and paraded out to meet his friends as if she was wearing her finest gown.

It took several minutes to get past all the people wanting to congratulate him. Steele shook hands with one acquaintance after another. With his fingers firmly clasping Sammi's, he still managed to get her close to his friends in a short period of time.

"Carlyn and De-Ann I would like to introduce you to my fiancée, Miss Samantha Thatcher." He turned to glance at Sammi with an amused look. "Sam, these two big brutes behind the ladies are their husbands, Nick Sandini and Derek Howell. Nick owns Nick's. Remember the excellent restaurant you ate at the first day you arrived in San Francisco? Derek owns Hidden Coves, where you stayed last year."

Sammi returned their friendly greetings with a generous smile. She liked both women and their attentive husbands immediately.

"Take care, Samantha," Nick teased. "Or you'll soon be as pregnant as my beautiful Carlyn."

"And my lovely De-Ann," Derek reminded.

Both husbands placed broad palms on their wives' stomachs with such tenderness Sammi felt a twinge in her breast. She experienced a sudden yearning to carry Steele's child as proudly as these women were carrying theirs.

"No doubt there will be three additional babies at our . . . Second Annual Picnic. Agreed, Sam?" Steele teased, squeezing her fingers to stop any rebuttal.

"Nick and Derek supplied the wedding cake and champagne, which the caterer is bringing at three."

"How nice," Sammi responded, turning as she was greeted enthusiastically by the dark-haired man escorting Monique and Kay.

"I'm Vic, honey." His smile showed even white teeth. "If you want to change your mind about marrying a trucker, it's not too late. I'm the last one of our group still uncommitted, and I'm partial to black hair."

Vic ignored Steele's glare and pulled his dates forward. "I'd like you to meet Monique and Kay."

"We've met," Sammi said in a syrupy-sweet voice, though reeling with antagonism. Any single women as elegant as these two were a major threat until Steele was safely married.

"Excuse me," Sammi said. "I have to greet my aunt and some dear friends of mine from Burbank."

Pulling free of Steele's hand, she rushed to Margaret, embracing her with strong affection as he walked over to the youths.

"How did you know I was planning a hillbilly party?"

"Steele told me several days ago."

"How did he find out?"

"Honey, the man knows everything you do," Margaret reminded her smugly. "You don't look much like a bride, but the guests appear to be having a great time."

"They are, and so will you. Who's the handsome man I saw helping you out of Steele's car?" Sammi asked.

"Steele's accountant. A widower having a hard time adjusting to single life. He felt we had a lot in common—math and the loss of our mates."

"Come with me," Sammi persuaded softly. "I want you to meet some of the sweetest ladies in the world."

After hugs and kisses were exchanged, each had to tell how wonderful Sammi's fiancé was. They had been flown to San Francisco and were being treated to a week's tour of the local wine cellars and other points of interest in Northern California before returning to the rest home. It was apparent they were as much in love with Steele as she was.

"Uh oh, here comes Steele now. Have fun, auntie dear, and ladies. We'll talk later."

Sammi walked forward, smiling at each youthful face as she moved into Steele's arms.

"Sam, I'd like you to meet the men responsible for my two weeks away from you. We go backpacking in Alaska every year this time. Since this is such a special event, I brought them back on the plane with me."

"You were in Alaska?" Sammi exclaimed. Steele's orgy was nothing other than an innocent camping trip, the companions who needed love more than her only awkward young boys. She had really misjudged him this time.

"Excuse us," Steele told them after introducing each to her. "Have fun while I take my fiancée into the house and see that she dresses properly for our wedding."

"What's wrong with what I have on?" Sammi yelped, protesting with bunched fists as Steele picked her up without warning and slung her facedown over his wide shoulder amidst the flashing of photographers' cameras.

With one hand across the back of her knees and the other on her rounded bottom, he walked through the amused, wildly applauding crowd in the shortest route to his front door.

"When the hell is the band going to quit playing 'Okie from Muskogee'?" Steele complained. "Don't they know any other songs?"

"Oh, dear," Sammi cried out, raising her flushed face. "I forgot to motion to Buck to stop."

"Buck?" Steele flared back, giving her a swat.

"The leader," Sammi explained. "Jerry!" she called out behind Steele's back. "Will you tell Buck to take a break until it's time to play the wedding march."

"I hope he does a better job than he's doing imitating Merle Haggard," Steele complained, not missing a single step as he slammed into his house.

"He's good!" Sammi argued, demanding to be let down. "The best of the many I had audition."

"God help the others," Steele exclaimed through clenched teeth. "Now, my impertinent wife-to-be, get out of this hillbilly getup you thought would embarrass me and into your wedding dress."

Set none too gently on her feet in the center of the master bedroom, Sammi put both hands on her hips and flared back, "*This is my wedding dress*! Turnabout's fair play. I dressed in my fanciest clothes for our first date and you played Li'l Abner. Now you can regale our guests with your taste in attire and I'll be Daisy Mae!"

"You think so, wench?" Steele returned with an icy gleam in his eyes that boded ill for Sammi if she disobeyed. "Get your clothes off and fast!"

"This is the only thing I bought," Sammi told him. "I've been too busy planning this party to shop for a proper wedding gown."

"My God, you're something else." Steele laughed. "It's a damn good thing I kept the twenty-four-hour tail on you or I wouldn't have purchased this and had Burt put it in your closet after I arrived home."

He went to the dressing room and slid back the door, waiting for Sammi's approval of the designer gown hanging on its padded rack.

"Oh, darling," Sammi whispered in a reverent voice. With trembling fingers she touched the elegant lace decorating her full-length traditional ivory satin gown.

"It's the most beautiful wedding dress I've ever seen."

"I'm glad you like it, Sam. Now get your little fanny over here and let me undress you."

"Undress me?" Sammi questioned. "What will our guests say?"

"How will they know, and who cares what they think if they do?" Steele took her by the arms and sat her down in a comfortable velour chair. He slipped off both sandals and carelessly dropped them on the carpet.

Sammi didn't utter a sound when he stood her up and pulled her blouse out of the waistband of her skirt. With one tug he pulled it over her shoulders and threw it on top of her shoes.

"Samantha Thatcher, I don't want you parading around again without a bra unless it's for my private benefit."

Sammi stood with hands on hips, breasts bared and moving up and down with each breath she took, and argued, "I'll go braless if I want! It's impossible to wear off-the-shoulder blouses and a brassiere too."

"You won't," Steele shot back more determined than she could ever be.

"No man—not even you—will ever control me!" Sammi taunted. "I refuse to bow down to any man."

"Haven't you realized yet that I never intended to bring you to your knees, Sam?" Steele scolded. "From the first my only interest was bringing you to my heart."

"Is that true?" she whispered softly. Her eyes changed, shining with love that had quickly replaced the sparks of temper.

"Of course," Steele answered dryly. "Now stand still."

She inhaled, trying desperately to keep her limbs from trembling when he bent forward and unbuttoned the belt of her skirt. With his fingers in the waistband of both garments, he deftly removed her red panties and skirt at the same time.

Steele threw the last of her clothes on the rug, rose to his full height, and stared through narrowed lids. He surveyed her from the top of her glistening head to her shapely bare feet.

Sammi watched his eyes darken, knowing his mind was churning with thoughts as passionate as hers when he removed his jacket with purposeful intent.

"Get on the bed, Sam. I want you badly, I want you now, and I want you hot!"

"What about our w-wedding?" she stammered.

"As aroused as I am, I sure as hell won't delay the ceremony very long."

"You do every damned thing backward!" Sammi chided. "You start the honeymoon before the wedding. You undress me before the ceremony instead of afterward. Now you want a, er . . ."

"Quickie," Steele filled in when she broke off.

"While nearly three hundred people wait outside to see what we do next?" she continued.

"Let 'em wait," Steele disputed arrogantly. "I can't."

"You're acting more like Benny and Alan all the time."

Steele leaned forward, swooped Sammi into his arms with a deep growl, and warned, "We'll see who I remind you of when I'm inside you, you willful little wench."

Steele threw her down onto the soft mattress of his bed and had shed his clothes before she could decide whether she wanted to scoot off the other side or not.

Deciding she didn't, Sammi threw her arms around his neck when he leaned down to gather her into his arms. She was wild for the man, as eager as he for a quick, passionate coming together—so anxious it didn't matter in the least that she was the hostess and he the host. There was plenty happening outside to keep their guests busy while she let the man she loved know how much she had missed him.

Their mouths joined, locking as erotically as their bodies when Steele eased between her limbs with an urgency that left them both breathless. There was no hesitation when he entered her. She was ready, lifting her hips up to encourage the fiery pleasure of each deep thrust. Despite the obvious frustration, he held back until a soft flush covered her body and he felt the convulsive shudders of a mutual climax consume them both.

As soon as Sammi came back to earth from the exquisite pleasure of deep sensual satisfaction, she nuzzled Steele's face.

"Do you think our guests will be able to tell I've been, er . . .?" she trailed off, tenderly rubbing the marks her fingernails had left on his shoulders.

Steele laughed loudly, bent over to nip her gently on the side of the neck, and said, "My good friends will know the minute they see my smug smile and your soft, cushiony mouth."

He kissed her lips with unabated hunger. "Not to mention the rakish gleam in your expressive eyes that proves you're a woman who's just been had."

"Aunt Margaret should hear your blunt talk." Sammi chuckled. "She thinks I have a terrible tongue."

She threw a pillow at his face and fled to the supposed sanctuary of the bathroom, only to be dragged into the huge tiled shower where Steele soaped a cloth and tenderly scrubbed each freckle from her uptilted nose.

"Keep your hands off my body," Steele admonished when she groped to cleanse him as intimately as he was doing to her.

"Why?" Sammi asked mischievously.

"Because you're playing with dynamite if you don't," Steele warned as he tenderly soaped each lush breast.

"I know, my darling husband-to-be." Sammi smiled, laying her face on his hair-roughened chest as the water streamed down his broad back. She hugged his waist, stood on tiptoes, and rubbed her soft stomach slowly against his until she felt his body start to harden and press insistently between her limbs.

"I think, Mr. Whitfield," she teased in a throaty whisper. One hand reached down between their bodies, wrapping fingers around his pulsating hardness as her mouth parted over his flat nipple and eagerly kissed it into an erect bud.

"Think what, Sam?" Steele moaned, sliding his hands over the sleek wet curves of her body. He cupped her bottom in both broad palms and pulled her up as tightly as physically possible without penetration.

"I think that you, my adored redhead, are definitely a *man . . . out of . . . control*!"

LOOK FOR NEXT MONTH'S
CANDLELIGHT ECSTASY SUPREMES

37 ARABIAN NIGHTS, *Heather Graham*
38 ANOTHER DAY OF LOVING, *Rebecca Nunn*
38 TWO OF A KIND, *Lori Copeland*
40 STEAL AWAY, *Candice Adams*

An exceptional, *free* offer awaits readers of Dell's incomparable Candlelight Ecstasy and Supreme Romances.

Subscribe to our all-new CANDLELIGHT NEWSLETTER and you will receive—at absolutely no cost to you—exciting, exclusive information about today's finest romance novels and novelists. You'll be part of a select group to receive sneak previews of upcoming Candlelight Romances, well in advance of publication.

You'll also go behind the scenes to "meet" our Ecstasy and Supreme authors, learning firsthand where they get their ideas and how they made it to the top. News of author appearances and events will be detailed, as well. And contributions from the Candlelight editor will give you the inside scoop on how she makes her decisions about what to publish—and how *you* can try your hand at writing an Ecstasy or Supreme.

You'll find all this and more in Dell's CANDLELIGHT NEWSLETTER. And best of all, *it costs you nothing*. That's right! It's Dell's way of thanking our loyal Candlelight readers and of adding another dimension to your reading enjoyment.

Just fill out the coupon below, return it to us, and look forward to receiving the first of many CANDLELIGHT NEWSLETTERS—overflowing with the kind of excitement that only enhances our romances!

Return to: DELL PUBLISHING CO., INC. B287A
    Candlelight Newsletter • Publicity Department
    245 East 47 Street • New York, N.Y. 10017

Name_____

Address_____

City_____

State_____ Zip_____

CANDLELIGHT Ecstasy Supreme

☐ 29	**DIAMONDS IN THE SKY**, Samantha Hughes	11899-9-28
☐ 30	**EVENTIDE**, Margaret Dobson	12388-7-24
☐ 31	**CAUTION: MAN AT WORK**, Linda Randall Wisdom	11146-3-37
☐ 32	**WHILE THE FIRE RAGES**, Amii Lorin	19526-8-14
☐ 33	**FATEFUL EMBRACE**, Nell Kincaid	12555-3-13
☐ 34	**A DANGEROUS ATTRACTION**, Emily Elliott	11756-9-12
☐ 35	**MAN IN CONTROL**, Alice Morgan	15179-1-20
☐ 36	**PLAYING IT SAFE**, Alison Tyler	16944-5-30

$2.50 each

At your local bookstore or use this handy coupon for ordering:

DELL READERS SERVICE— Dept. A 107
P.O. BOX 1000, PINE BROOK, N.J. 07058-1000   B287B

Please send me the above title(s). I am enclosing $_____ (please add 75¢ per copy to cover postage and handling.) Send check or money order—no cash or CODs. Please allow up to 8 weeks for shipment.

Name_____

Address_____

City_____ State/Zip_____